MENOETIUS

A NOVEL BY
ERIN CROCKER

COVER DESIGN
BY
LESLIE SAFFORD

Menoetius

Erin Crocker

Visit Erin at http://www.authorerincrocker.com

Thank you. If you're reading this right now, it means you trust me enough to continue the journey and, for that, I cannot write 'thank you' enough. I'm grateful for the support, the emails, the comments on Instagram, Facebook, and my blog. I've had awesome editing help with both novels by Linette Kasper, author of 'Daimon' and Amber Newberry Izzo, author of 'Walls of Ash' and editor-in-chief of FunDead Publications. I'm also extending another gigantic thank you to Bret Valdez who helped a lot in the editing process and is working on a magnificent novel that I hope he'll release soon. To all my beta readers and everyone who helped in the process... thank you, thank you, thank you, and thank you. To my kids, who endured many skeevy boxed dinners throughout the writing process... THANK YOU!

WESLEY

The trees served as our only canopy as heavy drops of rain fought to escape dark clouds. I found myself in a place I didn't recognize, with people I didn't know.

"Push!" a woman yelled before her desperate eyes met mine. "Ashley, go to the creek. Fetch us more water. Surely, soon we will need it boiling," she commanded, leaving no room for argument as she knelt to tend to a young girl.

"But my name's not Ash—" I began. There wasn't time to argue. I grabbed a pan and started down the steep rocky hills, being careful of my footing, until I reached a small creek. I dipped the warped container in the flowing water and filled it before hurrying back to the woman.

Once I arrived, she wasted no time. "Stir the fire before the rain puts it out. Heat the water." I did as she ordered, only glancing once at the young girl, drenched in a mixture of rain and sweat. "Push!" the lady yelled again, the pitch of her voice resembling an alarm. "Push harder or you shall both die," she warned.

The girl strained and fell back onto a tattered blanket. "Perhaps I am of the devil!" she screamed between pushes. Her response was nearly muted by the rain.

"Do not speak of your magic in such a manner. It is of nature. My husband, Ashley, shares this magic. He is like you. You two are not of the devil," she responded.

The girl screamed one final curdling screech that blended with the shrieks of a tiny thing covered in white film. I peered over the woman claiming to be my wife and stared into the girl's green eyes.

Lila? I mouthed, more than confused.

"My baby," she whispered. "Please care for her."

"Ashley and I are moving north this night. We shall live with my family and raise her as our own," she promised as she held the infant up to the mother.

The girl forced a smile smiled and tried to outstretch her arms to take her newborn but was too weak. She lay her head back down and the dim light in her eyes flickered until she was dead.

"No!" I screamed. "Lila, you can't die!"

"You mustn't speak of such things." The woman's mesmeric stare caused my feet to remain planted in soft pools of mud. "'Tis the…"

"Hand of Fate" by the Rolling Stones blared through the speakers as I struggled to stop shaking. "You are listening to *the* station for rock music, WTKQ 102.4!" an enthusiastic DJ finished as I lowered the volume.

It was only a dream, but those frantic eyes haunted me as I sat up, put my truck in drive, and left the busy roadside stop. I started heading west the afternoon before and went as far as possible until staying awake was intolerable.

Fredericksburg was close. Maybe they didn't take her there, but there was always the possibility that if I could find

Sara, she'd be willing to help. If she had a key to Lila's house, I could search it. I would also have to find Peter, unless they'd gotten to him, too. The passenger seat was empty— *she should be here, next to me.* Flashes of her green eyes teased my memory. The one thing I could count on through all this— Lila was a fighter.

LILA

The 'Facility' was harbored inside the Appalachian Mountains. I'd never been around the area, but friends who'd taken vacations to Massanutten talked about Mount Hurricane or at least the clouded rumors they'd heard from residents from the nearby town of Harrisonburg. Conspiracy theory wasn't my forte, but considering recent events, perhaps it should've been.

I recalled their accounts and noted the Harrisonburg city limit sign looming in front of us. Sullivan didn't stop the vehicle, nor did he acknowledge the onlookers who glanced up from their phones to stare at the dark, four-passenger vehicle being guarded by two equally black SUV's, one in front and one behind. They looked about my age, college students most likely. One of them, dropped her papers and panicked as they went flurrying with the wind. A few people came to her aid. Stressful, no doubt, but I envied the normal version of stress. I'd have traded places in a blink. I mean, what was a few notes in comparison to being a government lab rat?

Sullivan's face maintained a somber expression as we followed the unmarked Suburban leading us out of the city limits. The hills rolled by as I took in the sparsity of houses due to the plethora of farmland, the mountains off in the distance, and the lack of alternate routes. There were no specific landmarks to memorize, just fields of corn and soybeans. Each tree was similar in size and type. There were no road markers to denote our location.

Having only eaten lunch that day, I lacked the stamina to read into Sullivan's thoughts, but kept a sharp eye out for menial changes in scenery while fidgeting with the charms on my silver bracelet. He turned down a dirt road garnered with a rusted sign that read, 'No Trespassing Violators Will Be Prosecuted'.

"Almost there," he said as though I should feel relieved somehow. "You made up your mind yet? You ready to cooperate?"

"Do I have an option?" The bland words tumbled from my mouth; there was no meaning behind them.

"The alternative *is* rather grim," he agreed.

The Suburban in front of us slowed down as it approached a checkpoint boasting barbed-wire reminiscent of a state penitentiary. A few armed guards approached the first vehicle and I leaned to watch its driver hold out credentials and the soldiers stepped away as the cross arms lifted to let it pass and settled back in their restrictive positions. Sullivan drove up and more men surrounded our vehicle.

One soldier stared and despite orders, gave me a confused look. He could have been Wesley— tall and serious and somehow still compassionate. His eyes were chocolate and his hair too short to have distinct color. I could only imagine that it, too, would be dark and somewhere he had a wife or girlfriend waiting for him to come home after a long shift. I smiled weakly at him.

"Private Stevens! Take a break," barked a heavy voice.

The young soldier peered in the SUV one last time and back up at his commanding officer. He saluted and turned to leave. He was the nicest person I'd encountered in a while, but I doubted I would see him again. I certainly couldn't read his thoughts through my daze of fatigue and hunger. Cooperating was the only way I could regain strength. If they wanted a firework show, then they'd have to give me some form of nutrition.

My attention turned back to Sullivan who made a few more comments to one of the officers before the hands were lifted and we entered the Facility. He sat back, relaxing in his seat like a slug... a slithering, fat slug I wanted to sprinkle salt on and laugh at as he dissolved on the pavement.

"So, the stories were true? The ones my friends would tell at school." I sniffed, overcome with a sudden desire to antagonize him, "But, really, the mountains? Isn't that kind of cliché? Like, *all* of your top secret places are in the mountains or under them, between them?" I let out an arrogant chuckle. "I thought you were secretive?"

Sullivan raised an eyebrow. "Out of all these fables told by your friends, how many of them knew the truth about this place?"

I didn't answer. Instead, my attention turned to the tall fence, much too high to climb and obviously electric, even if I could get to it. The only way out would be through the entry gates. Surrounding the barriers, were layers of trees keeping any buildings entirely out of view.

"So, I guess we have succeeded in retaining anonymity despite the commonality?"

I couldn't argue with that, nor did I have the energy to. I wanted to change the subject. "You're right," I lied, "I've thought about it a lot during our trip. I can't control these abilities and I don't want anything else like Evansville to happen." I slowed my voice in an attempt to keep from sounding too eager to help.

9

"I figured you'd come around. Well, great. Then I'll make the arrangements. We'll begin tomorrow morning after breakfast with a basic health assessment. You might feel overwhelmed through the initial testing. Keep in mind that it will settle down after a couple of weeks."

He was lying. I didn't need to read his mind, and I could thank intuition for that. Sullivan pulled off the gravel and onto a smooth, gray path covered in white petals from the lines of dogwood that garnished either side. The end of the long road was invisible. "Where are we going?"

"You'll be shown around soon enough. Right now, I'm taking you to the main house..." Something about the pause and tasteless tone irked me. "My house. There's something I want to show you," finished his nails-on-chalkboard voice.

At the vague answer, I turned back to the canopy of trees, their beauty ruined by the presence of slime sitting next to me. He continued driving and soon a pristine, two-story, light-blue house stood before us. Sullivan pulled into the circle drive and was met by a few men in suits who opened our doors. Not bothering to thank them, I stood and studied the face of a stone-stairway leading to a glass door with floral etchings.

"Mr. Sullivan," acknowledged one of the men as he closed the door of the SUV.

Sullivan looked at the worker, his nose flaring as he huffed, "I want a group of you cleaning the white shit off the driveway," he barked in disgust; not that it was a surprise that the vile little man despised beauty. "It looks like we're arriving at a goddamned wedding," he added, frowning.

The worker seemed undisturbed by Sullivan's disrespectful manner. "Right away, sir," he nodded and took off.

Sullivan looked to me. "Come along," he urged, waving his hand toward the doorway as an indication that that was where we were going.

I started up the stone steps with him following a tad too close behind. Before I reached the top, the door opened to a well-dressed man with dark hair, although it was beginning to recede, and hazel eyes. "Welcome, miss," he greeted.

"Hi," I replied, not sure what else to say.

"That will be all," came Sullivan's short voice as he made his way into the foyer.

The man left and as Sullivan passed me, his hand grazed the side of my jeans. It was no accident. I cleared my throat to indicate the move was unacceptable. A part of me was frightened, but on the other hand, I could take him even if using my abilities killed me.

I shook the thoughts and looked around. The inside of the house was decorated like I'd expect a government-type house to look: political pictures lining the hall, shiny wood floors, antique-style furniture, flags everywhere—none of it welcoming. As we started down the hall, he pointed to a faded, sepia photo of an elderly man standing behind a podium. A few other men in military suits were trying to shake his hand. "That's Alexander Stutesman. He's the founder of FDRA. July 7, 1878—that's the day he retired."

"Okay." Outwardly, I kept my cool. I was fuming on the inside at the thought of Sullivan's passive-aggressive walk down memory lane.

"He was one of the first scientists to take claims of telepathy and telekinesis seriously." Sullivan looked at me. "He also realized the importance of eliminating...although the measures he took were a bit more inhumane than today's, but they were effective." We continued down the hall and on to another group of pictures. "This was taken shortly after states began banning forced sterilization. The people you see here believed they weeded out the possibility of anyone having abilities for good. The FDRA took a hiatus." His eyes bore into mine and I studied his, refusing to break the stare as he continued. "They were wrong."

We reached the end of the hall and took a left continuing down another long corridor lined with photos that Sullivan didn't bother explaining. We arrived at two tall doors that led to what I guessed was a boardroom. He took out his keys and shuffled them until coming to a gold one which he used to unlock the door. He held it open and motioned. "After you."

I entered hesitantly. The last thing I wanted was to be in a room with him, alone. Chairs lined both sides of a long meeting table and I stopped and stood in front of the one positioned at the head. Crowding the walls were photos, some recent and some from years ago.

"What is this?"

"Take your time. Study each face carefully," he advised, his tone becoming eerily stiff as my eyes wandered from face to face. Some of the people were old, some young; the ages varied as did the gender and ethnicities. It looked like the worst episode of Crime TV ever, like the killer was never caught and was somehow immortal. "Those are all the victims of monsters like you."

My skin crawled. "No," I whispered.

"Yes," he rebutted, "Every single person who's ever been harmed by knowing or having contact with those who have your abilities." He walked to a group of photos I was looking at and pulled a snapshot of a dark-haired lady— Linda. He took out a pushpin and fastened it to the wall. "And now we add her." He paused as he turned back to me. "How many more, Lila?"

Linda's cold eyes accused me. I cocked my head to the side still in disbelief. "What?"

"How many more people, innocent *people*, should die because of you freaks?" His voice grew louder and echoed through the otherwise empty room. "It's not natural, this telepathy, telekinesis, how you can manipulate others with your mind. It was never meant to be."

In a moment of what I'd call untapped brilliance, I argued, "Where's everyone who's been murdered or harmed by people without abilities? In war, for example. Like, did you ever think that if the government just told us all this in the first place, maybe these things wouldn't happen?" I asked, motioning to the wall of pictures before continuing, "That if it wasn't for *people* like me, you'd be pointing the finger at something else, or someone else? Hasn't that been the case since the beginning of forever? A few people get together and decide that whatever they are is normal and everyone else is no more than an afterthought and that everything bad that happens from then on is because of the 'freaks'? That's how it works." I blinked and inhaled a deep breath.

Sullivan smirked and sauntered closer to me. I froze. Closer. I was unable to move as uncomfortable static pulsed through me. Closer. I ran my suddenly dry tongue over the roof of my mouth. Closer. His ripely-sour breath strangled my nostrils. Closer. My eyes widened as he reached for my shirt with his index finger and thumb. My heart beat through the floor. Closer. His wormy fingers picked off a stray hair and tossed it to the ground.

He licked his bone lips. "I don't need a history lesson, young lady. I brought you here so, you'd have a chance to witness firsthand why your kind of peop—well, whatever you are, shouldn't be."

"And here all along I thought you had a supervillain backstory. Like maybe someone with telekinesis threw you into a vat of acid or murdered your wife and first-born. Some reason to waste your life on a grudge. The whole time, it was all about hate."

He raised an eyebrow and moved away from me. "We're not going to see this eye-to-eye. I thought bringing you here would solidify your cooperation," he responded as he gestured once again at the mural of victims.

I silently admitted that, yes, the amount was horrific, but without knowing the individual circumstances or the FDRA's involvement, it was hard to make any judgment, so I didn't speak at all.

"I guess this is how it's going to be then," he nodded and cupped a hand over the top of one of the burgundy chairs. He used his other to pull a radio from the side of his khakis. "Dan, come see Miss Daniels to her room."

"Yes sir," answered the crackled voice on the other end.

After a length of time, a well-dressed worker came and indicated I should go with him. The doors shut behind us leaving Sullivan to his thoughts... his narrow thoughts, like a shallow kiddie pool.

"You must be Lila," the older man assumed as he motioned for me to follow him.

"Yeah, I take it you're Dan?" I asked.

"Yes ma'am," he answered. We continued on our way in silence. He opened the front door and I looked out.

"Are we walking?" I recalled the length of the drive and knew I was too fatigued to make the journey.

"No," he chuckled. "My old legs won't take me that far." He motioned to a golf cart sitting to the side. "There's our ride. You're not planning to run, are ya?" he half-joked.

I shook my head. *Not yet,* I thought.

We hopped in the cart and he started down the driveway, making sure to slow down for the workers who, at Sullivan's demand, were cleaning the flowery mess. Eventually, we pulled into some type of garage that held rows of SUVs and cars. "When we get inside, we'll part ways. Peter'll be showing you your room."

"Is this 'Peter' your boss, too?" I was interested in learning more about the mysterious man I was being handed off to.

He laughed, "No, he's just an intern. First one we've had so far as I know." He leaned in and whispered, "I don't think Sullivan trusts the kid. I think he's all right, but then I'm not the one in charge," he chuckled under his breath as we pulled up to an unassuming building.

When Dan came around to my side, I jumped off the cart and we walked up a ramp, before waiting on a gray door that opened to an off-white hallway with blue carpet. Was it the same place they took Sara? Or did they just grab her up and bring her straight to me?

What did they do to Sara? What about my parents? They had their questions and I certainly had mine.

A tall, lanky boy with dark hair and green eyes, hidden behind glasses, approached us with a clipboard. "Dan."

"Peter," Dan greeted warmly, despite Peter's stern demeanor. "I suppose you can take it from here. Make sure she eats; that was Mr. Sullivan's orders. High protein, carbs— the whole nine yards," he informed the indifferent Peter.

"That'll be all, Dan," said the younger man without looking up from his clipboard. With that, he was off. That just left Peter and me standing in the long hallway.

"Needless to say, I won't take you on a grand tour. I'll show you to your room and make sure you get food. I'd advise that you *eat* as it will ensure you regain strength, unlike your friend— Sally, was it?"

"Sara," I snorted. "Wow, you really think you're badass, huh? A true legend in your own mind? God, you're only an intern." Suddenly, I felt less intimidated around someone closer to my age.

"I'm not the one being treated like a lab rat," he snapped.

I refrained from a retort. He seemed like the type to run and tattle to the nearest ranking officer. He began walking and I followed behind, etching his name into my mental shit list. He turned right, and we came to a set of doors.

"They need a fingerprint to open," he said in a matter-of-fact voice.

What was up with everyone trying to sound so impressive? He set his thumb on a monitor and the two doors swung open. The hall continued at length. When we reached the end, we were met by another door.

"This is your room," he stated as he placed his finger on a scanner and waved an ID card at a camera. The doors opened to a sitting area that contained a leather sofa and chair facing a flat screen TV mounted on a wall. On either side of the couch rested two plastic end tables—everything bolted in place. I gave Peter a what-the-hell look. "You're lucky they left the TV in here. Guess they didn't feel like anything would be safe around a telekinetic."

"Whatever," I grunted, crossing my arms in front of me and continued to evaluate the rest of the space. The walls were bare and to the right was a small dining area with a wooden table and four chairs. Beside it was an island. Behind that, a sink which I guessed was supposed to be the kitchen.

"The cabinets are stocked with plastic dishes and cups," Peter informed.

He led me over to a door and opened it, this time with no clearance required. The room was simple and contained a bed, dressers, a small closet, and another door.

"Let me guess...bathroom?" I asked, opening the door. Again, basic—a stand-up shower with a towel rack, a toilet, and a sink with some type of plastic mirror.

Peter broke the silence that filled the space around us. "I'm going to get you some food. I'll also ask about clothes and stuff for you."

"My size is—"

"I already know. No food allergies. I'll be back shortly." When he turned to leave the room, I realized he probably knew almost everything about me. Wesley crossed my mind and I smiled. Well...almost.

I strolled around the empty apartment. I couldn't cry or else I'd lose myself. I'd never be able to stop. I wanted my mom, my dad, Sara, Wesley—I wanted to be chewing on the end of my pencil wondering if the answer was 'A', 'B', or 'C', or preparing to give an oral report alongside Wesley. I wanted to come home an hour after curfew and sit down to a lecture about breaking trust and how I'd be grounded until I was old enough to get the senior citizen discount on small cups of coffee at donut shops.

I walked into the living room and sat on the brown couch, concrete beneath my tired body. I stood and used the last bit of energy to pace. My frame shook from hunger. My stomach grew nauseous, but I wouldn't show weakness. I turned back into the bedroom and lay down on the bed. The ceiling was white. I tried to stay awake by making pictures with the rivets.

My mom's soft hand combed through my hair, her lavender scent filled my mind.

"Lila," she called. *"Come here, come to mommy."*

I jumped through the puddles, but they quickly turned to glass. It cut the bottoms of my feet and blood streamed into the rain.

I was getting too used to those dreams and had started waking myself from them. They were always the same—Mom would call my name and I'd eagerly jump through the muddy puddles to get to her, but she'd disappear, and the water would turn to glass or blood. I sat up just in time to hear the main door open.

"Lila?" It was Peter.

"In the bedroom." I was too weak to get up at that point.

"Okay." He shuffled through the doorway loaded down with a tray of food and several bags, which he dropped at the foot of the bed. "So, here's food. I'm going to set it on the nightstand. If it's not enough, just let me know. I'm hooking up a phone to your room, but don't get too excited; it only communicates within the Facility. Push '0' and you'll get me when I'm here. After that, you'll have to deal with Sullivan. You have clothing in the bags. Somewhere there's soap, shampoo, conditioner, and other toiletries."

"You realize I'm a person, right?" I ran my hands over the bracelet, Wesley's bracelet.

"Come again?" My question caught him off guard and he lowered his eyebrows.

"I'm a human being," I explained. "You know that? I have parents—I *had* them. They're dead now."

"Your file indicates they are very much alive."

"You're in college. You know I wanted to be also? I'm a person, not a machine or an experiment." I didn't want to get sentimental but hoped by appealing to Peter's humanity, we could make a connection.

He paused for a minute and let out a deep breath. "Come with me. There's one more thing I need to show you in the restroom. It's about flushing the toilet."

I gave him a strange look but followed. He pulled the handle to the toilet and it flushed loudly. "Watch what you say and do. There are cameras in every room but this one." He quickly left me standing bewildered in the bathroom. *Did he just give me an out? Did he let me in on something I shouldn't know? Why?*

"I take it you'll be fine for the evening," he commented, acting as though nothing had happened. "If you have any troubles with the toilet, feel free to call me." With that, he turned and left me to eat dinner alone.

The tray was loaded down in turkey in gravy, mashed potatoes, pasta, a roll and a piece of cake for dessert. At the time, I was starving, and the idea of the food being laced with sedatives—or anything else, alluded me. Sullivan was right—it was good, or I was just famished enough for it to seem that way. I shoveled it down and without bothering to change, fell asleep.

"Sullivan is evil. He's the head of FDRA and don't believe it if he tells you that he isn't." Wesley's figure stood next to me and the lake glittered beneath us as the sun rested in a clear sky at Garvin Park.

"How do I get out?" I asked as he reached in his pocket to pull out a wrapped box with a tiny ribbon.

"Here, open it," he smiled, and his eyes shimmered into the water.

Despite myself, I loosened the fragile ribbon and gently took the lid off the gift only to find the severed head of Mom's porcelain figurine staring blankly at me. I dropped it and jumped back.

"It was you. It was your fault," Wesley accused as the background behind him faded into Sullivan's wall of photos.

I woke with a jolt. It took me a long while to figure out the scene was nothing more than one of my many nightmares. Memories of my mom and dad filled the confusion and my chest heaved with regret. Why couldn't I have been there that Friday evening? Maybe they would still be alive.

The version of Wesley that plagued my dream was right— their deaths were my fault. I couldn't bring them back, but given enough time and energy, I could tear the FDRA apart and make them pay for what they did, make Sullivan pay. What about the others, though? What were the circumstances behind their deaths? Did the blame rest solely on those with abilities?

I'd barely sat up when the main door creaked open. "Lila? I brought breakfast," Peter's unpleasantly chipper voice resounded throughout the room. I stood up by my bed and made my way to the living room. "There you are." He scowled as he looked me over. "Not ready, I see. Well, you better eat and get washed up because from what I understand, we have a long day planned."

"We?" I walked closer to the table.

He answered, "You, me, and Sullivan. I'm sticking around as part of my internship. Extra credit, really," he smirked. "I believe this will be fascinating." He pushed his thick glasses up on his nose.

"I guess I'd better get a move on then." I sat down and opened the tray in front of me. I was met with eggs, bacon, toast, and a couple different types of cereal.

"There's juice and milk in the refrigerator. I can get it for you if you want."

"Sure. That'd be great. Thank you," I replied and picked up the fork as Peter walked over to the fridge. He placed the cartons in front of me and moved to the side while I continued to eat.

"I suggest you eat everything, especially if you happen to be saving any of that energy," he said nonchalantly, as if he knew that I wanted to build up my ability in order to escape the prison.

I stopped chewing mid-bite. *Should I read into that comment?* I didn't argue with him, though and poured the milk over the multi-grain flakes and when I finished that small box, I opened the next. Despite my stomach being full, I poured an extra glass of milk, knowing how many extra pounds I'd be putting on by binge eating. Dieting, however, was number five-hundred thousand on my list of priorities.

"I'm off to get ready. Feel more than free to wait out here." I stood to leave. "I've been known to take a while," I added.

"Remember, this isn't a fashion show. No need to dress up." He rolled his eyes and picked up some news magazine back issue that was left on an end table.

Taking note of his freshly ironed khaki pants, white tennis shoes, and navy polo, I replied, "Like I'm taking wardrobe advice from you."

Once the door was closed behind me, I searched through the bags and found everything I needed for a shower. Rummaging through the others revealed jeans and plain t-shirts. I took it all into the bathroom. Privacy.

The false mirror worked to expose tiny creases that were popping up on my forehead. My green eyes looked dull and were highlighted by the charcoal indentions underneath. My face was pale and oily and my typically full, light brown hair was lifeless. Being captive in that place was doing nothing for me. I shook my head in resentment.

I needed to pull it together and, on that thought, I remembered Wesley's demeanor from the night we went on the run. He was so cold after we left my house. He had emotionally detached himself from the situation to survive. He'd placed practicality over his emotions. That's what I needed to do. I couldn't let myself mourn my parents, nor could I think about Sara or Wesley. I had to go into survival mode, to find out what really happened to my mom and dad.

As warm water from the shower hit my body, I made the decision to not allow Sullivan to break me down. Wesley had warned me he was dangerous and manipulative. What about Peter, though? It felt like he was trying to help me and yet he was interning with those people.

I turned off the shower faucet and grabbed the soft towel. I brushed my hair and teeth and was surprised at how well the clothes fit. Rummaging through the bags yielded nothing. I was hoping they included mascara or lip gloss, but only found the basics— more soap and extra deodorant, not even a band to pull my hair up. I scrunched it so it would wave and took one last look at my dull complexion. It made sense that Sullivan didn't care about my appearance, but cleaning up would at least make me feel better. I still looked like crap. I grabbed a clean washcloth and ran some hot water on it before placing it over my face. A couple minutes passed, and I removed it. A little more color surfaced on my cheeks. How long would it last? I turned off the lights and walked into the living room where Peter sat, waiting patiently.

"I think something is wrong with the toilet again. Like, the way it's not flushing right." I needed more information out of him and he'd been the one to drop the hint.

"Okay, I'll look at it when we're finished this afternoon. As it is, the time is now 7:25 A.M. and we're almost late. Don't want to lose my internship, so let's get going." Peter opened the door and motioned for me to leave the room.

"Where are we going?" I was genuinely curious.

"General testing, real easy, just like your checkup at the doctor. They want to get some vitals on you and stuff." His voice was matter-of-fact as we walked down the long hallway. He swiped his card in front of a large door. "This is the main door. You can see the front of all the buildings from here. The only one not visible is the control center. Say, if someone ever tried to escape, it'd be bad if they made it into the control room."

Why was he telling me that? I shouldn't ask. "Why?"

"Because it's home to the computer mainframe. If that system was disabled, then security would be compromised. But we don't have to worry about that," he chuckled. "No one could get through the safety measures."

He obviously didn't know what I was capable of; by continuing to use my abilities, they would only grow stronger. I needed to stand firm. They couldn't break me down or cause me to doubt myself. I had to stop being intimidated by Sullivan and his minions, whoever they were.

The front doors to the structures faced one another at an angle, each having a letter and a number over them. The front door of my building read, 'E101'. "Which one are we going to?" I asked as I continued to follow slightly behind Peter.

"We will be in 'E110'." He didn't turn back to answer.

Well, that was informative. I didn't bother to ask more questions and continued to walk, taking in the fresh air and warmth of the day. What Wesley was doing? I caught myself. I couldn't break down, no emotion. After a few moments, we arrived at the green door of building 'E110'. "So, this is it." My stomach began to twist a little and I took in several deep breaths. Once inside, we walked down a hall with no windows and a single door. Peter knocked, and it opened.

"Peter, hello again. Oh, and you must be Lila." Her lips were slicked with pink gloss and her dirty blonde hair was pulled back in a ponytail. She was slender and petite and was a far cry from crusty Sullivan. In different circumstances, I would've felt perfectly comfortable with this lady as my doctor. The situation being as it was, though, she was nothing more than an old witch...a totally cute and coordinated old witch, but one nonetheless.

"My name is Dr. Sawyer. It's nice to meet you." She held out a hand, and I took it, trying to make it look as though I'd decided to comply. It worked, because she seemed surprised.

"Well." She paused. "Let's get started."

She asked me a battery of questions about my overall health and took my blood pressure. She listened to my heart and lungs, checked my pulse, eyes, ears, throat, and reflexes.

"You seem perfectly healthy, young lady," she assessed after a long bout of silence. "We're going to run some blood work though, just to make sure."

I squinted as she took out a sterile needle accompanied by a parade of tubes. After scanning the room in desperation, the only thing I could focus on was Peter. My arm pulsed as she tied the rubber band around it.

"There's a good vein," she proclaimed happily.

My lanky escort continued staring at the sterile floor but glanced up and allowed his green eyes to meet mine as I winced when the cold tip grazed the top of my arm. It penetrated, and I tensed up.

"Relax and this will all go quicker," said the shiny set of lips as she filled tube after tube after tube of blood— and Sara had accused Wesley of being the vampire. I almost laughed.

"There, all done! I'll have results back this afternoon." She looked down and began typing something into her computer.

"That fast?"

"We have a lab on site." Her voice was upbeat. Did she know why I was there? Of course, she did. Like everyone else, she knew more about me than I knew about myself.

"Are we finished here?" Peter's voice came out of nowhere.

"Oh, yes, she's ready," she responded, still busy typing. "Goodbye, guys." She glanced at me, "Good luck."

We left the room, but surprisingly Peter didn't go out of the building. Rather, we walked to the end of the hallway and he placed his finger on the reader and the door slid open to a set of stairs. He started down them and I followed. We came to another door and he entered a code and his fingerprints, and it slid open. The room looked like one of those observation cells in crime dramas. The glass was one way, and in the vestibule, rested a wooden desk and two chairs.

"Why hello, kiddos," boomed a voice from the corner. It was Sullivan dressed to the nine's—a black suit, red tie, and patented black shoes. He left the group of other well-dressed men and women and walked toward Peter and me. Peter nodded at him. "You got her here in one piece, son." He patted Peter on the back and smiled. "Well done. Maybe you're good for something after all." I stood quietly as he insulted Peter through his smile. I was desperate to get back in Sullivan's head, but saving my strength was crucial if I wanted to escape.

"Are you ready for experiment number one?" He turned toward me and smirked.

"I thought I was going to get information," I responded coolly, trying not to show too much emotion. Dad would've called that a poker face. Maybe Wesley would've had some complicated term.

"You give us what we want, and we will certainly return the favor," he bargained.

"And what will that be?" I calculated my words.

"We've seen telekinetics and telepaths," he mused, "but the power of suggestion? Not one of them could do it. They were useless to us, so we had to dispose of them. I'm sure you want to be useful." He raised his eyebrows and reveled in his subtle threat.

"I suppose I do," I answered blandly.

"Good to hear. Well then, young lady, why don't you and Mr. Peter here make your way into the room." He outstretched his arm to another wooden door and stepped to the side.

Peter hesitated. "Me?"

"Yes, did you think it'd be one of us? Or that we'd bring in an outsider?" Sullivan raised his eyebrows in a warning. "Is there a problem?"

"I just didn't know that—I mean, no one told me that..." Peter looked unsettled by the new development.

"It's okay, boy. She's not going to harm you, if that's what you're afraid of. Now, go on, don't keep us waiting." He turned to me. "We have Peter's internship application and I'll be reading you a question or two from it over the speaker. To make sure you know the basics, get into his head and answer them. After that, we'll proceed to suggestion. If you fail... well..." Sullivan cleared his throat and ran his tanned hand over his Rolex. "Just don't fail. Now, on you go." He stepped to the side again as Peter and I made our way into the room.

The chairs were hard, and the naked space made the process more uncomfortable than it already was. We had no more than sat down when the baritone voice sounded through the intercom, "Where was Peter born?"

Peter took in a deep breath. "Relax." I tried to smile. "Don't make this harder for me."

I pushed my energy into him and let myself into his mind. I sifted through his thoughts—likes, dislikes, past, present. I stopped in the present. He'd seen Sara, a lot. My face must have had a confused look on it. Before I could think too much, something pushed back at me.

Stop and I'll give you the answers. Get out of my head. I paused. His voice lingered in my mind a second before I realized Peter was also telepathic. It was shocking since no one had been in my head since Wesley. Why weren't Peter's eyes sharp? Perhaps the glasses concealed their brilliance?

Over the intercom, came the impatient voice of Sullivan, "Could we get the answer sometime today?"

I shouted back, "It's sort of been a while, and he's harder to read. Let me get warmed up."

What the hell? How are you doing that?

The same way you're doing it. Peter stared at me as though nothing was happening. *The answer is Austin, Texas. I was born in Austin, Texas.*

You better not be messing with me. "Austin, Texas," I answered loudly.

"Question two," Sullivan began, to my relief. "What's Peter's major?"

I returned my focus to Peter. *Looks like a trick, you graduated... with a Master's. What are you doing here?*

Don't worry about it right now.

I glared at him. *Tell me or I'm letting Sullivan in on your secret,* I threatened.

I promise to tell you later. Right now, just answer that my major is political science.

I sighed, *Fine.* I looked toward the dark glass. "Political Science." I rolled my eyes. "Can we just get on with it? This is boring." I wanted to fish through Peter's thoughts but didn't think it'd be a good idea to keep wasting energy doing so.

The voice came over the speaker, "Okay, now try some suggestion. Make him think he's on fire."

I welcomed a deep breath of stagnant air and stared at Peter, feeling guilty for what I was about to do, but recognizing if I wanted revenge, I had no option.

I'm sorry, I don't have a choice.

I know. Just do it. He braced himself.

I focused and pushed the waves through his entire body and concentrated on fire. Flames of heat scorched my mind and I thrust them at him. At first, it wasn't working. Eventually, though, beads of sweat formed on Peter's forehead. The fire wasn't real, but I felt bad for him. He began to pull on his shirt and fan himself. Then he started screaming and jumped from his chair.

"Make it stop! Please, no more!" he shrieked as he tried to put out the invisible flames by frantically patting his shirt and pants.

I wasn't going to back down until I was told. That was how I'd prove my loyalty to Sullivan. He wanted to see how bad I'd be willing to torture Peter to obey his wishes.

"Damn it! It hurts!" Peter cried out, falling from the chair while I hoped that soon Sullivan would instruct me to quit.

After a while, "Okay Lila, that's enough."

I pulled away and sank into my chair from exhaustion. *So much for saving energy.* If they kept pushing me like that, then I'd never be able to take them down. Sullivan and his group walked through the open door. He turned to Peter. "Leave us and come back in one hour. It'll be lunchtime by then and you can escort her back to her room." Peter didn't look up at me. His eyes were straight on the door as he made a swift exit.

Sullivan addressed the group. "Would you excuse us, please?"

Without question, they turned and left. The chair scraped across the concrete floor as Sullivan pulled it out from the table and took a seat. He leaned back and clapped this slow golf clap that reverberated through the concrete room. "Well now, I'll say that was impressive." He loosened his tie. "I've seen my share of those with telekinesis and basic telepathy, mental communication and such. I haven't had the pleasure of running into one so talented as yourself. Hmm, Thomas and Jennifer broke the mold with you, girl."

"Who killed my parents? You? Did you order them dead?" No time for niceties. I wanted to get the important information while I had a chance. Being weak, there was no way to know if Sullivan was telling the truth.

"It was a miscommunication, really. We only came in to talk and everything just spun out of control."

Liar. "What happened to their bodies?" My stomach turned as I forced the dry words out of my mouth.

"You have a family plot, right? Down in Florida? You'll find them buried there." His nonchalant tone made me want to kill him right then, but I didn't have energy, so I stared down at my feet.

"Did it occur to you that people will be looking for me? My aunt and uncle. What about my school?"

"It did," he mused. "It's all been taken care of— after you took off with Wesley, your parents went searching for you. They were in an unfortunate accident."

His words were daggers. I blinked hard. "What about me?"

"You were found, thank God. You're safe in government custody where we can interrogate you," he explained.

"And Wesley?"

He waved the question off. "Yesterday's news. His mom's in the nut house. That just leaves Billy and a little sister."

I struggled to process the information. "I'm tired." It wasn't a lie. My head started to spin.

"We have more testing to do," came his uncaring reply.

"These abilities take energy. I've only even known about them a little more than a week. I don't have the stamina right now. There's nothing more I can do," I argued.

Sullivan's face reddened, and I feared he would lose his temper. He pushed his chair in and paced over to the wall. He leaned against the concrete and straightened his tie. "Okay, I'll send for Peter. Go to your room. Eat, nap. We're going to continue tonight with telekinesis."

"But you've seen that."

He motioned to the observation room. "They haven't."

I got it. I was a freakshow. "I see."

Just then the door opened, and Peter entered, his face pale. "Take her to her room to eat and rest. We'll continue this in the evening."

Peter nodded his head at Sullivan and looked to me. "Come on, then."

As we walked down the hallway, I tried to apologize. "I'm sorry...but I didn't have a choice."

He didn't respond, just continued down the halls until we came to the door to my room. Once we entered, I reminded him, "Hey, can you check out the toilet? Remember, it wasn't flushing right..." He owed me an explanation, and I was going to make sure I got it.

"Okay, show me what's going on."

I followed him through the bedroom and into the bathroom. Once we got there, I whispered, "What happened today? You're also telepathic? Does Sullivan know?"

"Yes, I'm a telepath. I can also make suggestions, sometimes, which is how I landed this internship, by saying

I'm attending school at George Washington University." He paused for a bit and pretended to tinker with the toilet. He took in a deep breath, "Lila—I'm your brother."

The words were bullets. Just when I thought there was nothing more for me to find out, I was standing in front of a guy who claimed to be my brother. "Wait—that was too much info wrapped up into one sentence. How...how are you my brother?"

A muted expression crossed his face as he explained. "I'm your half-brother—you can thank Tom. He and my mom, Valerie, had a few wild nights and, well, you know the deal. I was five when he was told about me. After spilling the beans to Valerie about the implications of having a biological child, they thought it best she raised me by herself."

"You're my brother? I have a brother. Was your mom—"

"No, my mom didn't have any abilities," he interrupted. "I got Dad's. You obviously got more than I did," he added. *We need to get out of the bathroom. They're going to think something's up eventually.*

We both stood, and I struggled to wipe the look of surprise off my face.

"Okay, so everything looks like it's in working order again. I'm off to get your lunch."

When will you see Sara? I missed my best friend so much.

Tonight. She's sort of been staying with me.

"Good, I'm starving." *Is it safe to talk like this?*

"I'll be quick, then." *I think so. We have to get you out of here. Sara and I have a plan.*

"Good." *I already have a plan and you can't be around when it goes down.* I knew exactly what I was going to do, and the last thing I needed was too many people involved. That's the downfall of any sinister plan; a whole bunch of people and wires get crossed, everything gets convoluted— I'd seen *Almost Got Away With It* before.

We'll talk more when I get back with your food. He turned and headed for the door.

He left and, feeling exhausted, I lay down on the queen bed and let the new information sink in. In the past couple weeks, I had lost my parents, traveled halfway across the country, developed feelings for Wesley, learned about Tom and Jennie, was drugged and taken in by a secret government agency, and *then* discovered I had an older half-brother. I just needed time and space and couldn't have either until I escaped. I stared at the indentions in the ceiling and tried to make patterns out of them until my tired eyes couldn't take anymore.

***

I was awakened by a knock on my bedroom door. "Peter? Come on in." I was anxious to get to know Peter better, but when the door opened, an older man with dull blue eyes stared back at me—Sullivan.

"Sorry, it's late and Peter went on home for the evening. He came to bring you lunch and reported back that you were sleeping. Of course, we could see that." He gestured toward the camera. "The research team and I agreed that it'd be best to allow you to rest. Today was probably a big day for you. As it is, tomorrow is going to be an even bigger one."

He sat the tray on the stand beside my bed. I opened it and began eating while he continued to talk. "Your blood work came back fine. Everything is normal, but the doctor recommended increased protein intake," he mentioned. "So, *we* might be spending more time together." His mouth twisted into a slithery smile, like a snake I wanted to smash with a shovel. "As I said earlier, tomorrow we're going to begin with some simple experiments using your telekinetic abilities. We might move on to more exercises in telepathy..."

His voice trailed off and I stared at the tray, trying to pretend that I wasn't in his head. The last time I attempted it, I'd merely grazed the surface and found myself confused that Sullivan could be so evil and yet seem like such a peaceful person. I began to push harder with the knowledge there'd be time rest and eat again before morning.

I weeded through his disgusting thoughts and violent memories until I found my parents. The porcelain figurines shattered against the wooden floor. The blank eyes from that night stared into mine. My mind jumped to the worried looks on my mom's and dad's faces and Sullivan's hand tightened on the trigger—once, twice. He killed them. What a damn liar and fool. I fought hard not to get sick or show any sign of anger toward him at that moment. My mind separated from his and drifted back to the present; I'd seen enough.

"Does that sound good?"

"Huh?" I paused, the only thing sounding good was suggesting to Sullivan that he throw himself off one of the tall buildings. "I'm sorry, I was starving and I'm afraid my food got the best of me."

"Tomorrow is going to be quite rigorous. I was thinking the day after, you could stay in your room and rest while my team assesses the data we've been gathering."

"Confined to my room, huh? A prisoner. Just what every teenage girl dreams of," I scoffed.

"Oh Lila," he began, waving his hand as though I should be grateful for the day off. "You're not a prisoner, really. You agreed that it was safer for you and everyone else in the world to just stay here with us. I have my team working on better accommodations for you. Unless, of course, you've changed your mind, again, my dear." He leaned closer, resting his brittle hand on my leg, his rotted breath nearly making me gag.

I closed my eyes. I'd always been okay defending myself, but alone, with weaselly Sullivan, I'd never wanted to watch Wesley materialize and beat the shit out of someone as badly as I desired it at that moment. "No, I think it's better that I remain here. For everyone," I lied, moving away from him out of disgust.

"Well, hun, it's late and tomorrow will prove taxing. Get some sleep." He abruptly took the empty tray, turned, and left the room without looking back.

My stomach churned from the vision of my parents' murder and the realization I'd been face to face with their killer. The fact that I didn't execute revenge then and there made me furious with myself, so I took in deep breaths and noted that all would happen in due time.

I was too tired to get up, and I lay in bed and recalled the layout of the Facility. I pored over the details Peter had pointed out as we walked through the buildings and fell asleep piecing together my plan.

"I'm leaving soon," I said as our fingers locked and unlocked. His chest was warm and his shirt soft as I leaned my head against it and stared into the bits of sunlight as they weaved their way in and out of leaves that hung on a sprawling green tree.

He brushed his lips against the top of my head. "Good, I want to know you're safe," he whispered.

"I know this isn't real, but I wish it was," I admitted.

"As do I." His mint breath rested on my head and I closed my eyes, welcoming our small moment of seclusion.

I was awakened by the dream itself, like being with Wesley was something too good to happen. I used the bit of solitude to steady my breathing and arrange my thoughts. I had to forget about Wesley and the dream and focus on revenge. Since they were murdered, my parents consumed the majority of my thoughts. My emotions were running high, but I had to put it out of my mind. I tried returning to Wesley and his no-nonsense attitude when we first left Fredericksburg to hide out in the Midwest but became overwhelmed by more emotion. I shoved him out of my head again.

I flicked the bathroom light on and splashed my face with cold water from the sink before stepping into the shower. When I was finished, a knock sounded on the door to my bedroom. It was Peter. "Just a minute," I called out, and then hurried to dress. Even though it was summer, I picked up a pair of jeans and a plain t-shirt because it's not like they left me with another choice. No one really cared how I looked; besides, I needed to wear something comfortable. Before leaving, I slipped my bracelet on. Even though I needed to keep my emotions in check, it couldn't stay behind in the room.

"You're ready today!" Peter exclaimed looking at me as I opened the door.

"Yeah, and ready for breakfast," I responded, sitting at the table. Peter sat across from me and pretended to read the local paper.

You live in Fredericksburg? Is Sara there? Did you see her? The fact that I could eat and talk at the same time amused me.

Peter tried not to laugh out loud. *One question at a time. Yes, and it's one hell of a drive. When I first started here, I stayed a few days at a time before going home. And yes, Sara is there, we went to the mall yesterday.*

I wanted to ask about Wesley. Did Peter know about him? Wesley was probably still in Missouri because it wasn't like he'd forgive me that fast for killing Linda. Peter glanced at my bracelet, the one thing about me that stood out among the plain clothing and drab hair.

Yes, Wesley's back too. He glared over his paper and studied my reaction. I played with one of the hearts that dangled from the band.

He came back for me? My heart leapt.

Until he moves on to the next girl. That's a nice bracelet, though.

Wesley gave it to me for my birthday, I explained. *It's not like that with us. What makes you think he's playing me?*

You don't know his past, Lila.

I tried not to look at Peter like we were having any kind of discussion. *What about it?*

Oh my God! A total revolving door. The shorter list would be the one of girls he hasn't been with, Peter contended.

As quick as hope came, it went away as I recalled all the girls we'd met during our trip. What if he was just trying to sleep with me the entire time? What if Peter wasn't joking? Wesley would say anything, right? *Why'd he come back, then?* I challenged. *If he's with other girls, why would he come back for me?*

Peter shrugged. *Good question. Maybe because you're the one girl he hasn't had.*

Every piece of my body came unglued. *Then I'll be the one girl he won't get,* I resolved. I finished breakfast and we exited my room and started for the hall.

"What's on the agenda today?" I asked Peter, who walked beside me. It was totally weird to have a brother, but oddly I wasn't mad at him for not revealing himself sooner. He was probably in the same position I was.

"Telekinesis," he answered as he opened the door and we stepped outside. It was cloudy and humid; perhaps it would rain. *You up for it?*

I haven't practiced much, I admitted. *I might be better at suggestion and telepathy.*

You'll do fine, he assured me, and I believed him.

"Where're we going?" It seemed we were headed toward the medical building, but I wanted to be sure.

"Same place." Peter's answers were short. It was part of the act. I chewed over what he'd told me about Wesley, but parts of it didn't add up. Why would Wesley spend so much money on a bracelet just to mess with me? Was it part of some game? If so, he'd lied to me as much as I'd lied to him.

The metal door in front of us buzzed open, and I followed Peter to another door that led to the stairs. Once again, we met Sullivan, who was busy talking to the same group that had been there the day before. He didn't look away, but when the door buzzed open, Peter motioned for me to enter.

I made my way into the room. Everything was concrete, and it was empty. They'd removed the table and chairs. I felt so vulnerable, truly like research more than a person. They could see me from the dark windows, but I couldn't see them. It made me super uncomfortable. While I waited, I turned my bracelet around and thought of Wesley's smooth lips as they pressed against mine, the way our tongues danced and his explored every angle of my mouth, the overwhelming sense that moment was it, for me. Was it for him?

"Okay, we'll begin. Bring in object 'A'," Sullivan's unpleasant voice sounded from a camouflaged speaker. The doors opened, and a few workers came in carrying a block of concrete. They placed it several feet in front of me and quickly left.

I stood for a minute before asking, "What am I supposed to do?"

"Whatever you want," came the response. "Lift it, push it, throw it..."

I sighed, wondering how heavy it was and knowing the most I'd done was throw a mirror. I pushed some energy at the slab, no response. I pushed harder and it shook. When I threw out more waves, it lifted. At first, the weight went unnoticed, but after some time, sweat formed on my forehead and ran down my jaw. Static appeared in my eyes. I needed to stop but was not about to put it down until I was told. Finally, after a length of time, came, "Okay, lower it." I released a slow breath and pulled the waves back in and a crash reverberated as it slammed to the ground.

The men removed the brick and set up for the next item, which, to my surprise was a compact car.

"Seriously?" I shouted, still trying to catch my breath.

"Whenever you're ready," replied Sullivan through the speakers.

Impossible, I thought to myself.

Oh my God, Peter's voice rang through my head. *There's no way. This'll kill you.*

No, I got this. Though I didn't have it. I pushed harder than before and the vehicle moved a little. My heartbeat sped when I shoved more energy at the beast. I had to think fast. I wouldn't be able to lift the vehicle; it'd be impossible. What would Sullivan do to me when I couldn't? His words about doing what I wanted surfaced, and I smirked when an idea came to me. I shot a small amount of energy to the ignition, sending electricity through the vehicle until the headlights turned on and the engine whirred. I moved the gear from park to drive and sent more waves to the gas pedal. The small car crashed into the side of the wall.

The morning turned into afternoon as they sent object after object in. Some small and light like feathers or basketballs, others were heavy like anchors and furniture. Sullivan was relentless, barking orders through the entire ordeal until finally they called for a lunch break.

Peter came in to get me. *You look like shit. Are you okay?*

No, I'm not okay. Am I going to have to do this later? If they asked me to do more, I wouldn't be able to.

I hope not. You can't take much more, I can tell. I don't want anything to happen to you.

We walked back to my room and when we got there, Peter left. I used the time alone to sleep. If I dreamed I didn't remember, but when he returned with my meal, exhaustion overwhelmed me. Seeing that, he brought lunch to me.

They want me doing paperwork in the office the rest of the day. Will you be okay?

Yeah, I answered him. Some energy had returned even after the short nap.

I'll be back early tomorrow morning. I also spoke with Sullivan and you're done for the day.

Good, I responded, finishing the food.

See you tomorrow. He picked the tray and plates and then left. I fell back on the bed and went to sleep.

***

The sheets rustled, and my eyes snapped open. The light in my room was on and Sullivan was sitting on the side of the bed. He stared at me, which was totally creepy. "I brought dinner. Peter's tied up in paperwork."

Remembering not to let on, I replied, "Oh, he didn't tell me." I sat up and took the plate of food from the slimy geezer. "So, what's next?" I almost didn't want to know.

"Like I said, tomorrow you get free time," he answered. "What I'm curious about is where does the energy go once you're finished using telekinesis?" he edged toward me. "It's just…it's a lot of *vigor* for a young girl to keep penned inside."

"W-what do you mean?" I stuttered, knowing exactly what the filthy predator was getting at. My appetite failed.

"Basic science, hun." I cringed every time he called me that. "Energy can't be created or destroyed, and a girl like you…" his vinegar voice left nothing to the imagination and my stomach tossed about in disgust as he tried to fold a piece of stray hair behind my ear.

I yanked my head back. "I don't know. I have a 'C-' in chemistry. I'm not good at science," I responded in a tone warning him to stop.

"Hmm, that'll be an interesting study to conduct before we administer the shot. If it works, you might be free to go." His sordid wink sent shivers up my body. Not the warm electric jolts like when Wesley would touch my arm or look at me just right; the gross kind, like seeing a group of small spiders and itching the rest of the day.

I blinked. "I'd think you'd want to keep me how I am, weaponize my abilities. Like in some of those movies."

He chuckled and small beads of spit slipped from his mouth when he did—nasty. "All those films, huh? We're not that ignorant in real life. We have weapons and intelligence of all sorts, many you wouldn't be able to imagine. We couldn't control you. Don't you understand? The longer we experiment and keep you the way you are, the larger the risk."

"Seems pretty ignorant to me. Destroy an entire group of people, not a few, but tons of them, just for being different," I huffed. "Why not negotiate with the vaccine you've made, let us decide if we want psychic powers or not? Or, only force it on people who use the abilities to do bad things? Honestly, I don't want it. I know I made mistakes, but that's only because I wasn't given proper information to begin with. Because of you—my government- nearly everyone I cared about was murdered and the rest, I may never see again. Maybe if I'd known about this from an early age and it wasn't sprung on me over the course of a week, I never would've killed Linda and hurt her friend, Amy," I challenged, even though it wouldn't do any good.

"No negotiation. When we're finished collecting data, you'll get the serum, so we can test its effectiveness." He tried looking in my eyes, but I turned away. "Lila, no one with the abilities is good. How could you be? You're power hungry and if I released you tonight, you'd be running around with that boy, Wesley, stealing, murdering, and God knows what else."

Arguing with Sullivan was useless; the man was not only ignorant, he was stupid. It amazed me he could even get himself out of bed and dressed in the morning. I continued to look away for a long time until he finally stood, wished me 'good-night', and left. I remained until both doors opened and closed.

After a bit, I stood and walked into the main room. Thanks to Peter, I knew cameras were watching every move I made, but I wanted out of there so badly. Considering the bolted down furniture and my exhaustion level, there wouldn't be a way to escape that night.

I returned to the bedroom and lay down. I fell asleep immediately and didn't wake until the next morning when the door buzzed, and Peter called my name. I sat up as he entered the bedroom. "Hey," I muttered, stretching and taking in a deep breath.

"Morning, get up. I need you ready to go," he commanded. *Plans changed. They're administering the injection today.*

"Where?" I yawned. *How did you find out? Why would they tell you? You're only an intern...no offense.*

"I don't know," he answered. *You're not the only one who can get into peoples' heads. I don't know how you'll get out of this.*

I got up and opened the door. "Breakfast?" I asked, looking to Peter's empty hands.

"They don't want you to eat today." He paused. "Before we leave, I want to check on the shower; a few others weren't working right. I want to make sure yours is."

"Sure," I said, opening the door wider and stepping aside so he could get to the bathroom.

I followed him inside where he pushed the door half shut. "Eat these." He held out several protein bars. "Quickly, they'll get suspicious if we're in here too long."

I tore open the first package and shoved the grainy, dry stick into my mouth. I chewed fast, flinching when the rough pieces tore their way down my throat while Peter pretended to look at the shower, turning the faucet on and off and poking around.

"Those will give you the nutrition you'll need."

"For escaping?"

"For anything you feel like doing," he answered in a whisper.

He left the decision to me. He wasn't going to try to rescue me, because he knew he didn't need to. He understood I was staying to gather information, but at the same time, I had what I needed and remaining at the Facility was becoming increasingly dangerous each day.

"Well, looks good," he proclaimed loud enough for the cameras to catch as I crunched up the final protein bar. He left the bathroom and I rinsed my mouth with water from the sink, making sure to get the tiny granules from my teeth.

"I'm ready." I exited into the living room where he stood and we walked to the door. He entered his thumb print on a scanner and led me down the hall. My heart raced. *What if I mess everything up? What if they have a backup plan? Surely, they would. Sullivan wouldn't be so arrogant that he'd actually think I bought his line of crap and gave up trying to escape.* What was I going up against?

I followed Peter out of the building and into a familiar one. "This is the way to Dr. Sawyer's office," I remarked.

"Yep, that's where they want me to bring you." *Lila, I can't lose you. I'll help you however I can.*

My stomach tensed, and I nodded as we continued down the hall until we reached a wooden door. The top of her blonde ponytail bobbed in front of the window. Peter knocked, and she turned and let us into an examination room. "Lila, good to see you again. Good morning, Peter." She walked over to a counter where she opened a box and took out a vile of clear liquid. "Give me a few moments to prepare this," she explained.

"Is that the…vaccine?" I asked innocently, trying to sound like Peter hadn't told me.

"Yes, Mr. Sullivan sent an email out last night. We won't be needing any further testing data. It's time to move on to phase two," she answered as she fiddled with the small bottle of serum and a long needle. The tip glared at me under the fluorescent lights. Suddenly, I had an idea and struggled to hold back a giggle.

Dr. Sawyer who was still prepping the shot turned. "Sorry?"

"Nothing, it was nothing. I'm just, umm…needles s-scare me," I stuttered, trying to recover.

"Oh, well this is nothing. Probably won't even feel it and before you know, you'll be normal. Just like everyone else." Her white teeth glimmered beneath the lights as she turned with the syringe and faced me.

A few weeks ago, when I had the nightmares and heard Wesley's voice, I knew something wasn't right; I'd have given anything to be like everyone else. I once thought I wanted to be normal but realized I didn't need that kind of negativity in my life. Even if the serum worked like it was supposed to, would Sullivan ever really let me go? Dr. Sawyer readied a smiley-faced Band-Aid that laughed along with the pointed needle as she started toward me.

I pushed energy at the shot and, like the pen in the hotel, flung it into the ceiling. "Lila, that's not…" her voice trailed off and I focused on my thoughts. That was it; I had to get out of there. I had the information I needed and by taking the whole place down, I'd carry out the revenge I was seeking. "I'm calling Sullivan," her quivering voice threatened.

I grabbed Dr. Sawyer's hand and looked deep into her eyes as she tried to pull from my grip. "You'll do nothing. Sit down until I tell you what to do." I pointed to the floor.

She took out her phone.

She must be a block, I thought.

No, try harder. Push, commanded Peter.

I looked into her eyes again as she struggled to dial the numbers. "Sit down." I shoved the energy at her and her eyes broke and went blank as she sat.

Now for the hard part. I studied my brother's worried green eyes and forced my way into his mind. "Get out of here, Peter." I pushed the energy to him and he stared back. "This place is going down...I can't watch out for you. Get. Out. Of. Here. Take all this." I thrust the energy at him, pushing past his own abilities. I grabbed Dr. Sawyer's laptop and a stack of files on her desk that looked important. He took them, turned, and left.

I allowed him about ten minutes to get out and turned to Dr. Sawyer. "What was in those files?" I questioned. She looked away. "Answer me, dammit!" I yelled, knowing time was a commodity.

"No." Her nervous voice wavered.

She didn't have to say anything. I pushed into her mind and furious images flashed before my eyes. My anger evolved into pure rage. Allowing people with telepathy, or any kind of ability to remain alive was never their plan. In a strained voice, I asked, "How many people are in this building?"

"About twenty."

I flinched, *do all the workers know what's going on here?* "And how many on the property?"

"Around two-hundred."

"Kids?"

"No."

I released a deep breath and put a hand on the doctor's shoulder. Her bland eyes waited for a command. "Without saying a word about me, you're going to tell them that there's a fire." Yelling fire would stir things up just enough to get me alone with Sullivan.

"B-but...there isn't one."

"Not yet." I stared deeper into her eyes. "Do you have a lighter? Or matches?"

"In my purse, in the office."

"Stay here, call about the fire, and I'll be right back." I left the room and walked down the hall until I saw a placard on the wall that read 'Dr. Amelia Sawyer'. Most likely, surveillance cameras had already detected me, and I had to move quickly. I entered and searched around her desk, eventually locating the doctor's purse. Near the bottom, rested an almost empty pack of cigarettes with a lighter inside. I turned the lights off and made sure nobody was in the hall before exiting.

When I returned to the examination room, she was still sitting on the floor waiting for me. "You make the call?"

"Yes, they're sending a crew to put out the fire as we speak."

"Good." I opened the box of cigarettes and removed the lighter. "I'm going to leave and you're going to set the office on fire, but you are to remain right where you are."

Her pleading eyes glared into mine. "What did I do to you?"

Not wanting to answer her question, I nodded to the white and gold pack of cigarettes on the counter top. "They warned you those things would kill you." I turned to leave, and she flicked the lighter on. Once I was out, she set the room ablaze.

The alarm sounded, and a handful of workers frantically came running from the staircase. They nearly plowed me down. I had to get out of there as the smoke escaped from under the door and thickened. I focused, remembering the trick I'd used at the gas station when Wesley and I were surrounded. I stared at a balding man in front of me and gave him a quick command to stop. He listened immediately and a few of the others paused. Did they know what Dr. Sawyer knew? I had to find out.

I dug into the bald man's mind. *"So, what do we do with the girl once we're sure the vaccine works?"* The man turned and faced Sullivan.

Sullivan's grin deepened. *"Kill her! We're going to eliminate them all anyway."*

The man didn't miss a beat. "Gladly!" he responded.

A woman coughed and then shrieked, "She's that girl! We have to stop her!" She signaled at a couple guys standing near her. They grabbed me, and I started kicking to get away. The harder I fought the tighter they held on to me. I was gasping for air; my efforts were futile. I finally relaxed and shifted my energy to the one on the left.

"Put me down," I instructed him. He let go, and I told the other man to do same.

A few more people came at me. I concentrated, and when I found the rays of energy, I pushed them to everyone all at once. "I know the building's burning, but you all will stay inside." A couple of them looked at me and continued their exits, so I pushed harder. "You will stay in the building," I instructed, coughing. My eyes burned as fumes swirled in my head. I needed to get out. I couldn't see down the cloudy hall, where the once hysterical group stood, motionless.

Satisfied, I buzzed the main door closed as I exited. The fire roared and cracked against the screams of those still inside. I pressed my eyes shut and studied the mix of rocks and dirt underneath my feet and kept going. Men and women with guns closed in on me and I shoved the weapons out of their hands, leaving them staring in confusion.

The campus was surrounded by tall trees that I snapped like twigs and dropped onto the top of the metal building. Roofs caved, and debris slammed into the growing mass of people trying to stop me.

Stevens came running toward me, gun in hand. "Put it down," I instructed. "Do you even know what's going on?" I screamed to him.

"I-I'm only doing my job," he stammered.

A quick glance in his head told me all I needed to know. "S-shoot yourself," I mumbled as a tug of guilt filled my body. I shook it, reminding myself of everything I'd seen. "Shoot yourself," I commanded, louder than before.

I hesitated when something tickled my nose. Metallic liquid ran onto my lips. I wiped it away with my hand and looked down at smeared blood. So, what if the confrontation killed me? If I didn't wipe out the Facility and everyone working for it, I'd be dead anyhow. They'd torture and destroy everyone else with abilities as well. Truth was, I had nothing to stay alive for, no parents, Wesley wouldn't understand why I killed so many people, and Sara would never truly be safe with me nearby.

The dust beneath my feet separated as two choppers circled above, like vultures ready to consume prey. "Put your hands up and surrender or we'll shoot," their voices boomed from loud speakers.

I laughed. I didn't even need to look into their eyes anymore. I was in the heads of both pilots and the snipers when I gave a blanket command, "Crash your aircraft." Sun tinted flames soared as the two helicopters plummeted to the ground. I took cover as the copters slammed into what was left of the buildings and singed fragments fell, killing any survivors.

Sullivan was missing from the chaos. I surveyed the area to find a pair of khakis sticking out from under a large beam. I walked over to it and pushed it away. Sure enough, it was him. The thunderous sound of destruction muted itself. Everything paused. It was me and him. For merciless seconds, we were alone. I stared deep into the sordid, pale eyes of the man who'd destroyed my life. I was outside myself; empty, livid, satisfied.

"What the he..." he attempted to mumble.

"That's for my mom and dad, you bastard," I sneered, wiping more blood from my nose so I could breathe and kicked the metal over him. *He'll be dead soon enough.* But I wanted to make sure. "Relax, *hun*," I mocked. I focused on him until the rapid thump of his frantic heart pulsed deep in my ears and concentrated on the rhythm.

"W-wh- what are you doing?" he managed in a screech of triumphant pain.

"Whatever I'd like," I snapped back and adjusted his heartbeat—slower, slower. His breaths were the flapping wings of a monarch I once came across that was dying. The wings opened, closed, slower...and then nothing.

Too tired to celebrate, I tried walking toward the entrance. The gates blurred in my vision as I used the last bit of energy to force the bars open. I staggered out. My throat scratched. The scenery ran together. I quit. Sullivan was dead.

A faint figure stood over me, holding out a hand. The sun caught his blond hair and danced in his eyes. His cheeks were pink and he smiled, welcomingly.

"Wes-"

The sun leapt through my window as I sat in front of my vanity on a cushioned chair. Soft bristles grazed my hair and her smooth hand rested on my uncovered shoulder.

"I'm so proud of you, dear. We both are."

Without turning, I questioned, "Mom?"

"Yes, honey?" Her soft voice circled my ears.

"Mom, you're here."

"Where else would I be on your big day?" I turned to her as she beamed with pride and adoration.

I was confused. "What do you mean?"

She didn't answer but motioned for me to turn around and began brushing my hair again.

I stared in the vanity's mirror, but the glass was missing from it.

"Mom, what happened to the..." She was picking up shards of glass from the floor. "Mom!" Her hands were cut and bleeding. "Mom! Stop... you're hurting yourself!" I tried to focus and push my thoughts, but it didn't work. She continued collecting the tiny fragments as crimson liquid slid from her palms to her elbows. She maintained her calm, relaxed smile as she reached around me and began pushing the bloodied pieces into the empty frame.

She touched my shoulder. Piles of covered glass were strewn about the floor. "Mom! Mom...why won't you talk to me?" For the first time in a while, I started to cry. I covered my face and my body heaved as saline drops landed on the sharp shards and mixed with blood.

SARA

I couldn't believe we'd driven all night long without stopping. Seriously. No stopping, not even for one of those gas station bathrooms with piss all over the seat, floor, and walls. I thought of Lila, how she'd turned herself in to save me. *If* she even saved me. If the moron sitting in the driver's seat planned on letting me go. Maybe he'd actually been instructed to drive me to the Rappahannock, kill me, and toss my body in the water. I'd eventually wash up on shore and my chipped toenail polish would end up on the front page. How embarrassing. I sighed aloud as we pulled up to a corner bus-stop.

"Well, here we are." The government jerk-wad who'd been instructed to take me back to Fredericksburg handed me ten dollars and motioned for me to get out of the van.

"That's it? O-M-G! This will barely buy me a mocha. What am I supposed to do? Catch a bus?" I looked at the wooden bench surrounded by plexiglass. My unamused driver simply nodded, to which I made sure he totally caught my dramatic eye roll before opening the door and exiting the vehicle.

He pulled away fast, and I took a seat on the unyielding bench. I was officially back in the 'Burg, but I'd never ridden the Fred Bus and wasn't sure what time the routes were. *I'll never be able to schedule a manicure now,* I whined to myself.

A loud 'boom' sounded above as the clouds quickly gathered. A spring storm was exactly what I needed because it wasn't like I'd tried to fix my hair or anything.

I turned my thoughts back to the chipped paint on my toenails. God, it was hideous. Didn't even match my outfit.

What the hell was I thinking when I painted them light blue? The distant rumble of an engine interrupted my agony. A rusty pickup slowed down and eventually came to a stop.

"Looks like you need a ride," he smiled as he threw open the door. "Jump in!"

Without hesitation, I jumped off the bench and into the old truck. "How'd you...never mind, superpowers."

He chuckled before asking, "Where am I taking you today, Miss Sara?"

The rain drummed on the metal roof. I thought for a minute. "I don't want to go to my house, or to Andrew's, and Lila's not home...obviously. I don't know." I glanced at the floorboard and thought about the ten dollars in my pocket.

"How about my place? Then we can get that pedicure you were wanting," he offered as a smirk came over his face.

My head shot up in disbelief. "Can you please not do that?"

He sighed, "Oh fine." He put the truck in drive and I gulped. What would he want in exchange for help? He was cute, though he could totally lose the glasses and was in serious need of a wardrobe consultation, but he seemed nice. Maybe the exchange wouldn't be so bad.

"What are you thinking about?" He looked over at me.

"You don't know?" I challenged.

"You told me to stay out of your head. I'm not used to doing that. When I do, I get curious."

"Lipstick," I lied.

"Oh, yeah, purple...it's not going to match everyone," he added.

"Right? How will that even be a trend? It's almost as bad as horizontal stripes." I responded, immediately feeling at ease.

"Seriously, it's so biased," he agreed. "Oh, here we are." Before I knew it, he pulled up to a group of apartments and parked. "No luggage?"

"You're joking, right?" The door squeaked as I pushed it open and hopped out.

We walked up the stairs to the third floor and he unlocked the front door. I was shocked the living room was clean, decorated in a vintage motif with a picture of Marilyn hanging over a white couch. The kitchen was immaculate as well. Maybe I was wrong. What if Peter had a girlfriend?

He motioned for me to sit on the couch and sat next to me. "The apartment only has one bed." He scooted closer and my stomach flipped. I tensed my muscles in disbelief; he was asking for it already. It totally reinforced my whole theory that every single guy on the planet was a perv and I was baffled that this guy was Lila's brother, or at least claimed to be. I believed him, though, because not everybody had those deep green eyes...or crazy powers. He leaned in. "We need to discuss some things."

I swallowed hard and prepared myself to be taken advantage of, again. It was at that moment the door flew open and Peter jumped up. My eyes met a tall, attractive blond, well dressed, in trendy jeans, a plain navy shirt, topped with a plaid over-shirt. He was carrying a duffle bag and backpack.

"Peter!" He dropped his things and shut the door.

"Oh my God! Darryl! What a surprise!" The two guys embraced and then turn to me. "Darryl, Sara. Sara, this is my fiancé, Darryl," Peter beamed.

My eyes widened, and I stood. "I didn't...I mean..." my cheeks heated from embarrassment. The lipstick and the Marilyn poster, it totally made sense. "I didn't know that... congratulations, both of you!" I walked up to Darryl and reached out to shake his hand, but he wouldn't have it and pulled me in for a hug.

"You're relieved," Peter said simply.

"I just...I figured you'd want..." I glanced from him to Darryl.

"Sex?" He chuckled. "Sex in exchange for giving you a place to stay." He shook his head and a mischievous grin spread across his face.

"What did I miss?" Darryl asked as he picked up his bags and sat them lightly on a glass table.

"This is my little sister's best friend. She was in some trouble, so she's staying here for a while."

"Oh, okay. I have an air mattress, somewhere," Darryl offered. "I'm so tired."

"Rest up then. Sara and I are getting our nails done. I'll pick up dinner," Peter offered.

"Awesome! You're the best." They gave each other a short good-bye kiss and Darryl looked at me. "Get him a new wardrobe while you're out," He winked, and Peter rolled his eyes.

"I wouldn't know where to start," I joked back.

Peter stood by the door. "C'mon. This will give you a chance to relax and then we can regroup and discuss a plan to rescue Lila. She arrives at the Facility this evening, so I'll be leaving around two."

"That early?" We made our way back to his truck and got in.

"Long drive, about two hours," he explained. "With her there and you here, I'll be doing it a lot, though."

"I want to come with you," I jumped, eager to see my friend.

Peter shook his head. "No way. Too risky. You need to stay here." He paused and narrowed his eyes. "Isn't graduation coming up?"

"Yes, but I get a reprieve. You know, with my best friend missing and all," I answered back. "I probably won't even go. I didn't take my finals, either," I finished.

"You'll take them," he challenged.

"Umm, no." I raised an eyebrow and threw some attitude at him.

"No pedicure," he half-teased, half-threatened.

"Fine, but what's it matter anyway? People only graduate if they're going to college and stuff. I'm not." I looked down and fidgeted.

"Why not? You should," he suggested.

"It's not for people like me. My grades suck; I couldn't get in anyway."

"'People like you' totally deserve to go and with a 'friend like me', you can get in anywhere you want," he winked.

I didn't answer for a while. I didn't really have much to lose by taking Peter up on the offer. "You know what? I'll think about it!"

He grinned in response. "You're smart enough, you just have to tell yourself that you are. Don't let the life you were born in define you."

"Well aren't you just a walking inspirational meme?" I half-smiled as I looked in his eyes. It was like looking at Lila. She was the only person I knew who bothered to encourage me. Everyone else gave up a long time ago and Mom didn't care. Peter was right—I didn't want to keep jumping from house to house. Maybe I'd catch a ride to school, take my teachers up on their offers to complete finals, and graduate.

WESLEY

It was a little after nine in the morning when I reached my house in Fredericksburg. Overwhelmed with exhaustion, my mind spun. What would a guy do for love? Drive halfway across the country and turn around and travel the distance again. Surrender any control he thought he had over emotions, over life. Choke down pride and forgive— even though she hadn't asked to be forgiven, yet. Regardless of everything, her lies and what she'd done to Linda, Lila was it.

I sat on my couch and recalled how her silk hair melted in my hand, how that smile, or those eyes, with their deep sparkle could talk me into anything, how the warmth from her lips moving against my own entranced me until she was all I could think of— then she was gone. How would I figure out where they'd taken her? Finding Peter would probably be my best bet, but it was something I wanted to avoid.

Was it too early to stop by Sara's? My head dissolved in the thick cushions. I couldn't sleep. Lila wouldn't let me. I rubbed my eyes and headed out again. I drove until I pulled up to Sara's house. The grass was overgrown and littered with empty beer cans. I maneuvered around an old lawnmower as I made my way up an uneven sidewalk. The porch creaked beneath me. I shifted my weight and waited for someone to answer the door. Some washed-up douchebag answered wearing only boxers and a stained white t-shirt. His bloodshot eyes looked me up and down while mine returned the stare with disgust.

"Yeah, pretty boy? Wha' the hell you want?" He leaned against the door frame and moved his arms from behind his back to reveal a lit joint.

"Sara around?" I asked, trying to peer behind him into the dusty house.

Before he could answer, a redhead in underwear and a tank top slinked up behind him. She had frizzy hair and wasn't even worth a stolen glance. "Who's askin' 'bout Sara?" She reached over the guy and took the joint.

"I'm a friend from school. She wanted to borrow some notes," I lied as I choked from the pungent smoke coating my face and clothes.

"Good lookin' friend," she smirked and took another hit.

Ass-wipe glared at her. "Get the hell back in the kitchen and make breakfast, woman." She gave a curt shake of her ass as she turned to leave. The man's lips curled into an I-want-Wesley-to-beat-the-shit-out-of-me sneer. "Whores're only good for sex and food, right?"

I scowled. *No wonder Sara doesn't want to be at home. I'd like to leave, too.* "Well, do you know where she is or not?"

"Who knows." Another puff of smoke drifted toward me. "Took off again the other night, didn't hear from her for days. She called to say she was stayin' in an apartment... some guy... Paul," he choked, "...Parker...hell, I dunno." He coughed again.

"Peter?" I tried to sidestep the heavy clouds before I also wound up high, not that I was necessarily opposed to it, but that was not the time.

"Yeah, I suppose..." he replied, exhaling again. "Peter, Parker." He opened his mouth to reveal crusted, orange food around the sides of his teeth and chuckled. "Peter fuckin'

Parker," he stated again, coughing through his laughter as I struggled to keep from throwing up.

"Than—" I began, getting annoyed. The slamming door cut me off. I wasn't sure why I was even thanking the moron.

Peter was not someone I wanted to see or think about, especially since I ran off with his little sister. He was nosy as hell, and the minute I was near him, he'd be in my head and know everything Lila and I had done.

He'd be pissed I took her, but I had to get her away from Fredericksburg. It wasn't as though there was a choice. I couldn't risk taking her to his apartment because, most likely, Sullivan was on to him. It wasn't like Peter kept a low profile.

Frustrated, I walked back to my truck. The odor from the marijuana had laced itself in my shirt. The smell wouldn't dissipate until I took a shower and changed clothes. Sighing, I hopped inside, turning the radio on before backing out and heading across the city to Peter's apartment.

A visitor's spot stood open; I parked and got out just in time for the rain to start. I ran to the stairs and hurried up a few flights until I reached apartment thirty-four. Before I could ring the bell, the door swung open.

Darryl stood in front of me wearing workout shorts and a t-shirt, a surprised expression crossing his face. "Oh, hey Wesley."

"Hey, man. Where's Peter? I heard he had a girl with him named Sara."

Darryl took in a deep breath and scrutinized me. "Dude, are you high? You reek." His eyes lit up and he leaned forward. "Wanna share?"

I released a pent-up breath and explained, "I was at Sara's house. I'm not on anything."

He seemed to believe me. "Well, you just missed them. I think they were going to the mall. I'm sure he'll have her back later if you wanna stop by. I was just on my way out."

I sighed. I needed to get the smell off me before going anywhere else, but Lila wouldn't allow that either. "Thanks. I'll see you later then."

"Sure," he replied. He nodded before he took off and left me standing in front of the locked door.

"Dammit!" I muttered in frustration.

The windshield wipers screeched, trying to grab my attention, but Lila was my only focus as I pulled in the lot and headed for the mall. Maybe she was with Peter and Sara. Maybe they already got her out. Maybe she escaped by herself. Maybe, maybe... maybe's ran through my mind like a scrolling marquee until I wanted to scream but couldn't, because I was standing in a parking lot while shoppers walked from their cars to the mall and back again.

They didn't care. Why should they? Sullivan wasn't chasing them. He didn't have anyone they loved in his death grip. The rain died down until it became intermittent sprinkles. My phone rang.

"Wes!" her voice squealed over the strained speaker.

"Katie-bug!" I returned with fatigued enthusiasm. She giggled.

"Can you put Dad on for a bit?"

"Fine!" she huffed.

"Wes?" Dad's concerned voice shot out of the speaker. A lady walked by and gave me an odd glance but didn't linger.

"Hey, Dad," I started.

"I got your note." His tone grew sharp. "What the hell were you thinking? Why did you have Lila?"

"Dad—" I tried to cut in.

"You ran off on your mom, your sister. To do what exactly? You yelled in your mom's face!"

"Dad, it's not like that. I thought this was what you wanted."

A lengthy pause and then, "What're you talking about?"

"Mom said you wanted me to come out here in August and watch out for Lila, to take her to the lake house, if necessary," I explained.

"No...she told me you took off. That you'd had enough" He seemed confused. "Why would you bring her to Missouri when Peter is right there?"

"She told me you wanted me to, that you weren't able to come."

"Dammit...she lied to both of us. You know...she had a breakdown. They put her in an inpatient clinic."

I sniffed. "Maybe that's where she belongs," I muttered and immediately regretted it.

"Wesley!" Dad yelled.

"Dad, can't you see she set all this into motion? She had me get Lila and bring her out there so that Sullivan could take her. He probably promised he'd leave us alone. It's lies, Dad. When we arrived, she knocked Lila out." I took shallow breaths. "Dad, she's gone. Lila's gone..." Silence was the only sound from the other end.

I continued, "Lila is the only woman I've ever met who understands me. She's witty, independent, strong..." I paused, considering the way a pair of tight jeans sat on her hips. "Gorgeous." The words poured from me; I couldn't stop them. "I'm around her and I want no one else. I can't...I'm not able to explain it. Dad..." I paused, debating before admitting everything to him. I choked back a humid realization as it collided with some type of foreign giddiness and radiated through my body.

"So, let me guess, you're staying out there to look for her?" was his response.

"That's the plan."

"Be safe, Wes."

"Dad?" A pause on the other end. "I'm sorry... about Mom."

"Bye, son. Be careful."

We hung up, and I stood a while longer in the sticky air. Even in my certainty that Dad was thoroughly pissed. He'd be there if I needed him. Growing up, I could always count on him and I was glad that feeling would never change. I always thought as I got older I'd need him less but discovered just the opposite. If Peter and Sara wouldn't help, he'd do what he could.

Did Lila think I knew about Mom's plan? If she did, she needed to know the truth. I meant what I told Dad. My feelings for her were one-hundred percent real. The more I was around her, the closer the realization came—I didn't want to be with anyone *but* her.

I locked my truck and headed to the mall. As the sun emerged from behind the clouds, shoppers started to disperse. I took the opportunity to search for Peter and Sara but came up empty handed. My stomach growled, a reminder I hadn't eaten. Since when? I didn't know. I grabbed a cheap burger and fries at the food court. While I finished slurping down a soda, shallow giggles from a table across from me caught my attention. A brunette glanced my way and as I looked up, her eyes stole back down to the table. The moment was followed by laughter and reddened cheeks.

The dark-haired girl looked back up and I raised the corner of my mouth, just enough, so she could believe I was interested. I wasn't, but she thought I was. I studied her brown hair, but it was just that... brown. There wasn't a hint of blonde running through it and where deep green eyes should've been, rested the monotonous shade of brown. She wasn't Lila. I stood and walked away before they could come over and talk to me.

Hours later, when the final closing announcement sounded from the speakers, I left the complex. I'd spent the entire day watching for Peter and Sara. I walked back to the truck and had a sudden thought that if I drove around the lot, perhaps I'd find them parked somewhere.

After a few minutes of circling yielded nothing, I pulled into an empty spot. I should've went home and slept but couldn't. Adrenaline pulsed through me. Eventually, I ventured into a twenty-four-hour convenience store and grabbed a large coffee. No cream, or sugar. I only sought the fleeting buzz from a jolt of caffeine to alleviate nearly forty-eight hours of no sleep.

With the rearview pulled down, my attention turned to disheveled hair and foreign rings under my eyes. I looked like hell, felt like it, too, but I had to keep going. Something told me if I just drove around the city long enough, I'd find her. Whatever convinced me it was a good idea to mindlessly cruise the streets of Fredericksburg lied. Lila wasn't anywhere in that city and I knew it, just like I knew that confronting Peter would be the only chance to rescue her.

The sunlight started to creep into the sky when I reached the complex. I rang the bell. It was early, but I didn't care. I had to catch them before they left for the day. The door opened, and a messy-haired blonde stood in front of me.

"Oh my God...Wesley?" Her hazel eyes were wide as she struggled to straighten her hair.

"Sara," was all I could muster. I already felt closer to Lila seeing her best friend.

She invited me in and motioned to sit on the couch. "So..." she started.

"So..." I responded, unsure of what to say to the long-legged blonde sitting across from me.

She cleared her throat. "You just up and took my best friend halfway across the country." It wasn't quite a statement, nor was it a question.

"Yeah," I mused, "I guess I did."

"Wesley! I could slap you right now. What the hell? Did you think?" Her voice was accusatory, her eyes furious.

I explained the confusion with my mom, telling her what my dad had said the night before, and she sat and listened until I finished. "So, you see, she screwed the communication lines. We were all thinking something different." I glanced around the place. "By the way, where is Peter?"

"Working."

"Working? Where?" I didn't know Peter had a job.

"With Lila." I cocked my head, a confused expression on my face. "So, he's apparently got these abilities, too. Somehow, he scored an internship at the same research center they're holding Lila at," she explained, shrugging.

"Where?" I leaned forward. "Where is she, Sara? Why hasn't he gotten her out of there yet?"

"Calm down, she can get herself out, but right now she doesn't want to. She's trying to gather as much information as she can. When she's finished, she'll escape."

"She's not safe." Concern grew in my voice. "They'll hurt her. Please, tell me where they took her."

"Geez, you seem more concerned than her own brother." She scrutinized me. "Do you know she dreamed about you?" I shook my head. "Yeah, she'd have these dreams all through the school year about being in your car, being pursued by someone. I guess it's safe to talk about now," she shrugged.

She'd told me about some dreams, but not those. "Sara, I care for her," I admitted.

"Peter was right. You'd say anything to get with her, huh," she pondered, her demeanor suddenly changing and growing defensive.

"Peter's an ass," I waved her comment off, not surprised she'd listen to Peter and all his gossip.

"Whatever." She looked away from me.

"He is. Yes, I had a lot of friends...most of which happened to be female, some may have been slightly attractive." I shook myself from my stupor. "This is different."

"She's my best friend. How can you prove to me that your feelings for her are different? Her world was taken from her, and I'm everything she has left from her old life. You're going to have to get past me to get to her," she stated with her arms crossed.

"Then I don't know. I'll find a way." I disregarded her comment, remembering she hadn't bothered to answer my question. "When does Peter come back?"

"The place she's at is pretty far away, but he's driving home this evening. You're welcome to stay until then," she offered.

"Okay, that's fine." I rested against the back of the couch while Sara picked up the remote and started channel surfing.

"There's just no selection," she complained and continued scanning the stations.

"There's only eight hundred channels," I said dryly.

She finally settled on some teen movie I hadn't heard of. "We should make popcorn, right?" she asked excitedly.

"I don't do the whole 'teen angst movie' thing," I responded, leaning my head against the plush couch and closing my eyes.

"Suit yourself." Her sharp sigh was the last noise I heard before drifting to sleep.

***

The bridge stretched over a ragged creek that gleamed under an iridescent moon and outlined the figure of a woman, hastily making her way across the wooden passage.

"Pardon me," I stated as she nearly ran me over.

"No, the fault was my own." The light from the moon shone against her dark hair, and as her forest green eyes met mine, I realized I'd known her forever.

"It is dark. Shall I offer to escort the lady safely to her home?"

"Yes, thank you," she smiled. "Mr.?"

"My name is Ashley."

Her cheeks hinted at a light shade of pink. "I am Delilah."

"A true Puritan name if there were one," I chuckled as we continued down the empty road.

"I do believe myself to be growing rather fond of you, at the risk of being too forward." She looked to the ground, trying to avoid eye contact.

We had come to a stop in front of what seemed to be her home. Her hand was velvet glass against a glistening moon as I pulled it to my mouth and my lips grazed her skin.

"How prove you, sir, that this be not a single scandalous interlude?" She took a step back.

"Call, shall I. Tomorrow, after your family has breakfasted and ask your father permission to court," I promised the striking woman in front of me. "We shall talk then."

"Wesley?" The voice jarred me, taking me away from the strange scene.

I nearly fell off the couch. "Huh?"

"You're totally trippin' over there. You okay?" Sara squinted her eyes and studied me.

"Yeah," I lied. "It was just a dream." I shrugged trying my best to act like it was nothing.

"About Lila?" She leaned in, acting way too nosy.

"No," I snapped.

"Geez, whatever," she huffed and flicked the channel again, putting it on the afternoon news.

"Turn that up," I asked.

"We'll take a look at your afternoon traffic patterns, and coming up, the CDC has released new studies supporting the claim that certain infections thought to be contained by immunizations are beginning to mutate. The director is telling citizens not to worry as the process is slow and vaccines are constantly evolving. But first, a story that has grabbed the attention of the entire nation. What really happened at Le Merigot, a hotel and casino in Evansville, Indiana where a mother wound up dead and her friend severely injured. Lead investigators are expected to release a statement later today negating speculation that this attack was caused by terrorists. We'll have more on that later. And in entertainment news—"

"Dammit," I spoke over the reporter.

"What?"

"The Le Merigot—that was Lila," I muttered.

"Wes? What are you talking about?" She tilted her head. She hadn't heard what happened.

"Maybe Peter can explain—" The clicking door interrupted my response.

"Maybe Peter can what?" His face was already red with anger. "You've got balls, man. What the hell are you doing coming around here?"

"Rescuing your sister. Ya know, the one you won't bother to help escape?" I scorned.

He slammed the front door and moved toward me. "You mean the sister you couldn't keep safe? She was taken on your watch, dumbass. You were too busy watching her to watch *out* for her," he snapped back.

The pressure in my head was building. "Get out of my thoughts." I pushed hard, trying to keep him from seeing an onslaught of scenes that'd set him off more. I didn't feel like kicking his ass, at least not right then.

"Yeah, your make-out sessions make me sick," he jeered.

"What? No way!" Sara exclaimed, obviously shocked.

I balled my hands into fists as he moved closer to me. "Where is she then? Why hasn't the protective big brother saved her yet?" I challenged.

His eyes filled with rage, but before he could come at me, Sara stepped in. "Guys, stop. This is ridiculous," she warned.

"He's messing with my sister and I'm kicking his ass," Peter yelled.

"I'd like to see that, beanpole," I shouted back. I could knock him out in one punch. Peter was the desk-job-computer-geek type. He didn't work out, probably didn't even know how to fight.

"Stop it! Both of you! Is this getting Lila back?" Sara snapped at both of us.

I paused, annoyed that she was acting as a voice of reason in the situation. "Fine," I answered back.

Peter took in slow breaths. "No, you're right."

I grinned. *You just don't want to get your ass kicked.*

Fuck you, Wes. He narrowed his eyes until I could barely see green between the slits.

"Guys, I'm serious. No mind magic either," she scolded again. "Is this how Lila would want either of you to act? Keep in mind, we're besties. I tell her *everything.*" She scrutinized me on the last word.

Peter looked at the wall and swallowed hard. "If I try to get her out now, she won't come. She's on a mission to avenge her parents. She thinks she's going to get a lot of information."

"Can she?" I asked, curious to see what he made of her abilities.

"There's no doubt, but at what cost to her? Wes, you know each time she uses telepathy, or anything else, it drains her," he explained. "Everyone there knows Sullivan's plan is to kill her and everyone like her. Us, for example."

"Then stop it." To me, the solution was simple— try to reason with her, let her know the dangers.

"I can try. I don't know what she's planned, and I can't get in her head. Unfortunately, I have to make the drive back early tomorrow morning. I might stay there for the night. Maybe I can try talking with her about it more. Make an offer to help her get revenge after she gets out of there." He thought for a minute. "Wes, I'll drive back the following day. Do you want to meet then?"

"Sure," I responded, a bit skeptical that he planned on including me or letting me know what he was going to do.

"Then it's settled. Meet us here around noon, and we'll come up with something," he assured me.

I didn't believe him. I couldn't. He was planning something. Maybe he wouldn't show up at all. Instead of leaving, I stayed in my spot and kept an eye on the apartment, which was boring. Hours passed. The the clock that revealed it was never hours, just minutes. I drank the cold coffee still sitting in the cup holder. I was hesitant to leave, but at least twice, convinced myself to drive up the road to use the restroom or grab a snack. At some point, my body gave up and I laid my head back and closed my eyes.

We were on the bridge in Evansville. I grabbed her, pulling her close to me and kissed her. I slid my hands down her arms until my fingers locked between hers. Our eyes met, and I stared deeply into the set of emeralds that glittered in the afternoon sun. "I love you, Lila," I whispered.

She didn't respond at first, staring at the graveled path beneath our feet. Finally, she looked up. "Wesley..."

Of course, she didn't get to finish what she was saying. A sharp tap rattled the truck window. What time was it? "Wesley!" Sara yelled through the glass. "What the hell are you doing here?"

I sat up and opened the door. "Making sure you and Peter didn't do anything without me." It was early afternoon, but already getting hot outside.

Sara rolled her eyes. "He already said, he's coming back tomorrow morning." She inhaled and exhaled a deep breath. "You might as well come inside. I took my last final, you can help me celebrate," she motioned for me to follow before adding, "since nobody else is around."

"Thanks," I said casually. I got out and followed her up the stairs. "Isn't it too late to take finals?"

"I missed graduation, but because of Lila, the school gave me extra time to make them up," she explained as she put the key in the door and opened it. We both entered, and she locked it behind us. "I'm an official high school graduate!" she cheered.

"Dare I ask how you were planning on celebrating?" I inquired and began stretching. Her answer was a coy smile before she turned and disappeared into the kitchen. When she returned, she was holding a glass bottle, a mischievous grin on her face. "What is it?"

"Banana Rum," she replied as she pulled the bottle back and took a drink. Then she looked at me. "You drink, right?"

I shook my head and crossed my arms. "Not that shit." I huffed at the ridiculous fruity alcohol.

"It's good," she remarked before taking another drink. "Plus, it's all we have right now."

I could've gone and picked up something else but didn't want to leave so I grabbed the bottle and took a couple hits from the sweetly flavored alcohol. I was surprised it burned on the way down. "You might want to mix it with something."

"Aww." Sara stuck her bottom lip out. "Wittle Wesley can't handle his alcowahl?" she mocked.

"Whatever, I could drink you under the table," I countered.

"Then let's see it," she challenged.

"Fine." I walked past her into the modernly decorated kitchen. I opened the cabinets to discover one stocked with champagne and wine glasses. To the right of them, was a set of shot glasses. I grabbed two. Sara was sitting on the couch. I plopped down on the other end. The bottle waited on a glass coffee table, and I gently placed the glasses next to it. "Let's do this."

"Wesley..." she started as she leaned away from the bottle.

"You chickening out?" I challenged and poured two shots.

"I'm not losing to you," she responded, sitting forward once again.

I picked up both glasses and handed one to her. "Cheers!" I said as we both took a shot. She grabbed the remote and turned the TV on. I looked at her. "What are you doing?"

She changed the channels until she came to a soap opera. "Okay, every time a character cries, we take one shot... every time they sleep together, we take two."

"You're kidding, right? This is stupid." The serious look on her face denoted she wasn't joking. I laughed. "Fine," I agreed to her ridiculous game.

We sat together watching the dull episode and took shot after shot after double-shot. By the time it ended, I was buzzed, she was drunk, and the bottle was three-quarters empty. "Oh my God!" she laughed. "Dance with me, Wesley!" She held out a hand.

I took another drink, but was too lazy to put it in a glass, so I drank straight from the bottle. "No, no way," I grinned. "I'm not dancing." But she was already up, blasting the radio and jumping on the sofa. "God, I hope you don't destroy the couch." I was laughing, but also watching the seductive way her hips rolled to the beat of the music. "Here." I handed the alcohol to her and she took another drink before giving it back.

"Your turn. I betcha can't finish it," she dared me. I chugged the remainder until it was empty.

"There, now we're out." She plopped next to me and crossed her long legs, turning her body toward mine as her tongue ran across her lips. She swayed with the couch. "And I can't drive to get more," I mentioned as she scooted closer. I reached up and moved my index finger down her temple before embracing her and lightly pushing her against the couch. She giggled as I stared into her brownish-green eyes and pushed some loose hair from her face and caught goosebumps on her shoulders and arms as I did so. Content with her reaction, I moved closer. Grazing her ear with my lips, I whispered, "By the way... I won."

She frowned, and her hand rested against my chest as mine moved to her waist. We were in that position when the front door clicked open. "Umm, did I interrupt something?" Darryl asked, setting some work files down and shutting the door behind him.

We parted, and Sara giggled as I pushed away from her. "No," I answered.

Attempting to redeem herself, she stood, turned down the music, and walked to Darryl. "I took my last final; we were celebrating."

He smiled, realizing she was drunk. "I'll join you," he responded. "After today, I need a drink or few."

"We're out," she informed him.

"Crap, I'll be right back. What do you want, Wes?" Peter was a dick, but Darryl had always been pretty nice.

"Anything. Beer's fine," I answered, trying not to slur my words.

He left, and Sara staggered back to the couch, throwing herself onto my lap. She grabbed the remote and turned the music back up. "What are you trying to do?" I asked, pulling her closer as the walls slanted inward and my heart sped up.

She giggled again. "You." She ran her hand over the top of my shirt as the sun shone crookedly through the window.

She would've been effortless. A few delicate whispers followed by a rush of kisses and I'd have her. The prospect dangled in front of me, taking the form of never-ending tan legs. She wasn't thinking. She was Lila's best friend and would never forgive herself if she and I went through with it. "I can't do that," I answered honestly.

 Sure, she felt good in my arms, better because I was drunk, her body, soft and warm against mine. She was pretty, her eyes set off by highlights running through her blonde hair, the fact I could see straight down the front of her tank-top, but she wasn't Lila. "You're drunk, I'm drunk— not a good combination."

She stood again, thinking for a minute before nearly falling backward. "Fine, dance with me," she demanded.

The alcohol in full effect, I didn't argue. I got off the couch and twirled her. We didn't hear the door open again. "Go girl!" came Darryl's voice. "Wesley's got some moves, too." He was carrying a couple brown bags and disappeared in the kitchen. He came back out, holding malt-drinks and a beer and handed one to each of us.

"Thanks," I said, stopping and taking it from him.

He held up his bottle and we clanked ours against it. "Here's to Sara surviving finals," he announced.

"Congrats," I answered. I hadn't congratulated her and felt guilty for not doing so.

She kept laughing. "Thanks guys!"

I wasn't sure how much time passed, but the three of us kept drinking. Eventually we ordered a few pizzas, a ridiculous amount for three people come to think about it and drank and ate and danced until I passed out on the couch.

SARA

My head spun like a train that had run off its tracks as the door slammed and woke me. "Peter… geez, you scared me," I mumbled before laying back down and closing my eyes.

"She escaped!" he exclaimed, jostling me. "We have to find her."

"Huh? Your words are as blurry as my vision. I had way too many last night." I sat up and rubbed the sleep from my eyes.

He smiled briefly and turned the TV on. "We are live in the mountains at the site of an explosion. More details to come tonight. So far, there are many fatalities, an exact number is not known at this time. We will keep you updated on this horrific situation."

"That was Lila? Is she okay?" my voice squeaked against the nauseous walls and blurry outline of furniture.

"I don't know. I don't know what happened." He pulled me up and threw clothes at me. "Put these on. We have to go. There's no time." He glanced at the couch. "What the hell is *he* doing on my couch?" he complained.

"He helped Darryl and I celebrate last night," I answered, yawning.

"Yeah, I bet he did," he said between his teeth. His expression changed from anger to concern that verged on tears. "She got in my head and made me think I was supposed to be coming back to Fredericksburg. It wasn't until I got out of my truck that I realized it. She used a lot of energy doing what she did. More than I've ever seen."

I unfolded the clothes and changed quickly. I seriously wanted to rescue Lila. It'd been so long since I'd seen my best friend. A part of me was excited, but I was totally worried, too. Like, what if she exploded or something. That could happen. Right? "I'm coming." I slipped on a pair of flip flops and followed Peter out the door. We jumped in the truck and sped off.

"Where should we start looking?" I caught myself keeping an eye out, as though she'd been able to get all the way back to town in the short amount of time.

"Woods and mountains surround the complex. If she blacked out, a wild animal could attack her, she could dehydrate. There's people up there, investigating. They know who she is and they're looking for her."

"But she'll be okay. Right?" I could imagine the grim possibilities that Peter speculated, but I wanted a glint of hope. "Lie to me...please."

He hit the gas harder as we merged onto 95. "Yes, she's going to be okay," his voice strained. "Wesley's right, I should've gotten her out. I didn't realize she'd do all that."

"This is Lila we're talking about. She'll find a way out; she'll fight. She's not the type of person to give up."

Peter nodded in agreement. "*So* true."

"And forget Wesley. Yeah, he's totally fine, but he's such a jerk. She better not look at him twice," I warned, seething at the thought of him taking advantage of Lila, especially after everything she'd been through— most of it thanks to him.

"Too late for that, sweetheart." Peter explained, "I'm nosy and I've been in both their minds. They're seriously obsessed. It's all they think about…one another, totally weird. I can't figure it out."

"Oh," I frowned, remembering bits and pieces of him turning me down when we were drunk. After a while, I couldn't take anymore. "Spill," I insisted.

Peter sighed, rolling his eyes. "Oh, fine. Let's say they got real close on their trip," he paused. "Yes, you should totally read into that. He thinks about his fingers combing through her hair…" He shuddered. "Don't really want to talk about it. You get the picture."

"This *is* Wesley, right?" I had to ask because that seriously didn't sound like the Wesley I'd learned about since everything went down. "Has he changed?"

Peter shrugged, "Possibly. Don't know. We're not exactly 'besties', but he seems to genuinely care for her." He studied the rearview. "And he's following us." His hand smacked against the wheel.

Wow, I mouthed as Peter reached for the dial and Cher's "Turn Back Time" rung through the speakers.

I pieced together mental pictures of Lila and Wesley. They'd be a super-cute couple, no denying that. They seemed very different, though. Lila was sarcastic, bubbly, and unwilling to put up with someone's crap—Wesley's crap. And Wesley was self-absorbed. Despite that, he was basically flawless in every way, and he knew it, which put a bigger dent in his perfection than my ex-boyfriend's front fender the time I started making out with him while he was driving. All I could do was shake my head, knowing once we found Lila and made sure she was okay, she'd have a great explanation. *She better have,* I thought.

"No kidding," Peter agreed.

"Stop," I play hit him. "What are we doing about Wesley?"

"Nothing." His response shocked me. He'd been so angry with him and had to be pissed he was over partying with Darryl and me. What changed? "He wants to find her as badly as we do. Another set of eyes can't hurt. Especially with a connection like theirs," he added.

What was that supposed to mean? I was totally lost. Lila was lost, and Sara was lost. I wasn't even sure who was the most lost.

Peter's voice floated over the music, "Relax. Take a nap.

"I'm not tired," I responded trying to fight a sudden urge to sleep, but it didn't work. My mind turned to fuzz, and my body relaxed. I shut my eyes.

LILA

I sat up.

"Not too fast."

I slowly opened my eyes to an elderly stranger, yet he looked somewhat familiar. I stared for a long time, trying to recall where I'd met him before.

"Don't remember me, do you?" he chuckled as I continued to scrutinize him.

I studied the beginnings of a white beard; his thin hair was the same shade as the set of shimmering gray eyes. "The carnival?" I started.

"Right, right...little Lila with the cotton candy." He smiled at the thought of the memory.

"Am I dreaming? How...? You—"

"Not dreaming. And you're not in danger." He extended his hand and I took it. "Name's Paul."

"Are you with...them?" I looked toward the door. What if someone from the FDRA survived? They didn't...they couldn't have.

"I was." An old chair creaked as he took a seat. "Yep, a long time ago," he laughed to himself before continuing, "I was a lad, right about your age, I reckon. Got hired on as a newbie cop near D.C." He sighed. "Those were the days. I really thought I was somethin', getting drinks with the boys after work, meeting up with the ladies." He waved the memories on. "Oh, anyway. I happened to be talented, maybe not so much as yourself, but I was good at solving crimes. That ability got me promoted fast. Sometimes I had to let them go cold on purpose. Didn't wanna draw too much attention, ya know?" I nodded, anxious to hear more.

"I didn't know how I knew things. So, I sought advice from a local group who claimed to practice some kind of nature magic," he let out a loose chuckle, to himself. "Magic, can you believe it? But it was that or a nut house," he coughed to clear his throat. "I was working as a detective when I was approached with an offer I couldn't refuse. Seemed a young man had rejuvenated some sort of ongoing federal team and was looking for some of the area's most talented investigators. The hours were long; we'd get orders to seek out a specific individual. So, we'd find them. Everything was hush-hush in the beginning. Around the late seventies, I met with a man named R.J. Sullivan, a serious guy. No playing around with him... all business and he wanted me to track down a young man and woman. Finding them was crucial enough for him to entrust me with the agency secret over a few rounds of gin in his office." Paul pushed his rickety body off the chair. "Speaking of booze, wanna drink?" He made his way to the kitchen and grabbed a can of beer out of a rusty fridge.

"Oh, no...thank you," I managed.

"Okay, well anyhow. Sullivan tells me all about these telepathic abilities and why it was important to find this couple. I start thinking about my own talent, how I just knew things sometimes. Back then, we didn't have technology like the Google. No, we had to do research—*real* research. Days in the library poring over history and newspapers, but I discovered it was easier to use my ability to get information. I found the midwife who delivered you. She said they tried to get in her head, make her forget about your birth," he chuckled to himself.

I interrupted, "She was also telepathic, then."

"No." I cocked my head in confusion, and he continued, "Some midwives still practice a kind of old magic. They store diaries and books passed down for centuries. She entrusted me with one." He walked over to a dusty shelf and began sifting through books. "No... here..." Dirt flew, and he coughed as he continued shuffling. "It's right... aha! Here it is." He pulled out an old, weathered book that'd been taped and glued numerous times and handed it to me. I carefully started to open it. "No, no... don't read it now. I'm entrusting you with this because I think it might give you some insight."

"Into what?" Paul's house was small, but there was a lot to take in. Shelves and tables cluttered with stuff, like a dusty version of where I once lived. If the curtains weren't pulled shut, powder would've floated between beams of sunlight.

"You know what I was doing when I saw you at the fair?" He slowly made his way toward me. He was dodging my question.

"I was running from Sullivan. After I figured out that he and his workers were putting these people through torture you wouldn't be able to imagine, I went on the run. Everyone knew of the horrific things he did and ignored it. Most of them helped him. When you came up to me, I knew you were the one he was looking for. He sees evil; all I saw was kindness, compassion." He stared straight into my eyes. "Your talents don't control you. You're in charge of them. They don't make you good or evil; that's for you to decide."

I smiled, grateful for his reassurance. "How long have I been here?" I was already starting to feel better.

"Since you stumbled in my front yard? Oh, about early noon, I suppose."

"Oh…" I stood up, still a little dizzy and mumbled, "I have to go."

"You do need to leave, I agree. They're looking for you." He thought for a moment.

"Who? Everyone's gone," I admitted as I pushed back memories of death.

"Well, are you sure? I reckon they'd have someone else, somewhere who'd know about the FDRA," he shrugged. "Do you know where you're going?"

Closure was the only thing on my mind. "Florida, my aunt lives there. I'm sure that's where they…" He stared at me. "They buried them… my parents, after they di— were killed," I answered. Telling people my parents were dead was a foreign language and something an eighteen-year-old shouldn't have to do.

"How you gonna get there?" he huffed.

"Airplane?"

He raised his eyebrows. "You think it's a good idea?"

"It's the only one I have. Will you give me a ride?"

He gestured to the front door, and we walked to his beat-up truck. I wanted to open the book he'd given me and start reading, but it was getting dark.

Paul must have noticed my curiosity. "Be careful with it. The midwife who gave it to me said I'd know who to give it to when the time was right."

"Me?" I was confused. "Why do I need this book?"

Paul gave a quick chuckle. "To help you understand."

Before I could ask any more questions, fatigue overtook me, and I fell asleep.

***

"Hey..." His hand tapped my shoulder, jolting me. "Hey, we're here."

I stretched. "Hmm..." Where were we? I couldn't remember.

"This is your stop. And this is as far as I go. Been hiding out— right under his nose, for over ten years. I don't want to get too brave, now," he chuckled.

"It's okay. I can take it from here," I reassured him. Since my aunt and uncle lived in Florida, I'd gotten used to flying over the years. "Thanks for everything. Hope I see you around."

He shrugged and smiled. Knowing I wouldn't see him again, I grabbed the tattered book, holding it close as I entered the airport. The taillights of the beat-up truck faded into the flood of streetlights and billboards. "Bye, Paul and thanks," I whispered.

I found the flight information board and hurriedly searched for one to Florida. To my right was a ticket booth with no line and a smiling attendant, so I approached her instead.

"Hey there!" she greeted. "How can I help you this evening?"

"I need a ticket for a direct flight from here to Orlando International, please."

"Okay," she began typing. "Let me check on that for you. One second..."

I glanced around the building, looking for police, military, FDRA, I didn't even know if Paul was right about someone chasing me. She continued typing.

"Okay, the next available flight is going to be tomorrow evening, unless you're okay with a layover? I could get you on one around five in the morning," she offered.

My frustration rose. I had to manage it. She didn't control the schedules, but I couldn't risk switching flights. "When's the soonest direct flight?"

"There's one that leaves in two hours, dear. It's all sold out, I'm afraid." She frowned.

I stared into her eyes and pushed. "Bump someone to tomorrow afternoon. I'm taking their ticket."

She stared back for a split second and then began typing again. "Oh, look! It seems like we had to switch someone's flight. We have an open seat," she replied, excited.

"Nice! I'll take it!" I responded.

"Okay." Computer keys clanked underneath her manicured nails. "That'll just be six-hundred-forty-five-dollars and thirty-five cents. Will that be credit or debit?" she looked at me expectantly.

Shit, I thought; no money. I stared into her brown eyes. "I just paid you." I pushed more energy at her and prodded through her mind. Was anyone looking for me after what happened with Linda? Was the FDRA's cover-up true? Surely, if authorities were searching for me, she'd know. I came up with nothing and sighed, "Just give me the ticket so I can get on the flight."

She cleared her throat. "Well, you also need an ID."

A stack of business cards sat on the counter. I grabbed one and held it up. "Here's my Virginia license." Getting in her mind was exhausting.

"Oh gosh! My mistake," she said, seeming confused. "That's strange. It seems as though we have all your information."

Soon, the ticket was in my hand and I made my way through security. I held onto the business card and when the guards asked for identification, pushed my way into their heads until they were satisfied. I walked through the metal detectors, grabbed the book, and made my way to a full boarding section. There was an open spot on a tan bench, and I took it.

"Fly a lot?" An older guy sitting across from me shifted his body.

"No," I answered, not wanting to make small talk.

"Oh, didn't think so. I make this flight a lot. Hadn't seen you before."

"Yeah," I replied and shifted uncomfortably in my seat.

"You okay? You seem upset," he observed.

I turned toward him and in one impulsive burst blurted out, "No, I'm not. Okay? See, a couple weeks ago, I found out I had abilities. But not normal ones. *Noooo*, not like other people who can sing good or dance. I can move things and talk to people in my head. I could destroy a plane if I wanted. This guy I like, Wesley, well... he's telepathic. So we talk to each other in our heads, but no one can know because the government's out to get us. In fact, I just took down an entire military base they utilized to conduct crazy experiments. And I'm seriously afraid if I see Wesley again, he's never going to forgive me for it, but he has to understand I only wanted to save the rest of the people like me and get revenge for my dead parents. Do you think he'll be able to get over it?"

I stopped for a moment. To say the least about it, the expression on the stranger's face was stunned.

Lila, what are you doing?

I sighed and stared into his eyes. "Forget I told you anything at all. Get up, grab a cup of coffee and a newspaper and stay far away from me."

Without hesitation, he shook himself from the daze and smiled. "Hope you have a good trip. I'm gonna stroll over here and grab some coffee."

I nodded and sat back in my seat until they announced the flight. Once we boarded and all was settled, I opened the mysterious book. The pages were heavy, faded. Some were torn, and others had small holes in them.

June 6, 1666

Dearest Diary,

I find myself locked in my room where sat I all the day. Missing the sweetest pink of the tiniest flowers whereupon rest themselves in the garden of my dearest mama. Thee I ask, what shall I

To my dismay, the words faded until they were unrecognizable. Frustrated, I shut the book and contemplated just throwing it away as I gently reopened it and flipped through the pages looking for anything legible. The front cover revealed that it was the diary of Delilah Lynam, born in London, England on June 1st, 1649. *She was seventeen,* I thought to myself. We shared a birthday.

Annoyed, I turned my thoughts on other things as the pilot introduced himself and announced the altitude, speed, and estimated arrival time. The plane rumbled beneath us down the runway. I turned my light off and sat back.

When I arrived, what story would I tell Aunt Liv and Uncle Derek? What had they already heard?

Wesley—my stomach churned around the gamut of feelings, knotting and complicating them even more than before. My emotional side wanted his arms around me tight, reassuring me I was safe; no one could keep me safe. Peter said Wesley was only messing with me, anyhow. Even if he wasn't, would he be able to overcome the things I'd done to escape Sullivan?

Hours passed before the pilot announced we'd be landing and everyone needed to stay seated. Once the plane hit the runway and came to a stop, we unbuckled and started unloading.

In the airport, families hugged one another, and some people made their way to waiting cabs and bus pickups. I walked over to an unclaimed cab. "I need to go to Kissimee," I said.

The driver looked over at me. "That's fifteen miles away. It's gonna cost ya."

"Don't care," I answered nonchalantly.

"Okay." He opened his door and got out. "Where's your luggage?"

"Don't have any." I gestured with the old book.

He furrowed his brows. "Uh...okay." He shrugged and got back into the cab.

Once inside, I relaxed in the grateful silence during the long drive to my family's house. The fluorescent porchlights were a relief as the cab slowed and pulled over to the curb.

"That's gonna be sixty-five-dollars." He smirked, "I told ya it'd cost."

I pushed my energy to him. "I already paid you, remember?"

He shook his head. "Nice try, kiddo." His face dropped, "Where's the money?"

I pushed harder. "I paid you at the airport."

"Oh, yeah." He looked confused. "My bad. Have yourself a good one!"

"Yeah, thanks," I answered, scooping up the old book and exiting the dented vehicle.

I walked up to the tan house and knocked on the door. After a while, I worried—maybe they went out for the evening and left the lights on. What if they were on vacation? What would I do? Soon, the door whipped open.

"Oh my God!" Liv hugged me tight and Uncle Derek stood right behind her. She pulled away so Derek could hug me, too. Aunt Olivia, or Aunt Liv as I called her, was Mom's scatter-brained sister, a free spirit who majored in art, against the family's wishes. Regardless of familial expectations, she'd managed to earn a modest living selling her paintings and had even been featured in galleries.

"Oh my, oh my God!" My giddy aunt paced back and forth for a minute in excitement. "I can't believe—"

Derek, always the steady one, glanced at her. "I'll make some tea."

My stomach rolled at what happened the last time I'd been offered hot tea. My aunt and uncle weren't up to anything.

"You're right, Derek. C'mon you, let's sit down!" She grabbed my hand and pulled me over to the round table in their eat-in kitchen. "They told us you took off the night your parents died. You just ran away. They said that Chase and Becky thought you'd come down here. So they were on their way south and in a panic. They just... they hit the gravel..." she began to sob.

"Who's *they?*" I leaned in to get her answer.

"Umm, something 'S'...Saunders? Hun, do you remember?" she called to Derek.

Derek glanced over from the stove, "Sullivan, I think. The lead detective."

"But I know you. I knew you didn't just run away. What's really wrong? Are you in some kind of trouble?"

Liv had my mom's eyes, a dull blue that sparkled at any kind of excitement. I was talking to Mom; I was tired, and the response poured in one, nearly incoherent explanation. "We came home, they were dead, me and Wesley, I went with him. All the way to Missouri and I have these abilities like telekinesis and stuff and Sullivan is the person who killed Mom and Dad and he's after me and Mom and Dad aren't really Mom and Dad and I have this other Mom and Dad who I don't call Mom and Dad and I killed a lot of people at the Facility when I was captured after Wesley's mom drugged me in Missouri and I had to escape and an old man gave me this diary and I came here."

Dang, Lila. You did it again.

Derek stood, unmoving. Liv's mouth was agape. I studied their incredulous expressions; I could let them remember what I'd told them. How safe would they be if they knew the truth? Sighing, I harnessed energy from Derek and pushed it to Liv. "Forget that and whatever Sullivan told you. I was with my parents in the wreck. I was in the hospital for a while and am better now. You both had to come back to take care of the funeral, but knew I was in good hands with close friends," I assured them.

Liv smiled as Derek made his way over with the cups of hot tea. "I'm so glad you're okay." She cleared her throat. "I'm going to sound a bit insensitive, but we need to make a trip to your parents' attorney tomorrow. It's important he see you right away. You're eighteen now and you're the only one who can sign all the papers. I know this is strange, but your parents left copies of all your ID's with us. They're in a lock box in the master bedroom." Liv shrugged. "Maybe afterward, you'd feel like stopping by the cemetery?"

I nodded. Eager to change the subject, I motioned to a painting on the wall. "Did you do that? It's dark." I'd always admired Liv's paintings, how they were all unique to what she was experiencing in life.

"Yeah, well... right after B-Becky passed away..." she started but changed the subject as she looked down at her tea. "Do you still draw?"

"No, I gave it up." I looked down at my cup of hot tea, hesitating before taking a sip.

"Why?" she frowned, disappointed.

"I just had... bad dreams." She looked concerned. "But not now. They're gone. I don't have them anymore."

"Art, any kind of art really, is a good outlet." She stirred her tea. "Therapeutic."

"I know," I answered before yawning.

Derek broke in. "It's pretty late. I gotta go in to work for a while tomorrow. If you ladies are getting up to do all your stuff, you should get some shut eye as well. Lila, feel free to take the guest room. If you're uncomfortable, we can help you pull the couch out."

"No, Uncle Derek, I'm fine. Don't trouble yourselves. I'll take the guest room."

"Okay, night-night honey." Olivia smiled and then added, "I'm so glad you're finally here so we can get through this together."

I returned her smile with a nod. "Night, Aunt Liv."

I raced up to the guest room where my parents had slept during our family visits. The same old peach floral wallpaper hung on the walls, trimmed in paintings by my aunt. I envied her talent, how she so effortlessly translated raw emotion into haunting expressions. I didn't know a bunch of artists or anything. I stared at the haunting piece with a shadowed woman walking through a garden—the light floral roses contrasting her dark attire; The fog nearly swallowing them both. I missed drawing.

The cloudy air seeped from the painting and into my head, mixing with Liv's words. Would I be able to 'get through' my parents' deaths? How?

I yawned. I had nothing to change into. Exhausted, I fell asleep grasping the old diary.

"Mom!" I screamed. "Put the glass down!"

"Honey, what are you talking about?" I stared at myself in the mirror as she combed through my hair. "I told you to get good sleep. So did Wesley," she laughed.

"Wesley?" I turned to her, confused.

"Honey," she laughed. "You're so nervous. But yes, I'd venture to guess your fiancé would like a bride who's able to stay awake for the ceremony."

It wasn't until I turned back to face the mirror again that I saw it— a white silk robe that covered me. I toyed with something on my ring finger— a glistening diamond staring back at me. "I'm getting... married?" I gulped. "I haven't even dealt with everything that's happened yet. I'm too young."

Mom gently turned me toward her and put her hands on each of my shoulders. "Your father and I will always be in your heart, but sweetie, you have to keep moving forward. Anger is a swamp. Stay too long and you'll get stuck forever. You're only using it to masque your hurt and grief. It's just one of the steps you're going through while mourning. We want to see you happy. Wesley's so good for you." She smiled and wiped a tear as it beaded up in my eye.

Dreams blurred with reality as I woke to the sun shining through the curtains. I stretched, recalling the illusion that could've been nothing more than my subconscious working through everything. I thought of Wesley. It'd been so long since I'd seen him, and while I couldn't deny I had feelings for him, I wasn't sure what to make of them. After what Peter told me, I wasn't sure Wesley had meant what he said. Could an eighteen-year old be in love? Was that possible?

Remembering what Mom advised about moving forward, I decided to start my day. I opened the door to my room and walked down the hall.

"Mornin', girl!" Derek was straightening his tie.

"Hey, Uncle Derek, Aunt Liv!"

"You know we don't cook much around here. Grab some cereal," Liv held out a colorful box and I took it from her. I grabbed a bowl and took a seat, pouring some Frosted Flakes and milk. "I thought we'd start by visiting the attorney. If you'd like, we could go by the cemetery."

"Aunt Liv, I really appreciate it. But would you mind if I went alone?" As much as I loved Liv, I needed closure, and it was something I could only get by myself.

She paused for a minute. "No, not at all, dear. I have nowhere special to be. Take my car since it has GPS, and I can write down the addresses for you, even though I know you're somewhat familiar."

"Thanks! Do you mind if I shower?"

"Sure, hun. Do you need clothes? I'm a little bigger, but I might have some things you could use?"

We were close to the same height and I smiled. "Yeah! Thanks." I stood and rinsed the bowl and we headed up to her room. She tossed around items in her closet until she found a tank and capris. "I know it's not the greatest, but it'll work. If you want, we could always do some shopping later."

"Sure, sounds fun!" *Move forward, Lila,* I coached silently.

"Okay, then. I'll let you get to it." She gave me a warm smile that reminded me of Mom before shutting the door. It felt good to finally be around people I knew and could trust one-hundred percent.

As I stepped into the shower and turned the water on, the drops soothed away the weight of the past couple weeks. I dressed, brushed my hair, and gargled some mouthwash, figuring it'd have to do for the time being. Liv was switching out laundry as I came down the hall.

"Hey you! You sure clean up well," she complimented.

"What can I say? Guess I get it from you," I shrugged and we both laughed.

"Well, let me get the keys and show you around my car."

I followed her over to the side door and she handed me a list of addresses and gave me a GPS crash course. "I might be gone a while. I need to think and clear my mind."

She nodded. "Of course. Take your time. There's plenty of chances for us to talk more later on." Her eyes widened. "That reminds me. Hold on…one second." Liv turned and dashed back in the house. I sat in the car, my stomach knotted. I was too young to be talking to lawyers about wills or visiting my parents at a cemetery. Moments later she returned with a metal box. "Here." She handed it to me. "Inside is all your identification… birth certificate, social security card, and what not."

"Thanks, Aunt Liv. I'll be back soon," I promised and with that, she walked back to the house and disappeared inside. I programmed in the first address to the Law Offices of Simmons, Simmons, and Simmons. It was only ten o' clock in the morning, but the day was already hot, and I turned the radio on and lost myself in the sun and music. Surprisingly, the office wasn't too far away. It was pretty small and when I entered, an older receptionist greeted me. She recognized my name when I told her. "And who are you here to see?" she asked.

Remembering the name of the law office, I gave her a strange look. The secretary studied me over her glasses. I raised an eyebrow. Surely she knew who I'd be there to see. Regardless, I slowly replied, "Mr. Simmons…"

"Oh, okay. One moment, please," she requested and got up to knock on a closed door.

I stood, and the door opened. "Mr. Simmons will see you now."

"Thanks," I said and entered the musty office.

The balding man smiled, "Lila Daniels." He extended his hand. "Your aunt called this morning. I've been expecting you," he explained.

I shook it and replied, "Mr. Simmons."

"Have a seat." He motioned to a chair facing the desk and I sat. "I'm glad to see you're okay. A lot of us were worried, not knowing the circumstances of things. Anyways, no need to take all day with specifics. Basically, you and your aunt are the last survivors of the family. Your aunt forfeited her share to you. So, you, my dear, are the benefactor of the estate. I have some paperwork for you to fill out and my secretary can notarize for us. Once it's signed I'll file it with the court and you needn't do anything else. The money, in the amount of three-quarter of a million dollars will be sent to our office, deposited into your account, and you'll be the sole property owner of your family's Virginia home."

"Here's my identification, in case you need it." I pulled out the old box, opened it, and handed him the documents. He studied them carefully and then buzzed his secretary. When she entered, I signed the papers and she made copies of everything. She finished, and I wished them both a good day. When I reached Liv's car, I entered the address of the cemetery. I didn't turn the music on, then. I spun thoughts around and around in my head. I'd have given every penny of the inheritance if I could've thrown the football to Dad one more time, or to sit with Mom again and help dust her villages and collectibles. How would I even be able to step back into that house, much less own it?

I turned into the gated cemetery and parked. My eyes scanned the lot for the newer sites, the ones that had small blades of grass poking through mounds of dirt. I wandered until I discovered two plots resting side-by-side. The walk wasn't long, and I stood in front of the reddish-marbled slabs; never had it seemed so real—death.

They were in boxes, buried under piles of dirt, rotting away... because of me. I ran my hands over death, the cool, scratchy surfaces, tracing my index finger over the eloquently scrolled 'D...a...' up and back down the 'n' until I couldn't.

I lay between the stones, watching the sky through slender leaves of tall trees. I concentrated and pushed all my energy at the ground. I wanted to hear them, to be in their minds. Nothing. I sat up, determined. I put my head on my mom's grave and focused all my energy at it. Silence. I pushed harder.

"Dammit!" The palm of my hand stung after it collided with the cold, rough stone. "Dammit!" I screamed again, pushing harder than I had at the Facility, I forced my energy into the ground. If I could stop Sullivan's heart, I could start theirs; I concentrated.

"Let me hear you!" I pleaded. "You're not dead..." I pushed harder, still nothing. My knuckles reddened and throbbed. Hitting the stones wouldn't do any good. "You're not gone! Dammit, you're *not*!" Angry tears filled my eyes as something warm and familiar grazed my lips. I touched them with my index finger. Blood covered the tips of my fingers.

I lay back down, knowing I'd pushed too hard and waited to regain control and energy. As strength returned, I sat up again. Still sobbing, "I'm sorry... I'm so sorry... I'll stop." I obliterated an entire military base. I glanced at the lanky trees knowing I could uproot them at will. I could tell anybody to do anything, and they would; none of that would make my parents come back to life. I placed my hands on their stones. "Rest now," I whispered. "I love you, too."

I had to leave the silence and finality. I had to get out of there, somewhere I could think. The only place I could think of— Tohopekaliga. A stunning lake located in Kissimmee. We'd gone there on our visits when I was younger, and I'd play at the playground. Sometimes we'd see an alligator bathing in the sun.

I drove for some time before I came to the lake. I parked on the side of the road and crossed it. Continuing down the walkway to the end of the island, I took a seat on a wooden bench. Waves mix with wind and birds. A few clouds rolled in and covered the sun. I wished I'd brought sunscreen. The breeze blew in a fresh, cotton smell and I closed my eyes, breathing deep.

I thought of Wesley and my dream. Was he good for me? If I couldn't be happy without him, how would I be truly happy with him? He was everywhere, encompassing my thoughts like I wanted his arms to hold my body. Everything was enveloped by him, he was so close; the air soaked with his recognizable scent, his breath neared me. I gasped for thoughts. I longed for him to be close by as I swallowed citrus wind. Whatever the feeling was, it was inexplicable. *Wesley, where are you? What are you doing right now?* I pushed my thoughts out to the water, like they were messages in separate little bottles, floating, desperate for answers.

Right behind you. Checking out your ass in those pants and hoping you're okay and that I'll get a chance to apologize.

I stood up quickly and turned. He was walking toward me, a sexy smart-assy smirk painted on his face. I couldn't run to him fast enough. He caught me in his arms and I stared into his familiar blue eyes as waves of energy caused my stomach to jump. "I'm so sorry Lila. If I'd known what she was going to do—"

"Wesley," I started, "I know. I knew it all along. It wasn't you. H-how did you find me?"

Our bodies moved closer together, in sync, and he ran his fingertips along my cheek. "I'll always find you. Lila... I—"

"Don't, Wes—" I knew what he was going to say, but not because of my abilities. It was thanks to old-fashioned instinct. With all the thoughts flying around my head, my dream the night before, what Peter had told me, it was the best and worst thing I wanted to hear and as good as his strong arms felt around me, I found myself unsure of how I'd respond.

"I've said it to everyone else. Lila, you and I are unavoidable. No matter what, this is it." His voice grew a bit excited, out of character for Wesley. "I used to think... I used to see Mom and Dad... so unhappy. Fighting. I didn't think that... I don't know." He shuffled a little before looking into my eyes with a seriousness that could've penetrated the bottom of the bottomless lake spread out before us. "I love you." He let out a deep breath. "There, I said it." He smiled. "I love you, Lila. Despite anything I said before, or anything that happened."

He looked at me, expectantly. Without a doubt, I loved Wesley, but I wasn't ready to admit it. "Wesley," I paused, trying to figure out what to say next. "My thoughts are a mess. I care for you, I do. But I have to get my feelings straight... I—"

"You need to figure things out." He thought for a minute. "No, I get it." He lowered his eyes and inched away from me.

"I'm sorry..." I studied the crevices in the concrete sidewalk beneath my feet. I wanted to tell him the same but couldn't. "Wesley, I killed all those people," I admitted in a weak voice. "I murdered everyone at the Facility, but Peter."

His jaw tightened. "W-what do you mean?"

"What I said."

"Even the innocent ones?" He walked farther away from me. "What about cooks? Guards? Office workers? You killed all the people who were just there trying to earn a couple bucks?" His eyes were liquid fire when I caught his quick, furious gaze. "I can't...I forgave you for Linda. But this? I-I—" His head was down as he turned.

"Wesley, stop." I pushed energy toward him. "Sit back down." He was fighting, so I pushed even harder until he did as I said. Fury filled his face, but I remained firm. "I, at least, get a chance to explain myself."

"Get to talking, then," he said through clenched teeth.

I didn't say a word before grabbing his hand. "You need to see." My head mounted with pressure as he entered my thoughts.

Sullivan was the obvious target. Next, was Dr. Sawyer. I revealed the innocent-looking blonde and flung Wesley into the same montage of her merciless torture, some of which went as far as operating on people while they were fully conscious.

What the—Wesley mouthed as we continued to the group that I locked in the building. How they'd stand in the operating room, taking notes and filling out charts as they ignored the painful screams.

The soldiers, like Private Stevens who didn't blink before shooting a young boy, with telepathy, when he tried to escape from the Facility, or the cafeteria workers who Sullivan had ordered to slip cyanide in meals.

Wesley, everyone there knew exactly what the plan was. My head relaxed as he pulled out of my thoughts. "Tom and Jennie weren't just running because of a vaccine. It was never intended for us. Sullivan only planned to use it on future generations. Not ours," I explained. "I destroyed everything. The buildings, the people, the records. No one can chase us if they don't know we exist."

His expression evolved from anger to disgust before it finally relaxed, and he put an arm around me. He didn't have to say anything. It was hard to stomach, but he forgave me. The wind picked up. "We should go," he finally said.

"Yeah, I drove my Aunt's car."

"Can I get a ride? I don't think my cab is coming back." He tried to ease the tension.

We walked to the car and got in. The ride home was silent. When we reached the house, Uncle Derek was already home and when we walked inside, the smell of Chinese food permeated the air. Aunt Liv hurried to the door. "Did you have a good day, sweetie? Get everything done you wan—" she stopped mid-sentence when Wesley entered behind me.

"Aunt Liv, Uncle Derek, this is my boy—" I wasn't sure what Wesley was.

"Friend," Wesley finished, chuckling awkwardly and rubbing the back of his neck. "I'm her friend, Wesley." He outstretched his hand to Uncle Derek, who shook it with a smile, but Aunt Olivia was having none of it and pulled the good-looking young man close into a tight hug.

"Well, it's so nice to meet you, Wesley. Good to see Lila has a 'friend'." She shot me a look of approval and I rolled my eyes. "It's nice of you to come all the way out here to see Lila."

"Yeah, I was on business," Wesley added.

We talked over dinner, mostly getting-to-know-you type conversation. No one brought up the accident or the lawyers, or cemetery visit. When it was time to go to bed, Aunt Liv looked between me and Wesley.

"You're welcome to stay the night. Will you two be sharing a room?" she grinned.

"Ye—" I started. Once again, unsure.

"Oh, no," Wesley interrupted, to my disappointment. "I can sleep on the couch."

"We can pull it out for you, Wes." Uncle Derek offered eagerly as he started to gather up the trash and plates.

"No, it's okay. I have to be up early to catch a flight back to Virginia." As he explained that, my heart sank a little deeper.

"Oh, so soon?" Aunt Liv was a little upset, too.

"Yeah, I need to get back."

I waited until Aunt Liv and Uncle Derek were in their room and called Wesley. I wanted to talk to him more and tell him how I felt.

Okay, I'm coming.

The door creaked open and he entered, shutting it quietly behind him. "What's up?" he whispered.

"Wesley, I care for you, but I have a lot going on with me. I can't control these abilities. I'm young... we're young. When I'm around you, that's all I want to do, is be around you."

"And that's so bad?" he questioned.

"It's just scary," I admitted, sitting on the bed and playing with the plaid comforter.

He walked to the other end and straddled me, his strong body was behind mine. He wrapped his arms around my waist, the sense of security I longed for. My heart turned into a million butterflies as he enveloped me and whispered, "Lila, part of loving you is being patient. Standing back while you get used to all the changes. Watching you figure yourself out. I won't stop loving you. Before, we rushed things." A few

105

seconds went by and he continued, "Honestly, I want to rush them again." Goosebumps trailed behind his fingers, down my arms. His warm cheek grazed the side of mine. His breath hit my lips. If I turned, we'd be kissing. "Come back to Virginia with me tomorrow." He pulled me gently back until I was lying down next to him.

"I have to, eventually," I admitted. I wanted to spend more time with Derek and Liv, but I had a lot to take care of at home. Besides, I could always come back. Sullivan was dead, and I'd sent a clear message to anyone who wanted to come after me. "Okay, I'll go with you," I agreed.

That night, his strong arms were barriers, restricting nightmares as I slept soundly. I don't think I moved out of them until I felt him waking up.

I turned to him. "Hey," I smiled, not sure what to make of him staying with me all night, but thinking it was something that'd be easy to get used to.

"Morning. I didn't mean to fall asleep." He rubbed his eyes and sat up. "If you still want to, we'd better get going, don't wanna miss the flight. I bought two tickets, just in case."

We both got out of bed and made our way into the kitchen. Aunt Liv was eating a piece of toast. She smiled at us. "I cooked toast!" she beamed. "Want a piece?"

"Sure," I grinned at how proud she was of her accomplishment; cooking was never her thing.

"Uh, okay," Wesley also agreed, confused.

"Great!" She turned to pop the toast down. "What do you two want to do today?"

"Um, actually Aunt Liv, since Wesley's going back, I thought I'd go, too. I need to get something figured out with school and all that before summer," I grimaced hoping I didn't hurt her feelings.

"Oh." At first, she seemed disappointed. "I guess I understand." Then she perked up, "You two could come visit later this summer! We can go to Disney!"

"Good idea," Wesley responded.

That seemed to be enough to satisfy her. We sat and talked while we ate our toast. Afterwards, we hugged her goodbye, and I promised to keep in touch before we loaded up in the cab and made our way to the airport.

WESLEY

The flight from Florida to Virginia was short. Lila slept while the craziness of the past forty-eight hours soaked into me. The front door slamming at Peter's apartment woke me up. I threw my shoes on, jumped in my truck, and followed them to the highway. After a few hours, we ended up in a small town called Harrisonburg. Peter must've known I was behind him and pulled off on a side street.

"Why'd you follow us?" He was angry.

"Same reason you two drove out here— to find Lila. Fighting with me isn't going to help accomplish anything."

He sighed, "They were holding her at a classified base in Mt. Hurricane. If she escaped on foot, she couldn't have gone far. She's probably weak, which makes her an easy target. The best way to find her would be to start close to the Facility and work outward."

Sara and I both agreed. Most likely she didn't get a ride and was probably in no condition to drive— if she even had access to a car. We searched through the woods all afternoon with no sign of her. It was dark by the time we reached an old house sitting at a clearing next to the road.

Sara used the pause to catch her breath. "Should we stop?"

"Leave no stone unturned," she sighed and we made our way to the abandoned looking home.

Peter eventually joined us and Sara knocked. We waited for some time. Around the side of the porch there was an old truck. The paint was chipped, but it looked as though it still ran. "Knock again, someone's home."

She tapped hard on the door once more and when she did, a curtain swayed. Then footsteps, followed by the click of turning locks. An elderly man with soft eyes opened the door and Sara stepped in front of me, "I'm sorry to bother you, sir. We had a friend who was going through a lot of stress and she may have went on a walk through the woods and gotten lost. She's real cute, dark hair, super green eyes—"

The man raised his hand in a motion for her to stop and whispered, "Yes, Sara... I've seen Lila. Took her in for a while this afternoon. She's okay. Drove her to the airport to go to Florida. Said somethin' about visiting an aunt in Kissimmee."

"Yeah, her aunt and uncle live down there—" Sara paused mid-sentence and thought for a moment. "Her parents. I bet that's where they were buried... Thank you, sir."

"Not a problem," he answered back, looking closely at each of us. "You be careful out there. They won't give up."

What did he know? Who was he? The stranger looked passed us both ways before shutting the door. I tried to reach into his mind to find out something, anything he knew, but he pushed me out of his head. We stepped off the porch and started back to our pickups. Sara piped up, "I'm going to go down there and get her!"

"No!" Peter argued. "It's not safe. This is all over the news. I don't think you understand the danger."

"Don't understand? What the hell?" she shot back. "I was the one forced to live in a home makeover disaster for a few days. I totally get the danger."

"You're not going," I agreed with Peter who nodded. A soft breeze blew by us and then, "I am."

"Hell no!" Peter shouted. "You don't need to be anywhere near her."

My fingers tensed as my hands balled into fists; my face burned. "You going to stop me?" I swallowed. "Use your abilities to stop me? Because you know you can't beat me in a fight."

Peter shot me an I-know-I-can't-win-but-I'll-sure-as-hell-try type glare before asserting, "She's *my* sister." His hands turned to fists as he moved toward me.

He didn't need to see her. I did. I wouldn't back down. "She's *my* girlfriend... kind of," I argued.

It was everything I could do to refrain from punching the taunting grin off his narrow face. "Yeah... along with how many others, Wesley?" Peter snarled.

Before I could make a move, Sara placed herself between us. "Both of you, stop it! She's not anybody's anything. We've been through the fighting before." She looked at Peter. "You hid from her for eighteen years." And then to me. "And you let her get captured."

"Let me go," I pleaded to Sara as though somehow the decision was left up to her. "Let me go for a day. One day. You two can stay."

Unsure if it was the pleading look in my eyes, or the tone of desperation in my request, somehow, I won her approval. "Fine, but Wesley, I swear to God if she gets caught, or if you hurt her..." Sara's voice trailed off.

"Nothing's going to happen. I'll leave tonight. I'll find her, talk to her, see how she's doing." I shrugged the comment off in a ridiculous attempt to play off the excitement.

"Then you should go," Peter responded sharply. I hurried to my truck as if Sara or Peter would change their minds and somehow find a way to prevent me from going to her. As evening turned to night, I found myself at the airport hoping I'd be able to get a flight.

My mind leapt back to the moment; I was glad to be close to Lila again. Her hair pooled into lose curls as she rested against the seat. I picked up a soft lock and wondered how someone so amiable could kill so many people. Then, I thought of what she'd shown me; they deserved it, but what would it do to her? She had a lot to deal with, but maybe she'd be willing to give me a chance, to give *us* a chance. How would I be able to convince her? She was still sleeping when the plane touched down and only awoke when it jilted on the landing.

"We're there already?" she yawned as she rubbed her eyes.

"Yeah, good old Virginia. My truck is parked out here, so we don't need to rent anything," I told her.

When the all clear was given, I pulled my bag from the overhead and Lila reached for some strange musty book she'd been keeping close by. We exited the flight and walked through the terminal, taking the elevator to a parking garage. Her hair drooped as she waited by the passenger side while I unlocked the door. I walked around and stood in front of her, studying those tired green eyes, before moving my hand to her cheek. Her hair was silk as I pushed it back and stepped closer to her, slowly, desperate to feel her tongue curving around my own.

"Wes—" She looked away.

I released a deep breath and looked down. "I'm sorry." I shouldn't have tried kissing her. Maybe it was too soon, but after holding her the night before, our bodies so close together, I thought it'd be okay. Maybe jar her emotions a little. "After last night... I just, I don't know."

She still refused to look at me. "I was confused last night. I'm sorry I had you come into the room." Her eyes matched her monotone voice.

I gulped and opened the door for her. My heart sunk as I walked around to my side and pulled my door open. The ride back to Fredericksburg was going to be a long one. As I backed out of the parking garage and paid the fee, I finally acquired the courage to ask, "Lila, what do you want? I have to know." I needed her to be clear and honest, so I wouldn't cross any more lines.

"You have to know *now*?" she huffed. "You want to make me choose right now?"

"Choose what?" I hadn't thought about it that way. "Choose to be with me or not?"

"Yes, because if you want an answer now, like right now..." the palms of my hands were sweating as she inhaled a deep breath and let it out. "It's going to be 'no'."

The word was a dagger. All my cynical ideas about love, or finding a single person to focus my affection on, I'd thrown out the window. I convinced myself that she was worth fighting for, that she cared about me and I cared about her and why the hell was I holding back? She knew last night, but she didn't know now. I had to face the fact, maybe it wasn't fate, or synchronicity, or any workings of the universe. Maybe it was just two people in a stressful situation clinging to each other. I steadied my breathing; this was why the hell I held back, and damn me for thinking I needed any of it.

"Wesley, are you going to say anything?" she asked quietly.

What was there *to* say? I had my answer. "I think you said enough. Last night was just you being confused," I replied, sharply.

"When I was in the Facility, Peter told me some things about you... and all your girlfriends. I just don't know right now," she admitted in a soft voice. "All those girls on our trip," she sighed.

"I'm different. Everything changed, Lila." I argued, "Forget it. You made up your mind, based on second-hand information." I thought about Peter and the things he probably told her. My fist tightened.

"I didn't mean it like that..."

I could feel myself getting upset and clenched my jaw. "Then how did you mean it? Or are you confused about that, too? I don't want to play games." Frustration brimmed and I fought to push it back. If I lost it with her, I'd lose the one percent chance I had of her ever caring about me.

"Yeah, like you're not confusing... how last night you said you'd be patient, now you want some definitive answer. Today. Right now. About us. How should I respond to that?" Her voice began to rise.

"You should say 'yes'." To me, the reaction was simple, thoughtless even.

"Should I? Or do you just want to put words in my mouth?" she mocked.

Giving up the internal battle, I raised my voice back at her. "At least they're the right ones." Where was it coming from? Why was she suddenly angry? What did I do to elicit that reaction?

"I'm not a puppet," she huffed and then mumbled, "You're such a jerk!"

"Oh, now we're back to name calling." I didn't want to argue, but couldn't stop.

"You started it," was all she said as she folded her arms and looked out her window.

"I never called you a name. When did I call you a name?" At least I didn't think I called her one.

"You, trying to put words in my mouth. Trying to make me feel like my opinion is wrong," she contended.

"No!" was my response, because it wasn't true. I didn't say she *had* to say yes, I just said it'd be the right answer, the obvious, easy choice. "Is it your opinion or is it Peter's?" I asked bitterly.

"I'm not talking," she finished. "We're not talking. Just leave me alone, Wesley." She angled her body so it was turned toward her window and pretended to be interested in the passing scenery. It was a familiar episode, one that would be replayed many times during our lengthy trip together. In the past, I'd always gotten her back.

Yeah, no problem, I thought to myself. I wanted to believe she was a waste of time. Like if I could make myself buy into the idea, then her rejecting me wouldn't hurt so bad. Not that I was used to a lot of rejection. Ridiculous, I could get nearly any woman I wanted, except the one I was supposedly fated to end up with. How did *that* work out?

I clenched the wheel and glared straight ahead at the road. I wasn't going to look at her. I'd force myself if I had to. She was a siren, my name on her lips, hypnotizing, her mind seduced me, and her body, endlessly enticing. She was the only woman who had the ability to completely crush me between the letters, 'n' and 'o'.

I was happy to see the Fredericksburg city limit sign as we exited 95 onto Centerport Parkway. Downtown, the speed limit was twenty-five, but I went a little faster, eager to take her back to Peter's apartment as quickly as possible and get to my place.

I dropped her off without saying a word. And she didn't look back. *Good riddance*, I thought.

"See ya again, never, Lila Daniels," I vindictively told myself as I peeled out of the parking lot.

I drove the few blocks over to my place and pulled into the driveway. I fought with the lock on the front door until it finally opened. Exhausted, I slumped down on the old couch and groaned at the thought of making the thousand-mile trip once more.

A few beers were left in the fridge, and eventually I mustered up the energy to grab one. I returned to the couch and sat for a while longer, in the dark, enjoying my beer before getting up to start gathering my things. I hadn't planned on taking anything big like furniture. I just needed to bring the necessities, like books.

After I finished packing, I opened the fridge and threw out some old food and took out the trash. I wiped down the countertops before taking the last couple of beers and sitting on the couch. I'd have to keep paying rent on the place if I wanted to stick around the area and continue college in the fall. Truth be told, I liked the atmosphere of Fredericksburg, big enough for a mall and stuff to do, but still maintaining the small-town appeal. I'd even considered applying to Mary Washington, but wasn't sure if my credits would transfer. Lila was here... but that didn't matter anymore.

In any case, I wanted to go home for the remainder of summer. I'd made a promise to Katie and hadn't spent much time with her, or Dad for that matter, since I'd been asked to keep an eye on Lila. I wanted to make sure he was handling things okay before I took off for college and lost myself in studying, partying— and I smiled a vengeful smile— women. Lots of women, enough so that the name 'Lila' wouldn't have a chance to cross my mind.

Once I finished a third beer, I didn't bother moving from the couch, I covered up with a blanket and went to sleep, vowing to keep my mind off Lila and her soul-crushing rejection. I'd leave first thing in the morning; I'd clean up, take off, and be done with the whole ordeal. Peter was her brother, after all. He could help her figure out what to do. That's what she wanted.

I closed my eyes, welcoming sleep, and when I opened them again it was still dark. A quiet knock on the front door and the shuffling of feet woke me. I sat up and looked out my window to see Peter's truck. *Shit,* I thought. *What now?* I was done. I wanted no more to do with any of them. The sooner I told the irritating guests, the faster I could get back to passing out.

Not bothering to throw a shirt on, I answered the door, shocked to see the trio standing in front of me, Sara staring at me with huge eyes, unable to speak. Without being invited, they stepped in and Peter shut the door behind them.

"What? What do you want? It's five o' clock in the damn morning!" I exclaimed, irritated.

Lila wouldn't look at me. She stood against the wall, arms crossed.

"Wes, are you sticking around here or are you going back to Missouri?" Peter asked.

"Missouri," I answered. "Now can I get back to sleep?" I started for the couch.

Sara took in a deep breath, unable to stop checking me out, and complained, "He's drunk. He's not going to help us."

Peter glared at her, "Oh, yes he is." He looked back at me.

"I'm done with all this," I spoke up, my voice short.

"You're not if you want Lila safe," Peter answered back.

My stomach churned. What did they know? "Why?" Damn him for playing the 'Lila' card on me.

Sara looked around. "Does your television work?"

"You guys aren't making sense." They needed to leave. "Can you come back later? Maybe around five p.m.? I should be long gone by then; you can watch all the TV you want," I mused.

Sara grabbed the remote and started flipping channels until she came upon early morning news. The music was just starting and the wide-eyed anchor began reading off the daily headlines.

"Good morning Washington! Coming up at a quarter after five we'll take a look at your morning traffic routes, along with some fickle spring weather... Get out your jackets, today might just feel more like winter than early summer. But first, shocking new connections in isolated incidents. A few weeks ago, a Northern Indiana woman was found dead in an Evansville casino. Investigators first believed the death was caused by alcohol poisoning, but now believe there may have been fowl play. A young, brunette female was captured on a cell phone footage fleeing the scene. Though the picture quality is poor, detectives believe she is the same perpetrator of the act of domestic terrorism that occurred early this week on a secured military base nestled in the Appalachian

Mountains. Experts have reviewed the video and claim the resemblance is uncanny. Here is the footage we have so far."

The screen behind the reporter expended to fill the TV. The video of Lila running out of the restroom was grainy, but anyone who knew her could make a connection.

"Shit," I said, sitting down.

"Yeah shit," Peter replied. "Deep shit… one big ass pile of the smelliest shit you can dream up."

"So, what do you want from me?" I massaged my forehead with my hand. I didn't want to be around Lila, but I couldn't let her get into more trouble. I'd made a promise to see she was protected, and I couldn't walk away knowing she could be tracked.

Peter sat next to me before answering, "Take her to Missouri, with you."

"No!" Lila and I shouted simultaneously. At least we agreed on one thing.

Sara walked over to Lila. "We already talked about it. It's the only way you can be safe. It's just for a few weeks, until we figure out what to do next." She put her arm around her friend, a sentimental gesture that was ridiculous.

"I know, but he's such an ass." She deliberately looked at me. "I should turn myself in." She huffed, "It'd be better than being trapped with him."

"I'll do it for you. Are they offering reward money?" I snapped back. I wasn't going to let her get the better of me again.

"You're the one complicating everything. I mean, you just throw yourself at me and expect me to know how to respond." She moved closer to me.

I stood so I was face to face with her. "I don't throw myself at anyone. I was just *confused*." I said through my teeth, mocking her.

She flinched and a tiny part of me felt bad for throwing her words back at her. "That must be habitual for you... confusion," she raised her voice, leaning so her breath was on me.

The regret vanished and I was ready to slay her. "That only you—" I started, moving closer.

"Umm, wow... sounds like we went back to middle school," Sara interrupted us both. "How did you make it as long as you did? On the way out to Missouri the first time? You're going to drive me insane. Stop fighting."

We were still in one another's face. Her full lips so close to mine I could nearly feel them, my hand threatening to reach out and grab the back of her head and pull her to me as the rage turned into longing, passion. It did for her too— it pulsed within each nearly imperceivable creasing of skin when she blinked, through the gradual pink tone surfacing on her cheeks, and a discreet run of her tongue across her top lip, and somehow, without trying to be, I was in her head. I backed away and plopped on the couch next to Peter. Her body eased when I did.

"Okay, I'll get her out there, but I'm not driving. Not with her," I sighed. There was no way in hell I was going to be stuck in my truck another two days with her.

Peter looked at me. "What about your truck?"

"I'll figure out what to do with it. I'll probably buy a new one when I'm home. Either way, I'm not sitting in a car with her that long."

"Wow, another thing we agree on," Lila snapped and narrowed her eyes at me.

Peter shook his head, "For people who are fated to be together, you two sure do clash."

The exchange of angry glares stopped and we all looked at Peter. "Why do people keep saying this? My dad and now you. For I minute, *I* even thought it was true, but obviously, it's not."

Peter laughed and sat down as though we were around a campfire. "As much as I don't like this or you, Wesley, no one is above fate. I can see the connection between you. Even those without abilities can. Fate, she made you two that way. To need each other, want each other. When you're together, no matter how much you bicker...all you want to do is tear into each other...Lila, don't lie to yourself. You want those arms around you, his lips touching yours, and Wesley you want the same. In the end, you two would do anything for one another, forgive through nearly impossible circumstances." He looked from me to Lila, "Love, even though your world is broken. Fate has gone to a lot of trouble to keep you together. I'm afraid the more you fight, the more of a tantrum she's going to throw."

Sara was the first to speak, breaking the silence after Peter's revelation. "So...you're telling me that not only are you three young and beautiful with these super-crazy abilities that caused you to get caught up in some government underworld, *now* Wesley and Lila are being pushed together by fate?" She sat on the couch on the other side of Peter, eyes wide. "My God... it's like I just woke up one morning and got thrown in to some young-adult novel."

"That aside," Peter broke in, "Wesley, if you fly out there, will you take her back?"

"I said I would," I snapped.

"Lila?" Peter asked gently.

She sighed and crossed her arms. "Fine."

"I'll get online and book a flight. Sara, go with Lila to gather her things and come straight back. I may be able to book an afternoon or early evening flight, so hurry." He gave Lila a warning look before taking a tablet out of a black briefcase. "No stalling. The only thing we have working for us is the video quality. Mostly likely, someone who doesn't know Lila well, won't be able to recognize her that easily. Regardless, we need to hurry."

"Fine whatever," she sighed.

He threw the keys to her. "Here, take my truck." She nodded and left with Sara.

After the girls pulled away, he looked at me. "I want to apologize."

"For what?" I asked, wishing I had another beer.

"Doubting your feelings. You're young, but I got into your head. I wasn't lying about the connection. Realize, this doesn't mean I like you." He paused, "There's no use in either of you fighting it. I didn't want to say anything around my sister, but Fate might be using the devastation to forge a relationship."

I shrugged. "And Fate couldn't have found a better way?"

"Empathy and compassion isn't fate's obligation. She has reasons, responsibilities. I don't understand why she's fighting so hard for this, but she's not going to let it go. If you push against her, she will retaliate."

"Sounds farfetched. How do you, of all people, believe in Fate?"

"Do you believe in telekinesis? Telepathy? How can you live in our kind of world, see what we see, and deny that *anything* exists?"

"Touché," I agreed. Wanting to avoid more conversation, I grabbed the remote and changed the channel to an interesting documentary. It caught Peter's attention as well and he glanced between his tablet and the glowing screen.

The dynamic between Peter and I had changed from tense to some desperate need to get along, if anything, for Lila's sake. Still, an unspoken tension lingered, so we remained silent out of mutual fear of arguing again.

SARA

We sat in her driveway, and she looked over to me before staring at the floorboard. "The last time Wesley and I pulled out of here, I never thought I'd see this house again. I didn't know if I'd want to."

"I'm sorry." I touched her shoulder.

"I wonder if it's...if it's still..." She closed her eyes and took in a few deep breaths.

"No, someone cleaned it. When you went missing, I came and looked for you. That's where they found me," I explained, recalling the nightmarish figures with absolutely no fashion sense.

"Then, I should be the one who's sorry. The whole thing was my fault."

"Is that what you think?" She continued to look down. "No... no, Lila, look at me." She hesitantly glanced up and met my stare. "None of this was your fault. This was nobody's fault except Sullivan's, and he's dead now. Right?"

"Watched him die with my own eyes." She raised her eyebrows, which were in desperate need of tweezers and puckered her lips.

"C'mon, let's go inside." I opened the door to the truck and motioned for her to do the same. We both got out, and as we walked up the sidewalk she leaned against me, and I put my arm around her. She handed me the key and I unlocked the door, pushing it open slowly. The once overpowering odor of bleach had died out, and the house was still immaculate. We stood in the doorway for a long while before entering and shutting it behind us.

"I can feel his arms catching me." She let out a short laugh. "My parents were dead, lying in the living room, and all I can remember is falling into his arms. Damn him!" She smacked her hand into the wall.

"So that's why you pretend to hate him." I shook my head.

"No, I really do hate him."

"So...if I told you we got drunk together, and I tried to sleep with him, you're cool with that?" I totally knew she wouldn't be cool with it.

She frowned. "You what?"

I rolled my eyes. "Sorry, I was seriously trashed," I apologized, and she smirked and shook her head at me. "But he wouldn't do anything anyways. I'm your best friend. Practically your sister, and I know you better than anyone. You love him. Don't lie to me. You've been in love with him ever since those dreams."

"You seriously tried to sleep with him?" Not hearing anything else I'd said to her, she asked the question in disbelief, but I didn't know why. Wesley was hot.

"Like I said, sorry. Seriously, it was a mistake. I get it if you can't forgive me."

"On the positive side, I guess, it's a good sign he turned you down," she said before starting up the stairs. I followed her up and down the hall to her room. She pulled a couple of suitcases from her closet and plopped down on her bed. "What am I supposed to take? Clothes? Pictures? What do I bring with me?" She was starting to cry.

I sat next to her and held her. "What you mean, is 'what are you supposed to do,' am I right?" She nodded and sniffled. "You forgive yourself. You forgive Wesley, and you give yourself permission to move forward." I perked up. "And part of moving forward is going all cowgirl and visiting the great Midwest with your smoking hot cowboy stud muffin. Now stop crying before your mascara runs a marathon."

I stood and pulled the suitcases over, unzipping them while she sat on the bed watching me. "Let's start with clothes…" I shuffled through her closet. "Your outfits are so cute." I pulled out a few pairs of jeans, a ton of shorts, dresses, skirts, and tanks and started matching them up. Lila started to smile as she shook her head yes or no to my suggestions. "Admit it," I teased, "You're going to miss my fashion advice."

"Girl, you know I miss you already," she answered as she stood and walked over to her makeup. She held up a tube of lipstick. "Can't live without this, right?" She smiled through the struggle of holding back tears.

I laughed, "Duh!"

"Duh, yourself!" she giggled back.

"No, you!" We were both laughing.

"You!" she threw a pillow at me, and I tossed it back. Lila looked in my eyes, but hers were already far away, somewhere in the future. "I don't want to leave you again."

"It's only for a little bit. You know how things are when they go viral. Just that, viral. They last for like, two seconds, that's it." I'd begun rummaging through her drawers and pulling out bras and panties. "What color do you think Wes will like?" I asked with a coy smile.

"He won't get that far," she threw back.

I shrugged as I tossed some sets in and she continued packing up hair things and makeup. "Suit yourself, but I know if I was fated to be with fine-as-hell Wesley Turner, you'd never pull me out of that bedroom. Unless you two..." She cocked her head and blushed, turning away from me quickly. "Did you really? You didn't!" I squealed.

"No...not quite...just...I dunno," her voice got quiet. "I'm so freaking confused, and then he's just, like, there, and then I'm more confused because it's just like, all these bad things are happening, and I want him," she sighed.

"Be honest...he's totally hot, right?" She looked at me, a smirk coming over her face.

She paused for a minute and searched for the words. "Wesley is very...athletic."

My mouth dropped. "You mean, he has a body? Like a *body* body?" Recalling the sneak peek of Wesley Turner's abs when we'd been to his house earlier, but in the dim light it was hard to see details. I totally wanted those details, too. "Like all this time we thought he was a nerd and—" She looked up and shook her head as she threw more makeup into her bag. "Oh my God!" I was totally shocked. "And what about...you know?"

Lila wiggled her eyebrows. "No comment," she laughed, blushing.

I screamed. "He's ripped? I totally don't believe you."

"That was my first thought, too. He was working out. I didn't recognize him at first... totally embarrassing."

"He's hot...you're hot...you both have super powers... totally a young adult novel," I mumbled to myself. "You'll be in a Lifetime movie soon," I teased.

Lila smiled and tossed a bikini and a few pairs of pajamas in the suitcases. "Doesn't matter now. He and I, we fight too much. I don't know..."

"It's okay. It's nothing you have to figure out right now anyways." I took a few pictures off her dresser and packed them away.

"Anything else I'll need? Anything I'm forgetting?" She asked turning to me.

I shook my head. "I'll check on the house while you're gone if you want to leave me a key," I offered.

"Sara, come here." She sat on the bed and patted the comforter, requesting I do the same.

"This house is mine, free and clear. But I don't know if I'll ever be able to live in it. I want you to live here. You can pack stuff up, sleep in my room, the guest room, decorate it, or whatever. Make it yours. It'll be some work, if you're up to it. I'll ask my aunt to help me with any paperwork. She has a lawyer for all that."

I smiled and gave her a big hug. "Totally up to it! I love you, girl!" It'd feel strange living in a house where someone died, but not as strange as say mismatched stripes, or living through a morning without Starbucks. I certainly wouldn't miss the smoke-stained smell that never seemed to leave my hair, or clothing, or the boyfriends streaming in and out of the house. I shuddered. I knew I couldn't keep staying with Peter, he and Darryl would want privacy.

"Love you, too! There's no one I'd rather have living here."

We sat together, silent for some time before we stood and gathered the bags. We carried them down the stairs and loaded them in the back of the truck. We hopped in, and I drove back to Wesley's. Before we got out, I said, "All I'm going to say is something I never thought I'd say—give the guy a chance."

"Sara," she groaned.

"Whether you do or don't, I hope this thing works out because you know the whole California thing?"

"Yeah," she sighed, "and I totally can't go now."

"It's all good. I'm not going either!" I shrieked in excitement.

"Why? What's going on? I thought you wanted to go out there and do modeling or something." She was obviously surprised, which I supposed would be her reaction.

"Yeah, I totally was, but Peter convinced me that even though modeling was cool and all, maybe I should actually get a degree." Her jaw dropped. "You know, have a fallback plan in case it didn't work out in Hollywood. He pulled a few strings, well, magic ones, anyway, and got me into Mary Washington."

"Whoa! Seriously?" she squealed.

"Ya!" I screeched back.

"Oh my gosh! This is so exciting! See? You're so freaking smart! I'm so happy for you!"

She gave me a great big hug before we got out and walked to the door. Not bothering to knock, I pushed it open to find Wesley who, to my disappointment had put a shirt on and Peter engrossed in some totally boring documentary. "Tickets are ordered, we'll leave in a couple minutes. I'll drop you all off and Billy's gonna pick you up," Peter informed us without taking his attention from the show which I quickly learned was entitled, *Flightless Birds: A World Without Halophiles*.

"How the crap are you watching this?"

Wesley, still absorbed in the dull show remained focused and silent. Peter turned to answer. "It's amazing how a small organism has such a substantial impact on our ecosystem."

"No doubt," Wesley chimed in, nodding.

They were seriously bonding over that dorky show?

"C'mon man, we need to get out of here," Peter nudged him, but didn't break his stare.

Before turning off the TV and grabbing his keys and wallet, Wesley took a key off the ring and handed it to me. "Here Sara...take care of her."

"What?" I took the metal piece in my hands and turned it over.

"My truck, she's yours. No more borrowing your mom's old beater." He looked from Lila to Peter who were standing in shock. "What? I can be a nice guy," he added before grabbing his bags and heading to the door. "Come on, we should go."

A truck and a house all in one day? My next move was stopping at a gas station and buying some scratcher tickets. Lila gave me one last tight hug and Peter gave me a 'see you later' nod before they loaded up and backed away. Once again, my best friend disappeared, but at least I knew she'd be safe, that time, and in contact.

WESLEY

We were lucky enough to book another direct flight. I swapped seats and was satisfied to find myself sitting nowhere near Lila, who spent the duration of the trip reading some old book she'd been toting everywhere with her. It didn't matter what she was doing. I was glad to be going home and spending one summer of freedom before hitting the books.

Despite enrolling in a couple of online courses to get ahead in college, I relished the possibility of having the entire summer without Mom hanging on my every move, questioning everywhere I went and everyone I spoke to. I was always grateful she didn't have telepathy or telekinesis; were that the case, I'd never have privacy on any level.

I'd forget about Lila hanging around. She could find her own things to do and make her own friends. I started making plans, like hanging at the lake, chilling at the local bar at night, partying in neighboring towns...the possibilities, endless. I leaned my head against the cushioned seat, relieved.

Once the plane landed, we collected our luggage and looked around the pickup curb for my dad's truck. We didn't have to wait long, down the line of cars, a little voice shouted, "Wes! Wes! Over here!"

I waved and looked at Lila. "Over there." I tried to keep my tone even like I tried not to look at her legs in the short skirt she was wearing as she led the way, and I followed, wishing she'd wear loose sweats and a hoodie instead of outfits designed to drive me crazy.

Lila arrived at the truck before I did, and Dad jumped out and helped with her luggage stopping long enough to shake her hand and introduce himself. "Wow," he stood back for a second. "You look exactly like Jen, but I see a little bit of Tom in you." He thought for a moment. "No doubt in my mind that you're their kid."

Lila gave him a half-smile. "It's nice to meet you, Mr. Turner."

"It's Billy, and listen," he crinkled his brows. "I'm sorry about what happened with my wife...she's just not herself."

Lila smiled graciously, "It's in the past, but it's very nice to meet you." He opened the door for her, and she climbed in the front.

He caught my eye as I was tossing my bags in the back and raised his eyebrows, nodding his head and smiling in approval. I scowled and shook my head. *Don't even start anything, Dad.*

Me? Start something?

I glared at him, *It's not like that, anymore.* I got in the back, sitting next to a triumphant Katie.

"I'm *so* glad you're back, Wes. And you brought your girlfriend, too!" she added, excitedly.

"No, she's not—"

Katie pouted. "But you two are good together."

Lila turned and gave her a strange stare. "She has..." There wasn't a need to explain.

"I can see you guys kissing," she teased puckering her lips and smacking them in a mock kiss.

"Understood," Lila replied.

"Katie, stay out of their business," Dad scolded.

Lila smiled and turned back to an angry Katie. "It's okay. Wesley is a boy, and we're just friends. So, he *is* kind of a boyfriend."

Katie perked up. "You're nice. So much nicer than Tiff—"

"Enough, Katie." Dad shook his head.

Lila caught my eye in the rearview mirror as Katie snickered, and I wondered what she was thinking. *What?* I hadn't spoken to her telepathically since Florida.

Tiff? Tiffany?

It's not like that.

"Kids, I'd offer to stop for food, but some of the guys are coming over tomorrow night. I gotta get back and move stuff around in the shed. We're cooking out. Gonna do some practicin', too. You like music, Lila?"

She smiled, curious. "Yeah."

"Well good, I just happen to be the lead guitarist in our band," he stated proudly.

"Oh..."

"Dad, don't—" I started.

"Wes gets embarrassed. We call ourselves the Cowbells. We mostly play classic country and some older rock like the Eagles. We get together and cookout. You'll love it. It's good times!"

"Sounds like a lot of fun," Lila agreed.

"You know, we don't have to go. What if I drove you somewhere? I could show you around town." As much as I didn't want to hang out with her, it seemed better than hanging out with Dad's band.

"Wes has a few friends who come over, too. It'd be good for ya to meet people your age," he added.

"But, Wesley, we can do that during the day. I want to hear the band, meet your friends," she taunted, enjoying the situation too much. I shrugged and sat back, bracing myself for the embarrassment.

"Ya know," Dad started, "we've got together ever since Wes was little. Once, he was potty training, and boy did we have a rough time. Kid wouldn't go in the pot no matter what we tried—"

"Dad, no!" I begged.

He didn't listen and continued his story. "We're all grilling out, drinkin' some beer before we started rehearsing," Dad chuckled. "Wes comes running out, butt naked. He takes off runnin' behind a tree and wouldn't you know... he does his business right there."

Lila was laughing hysterically. "Really?"

"Oh yeah," Dad smiled. "That's how we got him trained...right behind the tree. Eventually he got the hang of it, started going where he was supposed to..."

I sat back and made a lame-ass attempt to pretend that didn't just happen, and to the one person I couldn't stand. "Can we change the subject now?"

"What's the name of the town again?" Lila asked, still smirking.

"El Dorado," Dad answered.

"El Do-rah-do?" she pronounced the Spanish word grammatically correct.

"You'd think," I responded. "No, it's El Do-*ray*-do Springs."

"Strange," was her reply, and then we were silent once more. Dad turned up the music and we continued the tedious trip south.

Another hour passed before we pulled into the drive and hopped out. I reached in the back and tossed Lila's luggage out, followed by mine.

"Make yourself at home, Lila. Wes, show her around. I'll be in the shed, working. Later I can run up town and grab some burgers."

"Thanks Mr. Tur—I mean, Billy," she responded.

"Sure thing, Dad."

Katie got out and started running around the yard in excitement, and I motioned for Lila to follow me as we grabbed our bags and headed to the porch.

I held one of the double front doors open, and she entered the foyer. "Foyer," I pointed out. We turned right. "Living room." We continued across the room until I opened another door. "Library, or study." We walked back through and across the foyer. "Dining room." Another right. "Kitchen, and out back is a pool."

We made our way down the hall and to the stairs. "All the bedrooms are upstairs. Your room has a bathroom attached, but it's only a tub, not a shower. Feel free to use mine," I said, a little uncomfortably.

"Thanks," she replied. "Really, I appreciate the detailed tour."

"Only for you," I met her sarcasm with more sarcasm. We started up the stairs and I went straight down the hall.

135

"The room at the very end is Mom and Dad's." I pointed to the room just next to it. "That's Katie's." I walked back down the other side of the staircase. "My room."

"Okay," she answered without looking inside.

I walked down a little more and opened the door to a bright room with a queen bed and built in shelves. "This is your room, bathroom's to the right."

"Thanks, Wesley." I stood, waiting for her to say more. "Can I be alone for a while? I'll come down later, maybe. I want to unpack, get cleaned up."

I shrugged, not caring what she did. I'd gotten her there and my job was done. I shut her door and made the way to my room. I unpacked my bags, hanging the clothes up and folding my socks and boxers in drawers.

A couple texts fell from a bag, reminders that I'd need to stay caught up in my classes. I fidgeted as the laptop screen lit and concluded I wouldn't get any studying done with my pent-up frustration. It was bad enough Lila and I weren't talking, but even worse that Dad brought up that embarrassing story.

I changed into jogging shorts and a t-shirt, grabbed my iPod, and headed downstairs. I pushed the front door open and took off down the drive. My shoes kicked up rocks as I turned left, watching for cars, running passed trees and white wildflowers, passed fields with cattle standing around in the early evening heat, passed my thoughts of Lila.

I'd have to keep every minute scheduled, plan something every day to avoid spending time with her. In Fredericksburg, it would've been easy. There'd always be an excuse to go somewhere with someone, or run an errand somewhere, but out there, in rural Missouri, excuses didn't exist. People traveled to town with purpose. No one living down a county backroad like we did drove fifteen miles or more into town just to waste time. If a person wanted to do nothing, they'd sit out on the porch or in a field or go running.

Not too many people had time to waste, at least the ones with farms didn't. There was always a fence that needed repair, sick livestock, or crops to harvest. I wasn't interested in farming and was glad Dad wasn't either. Our interest was seclusion, and the winding, rocky backroads that the state never bothered to name more specifically than by numbers, such as road 1,000 or road 1,300, and it worked perfectly. Dad never planted in our field and he didn't buy cows or chickens; he was a carpenter and worked in construction with a group of other guys from the county. I didn't have any interest in that, either.

I ran to the end of the road and turned, making my way back to the house; as I did, Dad's truck passed by. He rolled the window down and stopped.

"Hey Wes, pickin' up dinner in town. Wanna come?" I wasn't going to turn down perfectly good air-conditioning so I opened the door and hopped in. Classic rock blared from the speakers and he lowered the volume. "Lila was nice enough to watch Katie. She's a great girl, Wes." He glanced at me.

I looked away. "I guess," I muttered. "If frigid bitch is your thing." I finished under my breath.

"I thought you cared about her," he returned in more of a statement than a question as we turned on the highway leading to town.

"I did..." I sighed. "I do, but I'm trying not to."

Dad never said much to me about dating or girls, and I never had to ask him. "Better not be playing games with her, Wes," he warned.

I didn't answer him. The streetlights rolled by as he took a left and pulled into a local drive-in.

"I'm just gonna get cheeseburgers. Maybe some fries? Unless you want something special," he offered.

"No," I considered saying nothing for a minute, but then, "Get one without tomatoes...Lila doesn't like them."

I recognized the brunette carhop as she stepped off the sidewalk and walked around to my dad's side of the truck. She blushed and smiled. "Hey, Wes...didn't know you were back." She bit her lip and I chuckled, running a hand through my hair.

"Yeah, got in this afternoon." I remembered those lips, that body, but it was just a night, and I hoped she understood that.

"Maybe we can meet up sometime." She twirled a strand of hair around her finger.

I nodded. "Yeah, uh, sure." I turned away while Dad gave her the order.

She walked off to turn it in, and Dad and I sat for a while in silence. "Mm, hmm."

"It didn't mean anything," I assured him.

That time, he didn't respond, and we waited for our food in uncomfortable silence which continued indefinitely until, to my relief, a different carhop brought our order to us. Dad backed out and we drove home, listening to one of Dad's AC/DC tapes as I tried to resist tearing the bag open and eating before we made it back.

It wasn't long before we reached the house. "Dinner time," Dad yelled, to which Katie hopped off the couch where she'd been sitting next to Lila watching a movie.

Dad set the bags on the counter and pulled the food out of them. When Lila stood to make her way in the kitchen, I grabbed my burger and some fries. "I'm taking it to my room," I told Dad who just shrugged.

"Suit yourself," he responded.

I walked up the stairs and closed the door to my room behind me. Finally ready to sit down, I flipped my laptop back on and started eating while it booted up. I spent the rest of the night reading and researching an upcoming paper for a history class. It didn't bother me, growing up homeschooled, I was used to working independently and didn't need lectures or group projects to succeed.

Realizing how late it was, I took a shower and lay down in bed, closing my eyes to much welcomed sleep.

I woke up the next morning to the sound of thunder. With a storm coming in and Dad at work and Katie at daycare, I realized I'd have to spend the entire day stuck with Lila. I showered, dressed, and went downstairs for breakfast. I glanced around the corner—nobody. I grabbed a bowl from the cabinet and poured cereal. The rain pounded against the roof and windows as I scooped a spoonful and took a bite.

"Hey, anyone in there?" She glanced around the corner and I looked up. "Oh, you," she rolled her eyes and started opening the cabinets, looking for a bowl and spoon, I imagined.

I smirked and stood up from the table, walking over to the cabinet beside the sink and pulling a bowl out and then slid a drawer open and handed her a spoon. "Thanks," she forced a smile.

"Welcome." I sat back down, surveying her idea of 'pajamas' which consisted of a tight, white tank top and short, cotton shorts.

She looked up and pushed her hair behind her ears. "What?" she asked.

"Nothing," I remarked and quickly looked down at my bowl of cereal. *Every damn thing about you. Just go away,* I thought to myself.

She sighed and made herself breakfast. "I'll be in my room," she told me.

I shrugged. Like I cared. I watched her as she turned and left the kitchen.

I sat for a while before standing and walking to the sink to wash out my bowl. When I went upstairs, I thought about knocking on her door, but knew it wouldn't be of any use. She'd made her mind up, and as badly as I didn't want to, I had to accept it. No amount of small talk would work with her. She was different from the other girls; she knew my game and would use it to knock me on my ass.

I turned my laptop on and got started on the project, filling out the virtual worksheets and finishing my paper. When I looked up, the sun was coming from behind the clouds. What time was it? About three o' clock. I hadn't spent nearly as long as I wanted on classwork, but there was nothing more to do.

I decided to grab a snack from the kitchen. On my way downstairs, I glanced toward Lila's room; her door was open. Go figure. I peeked in, sorry I did as vanilla wafted into my nostrils and dizzied my head. "You coming out tonight?" I asked.

"I wouldn't miss it," she smirked and looked down at her phone.

"Did you bring a cardigan? It might get chilly once the sun goes down."

"All right, thanks," she said without looking up.

I left her to herself, shutting the door gently. I ran downstairs quickly and grabbed a snack, then retreated to my bedroom and opened a crossword puzzle. Lila was a puzzle; each time things started going well, she pulled away. Why? How many times had I told myself to forget about her? But every time we ended up together, again. *This time will be different*, I resolved to myself. I'd put her out of my mind. I'd find a different focus. But what?

The thud of car doors slamming jolted me from my thoughts. I'd show her, if she came. I got up and walked to my closet. Outfits hung from one side to the other. Which would be the best? I scoffed at my own thought; any of them would look good. I gelled my hair and sprayed on cologne, checking myself in the mirror and smiling before closing the door to my room. I passed by Lila's. I wouldn't knock—I forced myself to keep moving.

Her door creaked open before I reached the bottom and she came down wearing a pair of tight jeans and a dark tank-top that flared at the bottom. She gave me a once-over, and then a twice-over and as she did, I knew I'd achieved my goal and smirked.

"You didn't bring a sweater," I observed.

"Doubt I'll need it," she replied, matter-of-factly.

"Okay, stubborn," I teased, knowing she found my remark unamusing.

We made our way down the hall and out the back door attached in the kitchen. "Guess that's the pool you told me about," she noted.

"Yeah, it's all set for the summer, too, I suspect."

"Cool!"

Five or six trucks and cars had pulled up, and I recognized everyone as they set up their instruments in Dad's shed.

"Hey man!"

"Hey!" I greeted my best friend who looked at Lila, curious.

"Dalton, Lila. Lila, my best friend, Dalton." His brown eyes burned into her.

"It's very nice to meet you," he smiled at her.

She reciprocated the expression, "Nice to meet you, too."

"Where are you f—"

A shrill squeal interrupted his inquiry. All three of us turned to see a pair of red-headed wedge heels struggling to balance in the wet grass, but moving toward us, arms stretched out wide. When she reached us, she hugged me to her in a tight grasp I couldn't escape. After an unreasonable amount of time she pulled away. "Wes! You came back after all!"

I cleared my throat. "Tiffany, I'd like you to meet Lila." Tiffany smiled a fake smile and Dalton looked down at the ground, smirking. "What? What's going on?" I was confused.

Dalton spoke up. "She decided her name is Tiff-awn-i… not Tiffany. She won't answer to it anymore," he explained to Lila's amusement.

I glanced at 'Tiff-awn-i', incredulous. "What? I had an epiphany this semester. Tiffany is so boring. I needed to stand out, *Tiffani*. Make sure to replace the "y" with an "I"." She shrugged, pouting and then running her fingers up the buttons of my shirt. "Do I stand out, Wesley?" she asked, her voice whiney and lips pulled into an admittedly seductive kiss-me-I-want-you-to type pucker.

"Hi!" a voice came from the side, all too willing to interrupt the moment. "I'm Lila," Lila outstretched a hand.

"Oh." Tiffani didn't take it. "And you're here because..."

"I'm a friend of Wesley's," she grinned, entertained by the tension her presence caused.

"Yeah, we met...in college," I lied.

She looked at Lila condescendingly and placed a hand on her hip. "What do you study?"

"Art, painting, drawing." Lila continued my lie as the band started warming up and the fire grew in the fire pit.

"Did you tell her about us, Wes?" Tiffani draped a slender arm over me, and I pushed it off.

"There *is* no 'us'," I remarked before turning my back on her and catching up with Dalton who had walked away, probably because he was uncomfortable with the situation.

She grunted and walked over to the fire. Leaving Lila, standing awkwardly, by herself.

"Where's Connor? Is he still with what's her name?" I asked, once I'd reached Dalton who was watching Lila.

"Yeah...yes," he half-answered and touched my shoulder, though he hadn't heard a thing I said. He made his way over to Lila and struck up conversation.

I gave up and made my way across the lawn to listen to the band, who played a set and then decided to stop for beer and hotdogs before starting up again. I tried to stay away from Dalton and Lila. I wasn't going to be the desperate third wheel, but that didn't mean I couldn't listen. I pushed my energy into Dalton's head.

I overheard him. "It's chilly," he mentioned.

"Yeah, Wesley said it would be," Lila responded, staring into the fire.

"Take my jacket," he offered.

"Oh, no...I can't," she replied.

He took it off anyway. "Thank you," she responded as she turned toward him, a hint of a smile on her face.

"You're very welcome." And after a while he asked, "So, you and Wes. Are you two a thing?"

"Yea—well, no," she giggled. "No, we were, but we've decided to just be friends. It's confusing."

"Oh, cool! So why did you come out here?" he asked.

"Summer project, for credit," she answered shyly. "When I mentioned my idea of sketching agricultural landscapes, Wesley offered to bring me out here for the summer. It's an amazing opportunity to sketch and paint a different region of the country." The lie rolled off her tongue and for a moment took me back to Evansville. I shuddered. She was good at lying, too good in my opinion.

"Well, that's cool," Dalton answered. "Is art *all* you plan to do?" His flirting made me sick, but he was obviously interested Lila. She giggled, and I restrained myself from going over. I stood in the distance. Dalton leaned closer to her ear, and whispered, "Just a warning about Wes— he's a good friend, known him for a long time, but don't get too caught up in him. His bedroom kinda has a revolving door, if you catch my drift."

My cheeks burned. *Thanks dude,* I thought to myself.

"And what are you doing standing over here all by your lonesome?" Tiff-awn-i's voice came from behind me and she placed a hand on my shoulder.

I sighed; I'd been found. My focus dropped from Lila and Dalton and turned toward her. She was pretty, I'd thought so since we'd hooked up years prior. Her red hair curled against her light skin that glistened under the moon and accentuated her green, almond eyes. Freckles dusted her face, lightened by makeup she used to cover them. We'd been on again, off again; mostly because we'd start getting closer and Mom would put a stop to it.

No matter how hard she tried, Tiff never got me. She'd say weird things to convince me to 'lighten up', but how could I? How was I supposed to get over the fact I had telepathy, the constant surveillance, and the strain it put on my parents' marriage. It wasn't anything I could talk about with her. No matter how long I'd known her, I didn't trust her enough. Maybe I should've.

"Hello? Earth to Wes?" She waved her hand in front of my face.

"Oh, sorry," I finally acknowledged her.

"You're gonna burn a hole through her and Dalton if you keep staring. She's good," Tiff laughed quietly. "Only been here a few hours and she's got him reeling." She seemed satisfied that Lila was preoccupied with Dalton, not me. "What's the deal with her, anyway? Why would you invite her here?"

I didn't have to dig too hard to find the source of Tiffani's attitude. She was threatened. In her mind we were still a couple, and with Lila staying at the house, and my track record with other girls, she was riddled with insecurities.

I pushed harder in her thoughts. *God she's totally gorgeous. I'm seriously prettier, though. I wonder if she and Wes screwed. I should ask. No, I can't do that. There's definitely something between them, though. Ugh, what a*

145

bitch, but I guess she could be kinda cool, if Wes likes her. I wonder how many calories are in a marshmallow...

"Ninety," I popped up, forgetting I was listening to her thoughts.

"What did you say?" she scrutinized me. I'd have to come up with something, quick. That's why I didn't get into many peoples' heads—confusion. Thoughts blur the line between what's said aloud and the unspoken.

"I said ninety...as in there's a ninety percent chance Dalton's going to ask her out by the end of the night," I grinned, happy with myself for coming up with the nonsensical response.

"Would you care? I mean, if he did," she asked, hesitant, not wanting a real answer.

I pushed my hair back. "No," I chuckled, "You know me..."

"Boy, do I," she raised her eyebrows. "I also know how many girls you had going in and out of your room."

"Tiff, come on, that was a long time ago." I gave her an apologetic glance as I recalled the days when she thought we could be in an actual relationship. I couldn't lie to her, I didn't feel the same way she did; to me, it was just another night of sex.

"Whatever, Wes. Where's she gonna go when she finds out what a player you are?" Tiff shrugged and walked over to the shed, leaving me standing by myself.

I was glad when the guys in the band called it a night. Dad came out with them and they welcomed me home. He introduced them all to Lila who greeted them happily. While they were making small talk, I walked over to Dad and asked him for his truck keys.

"Why, Wes? Whadd'ya need them for?" He pulled them from his pocket regardless of the question.

"Just want to get out for a while."

"Okay," he finally answered. "Remember, I want the yard mowed tomorrow," he warned as I took the keys.

I nodded and headed toward his dusty pickup. I jumped in the cab and pulled out, driving the lengthy distance down our dirt road before coming to the end and turning right onto the highway. A few miles later, I stopped in the parking lot of the local bar, Tornado's. I got out of my vehicle and walked across the rough gravel.

The door swung open, releasing a cloud of smoke as a staggering couple tried to exit. I managed to catch it before it closed. A terrible noise wailed from the front of the dance floor, and that's when I noticed the glow of the TV screen. I shook my head and walked up to the bar.

"Hey guy, long time no see." My husky, dark-haired friend finished drying a glass with a dish towel, setting it carefully with the others before making his way toward me.

"Hey, Ben," I greeted, realizing he was the only person in the bar I knew. I pointed to the karaoke set-up on the makeshift stage. "When did this start?"

"'Bout a month ago. Boss says it'll bring in business," he smirked as we both listened to the sour screeches coming from the front of the building. "I think it's runnin' people off," he laughed.

I took a long look at the lanky blonde holding the microphone. I noted her short skirt paired with cowboy boots and her tan skin against the mid-riff. "She's hot, though," I mentioned, even though blondes weren't my forte.

Ben shook his head in agreement. "What'll it be tonight?"

I thought for a while. "I'm driving myself, just a Miller Lite," I replied.

"Boy, you know you say that now, but you'll be drunk and walkin' out of here with three or four of 'em girls in a couple hours," he teased.

Lila crossed my mind—Dalton and Lila, and his coat wrapped around those shoulders. I shook my head. "Not tonight, man. I have to be up early tomorrow; Dad wants me to mow the yard."

Ben narrowed his eyebrows. "Well, ain't that an excuse if I ever heard one. Mmm, mmm, mmm." He shook his head. "Wesley Turner turnin' down a night of raging summer sex. Somethin' ain't right. You have a woman or something? That's the only reason a guy'd turn down one of them girls."

I wanted to tell him how I felt about Lila. It'd be better than bottling it up, but everything was complicated. I wanted her, but I wanted to hate her. I took a sip of my beer. "It's not like that. I've decided to focus on college."

Ben leaned toward me. "I talk to a hundred people a week and you're the worst liar I've run into," he laughed. "You're not ready to talk about it." He stood back. "It's cool. The great Wesley, turning in his wild nights for some girl he met at college."

Ben's intuition was undeniable. He didn't have abilities like me or Lila, but still, he was impressive. Not wanting to insult his intelligence, I took a long drink from the bottle and started, "Okay, you win. We met last semester," I lied, trying to keep up the college façade. "She's hot as hell—dark hair, green eyes, bangin' body, nice ass. Smart, too, sarcastic." I looked up and Ben was giving me a genuine smile of happiness. "She really gets me. When I'm with her, it's not suffocating. When we're together, commitment doesn't seem like such a bad idea." I finished the thought before finishing the rest of my beer.

"Wow, dude. Sounds like you got it bad. So, what's the hold up? Where's your girl tonight?" He questioned.

With another guy. "Here's the catch—she doesn't like me like that. She's been through a lot of trauma recently." Suddenly the reason became all too apparent and I wanted to order another beer and do exactly as Ben said earlier, get drunk, have sex, and get over Lila.

"You got friend-zoned, huh?" he asked, empathetically. "Man, you don't need all that shit right now."

"It's complicated." I smirked, "Wesley doesn't get friend-zoned." Ben smiled back at me in agreement. I was convinced my attraction wasn't one sided, but my friend had a point, I really didn't need that. I remembered her lies, how she'd lead me on, but I was the player? I didn't need any of it and I certainly didn't need her. Not then, not ever.

That night I drowned my attraction in the single bottle of Miller Lite, it died and choked on its own memories until it was no more. Lila was no more, not to me—not then and not ever.

LILA

I woke the next morning to the pulsing roar of a motor moving back and forth somewhere below my window. I glanced out, which turned out to be a total mistake. I found Wesley mowing the yard—shirtless, sweat beaded and soaked through his hair, running down his bare back, and over his flexed muscles as he pushed the machine through the grass. My heart raced. I pulled the curtains closed before I had a heart-attack, or he noticed me gawking. What time was it? The clock read ten-thirty, and I felt bad for sleeping that late. I ran a warm bath and soaked for a while, thinking of how good it must've felt to be the drops of sweat pouring down that muscular body.

When I stepped out, I took a long look at myself in the mirror. I couldn't place it, but I looked dull, almost lifeless in ways, like a part of me died at the Facility. Everything I'd been through had taken its toll, mentally as well as physically. I'd killed Sullivan; I'd visited my parents' graves and felt the grievous wounds turn to scars. I was never one to judge myself too harshly when I looked in the mirror, but I totally looked like crap. I needed something but couldn't place it.

That's when the idea came to me—I needed sun. A little vitamin D would surely knock me out of the funk so, I dressed in my bikini and grabbed a towel. I thought about bringing the journal but didn't want to chance the already fading words being exposed to sunlight or take the risk of the book getting soaked. I shut the door to my room and descended the stairs. When I reached the landing, I looked into the living room and then the kitchen to find that Billy and Katie were nowhere in sight. I walked through the kitchen door and out to the pool and sat down on a wooden lounge chair, closing my eyes and enjoying the sun as it rested in the sky, warming the day as it did so.

Already, I was feeling better. The heat from the rays soaked into my skin and rejuvenated my entire body. I took in deep breaths, trying to convince myself to relax, which was not something I had the luxury of doing over the past few weeks. Everything was settled. I'd taken care of Sullivan. I had no reason to use my abilities, and not using them, I thought, was the way to get control. The only thing I had left to figure out was Wesley.

Did I push him too far by being indecisive? Maybe he couldn't get over what I did at the Facility. What *did* I want? Confusion overtook me, and I tried reminding myself I'd come out there to relax, but instead I replayed the moment he tried to kiss me, which only added to the mounting stress. Everything with him felt so right—*too* right. With recent events spinning in my mind, how Wesley made me feel was terrifying. Maybe someone like me didn't deserve to be happy.

No. I could change. With time, I could do better and regain the confidence and security I'd lost. I pushed all the thoughts as far away as I could and closed my eyes. I was almost asleep when the gate clanked open. I sat up to see him kneeling next to me. "Wesley...what are you doing here?" I tried not to stare.

"Well...I do live here. Thought I'd cool off in the pool." He studied me for a moment. "I thought you didn't swim."

"I don't, but I'm really good at tanning."

He chuckled, and his eyes glittered in the sun. "So, we're talking again?"

"Yeah, until one of us pisses the other off," I answered sarcastically, and as I did he moved his shirtless body toward me.

I braced myself as he put one hand on the arm of my chair and bent down until his chest was almost pushing against my breasts. His arm flexed as he used it to prop himself up. Time stopped when he hovered close enough for his sweet breath to hit my lips; his glistening blue eyes pushed into mine. My breathing sped up. Was he going to kiss me? His mouth approached mine as his skin lightly caressed my own. He reached with his left hand and premature goosebumps appeared on my arms, awaiting his touch. His hand reached all the way around, to a table I didn't see, and quickly grabbed a bottle of sunscreen before sitting back down beside me.

His lips curled into a mischievous smirk. "You should really use some of this if you're planning on being out here long," he lectured. I was having trouble forming words, so he waited a while before asking another question. "Why don't you swim?"

"Long story…" He gave me that look. He wasn't going to leave me alone until I told him. "The short version? We went on a summer visit to Florida and Aunt Liv took us to Key West. The tide was coming in, Mom warned me not to go out too far. The waves were bad, but I didn't listen. I got caught in an undertow; it took me down, and I hit my head on a rock. My foot got tangled in a piece of seaweed. Aunt Liv was able to get me out."

"Ouch! That sucks." He furrowed his brow and concern replaced the smart-ass grin. "What if I promised that there'd be no waves in the swimming pool...could I talk you into getting in?" He licked his lips and the only thing I wanted to do was be in the pool with his built arms around me.

"I don't think—" I was about to protest, but the prospect of being close to him, even though I was supposed to be angry, tempted me. I mean, we were talking and maybe I needed to listen to Sara and my crazy dreams and move on, to believe I deserved better than what I was giving myself. Wesley had been nothing but honest and understanding about the reckless use of my abilities. I readied myself to hesitantly agree but was interrupted.

"Wes! Wes!" came an excited voice that was getting closer, it was Tiffani followed by Dalton and another couple I didn't recognize. She ran quickly fanning her arms like she was trying to land a plane. She pushed the gate open and the others followed her into the pool area.

"Lila, you remember Dalton and Tiffany—" She interrupted him by clearing her throat "Okay, Tif-*fawn*-ee," he tried again, correcting his syllabic emphasis. "This is my other friend Connor and his girlfriend Alana."

"Hey! Nice to meet you guys," I greeted warmly.

"Back at ya!" Connor called as he walked over to talk to Wesley.

Alana came closer to me. "Cute bikini!" she exclaimed.

"Thanks!" Tiffani narrowed her eyes and shook her head.

"So, you're from the East, right?"

"Yeah..." I started.

"I bet it's so different for you—being out here, I mean." Alana had a sweet personality. She was a little shorter than me, at about 5'4, and she had beautiful, thick brunette hair that landed against a pink tank top and hazel eyes.

Tiffani muttered, "The only thing different is *her*."

I glanced at her, trying to contain my irritation by reminding myself of what happened in Evansville. "I'm going to get a glass of water." I excused myself. It was the only way I could get control of my abilities.

Dalton turned and followed me into the kitchen. "Hey," he said, shoving his hands in his pockets and rocking on his heels.

"Hey back," I smiled at him. A part of me was glad he followed and a part of me wasn't.

"So, I have to ask… how's the Wesley thing going? Last night you said you were confused."

I recalled the intensity of his body so close to mine; I should've told Dalton we were working things out. But when I glanced out the window, Wesley was standing next to Tiffani, her hand on his shoulder and him leaning into her, laughing and smiling. "No," I said, realizing Wesley knew exactly what he did to me. But why was he doing it? "No, Wesley and I are friends," I answered.

"Well…umm…I was wondering…" Dalton crinkled his nose, shyly and I noticed light freckles splayed across the top, probably from working in the sun all day. "Would you like to go out? Like on a date? Dinner or something? It's probably boring out here with where you're from and all but—"

"Yeah, I'd like that." I turned away from Wesley, who looked cozy next to Tiffani, and studied Dalton's reaction.

"Really?" his brown, puppy-dog eyes widened.

"Yeah, really." I giggled. I didn't want to be a part of Wesley's games. Dalton seemed down to earth, strong, and cute.

"Awesome…Well, I'm gonna get back out there…" He turned, still beaming, and left quickly as though I'd change my mind if he waited around.

I stood, holding the glass for a minute. I'd just turned eighteen and I needed to keep my options open. Sure, Wesley was damn fine and anytime he was near me I felt like I was drunk, like even after our time apart and the fighting, I was madly attracted to him, but he was a player, and I was more than a game.

When I made my way back outside, I immediately picked up that Dalton hadn't kept our date a secret. Wesley's jaw was tight, his expression serious as he glanced from his friend to me.

Tiffani strutted over. "I think it's cute…you and Dalton…on a little date. Maybe…we should all go, make it a double-date," she taunted.

Dalton sheepishly looked at her. "Oh, I dunno," he started, but he was too late. It was apparent when Tiffani made her mind up, that's how things went down.

"Where are you taking her?" she insisted to an embarrassed Dalton.

He looked to me. "Do you have Fourth of July plans?" I shook my head, embarrassed that in all the chaos I'd totally forgotten the upcoming holiday. "Cool. There's a guy named Wayne on the other side of town a ways who puts on a yearly fireworks show on the fourth. People either go there or to the lake to watch shows, but I like his the best," he shrugged. "It's not fancy or anything, we just bring a blanket and park in a field. There's music and stuff, and we could get something to eat before it starts. Only if you want." He came off as really shy and I found it super attractive.

Wesley scowled, but I turned back to Dalton and smiled. "Sounds great. What time will you pick me up?"

"I get off work at five. Is six okay? That way I can clean up."

I smiled. "Sure thing! I can't wait."

"That's still a few weeks away," Tiffany mentioned, interrupting our dialogue. "Are you going, Wes?"

He shook his head. "No, I'm not."

She moved closer to him. "It'll be fun. You've never been to one," she complained.

"I'll think about it," he finally answered before walking to the gate. "I'll text you," he finished without turning as he headed in the house.

"Well, we were headed to the lake. Just needed to stop by because Dalton here finally worked up the courage to ask you out," she explained in a taunting voice.

I winked and smiled at him as his cheeks reddened. "I'm glad he did."

Alana, who'd been in the corner hanging all over Connor looked at me. "It was nice to meet you. Connor and I might be there, too," she said before kissing him again.

"Nice meeting you too," I answered.

Tiffani rolled her eyes. "C'mon guys, let's go before it gets late."

"I'll text you tonight," Dalton promised before leaving with the group.

I waved at him and sat back down to continue my time in the humid, mid-afternoon sun. The cicadas buzzed, and the wind breezed past me. It was a perfect moment. Going on a date with a boy was a perfectly normal moment. I was moving forward, but could I leave Wesley behind?

I sat up and wrapped a towel around me, making my way into the kitchen, I grabbed an apple and washed it before continuing up the stairs and to my room. I cracked the door and dialed Sara.

"Hey girl!" came the voice on the other end.

"What are you up to?" I bit into the apple.

"Nothing much. Hanging out, applying for part time jobs."

"Hey, that's cool!" I responded, happy to hear she was getting it together. "You'll never guess what just happened," I teased.

"Do I want to know?" she replied.

"Totally! So, get this...I'm beginning to think every guy out here must be totally easy on the eyes. One of them asked me out...*aaand*, I said yes!" I giggled, falling back onto the soft bed and sitting right back up.

"Seriously?" she shrieked from the other end. "But what does Wesley think?"

My stomach dropped. "I don't think he's happy about it."

"Oh...hold on," she must've pulled the phone away and was talking to someone in the background. "Hey girl, can I call you tomorrow? Peter and I are catching a movie."

"Yeah! No problem. Tell him hi for me, too." I ended the call and turned to see Wesley standing in the doorway.

He sneered. "Congrats on your date." He used his index fingers to place quotations around the word 'date'.

"What's that supposed to mean?" He couldn't possibly be happy I was going out with Dalton.

"Exactly what it means." He shrugged. "I'm glad you're having fun," he answered and headed toward his room.

I shut the door, confused. My heart slowed a little and my stomach sank. What was I doing? Sure, Dalton was hot, but I had something deeper with Wesley and each time I got the chance to explore what was there, I ran from it.

I changed out of my bikini and went downstairs and turned the TV on. With the tension between Wesley and me and Dalton at work all day, summer was going to be pretty dull. As I scrolled through the channels, I played with the idea of getting a ride to town and applying for a part time job. There had to be something, right? I could be a waitress or work at a grocery store, anything to pass time until I could return home.

I got lost in a few daytime shows and before I knew it, Billy and Katie were home. He'd bought chicken and some sides. I got up quickly to help him with the bags.

"Sorry," he started, "I don't cook much during the week."

I laughed, "I'd volunteer, but I don't cook at all."

He sorted through the food, taking out the containers and lining them along the countertop. "It's okay! Plenty of time to learn stuff like that. If not, there's always take out."

I turned as Wesley came down the stairs. He was dressed in jeans and a black t-shirt. The warm scent of his cologne followed him. "Catch you guys later," he yelled without looking at any of us.

Billy nodded at him and my heartbeat sped until it became quick, sharp taps and my head lightened. *Where's he going?* I wondered but wasn't about to ask.

My answer came later—a lot later—after I tucked Katie in and Billy had made his way to his room. I was about to turn the TV off when the front door clicked, followed by

159

giggling. Wesley stumbled in accompanied by a girl I hadn't met.

"I'm totally buzzed," she squealed flicking her bleach-blonde ponytail as Wesley shushed her and tried to stifle his own laughs.

I came around the corner. "Seriously?" I raised an eyebrow at the way his hand traveled the length of her waist to the bottom of her skirt and up her bare legs.

"What?" Wesley mused and leaned against the wall. She fell into him when he did.

"You're both drunk," I said. I sort of sounded like an old schoolmarm.

"Obviously," she giggled and twirled a lose piece of hair before whispering something into Wesley's ear.

He sniffed and flashed her a grin. "C'mon." He coaxed her up the stairs, to his room.

I fumed. *There's no coming back from this, Wesley Turner.*

He paused but didn't respond. Somewhere in his drunk head he heard me.

That night I tried to sleep. I tossed and turned, finally getting up and going downstairs for a drink. Wesley had the same idea. He stood by the sink with a bottle of aspirin and a glass of water.

"Happy?" I asked.

"I am," his mouth had twisted into a devilish smirk. "I had a good time."

I shrugged. "Like I care." I suddenly wasn't thirsty, but I did care. What were they doing in his room? *What a stupid question, Lila,* I lectured myself. My stomach was queasy, and I shivered.

Wesley lifted the glass to his mouth. "You should go back to bed," he insisted. "You look pale...or preoccupied." He cocked his head. "Is something bothering you, Lila?"

The only way I could find out what he was thinking, or what he was trying to do was by getting in his head, but if I tried it, he'd know. I figured it'd be wise to spare myself from the details. Truth was, I pushed him away so I only had myself to blame. My eyes were flaming, but I wouldn't let him see me cry.

I shook the feeling away, without answering and took off for my room, shutting the door quietly behind me when I arrived. I crawled into bed and pulled the comforter over me. I fought to hold back sniffles, knowing if I started I wouldn't be able to stop. Why did life have to be so damn abrupt and confusing? Why did I feel like it was all my fault? How should I begin to get over it?

I must have passed out from mental exhaustion because when I woke up the next day, it was afternoon. I rubbed the sleep from my eyes and stretched. One look in the mirror reinforced Wesley's comment—I looked like I hadn't slept in forever. Defeated, I threw my hair up in a bun and decided the best way to get everything off my mind was to keep busy.

Although it was late in the day, I didn't have an appetite. Instead, I went to the kitchen to look for cleaning supplies. I searched for a pantry or cupboard and eventually came across a small closet. I opened it and found some household cleaning sprays and started wiping down the kitchen counters and sink.

My mind was so focused on unloading the dishwasher, I didn't think about Wesley. Instead, when I was finished with the kitchen, I sat down and flicked through TV channels until I fell asleep without realizing it.

I could feel my body shaking. "Lila! Lila!"

I groaned and rolled over. My eyes focused on Katie who was still pumped from daycare. "Come play a game with me!" she shrieked.

Not wanting to tell her 'no', I sat up and grinned. "Okay, let me get changed and put shoes on."

"Fine! But hurry!" she insisted.

I tousled her frizzy curls and took off upstairs. After changing into shorts with a t-shirt and sandals, I opened the front door to see Wesley holding a squealing Katie and spinning her wildly through the air. "Faster! Faster!" she screamed.

He was out of breath and sat her down. He put his hand on his forehead and bent over. "Oh my God," he huffed. "I can't." He smiled so big it brightened up the already sunny day.

"One more time!" she squealed and giggled before she fell into him and knocked him to the grass. He reached out to tickle her, their laughs echoed through the yard.

"Fine!" He lifted her and swung her through the air. Neither one of them noticed me leaning against a beam on the porch, watching the carefree scene.

Suddenly Katie yelled. "Hey! Put me down now!"

Wesley was confused but sat her down and paused to catch his breath as she took off running. "Lila!" Her arms were spread, ready for me to catch her. I stepped off the porch and braced myself as she came at me, full force.

When she reached me, I grabbed her and flung her upwards before setting her down. "You're both here!" Her eyes were happy and wild. My heart sunk when Wesley noticed me. He wiped the smile off his face.

"Katie-bug, I'm going in to get cleaned up," he announced before starting toward the house.

She ran to him and he stopped. "No!" she protested. She stood firm between him and the front door.

"It's late. I have somewhere to be…" He paused for a moment. "… And I have to turn in homework."

"Stay! It's no fair. I want to play with both of you guys," she crossed her arms. She wasn't taking no for an answer.

He sighed. "Fine, fifteen minutes," he relented.

She clapped her hands together and jumped up and down. My stomach turned, I tried hard to avoid Wesley, but there we were, together, because neither of us were going to tell Katie we wouldn't play with her. It wasn't her fault we were fighting, or I made a mistake, or Wesley enjoyed indulging himself with drunken hookups, or whatever was happening between us.

We stood, waiting for her. "Okay. Everyone, join hands," she instructed as she put out both of hers.

"W-why?" I asked, noticing Wesley's eyes narrow and the menacing way he pressed his lips together.

"Ring-around-the-rosy," she explained. "Now grab my hand and Wesley's," she demanded.

Wesley and I both held her hand, and I reached to take his. Instead of cupping his hand over mine, he locked his fingers between my own. Sticky sweat separated our skin and fireworks popped in my stomach. My theory? Katie was trying to torture me.

"Okay," she said through her toothy-grin. "Let's go!" She started singing the song and bounced as we all went in a circle. "...We all fall down!" She screamed in delight.

Poised to fall straight down in the grass, a sharp tug jerked my body until I lost balance and landed on top of Wesley. I started to push myself up quickly, wanting to get away from him, but his stare paralyzed me. The deep blue of his eyes, which I hadn't really looked at since I escaped the Facility, pulled me in and forced me to remain as my body hovered close to his.

I gulped as Wesley glided his hand toward my face. He swept a lock of hair from my eye and pushed it behind my ear. "You should be more careful," he whispered. "I'd hate to see you get hurt," his tone was more of a leer than the expression on his face.

His teasing hurt; first with the blonde from the night before and then pulling me onto him. I needed to show him enough was enough; I pushed myself up before staring him dead in the eye. "You can't hurt if you don't feel," I mouthed with a nonchalant expression on my face. Seconds after, I regretted it as his face dropped and he swallowed.

I stood and wiped the grass off my shorts and legs. "Dinner!" Billy called from the front porch. Katie took off to the house and, even though I wasn't hungry, I followed, leaving Wesley standing alone, facing the road in front of his long driveway.

Everything was so wrong, and I'd certainly done my part to screw it up; but so did he bringing a girl over, doing who knows what with her. That was Wesley— Peter had warned me, and I'd promised him I'd be careful. One thought continued to eat at me, though—was that really Wesley? It certainly wasn't the guy at the seafood restaurant, on the bridge, or in the hotel room. And these thoughts only led to one question. Who was Wesley, really?

Too lost in thought to pay attention to the conversation and teasing between Billy and Katie, I picked at my food and only glanced up briefly as gravel crunched under truck tires followed by Wesley coming down the stairs, ruffling Katie's hair, and heading outside.

Later that evening, while they watched television, I sat on the porch and stared at the graveled drive. What was Wesley doing? Where did he go? It didn't matter; I was the one who couldn't make up her mind. An old pickup made its way down the dusty road.

At first, I couldn't make out who it was and stood to get Billy, thinking it'd be someone coming to see him. As it neared, I recognized the driver as Dalton. He parked in front of the house and got out, shoving his hands in his pockets as he did.

I walked down the stairs, embarrassed because I hadn't really gotten cleaned up at all. "Umm, hey," he started, his wide cocoa eyes immediately calmed me. "I-I thought you'd be at the bonfire. When Wes showed up with Tiff and you weren't with them, I figured I'd come out to check on you," he flicked his head to move a piece of loose hair that was bothering him.

"Oh," I replied. I was unsure of how I'd explain that. If I told the truth, that Wesley took off without telling me, things would look tense and Dalton would wonder why Wesley hadn't extended an invitation to begin with. My only choice was to lie and hope for the best. "I didn't feel like going." It was a simple answer and I hoped it'd suffice.

His face dropped and he grinded his foot in the rocks. "I thought you would." He took a deep breath and quietly offered, "W-want to go with me?" When his nose crinkled nervously, I could make out all the freckles that formed over his sun burned cheeks.

Wesley would be there, and, thanks to Dalton, I knew he'd be there with Tiffani, but how could I say no? If my feelings for Wesley represented an untamable storm, then Dalton embodied calm and stability. They were both handsome, Dalton more so, in a rugged sense. *Maybe I should go*, I told myself. I hadn't done much of anything since I'd come out there.

I lightened my face and answered, "Yes!" Relief mixed with nerves overpowered me. "I think I will go," I answered despite the confusing emotions. "You want to come in and give me a little while to get ready?" I offered.

The muscles in Dalton's face relaxed and he grinned. "Yeah, sure."

He followed me up the steps and I led him into the living room. He smiled and nodded to Katie. "Hey!" He called over to Billy who was sitting in an arm chair trying to stay awake for another episode of *Bubble Guppies*.

"Dalton," he sat up and waved at him. "What's been going on?"

Seeing that the two of them were busy talking, I made an exit upstairs and shut the door to my room. I sifted through my outfits, remembering that Dalton was dressed in blue jeans and a tee covered by a plaid, button-up shirt. Earlier, Wesley was dressed a little nicer in jeans and a navy, collared shirt. He'd spiked his hair; Dalton combed his to the side. A sundress would be a good compromise, so I pulled out a navy one with white flowers on it.

I clipped half of my hair out of my face and applied mascara and lip gloss before slipping sandals on and heading downstairs.

"...Well, if we don't get more rain, what're you guys gonna do about the soybeans?" I caught Billy in mid-conversation. As soon as my shoes tapped the floor of the wooden entry-way, Dalton's eyes stole from Billy to me.

Billy gave him a knowing look. "Bye, kids. Get her back in one piece," he teased a red-faced Dalton.

"Yes, sir," he answered back, quickly shuffling me out the door.

Once we were alone on the porch he motioned toward the truck. "Shall we?"

"Let's do this." I released a breath, allowing humid evening air to soak up any worries still brewing in my stomach and carry them far away.

He offered his hand and I took it as we continued down the porch steps and to his truck. The cab smelled like chewing gum, minty and clean. I looked back and saw some of his work stuff. "So, what do you do?" I asked.

"This summer I'm working on Mr. Seward's farm, tending to the cattle and chickens. He's gotta couple 'a pigs, too. Right now, I'm repairing the fence. It went down in the last storm. I help my parents out on our farm, too. Someday it'll be mine."

"And that's okay?" It was interesting that he seemed perfectly happy working on a farm.

"Why wouldn't it be? Sure, it's hard work, but it pays off. We sell our crops and our cattle for money and keep some for food. What else do you need?" His cheeks turned red. "A good woman, that's it." For Dalton, everything was that simple. He had the rest of his life figured out, and there was no doubt he'd be successful. "Everyone else wants to go away to college. They don't understand why I stay here. I'm happy with this." He turned the music down. "I bet the city's a lot different, huh? You miss it?"

I giggled. "Maybe the Starbucks," I admitted. "I like it out here. Everything's slower…in a good way," I added.

"Sorry princess, no fancy coffee shops," he teased as we turned down the road and onto a narrow street. After a little longer, he pulled to the side, behind a small, green car and parked. "We're here."

I sighed in response and his eyes filled with concern. "You okay?" He didn't wait for an answer before jumping out and coming around to my door. He opened it and held his hand for me to take. "It's probably hard being in a new place, around new people, huh?"

When I took his hand in mine, it wasn't quite the fanfare I'd experienced with Wesley, but butterflies stirred, nonetheless. Maybe I could be okay after all. We walked in a shallow ditch along a string of cars and trucks and eventually reached an open field where a couple guys were stirring the fire in an attempt to get it going. A few girls worked on getting food from a stalky boy cooking on the grill and pop music played over loud speakers. "Huh…"

"Something wrong?" Dalton glanced at me.

"I figured you guys would play country music," I answered, confused.

He huffed, his lips bending into a playful smile that sparkled against his bright eyes. "Guess us country folk really know how to throw a party."

I tapped his shoulder lightheartedly, feeling its hardness as I did. Instead of taking my hand off, I held on and leaned into him. Instinctively, he curled his arm around my back, so my body was against his.

I studied the groups standing in semi-circles, chatting, satisfied when I didn't see Wesley anywhere. Ironically, Dalton piped up, "Hmm, I don't see Tiff or Wes." He shrugged. "Maybe they went back to her place. They usually leave parties early," he added without explaining more. He didn't need to. "So, what do you want to do?"

I was saved from answering his question by Alana and Connor, who bounded up to us. Connor high-fived Dalton and Alana waved. I pulled away from Dalton and turned to talk to her. "Have you seen Tiff?"

I looked through the crowd again. "I haven't."

"Did you come here with them?" she took a drink from the cup she was holding.

"Dalton picked me up," I responded, nervously rubbing my arm with my hand.

"Oh," she cocked her head back and gave a half-smile. "That's unusual for him." She leaned in close to me so the boys wouldn't hear her. "He must really like you."

I pulled on a loose strand of hair. "Really?"

"Totally, and that's good because he'll treat you like a princess." She leaned in closer. "He's a lot better than Wesley. I tell Tiff all the time to find someone else, but she always thinks she can just change him." She huffed, "There's no changing a guy like Wes. I'm glad you're not tangled up in all that." She pointed to a girl standing near the grill. I recognized her as the blonde from the other evening. "See her? Uh, yeah." She shook her head. "I guess Tiff found out they were together, and all hell broke loose."

My stomach ripped to shreds. Or was it my heart? If he'd known Tiff for that long and wouldn't change for her, why would he for me? What did the week we'd spent together actually mean to him? I thought of the girls he'd flirted with, Linda...was *everything* a lie? I caught Dalton in the corner of my eye and he stared back, flashing me an adoring smile. I turned my attention back to Alana. "I'm only here to fill an art requirement," I reminded her.

"Oh, right. I totally forgot. Can I see some of your stuff sometime?"

I thought for a minute, if she ever stopped by, I could persuade her that she'd seen my drawings. "Yeah, anytime."

A set of warm hands ran down my bare arms, causing goose bumps to emerge as they did. "Lila?" A whispered voice soaked in my ear; it was Dalton. "Connor's been drinking so I'm gonna run him up the road. We need to get ice and he's parked closer than we are. Will you be okay?"

Before I could answer, Alana leaned in to reassure him. "She'll be fine, geez," she teased.

I was surprised as Dalton ran his dry hands down my arms once again. He closed in and gave me a soft peck on the back of my head, allowing his lips to linger on top of my hair. Being so close to him, I took in a rich outdoorsy scent. We stayed like that for a while until Alana's voice catapulted me back to reality. "Well, speak of the devil." She leaned on her right foot and crossed her arms.

I glanced up from Dalton's embrace just in time to catch Wesley, making his way across the field with Tiffani. His ocean eyes cornered my own until I couldn't look away. *You should pay attention to your date.* His voice rang through my head.

Ignoring Wesley's repulsive comment, I looked up at Dalton who was standing next to Connor, still waiting for an answer. "I'll hang with Alana. We'll be fine," I assured him.

The guys left us alone. "Hey, want me to get you something to drink?" Alana offered.

"Yeah, thanks. Anything's fine," I responded, trying not to focus on Wesley and Tiffani who had picked up a stick and were making a scene of feeding each other melted marshmallows.

Alana took off for the drinks and I crossed my hands over my chest—awkward. The music slowed down, and Wesley pulled Tiff close and leaned to whisper in her ear, reverting his eyes to me, every once in a while. Against my better judgment, I pushed energy at them, wanting to hear what he was saying, vowing to make his life hell if he was talking about me.

He was singing to her, in a hushed, low tone, the notes vibrated from his chest, perfectly on pitch. *"Play that song,"* his voice was airy. *"The one that makes me think of you..."* his velvet echoes coupled with the cracking fire caused me to snap.

Wesley wasn't supposed to be with her, those strong hands clinging to her waist. No! We were supposed to be *together*, me and him. *Not* Tiff-*awn*-ee. I didn't even know he could sing.

In a single moment of anger, I pushed energy past Tiffani and her obnoxious giggle and straight to the stick she held behind her back, causing it to catch fire. "Ahh! Shit!" she screamed. "What the hell!" she dropped it before the flames reached her hand and jumped back into Wesley's arms.

His head snapped up and he looked straight at me, his jaw stiff and tense, his eyes were the fire. My chest caved, and I took off to the woods. Shards of sharp twigs threatened to stab my toes, but I didn't care—I kept running. I had to get out of there. I thought of Dalton, I'd explain myself to him later. I'd make up something, some lie, because it couldn't be the truth. I wasn't able to be honest and tell him about my parents, Sullivan, my abilities, or the real reason I'd come to Missouri.

"Well, whad'we have here?" A low voice slurred from behind me. It was some black-haired guy I hadn't met. He moved closer and I backed into a tree.

"This isn't a good idea," I warned. I felt bad enough nearly burning Tiffani's hand. I didn't want to use my abilities if I could avoid it. Every time I did, someone got hurt.

"Look a' tha tight li'l dress," he stumbled toward me. "Girls like you'r askin' fer it."

Volcanic fury filled my body. He was in my face; his alcohol breath stained the air. I stared in his eyes, harnessing enough energy to push into his intoxicated head, but before I could, he dropped to the ground.

The guy turned, and his face met Wesley's thick knuckles. He collected himself and staggered to Wesley and managed to get a punch in before Wesley knocked him down a last time.

Our eyes met, his expression softened to concern. Still shaking, I moved slowly toward him and stretched an unsteady hand to the red mark on the side of his right eye. Before I reached it, his cold, stiff hand caught it mid-air. A stern expression clouded his face as he dropped my hand back to my side and let it go. His eyes were rocks. "Play what games you want with me. Leave Tiff out of it."

And that's exactly how Dalton found me and Wesley. Standing apart, dead air suspended between us, my eyes frantic and his frozen. "Wh-what happened?" He looked to the guy on the ground and ran by Wesley to me. "Are you okay?" His strong arms enveloped me, and I fell into them.

Wesley spoke up. "I'd seen Mark take off into the woods earlier, probably to take a piss. For whatever reason, Lila decided to play jungle girl and go exploring. I know Mark's trouble when he drinks, so I followed her to see that she'd be okay," he lied.

Dalton looked at his friend. "Okay. Thanks, man. I guess it was a bad idea to leave, huh?"

He kept his arms around me. They were warm, safe. The leaves cracked; Wesley had returned to the party. Dalton inhaled a deep breath and stroked my disheveled hair from my face. "I bet you're terrified." He stepped back so I could see his apologetic eyes. "I'm so sorry, Lila."

I believed him, but I didn't want his apology. We were facing one other; body drew closer to his and was held once again in his safe arms. His hand glided to my hair as his other arm wrapped tighter around me until our lips met and the leaf-laced ground spun below our feet. It wasn't the soft, thick lips Wesley had, nor was it that burst of fireflies spinning from head to toe, but it was security. Dalton was faithful and consistent; he was what I needed. My arms curled around his neck as he backed me into the thick trunk of a tree and pushed against my hips with his hand.

After some time, he pulled away. His cheeks were the darkest shade of crimson I'd ever seen. "W-wow, umm," he started, and paused to collect himself. "Do you want to go back to the party?"

His cautious manners were cute and refreshing. "I don't know," I admitted. "I'm pretty shaken up." I nodded to the passed-out guy lying to the side of us.

"I can take you home?" he offered.

We made our way to the party and he grasped my shaking hand in his steady one. Once we arrived, Alana ran up to us. "Are you okay?" she lowered her brows. "Wesley told me what happened. I went to get you a drink, but got caught up talking to Kimberly about her new job at—"

I put a hand on her shoulder. "It's okay...not your fault. I should know better than to walk through a strange forest."

She tilted her head. "It's a good thing Wesley showed up when he did. I don't know anyone else who could've taken Mark down like him..." her voice trailed off as she caught a look from Dalton.

"If I'd been there, I would've done much worse," he threatened, glaring as he did.

"It's not your fault," I reassured Alana before turning to him. "Hey, let's go," I choked out in a combination of nerves and sadness.

The walk to his truck was a blur as was the ride home. The only thing I remembered before making my way to my room was him walking me to the front door and asking if I'd be okay. "I'll call you during lunch tomorrow," he promised.

The front door swung open; it was Wesley. "I'll make sure she's all right."

Dalton nodded and walked back to his truck. When the door shut behind us, I was surprised to come face-to-face with a gentler Wesley. He put a hand on my upper back and guided me up the stairs and to my room.

He helped me sit on the bed. "Hey," my attention turned to his calm expression. "I'll get pajamas."

I motioned to a drawer and he pulled out shorts and a tank top. I sulked to the bathroom and changed, half-remembering the desperate, but comforting kiss Dalton and I shared earlier that evening. When I came out of the bathroom, Wesley had the sheets pulled back. I hesitantly lay against the plush pillow and he leaned toward me.

His nostrils slowly flared as he grazed my cheek with the back of his hand. I hadn't noticed how swollen the side of his eye had gotten, until that moment. He pressed his lips together before speaking. "Dalton's so much better for you," he whispered. "Stay with him; he's exactly who you need." His soft tone faded into my closed eyes, and before he spoke again, I fell asleep.

WESLEY

To keep my distance, I had to stay distracted which was easy enough to do with Tiff flaunting her cut-off shorts and mini-skirts. Days had passed since I found Lila with Mark in the woods and anger filled my body each time I recalled the scene.

I spent a lot of time in my room reading and working on papers for college along with research to get myself prepped for fall semester. Katie and I would take walks together or she'd talk me into going swimming, since Lila wouldn't go near the water, not even for Katie. Katie would crinkle her nose and complain it was boring to go to the pool with her. I'd laugh and think that seeing Lila in one of her bikinis was a plethora of things, but boring was not one of them.

Everything seemed to be smoothing over; she'd fallen into a routine with Dalton. I didn't pay much attention but noticed them talking on the phone during his lunch breaks and most evenings he'd stop by, take her into town for dinner or a shake, and sometimes, to my chagrin, a drive down the backroads. What could I say? If she felt she needed anyone, he was her guy. He didn't have the history I did. He was simple, predictable.

I tried to pretend I didn't care, but after the incident in the woods, something changed. Despite my efforts to suppress or ignore them, my feelings for Lila poked through the surface and I struggled to hold them back. *It's all for the best*, was my half-assed attempt to comfort myself and it worked for a couple weeks.

I woke up early one morning and slipped downstairs to grab a quick bowl of cereal before heading out for the day. I was rinsing my dish when someone tapped on the door. I put it in the sink and answered. Dalton greeted me. "Hey man." He was beaming. I hadn't seen him that happy in...well, forever.

I ran my hand through my hair. "Hey, you ready?" I asked, nudging him.

He pushed back at me. "Let's go." He paused before I shut the door and his eyes scanned the background.

"She's asleep, I guess," I answered, knowing he was looking for Lila.

He sighed, pretending to blow it off. "Oh, that's cool." We got in his truck and he pulled out. "Truck shopping, huh? What happened to your old one?" He turned the radio down, so we could talk.

"Wrecked it," I lied and hoped he wouldn't ask anything else. Then, I figured out how to deter him. "I guess everything's going well with you and Lila?" I swallowed hard, the words were knives as they poured from my mouth.

"That sucks, man." He looked away, probably so I wouldn't see his cheeks redden. "Yeah...dude...she's hella perfect. I'm surprised you backed off from her." Then he let out a chuckle. "Maybe she figured out your game." On the surface, he was joking, but I noted the hint of worry weaved into his comments.

That wasn't quite where I wanted the conversation to go, so I straightened my jeans and tried again. "I'm leaning toward a Chevy. What do you think?"

Dalton paused and quickly glanced at me then back to the road. "I think you know as much about trucks as I do. Chevy's are shit, dude." He cleared his throat and took a piece of gum from the center console. He grabbed an extra piece. "Want one?"

I shook my head. "Thanks, though." The air between us was uncomfortable at best, he knew I was dodging certain topics, I could feel it in his fast glances and the way he twisted his face and narrowed his brows. "Just wanted your opinion," I added, trying to sound like it wasn't killing me to sit in the same seat he'd probably made out with Lila in.

"Wes?...Man...are you okay?" We were nearing town.

"Yeah, great," was my short answer. *No, I'm angry, hurt...pissed that my best friend is hooking up with the smartest, hottest girl I've met in my life and I'm letting him because she's totally right—I'm not good enough for her, so instead of redeeming myself, I'm meeting Tiff at the bar and having drunk sex with her,* would've been the longer, honest response that most likely would've resulted in me getting my ass kicked. I shifted in the seat.

"How's everything with Tiff?" he questioned, an I-know-Wesley's-lying-so-I'm-going-to-dig-into-the-wound-as-deep-as-I-can-until-he-loses-his-shit expression coming over his face.

"Good, she's great," *Shitty, all she does is bitch and expect me to listen.* I tried to smile so it might be believable.

"Umm, okay." He didn't buy it. "How about all the other girls?"

I shook my head and smiled, rubbing my index finger on my chin, "No, it's not like that, now," I answered.

He didn't believe that either. "Whatever, it's always like that with you, Wes."

I gritted my teeth and tried to stay calm. "Well...it's not, now, okay?" I shot him a warning look, hoping he'd back off.

"Uh-huh." He smiled as though he thought I was joking.

Maybe it was the idea of him and Lila sucking face on some backroad, his hands combing her silk hair. Maybe it was knowing her whispered breaths danced into his sunburned ear. Maybe it was the fact he was stable, and that with him, she'd never have to worry about being cheated on—although I never would've messed around on her. Maybe it was because I'd never considered the reality of losing her forever. Maybe it was the way my lips dried and cracked regardless of how many times I used my tongue to wet them. Maybe it was my empty hand where her body should've been. Whatever the case, I lost it. "Why?" My voice boomed inside the cab. He'd pulled into the car lot but sat motionless. "Why the hell can't anyone believe I can be with one person?" I stared into his off-guard expression, my eyes as wide as I could get them. "Why can't you just fucking believe that?" My cheeks were hot.

He put a hand toward me. "Wes—calm down," he gently requested.

"No!" I cocked my head. "You can be happy with Lila!" I licked my dry lips again. "Fine, be happy with her! But realize, *maybe* I'm happy with Tiff!"

"Dude, what's going on?" His expression denoted he didn't know what set me off when in my mind, it was clear. *I was supposed to be with Lila, not him.* "I didn't mean it like that. I mean, you're happy being with only Tiffani. That's great, man. I'm happy for ya!"

Get a grip, Wes. He's your friend, I reminded myself before releasing a deep breath. "Listen, Sorry." I shook my head, embarrassed for venting. "I umm...I need to cool down. Why don't you go on ahead? I know what I'm getting, I'll catch up to you later." I opened the door and started to get out.

"Sure thing. I'm working all day and have an early morning tomorrow. Mind telling Lila?" He was studying my expression and wondering why I went off on him.

"Sure," I answered. "Later." I shut the door to his pickup and watched him back all the way out before I headed to the lot to look at trucks.

***

I rubbed the dash of my new Ford F-150...nothing. Not a single speck of dust came off, and I smiled. The 2016 model would be a lot better than the one I let Sara have.

I crept up the drive to prevent loose gravel from kicking up and scratching her paint. I parked and headed to the house as I swung the keys around my index finger. I opened the front door and my nose was attacked by the smell of Pine-Sol. I'd no more than stepped through the foyer when Lila came around the corner. Her hair was pulled into a bun and she was rocking a t-shirt and sweats. In one hand, she held a mop and rubbed her forehead with the other.

"You're back," she started.

Why did she care? "The domestic look..." I scanned her as I stood there. "Nice," I continued, adding a little sarcasm.

"Save it Wesley," she pushed the mop toward me. "It's your turn. I'm taking a shower," she announced as I took it from her and she promptly headed upstairs.

"W-what's going on?" I stood, holding the mop and wondering what was happening when a series of coughs coming from the living room caught my attention. I made my way to the couch where Katie was bundled in a ball of blankets. "Katie! Are you okay?" I'd never seen her get sick. "Where's Dad?" Her face was sheet-white and her eyes, groggy.

"Daddy went to work, Wes," her little voice managed, despite fatigue. "Lila's taking care of me, but I threw up in bed and on the floor. She brought me down here and changed my sheets, and then she cleaned the floors up."

Instinctively, I put the back of my wrist to her forehead. "No fever. It's not the flu," I commented, shaken from seeing her tiny body lying so still.

"Daddy thinks it was something in my kid's meal," she squeaked.

"Shh…just rest." She scooted around for a little while. "Is your bed clean?" I fluffed her curls from her face.

"Y-yes, Lila cleaned it."

"C'mon," I grunted as I lifted her, and she placed her small arms around my neck. I carried her upstairs and settled her under the fresh seats.

"Will I be okay, Wes?" Her eyes were starting to close.

"Yes, Katie-bug." I sighed. "We have to wait it out." I pecked her forehead with my lips.

"Wes, I'm thirsty."

"I'll be right back." I rubbed her arm and made my way downstairs to get her some water. When I returned, she was asleep, and I didn't bother waking her. Instead, I pulled a chair next to her bed and sat, waiting.

181

I jumped at the deep sigh coming from behind me. "Good, she's resting." It was Lila and she looked as worried as I did. "Sorry I took off. I had puke all over me, if you didn't notice."

I hadn't; I was still caught in the ecstasy of owning a new pickup and wasn't paying attention to anything else. "It's okay. Thanks for taking care of her. You didn't have to."

"I love Katie. She's a sweetheart. How could I not look after her?" She stood to my side wearing cut-off shorts and an azure tank-top that managed to set her green eyes off and send my heart spinning to my throat. "I think she ate something bad. Billy and I couldn't detect a fever."

"I agree," I whispered. The weariness in her shinning eyes and deep breathing proved she was on edge over the ordeal. Despite my better judgment, I set my hand on top of hers and rubbed it gently. "She'll be okay," I commented. She didn't move her hand from under mine, so I kept it there— stupid, yes, but it seemed to comfort us both.

Lila sat at the end of the pink, ruffled bed. We were both nearly asleep when Katie's eyes fluttered open and she sat up "Katie!" I jumped to attention. "Lay down. If you get up too fast, you'll get sick."

The color in her face had returned and her eyes were wider than I'd seen them since I got home. "I can't rest! You guys are hand holding and Josie at day care says that if you hold hands, then you're married! You guys are married!"

Lila pulled her hand out from under mine and I jerked mine up, as well, and answered with nervous laughter. "Your friend told you that, huh?"

"Yes! And I'm so happy!"

"Katie, don't get in my head," Lila spoke up.

Katie didn't listen. "You love him so much." While Lila stood frozen, shocked, something whittled its way into my own head. "And you love her," she remarked with passion. "This is the best day ever, even if I *was* sick!" She looked from me to Lila several times. "There's all these colors anytime you guys are around each other."

Before she said anymore, I cut her off. "Katie, Lila and I are friends—nothing more." The words ground inside of me. "I'm with Tiff, and Lila likes Dalton."

Katie frowned in response to my statement.

"Umm, do you want to watch TV? I can put on cartoons and make soup," Lila was trying to distract her.

Good call, I pushed to her.

Yeah, it was getting awkward.

"Only if it's a princess movie," Katie demanded.

"Okay, let's go," Lila stretched out a hand and Katie took it. I stayed behind and made her bed, remembering to grab the glass of water on the way out.

When I got downstairs, I set the drink on a table next to Katie. "Wesley!" Lila called out. "I don't think there's any soup."

Eager to drive my truck again and knowing Katie was going to be okay, I responded, "I'll go to town for some."

I pulled my keys off the rack and headed out toward my truck. I thought back to Lila's hand and how warm and delicate it felt as it rested beneath mine in Katie's room, her worried eyes striking against her ice-blue top. Jealousy, hurt, loss, surged through my body until I couldn't place any single emotion. I wondered how much longer we could pretend to be happy with other people.

The answer didn't come that day, nor did it arrive days after. Not even on an afternoon when I emerged from a particularly time-consuming project to grab a snack. I picked up an apple from a bowl on the kitchen counter and washed it. After I turned off the water, a horrendous mixture of sounds came from the study. Curious, I walked through the living room and stood in the doorway.

Her back was turned to me, her hair a tangled, dazzling wave of curls. She must've been crazy bored to tinker around on the un-tuned piano. I crept behind her, taking care to remain silent until I slid next to her on the bench.

She jumped but didn't say anything as I leaned into her. Holding on to the apple with my left hand, I put my right one on the keys and played a short tune. My eyes didn't leave hers. Her mind tried to make coherent words, a fact I found amusing. I debated how close I could come to her without losing control. I could've lifted my hand and ran my fingers through her lush hair, pulling her toward me, allowing our lips to meet as my tongue laced around hers.

I walked my fingers across the keyboard, until my hand slid over hers and my body leaned closer to her. I ran a finger over her soft knuckles. Her eyes sparkled and mixed with my own. Her nail was smooth on my finger tip. She moved closer to me. Too close. I took a bite of apple and stood, hastily walking away.

I did what I knew how to do around Lila, protect myself. I could be attracted to her, but I was determined that she wouldn't play with my feelings any longer. She could pretend she wasn't interested in me as long as she wanted, but her reactions like her warm, rapid breaths and goosebumps crawling along her skin when I neared her, suggested otherwise.

The phone buzzed in my pocket. "Hello?" I answered.

"Wes!" came her excited voice, "Get ready!"

"Umm..."

"Tonight's Cutest Couple Night at Tornado's. Pick me up in an hour," she demanded in her giggly voice.

"Okay, see ya." It was the last thing I wanted—to be dragged to, a 'Cutest Couple Night'. I sighed and headed to my room to get ready. An hour later, I was down the stairs and out the door to pick up Tiff. As I walked to my truck, a set of headlights blinded me. Lila came out the front door, tight jeans, a black fringe tank top set off with a gold necklace. Her hair waved down her shoulders. She nodded and walked straight to Dalton's pickup.

I got into my truck and followed them down the drive but turned the opposite direction to pick up Tif-*fawn*-ee. Surely it was a coincidence and they weren't going to couple's night. Tiff didn't live far from me, so the drive was short, and she was outside waiting when I arrived.

She opened the door and got in. "You're like ten minutes late," she bitched as she crossed her legs and arms.

"I wasn't expecting to take you anywhere tonight," I responded, knowing it wouldn't make a difference.

She paused and studied me, mostly to see if I was lying to her. Her eyes narrowed. "You're not messing around with Lila, are you?" she pursed her lips, ready to 'read' my reaction.

I put my hand on hers. There was no doubt she was attractive. She'd worn a red dress with heels and pinned her hair up in a pile with loose strands hanging down. "No." was all I offered.

She shifted her body closer to me. "*No?* You're shacking up with her and all you can say is, '*no*'?"

"It's not like that. She's here for a summer project," I re-explained, even though I couldn't blame her for worrying.

"Yeah…a *'project'*. I talked to Dalton and they're coming tonight." My stomach dropped. "I'll be watching you and I swear to God if you get drunk and start making out with her or any other girl, we're done," she reprimanded.

I refrained from answering and locked my right hand in hers as we pulled into Tornado's. *It's all for the best*, I reminded myself as I walked to her side and waited with the door open.

She stepped down and slung her arms around my neck, kissing me. It was warm, the way our lips locked, and my hands curled down her waist. She pulled away and whispered, "We *could* just go back to your house."

The proposition was appealing, but we were already there so I figured we might as well stay. "You forced me to dress up," I teased. "We stay."

Her lips curled into a smile. "Okay, we stay." She straightened my shirt collar.

We made our way in and immediately Tiff started waving and pulled me to a table to the side of the dance floor. We joined Alana, Connor, Lila, and, of course, Dalton. "Hey, guys!" Alana beamed.

Tiff sat between her and the other girls. I joined the guys on the other side. "Are you drunk already?" she asked Alana. I wasn't sure what had put her in full-bitch mode.

Connor nodded 'yes', to which she answered. "No, just buzzed."

Lila narrowed her eyes and looked around the table. "No one's twenty-one. How are you getting alcohol?" She eyed the bottle of beer Connor had in his hand.

He shrugged. "Easy, everybody knows everybody. As long as we're not out driving, they don't care."

"Back home it's more difficult than that," she replied.

Dalton stood. "Speaking of which, anyone want anything? Wes? Tiff? Lila?"

I shook my head, but Tiff answered, "A margarita." Lila said she wanted something but wanted to be surprised—a mistake if you ask me. Nobody did.

We kept the conversation light, and soon Dalton returned with drinks. He looked at me. "Next round's on you, bud."

"Sure." I looked at Tiff who was slurping down the margarita. "Go easy on that," I warned, but she wasn't listening. Lila had some other fruity-looking drink.

"How're you liking the new truck?" Connor's voice broke through the music.

"She's great—" I didn't have time to finish before the DJ lowered the music and spoke through the mic.

"Hey! Hey! Hey! Tonight's 'Cutest Couple Night'!" she shouted and everyone clapped. "Here's how this works people...I'm gonna slow the tunes down and y'all get out and dance. Let's get some judges up here. C'mon now, who wants to be a judge for this? We need three." She waited for a moment while one of the waitresses, an older guy, and a lady came up to the front. "Great! You guys are responsible for voting on *the* cutest couple. Whoever wins gets a seventy-five-dollar gift card to Sammy's Stockton Steakhouse *aaaand* their snapshot up there on our 'Wall of Flame'." More clapping.

The three people who volunteered returned to their seats, and the DJ started up a slow song. Before I could ask her, Tiff grabbed my shirt and pulled me to the dance floor to join several other couples. Connor and Alana followed, as did Lila and Dalton.

Tiff-*awn*-ee laid her head against my chest and I looked over her shoulder. Watching Lila curled against Dalton was a torpedo. She leaned her head away and said something to him and they both laughed. I turned Tiff so I couldn't see them.

"Wesley," she hummed, brushing something off my shirt.

"Hmm?"

"What are you thinking about?" she whispered, not moving her head from my chest.

"You," I lied and added. "Taking you to my room later and—"

She interrupted. "No, that's not what I mean. Your mind is so far away...I feel like there's a lot you don't tell me."

I sighed. "No, there's nothing I'm not telling you." *There's so much you don't know, about telepathy, telekinesis, FDRA, Sullivan, the fact that Lila and I are supposedly fated to be together, how much I care for her and how hard I fight to hide it.*

She didn't respond, but finally the music lowered, and the DJ piped up again. "Now, we're switching things up in here!" She chuckled over the microphone. "Turn around and everyone switch with the couple directly behind you."

She raised her head up. "Oh, no," she moaned. I turned and was face to face with Lila and Dalton. Not wanting to let on that anything was weird or awkward, I approached Lila as Dalton made his way to Tiff.

*Great...*her voice sounded in my head.

Don't think I enjoy this. I'm trying to play it off, I replied as I took her soft hand in mine and placed my hand on her waist. Her arm coiled around my neck and my stomach spun.

Think—I know you like it. Her lips formed a smirk, and I fought back a smile.

And you don't? I teased as the lights hit the green in her eyes and they sparkled into mine.

As a matter of fact, I'd rather be finishing my drink. Her smile grew wider.

I can arrange that, I started to pull away. I wanted to ask her what we were doing, pretending to like Dalton and Tiff-*awn*-ee, but I didn't. I wasn't sure how she'd respond, and no way would I let her lead me on again.

But it's the 'Cutest Couple' contest. You don't want to forfeit, do you?

She raised an eyebrow. It was the two of us, alone, on the dance floor. We were floating on a level beyond anyone else, and I got it. She was the only one who understood me. I was unable to find my way out of the haze; the moment was unthinking as I took her silky waves in my hand and grazed my face against her. How close could I get without kissing her? Her deep breathing was the music, everything faded in the distance.

We stopped dancing for a second. "Lila," I whispered.

Before she could answer, the music lowered once more. "Hey! It looks like we have a winner! Will the couple over there please come up on stage?"

A lot of people motioned to see if she was pointing to them, but she wasn't. The spotlight panned and froze on me and Lila. All eyes were on us as I glanced at Tiff who mouthed a heated 'what the fuck?' I tried to answer back 'I don't know,' but I did know—I knew that Lila and I shared an unparalleled energy, a connection that couldn't be surpassed. I eyed Dalton who'd returned to the table and had started gulping down a beer.

What do we do? Lila asked as we remained on the dance floor.

Play along, I answered.

Are you serious? She had a deer in headlights expression on her face.

I took her by the hand and practically pulled her along until we reached the stage and made our way up the stairs of the makeshift platform. The DJ came to congratulate us. "First off, congratulations! How long have you two been together?"

Seriously? Lila panicked. "W-we're not together," she admitted as I caught her glance turning to Dalton.

"I'm just joking! Here's your certificates. One for each of you." The DJ handed the certificate to Lila and we smiled for a snapshot that'd be put up on the wall. When we were finished, we returned to the table.

"I can't believe you brought me to this!" Tiff complained as I neared her.

Alana put her drink on the table and looked up. "I thought this was your idea," she responded before I could say anything.

Tiff-*awn*-ee released a sharp breath. "Whatever! Fine. C'mon let's use the restroom...you too, Lila," she barked to Alana and Lila who was concentrating on something in the corner.

My stomach hit the floor. Lila could protect herself if Tiff tried anything, but how far would she be willing to go? The girls left and Dalton, Connor, and I walked to the bar to get another drink. Connor pat my back. "Damn that Wes, always stealing girls out from under us."

"Shut up, man," Dalton said, nudging him.

"Watch out, dude," Connor's eyes narrowed, and his forehead creased.

"Both of you should stop." They turned their angry glances to me. "It's not like that with her."

Dalton studied me. "It better not be," he warned.

I let out a short laugh. "If I wanted her, I could have her," I challenged him. How dare he think that she'd stay with him if I wanted back in her life?

When he stood up straight, Dalton was about an inch-and-a-half taller than me. He got off the barstool. "You wouldn't try it," he stared straight into my eyes. "Would you, Wes?"

I swallowed, hesitating and choosing my next words carefully, "If I was able to sweep her off her feet, perhaps, you didn't hold her high enough," I answered in a threatening whisper.

Dalton clenched his jaw and moved closer to me.

"Everything okay, guys?" her hesitant hand ran over my shoulder and down the front of my shirt as she leaned her body into my back. "By the way, anyone seen Lila? When I came out to wash my hands, she was gone."

I turned to Tiff. "What do you mean, gone?"

She shrugged. "Dunno, we thought she'd be here with you."

Connor's attention had shifted to Alana, who was chugging some neon colored mixed drink. Dalton and I exchanged confused glances. Whatever tension we shared fell away and I could tell we were both worried that she'd taken off. What if she heard our conversation and left?

Thinking quickly, I piped up. "Maybe she feels awkward about the contest. I'll look for her."

"No, I'll go," Connor put a hand up to stop me.

"Stay here," I argued. "When she returns, she'll be a lot happier to see you than me," I lied. Of course, it wasn't the truth. She wanted to see me, not him. Without waiting for an answer, I turned and left. While my eyes scanned the area, I pushed energy throughout the building to listen for her thoughts.

Fucking perv...you thought you were scary in the woods. Judging me by my clothes. Wes might've gotten to you the first time, but I'm going to finish what he started.

Shit, I mouthed to myself, and took off out the door. I ran behind the bar, a place that'd been my reserved make-out spot for some time. I paused when I saw them. Mike had pressed himself as tightly against the wall as physically possible and Lila was studying him, scanning his thoughts.

"W-why can't I move?" stuttered a shaking Mike. "W-what the hell?" I could see his wide eyes though I was standing far away.

"You like girls." Lila stood in a near-daze. "But they sure as hell don't like you," she finished.

"H-how do you know? I-I can stop. I won't ever touch another girl," he pleaded with her.

"You're right. You won't," she threatened.

Knowing it was time to intervene, I stepped into the dim streetlight that tinted the dark scene. "Lila, think about what you're doing."

She turned. "Wesley? You followed me?" She narrowed her brows and tilted her head.

"You should let him be or you're going to do something you'll regret," I responded, trying to talk her down.

"Why? So he can continue to violate and objectify women?" She yelled.

"Okay, you have a point about that." I conceded the point because it was true. I'd seen him at a lot of parties and even had to pull him away from Tiff once or twice. "But, what can you do?"

She thought for a long time as the terrified eyes of Mike panned from me to her. "I-I can't move and m-my nose itches."

Lila sighed and looked at him. "Good," she answered, and I snickered. "Now," I could feel the energy draining from her. "You're going to stand here until you're completely sober. When you're able to drive, you'll go to the Sherriff's office and confess everything you've done. You'll tell them all about taking advantage of unwilling women. In court, you'll apologize personally to each one." She glanced at me, hesitantly, and continued. "...And you won't so much as think about kissing another girl, ever again," she finished. "Got it?"

Mike stood still against the brick exterior. "Yes." His answer was mindless.

"Good," Lila's chipper voice broke through the silence. "I'm heading inside." She turned to leave but turned back to Mike. "By the way, your entire body itches. You know, kind of like there's ants crawling all over you."

I followed her back into the building and once the door shut behind us. *You're bad, but I get why you did it.*

Stay out of it, Wesley.

She glared at me, those fire-green eyes glistening in the multi-colored lights. She wasn't going to get the upper-hand. I looked from her to the dance floor. *I bet you'd be in a better mood if we were back on that dance floor. You miss me already, don't you?*

Hardly, she spat back as we reached the others.

The girls surrounded her while she made up some lie about feeling weird about the whole couple thing and needing fresh air. Tiff and I didn't stay much longer after that; we caught a ride with a friend of hers back to her parents' house.

Later that evening, when she was asleep, I stood on her back porch and thought about what I'd said to Dalton. Getting Lila back would be easy. I leaned my back against a beam and wondered if it would come at the expense of my best friend.

LILA

I woke up late in the afternoon, having been exhausted from using my energy on Mike the night before. I felt bad for sleeping most of the day, so I quickly dressed and went downstairs. I found the broom and started sweeping the kitchen and hall. Afterwards, I mopped, sprayed all the counters down and wiped them off. Then, I searched until I located the vacuum and went over the carpet.

I stopped to wipe my forehead and the front door opened. It was Billy and Katie. "Hey, aren't you supposed to be working?"

He laughed, "It's the Fourth of July—No one's working." He glanced at me and then noticed the clean floors. "...Except you. Wow, the place looks great," he smiled, thankfully.

"It's no problem. I just feel like I shouldn't be staying here without helping out."

"It's appreciated. Umm, Katie and I are going down to the lake in a bit. She's swimming and then we're checking out the fireworks. You wanna come?" Katie squealed in excitement and Billy's eyes sparkled as he winked at her. It was easy to see where Wesley got his looks from, Billy was tall with messy blond hair and the same cerulean blue eyes.

"Actually, I'm going to Wayne's fireworks," I answered.

"Oh, with Wesley?" he asked.

"No, Dalton." I wiped more sweat from my forehead. I hoped Billy wouldn't be upset I wasn't with Wesley; Katie seemed to be.

"Girl," he shook his head and smiled. "I like you more and more every day. Glad you're still with him. I'll see what Wes's doing."

With Katie outside playing and Billy searching for a hung-over Wesley, I returned to my room and checked my phone which had one new message on it. It was from Dalton. 'See you in two hours.' I checked the time. It was a little after four. I grabbed a pair of shorts and a black tank top and walked down the hall to Wesley's room. His door was open, so I let myself in and went into the bathroom. I shut the door behind me and started the shower. When I finished, I dressed and carefully opened the door, hoping he wouldn't be there. He wasn't.

I walked back to my room and started getting ready, pulling my long hair into a not-so-messy-messy bun. I grabbed some jewelry and came across the bracelet. I wasn't about to wear a bracelet Wesley bought me on a date with Dalton. After a while, I heard a knock at the front door and ran down the stairs. Dalton met me at the door wearing dark shorts, a black logo t-shirt, and sandals. He looked at me. "You look... wow," he complimented.

I smiled, "Thanks." The thoughts of dancing with Wesley the night before melted away as I stood in near him.

Dalton studied me for a while. "You okay?"

197

Turning my attention back to him, I replied, "Oh, yeah."

He held out his hand. "Ready to go?"

We loaded up in his truck and headed out. After some time, we pulled into a grassy field along with a bunch of other cars and trucks. People had folding chairs and blankets lined up on both sides of the street and children were throwing footballs or playing tag. Across the road, we faced a burgundy house with a large shed next to it. Dalton pointed diagonally, and said, "They'll shoot them off all the way over there. We got a good spot." He opened his door to get out and I did the same. He pulled a blanket from his truck bed and spread it across the lawn. "Is this okay? I have folding chairs."

"It's fine, thanks." Dalton made everything so simple. He was safe, once he found a girl, he'd love her, and only her forever. When I was with him, worries slipped from my mind. I completely forgot about my abilities.

He waved at a couple, the woman was ready-to-pop pregnant, before sitting next to me and putting an arm around me. I leaned in to him. "Who are they?"

He smiled. "Tim and Janet...Bentley."

I didn't want to sound nosy but couldn't help myself. "She looks really young."

"They're our age but married right after high school. They're happy together," he smiled and briefly paused before continuing. "I guess."

A truck pulled into the open spot next to us. I looked around Dalton to see if it was Alana, but to my dismay it was Tiff and Wesley. He nodded as he pulled a couple of chairs from the bed. I looked back to Dalton who waved at them. *I thought he wasn't coming. Guess he changed his mind...super annoying.*

"Hungry?" Dalton asked as the sun started creeping lower.

"Yeah, a little," I answered.

"I can get us some hotdogs and soda?" He started to stand.

I didn't want to be left alone next to Tiffani and Wesley, but I was hungry. "Sounds good. Thank you."

He nodded and walked off. I continued to stare off to the side and folded my arms across my ribcage. I decided to ignore them and wait for Dalton to return.

You look good tonight, rang a voice in my head.

Shouldn't you be looking at your date? I retorted.

I can look at you, too. Having fun with Dalton?

What the hell kind of game was he playing? *I'm not answering tha—*

Someone from behind me screamed. The shriek was followed by an "Oh...oh my."

I stood to see what was going on and made my way toward the noise. "My water broke," came a shrill cry for help. Wesley and Tiffani walked next to me. Wesley pushed through the crowd to Janet Bentley, who was in tears and panicking.

"Okay, you have to calm down," he cautioned her and then turned to the growing crowd. "We need clean blankets and towels." Everyone froze. "Someone get some," he demanded. A few people ran to their cars. "Tiff! Run down and get help."

She nodded and took off as fast as her wedge heels could carry her. He helped Janet up on the back of a truck bed where someone had layered blankets. "Your baby's low... there's not going to be time to get to a hospital."

"No! No! I can't do this here," she screamed and raised her head to look frantically at the semi-circle of concerned and curious faces.

"You need to calm down," he instructed. "Where's your husband?"

"Getting food," she answered, panting.

"Lila! Get over here," he shouted.

Unsure of why he asked me to help, I made my way passed a few people and stood next to him. *Do you know what you're doing?*

Delivering a baby, duh, came his sarcastic response.

Do you know how?

No, but she doesn't know that. Maybe I read about it before, but that's beside the point. She needs to calm down. You can do that Lila. Make her relax.

Wes—

Do it, he instructed. *Or she could lose this baby.*

Her husband had returned; he was as frantic as she was.

"It hurts!" she screamed.

"I'm glad you're wearing a dress," Wesley remarked, pulling it past her thighs. "Do you feel like you need to push?" He asked her.

"Yes!" she screamed.

I put my hand on her sweaty forehead and looked into her wide eyes. In a calm voice I told her, "You'll relax now. You're not feeling pain."

Her breathing calmed, and when Wesley told her to push, she was able to do so. She couldn't feel the pain, but as I pushed into her mind, I could. It was a cross between food poisoning, being squeezed, set on fire, and every period I'd ever had my entire life, all rolled into one. I backed off fast— no wonder she screamed. Poor girl, to think, she was my age. When I pulled out of her thoughts, she began panicking again, so I endured the horrendous pain. *Can you hurry the hell up?* I managed.

You think I'm enjoying this? Wesley's voice broke through the burning. "One more push on three. One, two..."

She sat up and groaned and then, a shrill shrieking noise escaped from something tiny, covered in an alien-looking mucus. Wesley plopped it on her chest. "He's a boy." He grinned victoriously. Tim came over and thanked him before going to his wife to meet their son.

Dalton and Tiff had returned with paramedics and an ambulance struggled to maneuver across the grass between the people and cars. One of the first responders approached me and Wesley. "You did a good job. Most people would've freaked."

"Thanks," Wesley responded, as he tried to wipe the mixture of slime and blood from his hands. I blushed.

"You should consider becoming a paramedic," he suggested.

"I'm actually beginning a pre-med program," Wesley answered.

The paramedic looked to me. "What about you?"

I giggled, but mostly because he was kind of good-looking, especially in the uniform. "I'm an artist, not a doctor.

That's as close as I want to get to having a baby." The pain was traumatizing, and I was weak.

He thanked both of us again before walking off. They wheeled the new mom and her baby into the ambulance and she whispered a weak, but sincere thank you to us.

I backed up, near Dalton, as Wesley was surrounded by people. An instant celebrity, he was finally in his element and Tiff was soaking up the attention as well. "It's awesome that you helped out."

I giggled, "I didn't do much." Though I had.

"Do you still feel like watching the fireworks?" He asked, those big brown eyes staring at me until I couldn't say 'no'.

So, we stayed. We walked over to his truck and watched as color lit up the sky. He stood behind me with his strong arms around my waist. They felt good, calming. I forgot about the pain, I almost forgot about Wesley. When the show ended, he turned me around and pulled me to him. One of his hands combed through my hair and the other slipped up my ribcage and back down as our lips met. I explored his firm back and wished for the same thunderous burst in that kiss as there'd been in the evening sky. When we separated, I looked into his desert eyes and the thought occurred to me, maybe he didn't feel anything either.

Whether he did or didn't, he remained quiet as we folded the blanket and loaded up the truck. We waited in an unending line of cars and Dalton spoke up. "Tomorrow we're going to the lake. Want to come?"

I yawned. "Maybe, I'm exhausted." Truthfully, I could've fallen asleep then and there.

"I'll bet. It's not every day you help deliver a baby. I'll text you and if you can't go, maybe we'll stop by for a while," he offered.

"That sounds cool," I answered.

The car in front of us pulled up and he inched forward. "You okay?"

"Umm, yeah."

In the silence, I thought about helping the girl with her baby—with all the bad caused by my abilities, I could do good as well. I felt what she was feeling, I could truly understand her pain. Telepathy gave me empathy. When Dalton dropped me off, I walked up the porch steps and noticed he waited to leave until I was inside.

Wesley's voice came from the couch. "You stayed?"

I turned into the living room. "I'm guessing you didn't."

He stood up and stretched. "I had to come home and clean up. Apparently, delivering a baby is a messy procedure." He laughed to himself, "Tiff bitched the whole way home about me dirtying up her truck."

I couldn't help but laugh. I stopped as he came closer to me. I backed up, but he continued forward. The farther I stepped, the more he closed in until I found myself against one of the brightly painted walls. His body grazed mine as he gently put his hand on my shoulder and whispered. "Do you like him?" I drowned somewhere in his ocean eyes.

Goosebumps rose on my arms as I answered honestly. "Not as much as I liked you." The words stumbled from my mouth before I could stop them.

He swallowed, "Well..." he began, his lips moving closer to mine. He was going to kiss me, and I was glad he'd backed me against a wall, otherwise I was certain I wouldn't have been able to stand. "That's unfortunate..." He gently brushed back several strands of humidty-soaked hair that stuck on my forehead and sighed, "...because I really like Tiff." He gave me a patronizing look, pushed away, and started for the stairs.

"I know that's not true," I called to him, but he didn't respond.

In fact, we didn't talk the rest of the week. He found things to do outside, like mow, a lot...even when the grass didn't need it. Some days I'd wake up and he'd be gone and wouldn't come back until much later, and usually intoxicated.

The following week it rained. Billy said it was badly needed. Wesley didn't leave, but Tiffani stopped by with Alana, Connor, and Dalton, of course. I was glad to see him. He apologized for being distant and explained that he had to work a lot the week before, but a part of me didn't believe him.

We sat and watched TV together until Tiff finally spoke up. "It's supposed to stop raining later, finally. We should go out to eat...all of us, like a big group date. What do you say Alana? Connor?" They both nodded. "Wes?" He didn't move. "I'll take that as a yes."

"I'm down," Dalton spoke up and looked at me. I nodded in agreement.

"I can't tonight. I promised Katie I'd take her to the fair. It's the last night," he finally responded, bitterly.

"Then we go before. Face it, it'll be too hot to go early. We'll go on a lunch-dinner date. Okay? Okay! C'mon guys." She motioned to the other three. "Let's get ourselves cleaned up. See you in a few hours."

The others said their goodbyes and left me and Wesley alone.

Without a word, he shut the front door, letting it slam behind him and headed up to his room. I followed him but went to my room instead. What was he doing? Thinking? I fought the urge to get in his head. I learned my lesson on that. Instead, I distracted myself with picking out clothes, and found two dresses that'd be perfect for the date. Then I lay on my bed and took out the old diary.

October 15, 1666

Dearest Diary,

Keeper of my biggest secret. Have I one secret more, for we have fled to the colonies upon Father's merchant ship. Dying were they all and exposed was Father. A mark of the reddest paint, taking the shape of an 'X'. Placed was it upon our door and left were we to die a quite horrid death. Die did we not and Father feared we must be labeled witches and hanged in towne square. Mother believes the inhabitants of the colony of Jamestowne to be savages. I know of them not, but am of the mind that I shall pass away an olde maid, all alone. Soon, shall I bring thee news.

My eyes stung from trying to read through the faded words, and the text made me wish I'd have paid more attention in history class. I closed the diary and looked at the time. It was a little after one. I sighed, not really excited to go on the date. Dalton and I hadn't been talking much and, surprisingly, I was okay with it. We should've talked about breaking up, not that we were officially together. It could wait. I grabbed some shampoo, conditioner, two dresses, and took in a deep breath as I made my way to Wesley's room, hoping to borrow the shower. I knocked lightly.

His voice was flat as he answered. "It's open."

I pushed the door open to catch him looking unfairly gorgeous in fresh jeans and a turquoise shirt that set eyes his off more than usual. His skin was tan from working in the sun, and he smelled like he'd stepped out of a Calvin Klein ad. "I was...wondering," I stumbled. "I need to shower."

He shrugged, a cold expression crossing his face. "That's fine," he answered, walking to his bed and grabbing a book. "I'll be studying," he added.

What was wrong with him? Why was he suddenly going all cold again? He seemed pretty happy with Tiffani and without getting into anyone's head, I didn't know what to make of it all. I tried to drown the stress away in the shower, but unlike sweat, it clung hard, refusing to give into the soap and loofah.

I went the whole nine yards, taking my time to shave carefully and wash my hair. When I was finished, I started getting dressed, deciding to try the black dress I'd picked. I slipped it on and was elated to find the zipper going all the way up... until it reached my shoulder blades and wouldn't budge.

I tried pushing it down and then pulling it up—nothing. I attempted to slip the dress off, but it was zipped too far and wouldn't budge. *I could ask Wesley* but shook the notion off thinking that I'd sooner eat my way out of the dress. I struggled for a while longer with the back and finally opened the door in defeat. "Wesley," I grumbled.

He looked up from his book. "Yeah?"

"My zipper...it's caught." I struggled with it again. "Damn dress," I muttered.

"Hold on," he stood up and walked behind me. "It's a nice dress; you're going to rip it," he warned as he moved closer and I took in the citrus smell mixed with peppermint.

"Here," He bunched my wet hair and indicated that I should hold it up. I took it in my right hand and tried not to think about his warm breath hitting my neck. Or how good I knew his lips would feel on my bare skin.

The tips of his fingers gently stroking my shoulder blades as he worked with the stubborn zipper and after a little while, "I got it."

He moved it up, and then back down, just a little, to ensure it'd work again. I swore his body neared mine, but figured he was messing with me.

"You're welcome," he whispered in my ear while he pulled the zipper down a little more. Did he know what he was doing to me? Of course, he did.

His voice, his words, his body close behind me, his hands on my skin, his breath in my ear. "Keep going." I whispered feeling that he hadn't pulled his mouth from my ear. He hesitantly slid the zipper down a little more and paused. "Don't stop," I insisted, and he pulled it down further. His cheek grazed my temple until I stood on my tip-toes, turning my head slightly and winding up in the kiss I'd been wanting, but too scared to accept, since he'd snuck up behind me at the lake.

Our lips met, and my body jumped. It wasn't safe and secure—it was wild, thunderous like the burst of fireworks, the crackling colors as they opened and exploded in unpredictable patterns. He turned me around fully and slid the straps completely off my shoulders before kissing them. The dress glided down my ribs and waist, settling on my hips as my shaky hands worked to slip his shirt over his head. My wet hair spilled down my back and chest and he ran his hand through it. "Are you sure?"

I was in front of him, in the daylight, in my bra; my dress rested on my hips. His blue eyes soaked me into him until the rest of the world stopped existing. His shirt was unbuttoned, exposing parts of his enticing abs as he waited for my answer.

"Wesley, I want *you*. I'm done lying to myself and you." It was no use. Being near him was hypnotic, kissing him intoxicating. Why fight something that made me feel so good? I gave into it. We gave in to each other. "Tell me you have—"

He chuckled, "I learned my lesson," he answered pulling a gold wrapper from his pants' pocket before they hit the floor. We fell onto the bed, the only sounds our short, rough breathing, and the rhythm of our lips as they parted quicker and fell back together.

He was on top of me, his muscles flexing to hold himself up; his neat hair fell onto his forehead and I swept it back. Our bodies were like the wick of a candle; individual strands intertwining, wrapping around one another moving down, melting at the touch of a flame as it made its way to the stick. The fluidity of motion ran from his body to mine, and back, swirling around entangled pieces of string and dancing back and forth, teasing the base with its motion until it couldn't anymore.

I pulled my lips away from Wesley, forcing him to lose his grip on my back as my head hit the pillow. Stars. A tremor paralyzed me, and I knew what I was feeling and as soon as it started to end, it happened again. The flame enveloped the stick as it melted to the base. Wesley's head landed next to mine on the pillow as he took in sharp, shallow breaths, his moans and gasps curving through my own.

I wanted more. *Do you have to stop?* I wanted more of him.

He chuckled, *No.*

The candle, whole again, was teased by flame that made its journey down the entangled wick, time after time, until we were so tired, moving wasn't an option. I closed my eyes and drifted off.

Sleep was peaceful; dreams and nightmare didn't exist in Wesley's arms. I rested against his rhythmic breathing, relaxed, for the first time in quite a while; satisfied.

I wasn't sure how much time passed before Wesley sat up quickly, his voice knocking me from my tranquil coma, "Shit!" He rubbed his hand against his forehead.

I stretched, my body shook from exertion. Did he think we made a mistake? I pulled the blanket over me and sat up behind him, feeling the warmth from his back penetrating the thin sheet. Then, I heard it too—the source of his unease—my stomach flipped at the faint knock on the front door. I'd totally forgotten about the date...and Dalton.

Wesley whispered as though they could hear us. "I'll rinse off quickly, dress, and stall them while you get ready."

"Okay," I answered, disappointed that I couldn't just spend the rest of the afternoon lying next to his seductive body. He turned, and our lips met once again, and twice. He put his hand on my forehead and combed through my hair and down my cheek as our kiss continued. "Wes—" I whispered between kisses.

Another knock. He jumped up and was in and out of the shower within minutes and dressed quicker than that.

I hurried into the shower, trying to keep track of the time. Once I was finished, I went with the light blue sundress without the zipper, scrunched my hair, and didn't bother to put on makeup. I slipped a pair of wedge heels on and rushed down the hall and stairs.

Tiffani scanned me up and down, "Wow, for taking *so* long to get ready, you sure don't clean up well," she taunted.

Dalton stepped up to my defense, "Lila, I think you look great."

Recalling Wesley's strong hand as it pushed into my hip, I answered meagerly, "Thanks," and gave Dalton a little smile while Wesley looked away. "You're not so bad yourself," I complimented him.

Tiffani piped up, "Are you sure you're feeling okay? You look...flushed." She studied me, and my pulse raced. She was the type of girl who could see right through me.

"Me? No, I'm fine..." The wooden floor spun counter-clockwise beneath my feet until I almost lost my balance. "No flushing at all. N-nope. The only thing flushing is the toilet..." Things were getting uncomfortable fast.

Calm down, you're going to give us away.

Wesley, this is bad. It's like, we cheated on them.

We're not exclusively dating either of them.

But this is a date...

After that bit of silence Tiffani raised her eyebrows. "Well, let's get going, shall we?"

To my dismay, they'd arrived in separate cars. Wesley rode with Tiffani, Alana with Connor, and me with Dalton.

"I like that dress. It makes your legs look long," he eyeballed me as he put his truck in drive.

"Umm, thanks. I like your...outfit, as well." I complimented, scanning his attempt at 'dressing up,' which consisted of dark wash denim jeans, and a t-shirt with a plaid shirt buttoned over it to hide dirt stains. Wesley aside, Dalton was attractive, but my mind was saturated with thoughts of Wesley's tongue turning with my own. The aching throb started again, and I stared out the window, riddled with guilt and desperate for the date to end. "Where are we going to eat?" I looked into Dalton's unknowing eyes, and guilt bombarded me.

"Downtown is blocked for the fair, so we're going to this place right outside of 54 highway called Chick'n Fixin's."

"Chicken what?" The name of the restaurant served as distraction enough from the earlier events with Wesley.

"Chick'n Fixin's...I guess maybe it may sound silly to you, but they serve some of the best fried chicken around."

"No, no...I enjoy new experiences. So, the fair is inside your city?"

"Yeah, they set up right next to the park. It's tradition." He turned the radio down so we could talk more. "Well," he changed the subject, "I bet you think you East Coast people have good fried chicken. I hope you're ready to be blown away."

I laughed, "For sure...can't wait."

We pulled into a gravel lot outside of a stand-alone building. I was surprised they had any business at all, but the full parking lot implied otherwise.

"I hope they have a table!" Dalton remarked as we got out of his car.

Too uncomfortable to laugh, I rubbed my hand down my arm as Wesley and Tiff got out of his truck, followed by Connor and Alana who'd just pulled up.

Tiffani slipped her sunglasses down her nose, "God, I hope they have a table."

We were all thinking the same thing but lucked out as a large group exited before we could get through the door. We entered and spoke with one of the waitresses who obliged us by pushing a couple tables together, so we could sit with one another. I found myself seated next to Dalton and across from Wesley, who's shimmering blue eyes melted my own. Tiffani was engrossed in a conversation with Alana about the restaurant changing some decorations around, which was quickly joined by Connor and Dalton who had stuck around for the year and was explaining details to the girls.

Wes, do you think they know?

No, but I can't wait to get out of here. I caught him trying to hold back a grin.

Why would that be? I smiled coyly at him.

This afternoon wasn't enough. All I can think about is making love to you, over and over.

My body warmed at his words, his tennis shoe slipped by my bare toes. My stomach was unsettled, and I wasn't sure if I'd be able to eat.

I want to be with you, too. This is uncomfortable.

Want to meet me in the bathroom? He smiled.

Wesley...

I'm serious, we could be quick.

No! I puckered my lips into a smile.

Why not? They'd never know. He struggled to hold back laughter. *The stalls are pretty big. I'm sure we'd both fit.*

I couldn't keep it in, the thought of Wesley and I synchronously excusing ourselves from the unnerving group date to do a quick hookup in the restaurant bathroom simultaneously frightened and amused me. I met his stare and snickered loud enough that it caught everyone's attention. They looked over at us.

"What did we miss?" Alana glanced from me to Wesley.

"I was...we were just..." Even Wesley waited for my explanation. I glanced down to a menu that sat right in front of me. "The Thundercluck— it's a sandwich, but it sounds hilarious."

"Easily amused, I see." Tiffani rolled her eyes.

Dalton smiled, "I think it's funny, too." Connor laughed, uneasy.

Nice save.

Stop, you're distracting me. I tried to keep from blushing.

From whom? Your 'date'?

As the attention turn back to me and Wesley, I sensed we must've been gazing at each other with intent, I chose not to respond.

"You two are gonna burn a hole through each other," Connor piped up.

Before anyone else could reply, the waitress flew over to our table. "I am so sorry. It's just been a madhouse in here, with the picnic and all. I can take your drink orders, if you want I can take your food orders, too. If you're not ready yet, that's okay."

We all ordered; I asked for the Thundercluck and Dalton did, as well. Everything seemed to have been forgotten by the time everyone was finished ordering and the waitress returned with help to pass out our drinks.

But Tiffani just had to pry. "So, I just think it's totally interesting that you're from Virginia. And I'm totally not getting why you came out here with Wesley. It just makes no sense. C'mon, spill... inquiring minds want to know..." A sly smile crossed her face, because she knew exactly how uncomfortable the questions made me.

I concentrated, entering her mind to find that she wasn't a bad person at all, but I also discovered how much she cared for Wesley. Heck, they'd known each other since they were seven.

She scooted her chair out and put her hand to her head taking in a deep breath. "Oh..."

"Are you okay?" Connor and Alana jumped to check on her.

Wesley glared. *Lila, get out of her head. You're not supposed to be doing that—self- control, remember?*

I sighed and backed off. Tiffani sat up. I tried to look concerned. "Are you okay?"

"Yeah, totally weird, just got so lightheaded suddenly, like, I can't even explain it." She tried to shake herself out of it.

Wesley put his hand on her shoulder and she smiled weakly, "Maybe it's just the heat," he surmised.

"Or maybe it's the affect you have on me," she answered, sheepishly.

He cleared his throat and broke her attention-seeking gaze, to her dismay, and took a long drink of soda.

Fortunately, our food was served soon after, and everyone watched as I gushed over how crisp the breading was on the tender, lightly seasoned chicken. They smiled, knowing the food from the Midwest had officially won me over.

When we were ready to leave, I got back into Dalton's truck.

"I hope Tiff's okay," he stated, obviously shook up.

Knowing what happened I responded, "I'm sure she will be. Wes is probably right; it's the heat."

We rode in silence until we pulled up to Wesley's house. Dalton turned the music down again and looked at me with his sweet brown eyes. "Hey, I had fun."

"Me too," I replied, because it was true.

"You sure?" he asked. "I know I've been distant lately. It just..."

I studied his eyes. "What?"

He looked down, embarrassed. "Nothing. Umm... We should talk, tomorrow."

"Okay," I giggled hoping that Dalton wouldn't suspect anything crazy happened between me and Wesley.

We said our goodbyes, and a few said that maybe they would show up at the carnival.

Wesley unlocked the front door. Once we were both inside and the door was shut behind us, he gently pushed me toward the wall, out of the way of any windows. With his hand behind my head, our lips came together in one smooth, rhythmic motion. "Let's go upstairs," he mumbled between kisses.

"Aren't you taking Katie out?"

We kissed again, our lips refusing to separate, his hands running down my waist.

"We have an hour," he breathed. "Or two."

I was convinced, but I thought maybe he'd forgotten about the 'going upstairs part' as his hand slid up the bottom of my dress and continued until his fingers caught the strap of my thong and played with it. He must have also assumed we were alone, when from the hallway, we heard a tiny snicker followed by little feet.

He moved his hand, fast, and we separated from one another before we were witnessed any further by two tiny blue eyes.

"Wes!" We both walked over to her. "Let's go, now! Let's go to the fair." The little girl hopped up and down.

"Ahhh, you have to get ready," Wesley reminded her.

She spread her arms to show off a pair of jeans, accompanied by polka-dot rain boots and a turtle neck.

I couldn't help but grin. "Do you think you might get a little hot in that? I do love the combination, though."

She crinkled her nose. "Hmm, maybe."

"Do you have a sundress? Or a romper?"

She shrugged.

"Who usually dresses you?"

Her little eyes dropped, "Mommy..."

The air was getting tense, "Okay, umm...what if we go to your room and see what you have? I can help," I offered.

"Do you know a lot about clothes?"

"Totally, just call me queen of Tyson's Corner," I proudly announced.

"What's that?"

"Never mind. Let's see what you got."

"I'll be watching TV!" Wesley announced, but we were already off to her room.

"Wow, you have a lot of pretty things to wear," I complemented, even though I didn't see too much in her closet or drawers that would fit her, anymore.

"You think so?" she beamed.

"Yeah," I continued to lie.

Her face dropped. "No, you don't. I can see that you don't."

Poor girl, I sighed. "No, I really don't. But these are cute." I pulled out a pair of jean shorts with a pink butterfly and purple flowers on the pocket. "And what about..." I sorted through a bunch of shirts and tanks, "This?" I pulled out a bright pink tank and held it against the shorts.

"Well, okay," she took the outfit and went in her bathroom to change.

I looked through her shoes in the bottom of her closet and found a pair of white slip-ons. *Perfect*, I thought. Her mood had changed when she came out. I was happy the clothes fit and handed her the shoes, which slipped on easily. "Do they hurt when you walk?"

"No."

"Okay, good. Now...what about your hair? Let's go in my room."

She grinned. "Really? Cool!"

We left her room and walked down the hall, I opened the door and let her in. She immediately went over to my dresser. "You have *so* much stuff." She rummaged through makeup and fanned through magazines, smelling the perfume samples.

"Here." I rubbed one of the pages against her wrist. "Now smell," I suggested.

"So cool!"

"Let's get the hair out of your face or it'll get sticky when you sweat."

"Like how?" She smelled her arm again.

"Want a French braid?"

"A what?"

"Never mind. I'll do it and if you don't like it, then we can try something else," I recommended.

"You're really nice," she said as I sat her down on the edge of my bed and sat behind her separating her hair at the part and combing through each side. "I'm glad you and Wes are in love," she mentioned casually. "Soon, you'll be married. Will we be related? Will you live with us? Can you do my hair every day? We could even go shopping together, right?"

"Whoa," I laughed, "slow down. I'm only eighteen. People don't usually just get married at eighteen anymore."

"Oh. Why not? Are there rules?"

"No, there's no rules, but there are a lot of reasons, marriage can be restraining... like what if I wanted to get a job, but then had a baby instead? Or, what if I don't know myself well enough? But, you know what the hardest obstacle is?" I asked, my eyes growing wide as I finished the first braid.

"What?" she asked expectantly.

"He'd have to ask me first," I answered.

"Would you say 'yes'?"

I remained quiet for a moment, not wanting to disappoint her as I weaved pieces of her hair in and out from one another. I'd never considered marriage as an option. "I don't know," I answered honestly.

"Oh," she said, a little disappointed.

I almost felt bad for telling her no, but the interrogation caught me off guard. "Are you seeing things? Or having dreams about me and Wesley?" I was curious.

"Just sometimes. It's just blurry things. I dunno. Sometimes it's hard being like this."

"It's confusing, huh?" I knew exactly how she felt.

"Yeah."

I finished up the second braid and showed her in the mirror.

The little girl smiled and turned before giving me a big hug. "Thank you."

"Oh, we're not done," I responded.

I searched through my accessories and found ribbon. I used makeup scissors to cut two pieces off and tied them into bows at the end of her braids. "See?"

"I love it!" Her smile grew bigger. "Tonight's going to be the best!"

"Come on, let's show Wes."

Her eyes were huge as she opened the door. "Daddy! Daddy, look!" She ran to Billy.

"Hey! Look at you, pumpkin." He lifted the little girl and gave her a hug.

"Lila did it!"

I stood in my doorway, smiling.

Billy returned the smile and nodded. "You kids heading out soon?" He asked, his smile mirroring Wesley's. I could imagine he was also a lady's man back in the day.

"I think so," I answered.

He gave me a warning look, "Be careful." His expression lightened. "But have fun!"

"Thanks!" I started for the stairs and followed Katie down.

Wesley was already up and grabbing his keys from the hanger.

"Wes! Look at me!" She spun in a circle to 'model' her new look.

"I like it!" He exclaimed.

"Lila's good, isn't she?"

"She sure is," he grinned at the double entendre and grazed my forehead with his lips.

On our way to the fair, Katie began telling us her list of everything she wanted to do that night and I looked down to find Wesley's hand heading toward mine. Katie paused for a moment, "So are you two boyfriend and girlfriend?" she sang.

Wesley glanced over at me and grinned. "I don't know. Are we?"

"Are you asking?" I teased.

The side of his lip curled. "No, I'm not."

"Then, I suppose we aren't." I folded my arms and crossed my legs.

Wesley sighed loud enough to grab my attention. "Lila, be my girlfriend already."

I raised an eyebrow. "I don't know..."

"Dang it, Woman. Say yes!"

I couldn't hold back the laughter. "Fine, yes," I answered, quietly.

He leaned toward me. "What?"

"Yes!" I squealed, still laughing as he squeezed my hand. I'd had boyfriends in the past. But, it was always assumed. No guy had ever gone out of his way to *ask* if I'd like to be his girlfriend. It almost wasn't a choice; you either were or you weren't. Despite the high, my stomach dropped. It occurred to me that when Wesley said he loved me in Florida, he wasn't joking. Despite all the stupid-ass crap he pulled since we'd been in Missouri, he meant it, felt it, and sincerely loved me.

"This is town, city limits," he announced as we drove by a Pizza Hut and a few other buildings and stopped at a light. He chuckled, "And the first of three stoplights, but you've probably seen most of this."

"Really? Three? Dalton didn't mention it." I hadn't visited many towns that small.

He nodded and took a left, and another right. "This is Main Street. As one might conclude, it's the main street, but, part of it will be blocked off for the picnic."

"How much is it to get in?"

"Nothing...we'll pay a donation for parking, but admittance is free," he explained.

"Oh wow! Totally crazy."

After a while, I could see what he meant, beyond the roadblocks were crowds of people and food trucks and arts and crafts booths lined up on either side of the street. From where we were in the road, a Ferris wheel towered over everything, even the old downtown buildings. It was a fantastic sight as we turned down an alley and into a parking lot, where we were waved into a spot. Wesley handed the boy a twenty.

"Wow, thank you, sir."

"Welcome!"

We got out and I helped Katie out of the back and asked her, "So, what are we going to do first?"

"I get to pick?" Her blue eyes lit up.

"Yeah," I answered, nowhere close to falling off the edge of cloud nine.

"It's too hot to ride rides...can we play games?" she looked at Wesley.

"Yeah...yeah, that's fine." He seemed distracted.

"Are you okay?" I whispered.

"I'm more than okay. I'm just surprised you said yes."

I deserved that. Being so sure of how I felt yet acting so unsure toward him. Blowing him off in Florida. I thought I needed time, alone, to get my abilities under control, but I made it so hard on him. "Wes—"

"It's okay, I've got the smartest, hottest girlfriend, and the cutest little sister at the fair. How could things get any better?" he interrupted my apology as we made our way back down the alley and to the road blocks. I'd never seen him that at ease. "Make sure you're holding my hand, or Lila's," Wesley lectured Katie.

"Should I hold the hand that you two aren't holding?"

"Ha, you're so funny," Wesley came back, sarcastically. "Maybe I'm just making sure Lila also stays safe."

I laughed as we continued past the smell of grease and corndogs saturating the summer air. We passed the Merry-go-Round and Wesley stopped at a ticket booth. "Let's see how much the tickets cost."

"Sir," the lady inside the booth caught Wesley's attention, "You can buy a band for twenty bucks and ride unlimited all night," she suggested.

"Okay, let's do it." He paid her and we all held our wrists up while she put bands on them.

When we were finished, we continued down the crowded midway until we reached the games.

"Oh! Balloons! Wes...I want to pop them!" Katie's eyes were huge as she pointed to a colorful wall holding a display of balloons.

The man working the booth hollered, "Every player wins a prize! Hit one balloon for a small prize, two for medium, and three for extra-large."

"How much is it to play?"

"Five dollars a try. But I'll give the little girl three chances for ten."

Wesley rolled his eyes but couldn't say 'no' to Katie. I sighed watching him, feeling guilty for wanting the evening to end quickly so we could be alone again. Just then, Dalton crossed my mind and the guilt surfaced. We'd never made anything exclusive, but still, Wes and I had, and I needed to talk to him about that, the sooner the better.

WESLEY

Were carnival games always so expensive? For what, a plastic sword or light up wand I could buy at Wal-Mart for a dollar? I wasn't going to tell her 'no' but remained incredulous at the outrageous prices as a dart flew by, missing the wall of balloons altogether.

She looked down, disappointed. The worker handed her another dart and she tried again, but it also came nowhere near a balloon. "I'm so bad at this." Katie turned as though she was about to give up and walk away.

Lila bent down. "No, you're not. Use your wrist, not your whole arm."

Katie smiled and snapped her wrist with Lila still beside her. The dart flew straight into a balloon, causing it to not only pop, but also four other balloons around it. Lila lifted Katie up and walked her over to the prizes.

"Looks like you win an extra-large one, huh?"

The man came over. "No, the dart only hit *one* balloon, not the others."

Lila stared at him. *Oh, no, here we go,* I groaned to myself.

"She won the extra-large prize," she insisted.

His taunting expression went blank. "Yes ma'am," he agreed while Katie pointed to a large stuffed penguin holding a surfboard. The man pulled it down and handed it to the glowing little girl.

"That's a lot to carry around all night," I mentioned, realizing immediately that I'd be the one stuck with it. "You two want to wait in this area and I'll run it to the truck?"

"Sure," Lila agreed.

And that's the story of how I managed to be walking down a carnival midway, in mid-July, sweating my ass off while hauling a giant penguin who grinned as he proudly held the surfboard. I maneuvered my way through the growing crowds, nervous about leaving the two of them alone. I made it to the truck and tucked the abomination safely in the back, hoping that would be the only game she'd want to play.

Lila was good with her, patient. I'd been floating since I asked her to be with me, only me… and she said "yes". I never thought I'd ask a girl that sort of thing, but she was magnetic. Everything about her, the way it felt to finally be with her. How that afternoon, I wanted to be gentle, but a part of me wanted her savagely up against the wall, her legs wrapped around my body. Suddenly, I wanted to take her home and lock ourselves in my room, I don't know…forever.

I left the parking lot, making my way back down to the girls, but when I arrived at the balloon game, they were nowhere to be found. I looked around and the world shrank as I panicked.

"Wes!" Katie's braids bounced as she came running toward me with a fist full of cotton candy.

"Really?" I looked to Lila who was following her. She shrugged. "Where did you get the money?"

"I can be very convincing." She smiled.

I shook my head. "You're supposed to be controlling it."

"Does Lila have more magic than we do?" Katie asked.

"It's not magic," I snapped, the humidity suddenly catching up to me. "But yes."

"She's double cool then!" Katie beamed and then forgetting the entire topic, asked, "Can we ride rides?"

I looked at Lila. "Sounds fun," she answered. "What do you want to go on?"

She pointed straight ahead of us. "It's a long line," I groaned.

"Please?" she whined, looking to the giant Ferris wheel.

"Okay, fine. Let's go." We made our way through the mess of people and stood behind a family of other kids who Katie claimed to know from her new daycare.

I moved a wisp of Lila's hair from her forehead and took one of her hands in each of mine. I was so fortunate that she decided to be with me, but Peter's warning had cast a thick shadow over us. If Lila had said 'no', would Fate have accepted it? Or would she have thrown another fit until she got what she wanted?

Soon, it was our turn to board and we walked up the metal platform with Katie. "Sorry, folks...two in a seat," the man informed us.

"I can sit it out," Lila offered.

One of the kids from the other family approached us. "I don't have anyone to ride with. Do you wanna ride with me?" She took Katie's hand and grinned. Katie smiled and nodded her head.

They loaded into a seat, with Lila and me in the one behind them. "We'll have a lot of time up here to ourselves," I teased, putting a hand on her smooth leg and running it under her dress and up her glossy thigh.

"You're bad," she said, moving close and pressing her soft lips to mine. She made me want her so bad, I would've jumped off the ride if she asked me to take her home right then.

"I don't want to do anything you're uncomfortable with," I began. "I don't have many limits, if you catch my drift," I warned her.

She stared back at me, a little embarrassed to be discussing the subject. "I guess I just don't have as much experience."

"Hey, no...no, I don't mean it like that. I got started a little early."

"There's a story here, isn't there?" She eyed me. I needed to be completely honest.

"Tiffani's cousin was three years older than us. She'd come to visit sometimes and we started talking. I was fifteen, almost sixteen and she was this eighteen-year-old goddess. Long blonde hair, evenly tanned skin, legs that went on for days..."

Lila cleared her throat.

"Okay, sorry. To a fifteen-year-old virgin, she was something straight out of Playboy. We'd find ways to be alone and one thing led to another. After that, we looked for chances to sneak away and mess around. Until one day, a storm was coming in and we'd run off behind the shed. Dad came looking for us. Well, needless to say, we were caught, and she got sent off to some boarding school in lieu of my parents filing charges."

"Fifteen? Wow! She seriously victimized you." Lila's brows lowered sympathetically.

"That's what they said, Mom and Dad. I never felt that way. It's not easy to talk about; it's kind of embarrassing, more so for her, but I won't lie, I didn't feel attacked at all. It kind of seemed like every guy's dream. Anyway, I learned... stuff. So..."

She scooted closer to me, running her hand through my hair and gently touching my face. "Wesley." She paused, and I braced myself for her to tell me to fuck off. "I love you, and I'm sorry I didn't tell you earlier."

The darkness of the conversation lifted. I raised my brows. "You mean it?"

Her green eyes flickered. "Yes, and I hope you still feel that way, too."

She said the three words I'd been waiting to hear. "I never stopped." I kissed her again as the wheel spun down and back up, overlooking the tops of buildings, and crowds who'd come to celebrate the historic tradition.

The entire night spun with the glow of lights fading into music blasting itself from the carousel, the funnel-cake flavored wind mixed with the salt of popcorn, sticky like snow cones. We rode a few more rides and shared a caramel apple while we sat on a bench and watched Katie ride a kiddie coaster.

"Wes...I'm so tired," she rubbed her eyes after the fifth time she'd gone through a multi-colored fun house.

I looked around, booths were closing and the crowds, clearing. "Let's go."

She held up her arms, and I carried her back to the truck and slid her in carefully and Lila helped buckle her up. We got in and looked back, snickering at her sleeping next to the oversized penguin still holding on to his surfboard. Smooth music wafted from the truck's radio. It wasn't very long until we were pulling into the drive.

"I'll get Katie if you want to grab the penguin?" I looked at Lila.

She nodded in agreement. I carried Katie upstairs while Lila awkwardly toted the stuffed animal behind us. I gently placed Katie in bed and slipped her shoes off. I shut the door quietly and Lila turned toward her room.

"Where are you going?" I whispered.

"I'll be back," she responded.

I smiled and turned to my room, entering and leaving the door cracked. I paced. Would she come back? Was she nervous? Why would she be? Wanting to find out, I headed toward the door and met her in the threshold. Unprepared for her body to catapult into mine, I almost fell backward. It was a dream—I was dreaming, we were—the curves of her waist and hips, a maze I wanted my hands to get lost exploring. I needed to memorize each facet just in case I woke up to the nightmare of her not being there.

I kissed her, our bodies fire as she tugged at my shirt and I pulled it off. My shorts hit the floor, and I reached quickly for my nightstand drawer and grabbed another condom. Her dress, soundless—a feather drifting and settling next to my shorts. I gently pushed her against the wall and lifted her.

If you're uncomfortable, let me know.

Again, she said nothing, and I started to second guess myself until her legs curved around me, spiraling down my bare back. She was air—weightless. Her fingers tugged at my hair and my neck burned as her nails pierced the skin. Her head bent backward, pushing deeper into the wall in an intense moment— her gasp was a song. Her body uncurled from my own and I put my arms around her until we reached the bed. I couldn't stop touching her, kissing her, and I wouldn't until she told me to. It had never felt that good.

This can't end yet...Wes—

Reach over and grab another condom and it doesn't have to, I replied.

"Crap!"

"What?" I breathed.

"We're out."

I started kissing her chest, between her soft, impressive breasts, and down to her first rib. "Wes, there's no more," she repeated as I continued down her second rib and moved to the third. "Wes? Are you hearing me?" she asked again. I fought the urge to laugh at her question; it struck me that she had no clue about what I was going to do. My lips drifted down her stomach, below her belly button. I licked them–her body was sugar.

"We—" was the last sound she made before her head fell back hard into the pillow. Her knees pushing against my head and her fingers lost themselves in my hair as I continued until she stifled her own scream and nearly choked me with the force of her legs until I had to stop.

"Shh," I hushed her, "everyone's going to wake up," I teased until I saw that she was a little embarrassed. "I'm sorry. I guess you liked that?"

"Maybe a little," she joked back, getting over herself quickly. She pushed me up and her lips were against mine as she directed me toward the bathroom.

Where are we going? I was remorseful that the condom stash ran out so fast.

I've always had this fantasy about showering... with somebody, she confessed without breaking the lengthy, but satisfying kiss.

I pulled away. "Somebody? Like anyone? Maybe an old grandpa or something?" I grinned.

"You read my mind, Mr. Turner." For a minute, I was confused until she giggled. "It'll feel good."

Her proposal was as intriguing as the way my fingertips lost themselves in her hair. I started the water and we both stepped in as it warmed. She squinted her eyes and her lips were fire against my chest.

Liquid beads ran off both of us, streaming down until I didn't know if I could breathe. I backed against the wall just to keep my balance. The water moved in a perfect back and forth rhythm, until I, too, moaned loud enough to potentially wake the entire house before closing my eyes in satisfied disbelief. Heat swelled in my body until I couldn't take anymore. I opened my eyes and she was in front of me. Her slender, wet hands rippled down my biceps and up my abdomen as I inhaled another vapored kiss. "Now did *you* enjoy that?" she asked.

"No, not at all." I tried to keep a straight face as I ran my hands through her wet hair, rinsing it, the water hitting our lips as they touched. Our bodies were against one another, and I still couldn't get her close enough.

I turned the water off and wrapped her up against me in an oversized towel. "I still don't have pajamas," she mentioned.

"We don't need any," I whispered. After I lay down, she rested her head against my chest and traced my abs with her index finger, mine were content to be trapped in her curly, soaked hair.

Only a few minutes passed, but I must've fallen asleep and jumped when I heard a timid knock at the door. Not wanting to wake Lila, I grabbed a pair of shorts off the floor and carefully got out of bed and tip-toed, hoping it wasn't dad knocking because we'd woken him up. I peered out and looked down to see two frizzy braids.

"Katie," I whispered.

"Wes, I had a bad dream. I'm scared. Can I sleep with you?" she yawned and looked over to my bed. "Is that Lila?" She squinted.

I thought fast. "She had a bad dream, too. But if you want, I'll tuck you in to your bed."

She nodded and held out her hands. I used the last bit of energy to pick her up and walk her back to her room, laying her gently in her bed and giving her a kiss on the forehead before leaving the door open just a crack so the nightlight in the hall would shine through.

When I returned to the room, I used the restroom and before lying back down. Moonlight streamed through the curtain and caught Lila's bronzed skin, turning it to stars. I kissed her bare back; sleep was impossible. Intense feelings couldn't exist—I used to mock people who believed that relationships were unique or dared to trust that their love could last forever. I mean, what was the divorce rate again? But Lila and I lived in some magical fantasy land where we had command of everything at our fingertips. Even fate was on our side, working as some kind of siren luring us together, making each touch a sensual inferno of desire that hungered for more.

Sullivan was dead. No one was following us. By the time college started in the fall, the viral news stories would be over. I wanted to share everything with her, to explore every nuance of her personality, and her body.

"Wesley?" she mumbled.

"I'm right here," I answered back.

"Wesley, please, come get me," she begged with a sense of urgency indicative of a nightmare.

"Lila, Lila, wake up..." Would they ever stop? She rolled over and rubbed her eyes as I clicked on the desk lamp.

"When did it start? What are you seeing?" I asked. Once she got her bearings she sat up, leaning her head against my arm.

"It's this diary that the old man gave me. Some girl's journal. I can't make out most of it, only bits and pieces. It's super old. I'm on this bridge, except it's made of glass, and the glass is cracked. And I see you, but it's not you. I ask for help, but you walk away. I can't move. I'm in these heavy clothes, I can barely breathe. I think it's the girl from the diary. I think *I'm* her, Wesley."

I let out a sigh of relief. "It's safe to say that it's not a premonition," I tried to reassure her. What about my own strange dreams? "Maybe you're more invested in her story than you think," I offered.

"But why?" She rolled over.

"Because it gets your mind off things. History is fascinating." I held her as she melted in my arms. "It'll be okay. Sullivan's dead, you're safe. We're together, fate can smile, and go about her business." I kissed her forehead and turned out the light. Our bodies teased one another as our lips met and my hands explored her waist and hips until I groaned in frustration.

"Wes," she moaned. "We can't..."

"Ugh," I whined. Was there a gas station open that late? No. Often, in desperate circumstances, I was able to conjure a solution. As luck had it, that happened to be the case. "Maybe we can." My hot breath swirled in her ear and her arm filled with goosebumps as I slowly ran my hand up it and across her ribcage.

She turned her head to me. "How, Wes?"

"Relax," I coaxed before pushing waves of energy toward her. *Don't fight this. I want to try something.*

But, what?

You'll see. At first, her mind was darkness until she eased up.

The space was void of anything recognizable, but pastel wisps swirled around us. *Where are we?*

In your mind. I looked around at the absence. *Thought there'd be more to it,* I teased.

Not funny, she replied. *Let me try...* Lila stopped, and her green eyes glimmered with focus until something scratched the bottoms of my feet—white sand.

A beach? I nodded. *Nice... but you don't like water...*

Wesley, it's my mind. How real can it be?

I moved toward her until she was close enough for me to tug at the strap of a light blue tank top she was wearing. My lips met hers as our tongues collided. *Did you feel that?*

The palms of her smooth hands were sweaty as she placed them against my bare chest. *Every bit of it. But how di—*

Don't ask questions, I interrupted her before we lost the momentum that allowed the telepathic platform.

Our bodies were cascading waves as they met flawless sands and moved in a melodic rhythm. We reveled in our alternate reality. No interruptions or fears existed as our energies swirled inside one another in a palate of patterns. She rolled on her stomach and leaned against her hand. *How long have we been here, making love?*

Does it matter? I chuckled, and she straddled me.

No, she giggled. Her cheeks flushed in response. I was about to kiss her again, but her weight multiplied. *Lila, you have to get up,* I warned.

She stood and wiped away a few grains of sand. *Wesley?*

I think my body's running out of energy. I couldn't stay, so I pulled away from her mind and gasped for air.

"Wesley?" she sat up and placed her hand on my sweaty forehead.

I had to lie. At first, it was bricks plummeting atop my chest. I was embedded in fictional concrete. "I'm all right," I managed, still catching my breath. "I'll be okay," I reassured her before pulling her back on the bed. It wasn't a huge lie—I was fine, really. I thought about our interlude on the untainted sand...I was more than fine.

She snuggled against me, grabbing my arm and putting it around her, and we both fell asleep quickly without waking until later that morning. I woke up first to the smell of bacon creeping under the closed door and seeping through the room. Lila quickly followed.

"What is that?" she asked stretching.

"Dad's cooking," I answered, looking forward to eating myself stupid. Lila stood up and started for the door.

"Where are you going?" I sat up.

"Clothes, remember?"

I stood, walked to my dresser, and tossed her a pair of shorts and a t-shirt.

"These won't fit me," she stated, holding up the shorts.

"They're drawstring, just pull them tight."

She put them on under the t-shirt, tying the string tight. "Won't your dad know?"

"Doubt it. I don't see him a lot, especially not in something like that," I laughed.

"Gee thanks." She pulled her long hair up into a bun, letting a few loose strands hang out. "I bet I look like a zombie, huh?"

I walked over to the mirror, standing behind her and pulling her close. "You look like a woman who got numerous rounds of amazing sex last night." I kissed down her neck, wanting her again.

"Narcissistic much? How do you know I liked it?" she shot back, and I grinned because I wouldn't have expected anything less.

I pretended to check myself in the mirror. "Then you must be a hella-good actress."

She rolled her eyes and we made our way out the door and down the stairs, walking to the kitchen like we hadn't eaten in a week.

"Mornin' Wes, Lila," Dad greeted without looking up from the pancake he was flipping.

"Wow, this smells amazing! You're a great cook," Lila complimented him.

"Heh, thanks," he answered, a little embarrassed.

"Did you have fun last night at the fair?" he asked as Katie strolled in the kitchen, sleepily rubbing her eyes.

"Oh yeah, and I won this great big stuffed animal, and we rode rides, and Lila got me cotton candy. We had so much fun and we came home and guess what, Daddy?" she said, her voice growing louder in excitement.

"What, sweetheart?" He finally looked up from the stove.

"Lila has nightmares, too, and she gets scared, and she sleeps with Wesley, too!" she exclaimed.

Lila's face shot up in a horrified expression and I shifted my weight as my stomach knotted. Suddenly, I wasn't as hungry.

"Oh, is that right?" He studied me and Lila carefully. "You must be swapping clothes, too, or you just have the same taste." He laughed a sly laugh.

I thought you said he wouldn't notice.

No thanks to Katie and her big mouth.

Is he going to kick me out?

Nah, he'll be mad at me, not you.

Despite the loss of appetite, I filled a plate and sat down at the table anyway. Lila also grabbed a plate and sat next to me.

As we finished eating, Dad stood. "Wesley, when you're done, come help me move some stuff around in the shed."

All I could think about was the lecture I was going to get. I wasn't scared of Dad, he'd never lost his cool with me or Katie, but I didn't want to let him down. I could tell him we were both tired and were up talking and fell asleep. That didn't explain Lila in my clothes, though. I thought about telling him Katie must have been dreaming, but it was still no good. Dad had already headed toward the shed, and I pushed my chair out and stood.

Lila put a hand on my arm. *I'm so sorry, Wes. What will you tell him? What are you going to do?*

I'm going to be honest, fess up. Own it.

Without looking at her, I walked out the kitchen door, letting it shut behind me. After the disaster when I was young, I'd been careful about getting caught, never thinking of how I'd react when I did. Truth was, I could make up all the excuses in the world, but Dad would know better. I loved Lila, only Lila. And I wasn't going to deny it or lie about it or make excuses for it. I knew I'd have to face him sooner or later, especially if things kept going how they were. Lila was an upward spiral; life felt better every second we were together. I felt hypnotized or drugged when I was around her and I didn't want it to end.

I took in a deep breath before I opened the door to the shed. "Dad," I said, nodding.

"She another one of your 'one-hit-wonders', Wes?" He didn't look up and I didn't answer that. "C'mon son, not more'n a year ago you didn't want to settle down, get serious. Hell, I didn't care. But now you're not settlin' down with my closest friend's little girl."

"It's not like that, Dad," I argued.

"Explain to me what it's like. I've got enough, with Katie, your mom nearly losing her mind...now you're fucking my best friend's daughter." He looked at me and a foreign anger shot across his eyes. "So you'd better start explaining. What's she gonna do when you hurt her, too? This is the only place she's safe right now. You stop and think about that?" He waited in silence. Another question I wasn't going to answer. "No, you're too busy thinking with your dick." He paused. He was sorry for what he'd said, and his expression softened. "Talk to me, Wes. What's going on?"

"I told you before, Dad, I love her."

He waved me on. "Easy words to say when you hardly know each other. No worries...Wesley, that's not love. You two aren't even living in the real world."

"We aren't?" I waited before continuing. "And why's that? Because we're chromosomal disasters? Because we've spent our lives being pursued? The only parents she ever knew were murdered, dead before we walked through her front door. *You* left *me* to protect her. I beat the shit out of a couple guys, she killed someone...I couldn't protect her. My own mother turned her in. That woman sitting in your house... *she's* the reason we never have to run again. Tell me about your *'real'* world, Dad. Lila and I know the real world, but it's not your world. It's one of death and violence, and secrets... *your* secrets. I'd say we've experienced the world in its rawest, uncensored form." I looked him straight in the eye. "It wasn't fucking. When I say I love her, I mean I'm loving her forever."

Dad didn't say anything for a while. "And I'm supposed to take you at your word?"

I gulped. I couldn't let him in my head, he'd see more than he needed to. I had no words. Somehow, he agreed with me, but how could I prove I'd never hurt Lila, especially with the terrible track record I thought I'd hidden so well? An idea shot across my mind and it was over the top as many of my greatest epiphanies were. My body shook to the point I couldn't hold it up and leaned against a table full of tools, surprised that one simple sentence could cause a level of anxiety near death.

Grease from the bacon and gravy mixed with nausea and soured along my throat. How did the idea come to me? Why? Was I losing my mind? Whatever the reason, individual letters stumbled one over the other when I responded. "Because, Dad." His eyes met mine, once again. I softened my voice so he'd know I was dead serious. "I'm going to ask her to marry me." The idea became palatable, the words—easy, but years away. Saying it out loud was near impossible; it was insane.

"Wes...I..." Dad also had no words. After the talks we had about girls and relationships and how I never wanted one. "That's not what I meant...I wasn't expecting—"

"No, you're right." Another shocking statement that widened Dad's eyeballs to the point I thought they'd fall out. "I don't have the best history with relationships. Well, okay. I haven't really had one for longer than a single night..."

"Wes, it's so soon. Is that what you want? Are you sure it's what she wants?"

Again, an answer I didn't have. I wanted to believe she did, or that I could get into her head and find out. I had to approach it the old-fashioned way. "I hope it is. Sorry, Dad." I turned to leave but was stopped by his voice.

"Wes, you're starting to grow up."

His words meant a lot. I couldn't help but smile and ran the distance back to the house. Lila was gone when I went inside, so I went upstairs. "Lila?" I called.

"In my room." Her voice seemed distracted.

I knocked and pushed her door open to find her sitting cross-legged on the bed, staring hard at the antique book she'd been dragging around. My curiosity had gotten the better of me. "Guess it must be intriguing, the way you're squinting."

"Like I said, the words are faded out and some of the handwriting is so loopy it's hard to read."

"Anything good?" I walked around and sat next to her, immediately understanding her struggles when I studied the text.

"It's written by a girl, she seems young. They lived in Europe and fled to Jamestown, something about a red mark on the door and her dad not wanting to be accused of being a witch." Lila laughed as she closed the book and looked at me. "She's my age and afraid she'll end up a cat lady or as she puts it, 'perhaps a schoolmarm,' if she doesn't get married soon."

Great, her response didn't sound promising. "When was it written?"

"The first date is 1666. What would've been going on back then to make them run?"

I thought for a while, through the history I studied and books I read. "It was the last round of the plague... that would've been in London, I think. If a person was exposed, they'd quarantine the entire household, servants and all. Everyone would be left to die. The red 'X' might have been a sign. Maybe to come back later and collect and burn the bodies."

"Eww, gross." Lila scrunched her face.

"Back then, women married young. Sometimes the marriages were even arranged. Good thing you all have a choice now, huh?" I chuckled, eager to get her opinion.

"Yeah, but I feel like I'd be way too young. There's so much to do besides dishes, cooking, and having kids," she laughed.

"But that's not what marriage has to be. Nowadays, you can marry and still do things you want...I mean, you can just be engaged for a long time...like a *really* long time." She gave me a strange look. I had to stop before I pushed too far. Debating her would be a surefire way to get caught. "Anyway, it doesn't matter, really."

"Yeah, maybe you're right," she agreed.

I leaned over the book and kissed her, our lips melting like usual, our bodies gravitating toward each other making me not want to stop, but knowing I had to. "Want to get out of here?"

"And do what?"

"Stop by a store," I chuckled. "Go downtown. I can show you more of the town."

"What about it being blocked off?" She shut the old book.

I laughed, "You'll see. Give me a few minutes." She nodded, and I headed to my room to clean up and change.

He tapped his fingers on the mahogany desk. Was it the same hand he used when his wife was out fucking the chauffer? I sat perfectly still, shoulders back, body tilted just a bit, to indicate I refused to back down from my position.

"Damn you, Robert!" His face reddened. "Damn you to hell! You got our men killed and if the medics didn't get to you when they did, you'd be dead too. I'm surprised they were able to get your heart restarted, but she still escaped in the process. I told you, she's not a guinea pig for your goddamn science fair..." he coughed from the yelling, "She's a threat. A significant threat. This is not a little girl, this is some slithering bitch who could take over the world—destroy it in one thought."

I'm gonna shove my pistol in your forehead and pull the trigger, you fucking moron. "That's why we're developing a cure!" I fired back at the pig.

"Damn you and your fucking 'cure'!" the moose grumbled before lowering his voice. "You've been at this a long time, Robert, and along the way you've made some great progress, but I fear it's not enough for some." The fat in his face jiggled as he spoke.

"What are you saying?" I leaned forward. "Not enough for whom?" I sat back after a while and shook my head. "You dirty bastard...you threw me under the bus, didn't you?"

He looked down, too much of a pussy to meet my stare. "I didn't have to throw you anywhere. DHS might cut your funding. One week—"

"Then what?" I was incredulous.

He leaned in and whispered, "They're giving you one week to clean up your mess. Between you and me, that gives you a little less than six and a half days to find the whore and kill her."

"This could take years, you know that. To find the right help—" *You dirty bastard; you finally got me cornered,* I thought, scowling.

"I bought you *one week*, you ungrateful son of a bitch, and you damned sure better use it! Now get out of my office!" The geezer yelled so loud, he'd gone into a coughing fit as he did so. I laughed at the fool before slamming the door to his office and storming to the elevator.

The doors opened to sex in black heels and a pencil skirt. She winked at me the same way she probably winked at her superior before she spread her legs all the way to an office at the top floor of the building. Slut.

One week, one fucking week, when it had taken eighteen years. I'd have to find someone who wanted Lila dead as much as I did, and as I entered the lobby on the ground floor of Headquarters, I caught a familiar news clip from Evansville, Indiana, and I knew exactly who'd want her six feet under. I smiled to myself and began humming the reprise from "Ragtime" which I'd seen some years back when I traveled to Chicago on a lead to Tom and Jennie. It was time to revisit the Midwest.

I was damn lucky to be alive after what that bitch had done to me. She stopped my heart...in one thought, she had the ability to kill me or anyone else. The world didn't have room for anything like that to exist. Lila wasn't a person, she was a monster.

LILA

Wesley left the room and I opened the journal.

Dearest Diary,

Late at night I sit, against the wishes of my mother. To you am I writing of the hope that hath bloomed upon my heart. Yesterday did I partake on an evening stroll with a few like-aged ladies from the colony. Came we upon a bridge whilst did they try to persuade me to stay. Made they claims of hearing the laughter of the devil upon the waters. Mother was correct in her assessment of the colonists. All of them, save one, a gentleman who did introduce himself as Ashley. Had he hair of sunlight and eyes that did shine of the bluest ocean. Upon meeting the gentleman, did he offer to escort me safely to my residence. Promise, did he, to come calling after we had breakfasted, to ask permission to court. Filled, my heart is, with hope. For upon this paper, never have I felt love until I gazed upon his eyes.

It was the same reaction I had to Wesley, who returned right after I closed the journal. I looked into his blue eyes and my stomach tingled.

"What's wrong?" he asked, getting serious.

"Nothing, it's just that...nothing," I smiled to reassure him that I hadn't just read a three-hundred-year old journal that described a guy looking exactly like him, written by a girl who reacted the same way I did.

"You still want to go?"

"Yeah," I smiled again and stood to follow him out of the room and down the stairs to his pickup.

We got in and he pulled out of the drive and onto the gravel road. We drove the same way into town, but this time, Main Street was no longer blocked. In fact, everything was gone.

"It looks abandoned compared to last night." I remarked. "Where did it all go?" I tried looking closer, where food stands and games had polluted the sides of the street; not even a piece of trash.

"Poof, into thin air," he joked, his face relaxing as he did.

"Funny, but seriously?" I was still mesmerized.

"People work all night cleaning it up," he stated, matter-of-factly. He'd pulled into a parking spot that faced a park with a cute gazebo.

"Still, there's no one here. Just super strange." The entire city almost felt abandoned.

"There'll be people here in a while," he reassured as we got out of the truck and stood on the sidewalk.

"There's a band that plays in the gazebo on Sundays," he informed.

"Seriously?" I was surprised at the uniqueness of the quaint city.

"Yeah, come over here." He took my hand and led me down a ramp. We walked past the gazebo and came to a very steep set of stairs. "That's the spring."

"The spring?" I was confused. "What about the spring?" I wasn't sure why he'd walked us down to see water pouring from a rusty-looking spigot.

"Come on, Spanish genius," he teased as he stood behind me and gently rubbed my shoulders. "El Dorado Springs translates into *golden springs*. That's the main reason the town was founded. Purportedly, the water has medicinal properties; it's supposed to maintain youth. People used to bottle it up and sell it. I guess it was kind of famous."

"Hmm...maybe I'll try some," I commented, starting to go down the steps.

"I think its only medicinal property might be Tetanus." He laughed at his joke. I looked at him, confused. "It rusts really fast," he explained, "You can try it, but be careful."

I laughed, "Maybe I'll pass." We started back up the stairs. Tired, I found a bench and sat down. Wesley sat next to me and I leaned into him as he put his arm around me. We stayed like that and enjoyed the shade and silence for some time.

"What is the right age?" he asked out of the blue.

I turned to look at him. "What do you mean?"

"To be married. You seem to be opinionated on the subject. Or engaged?"

"I'm not sure. It depends on the person, I guess. I've seen a few couples get married at eighteen and nineteen and end up bored and divorced. On the other hand, my parents married young. They were happy. What about you?" What was up with Wesley's sudden interest in my thoughts on relationships?

"I don't know. It's something that's never crossed my mind, something I'd probably never do. But, maybe it'd work with the right person," he contemplated.

"Like what kind of person?" I asked. The entire conversation was a tease.

"Hmm…I don't know." He looked around a while before continuing. A few cars pulled into empty spaces. "She'd probably have to have brunette hair, sparkling green eyes, be quick-witted." He looked at me. "She should be able to take my crap, too."

"And shove it right back in your face," I added. We both laughed, and he put his arms around me, pulling me tightly into his cologne-laced t-shirt. "Is that all?" I smirked.

"No… there's one more thing—she'd have to have some kind of crazy abilities, like telepathy or something," he shrugged.

"Well, I'm glad you've set your standards pretty low. Girls like that are common; shouldn't be a hard search," I joked back. For a fraction of a second, I wondered if Wesley was alluding to something with all the talk of getting engaged. The thought was fleeting and lost itself in the summer breeze that soared by us and toward the groups of band members who had begun unloading various instruments from their cars and making their way to the bandstand to get settled.

I changed the subject. "Do a lot of people come to watch them?"

"I think so. I didn't get to go a lot. You know, overprotective mother and all…" he rolled his eyes, something I hadn't seen him do very much. He was obviously learning to relax and take life a bit less serious.

"How do you think she's doing?" I asked, genuinely concerned.

"Okay, Dad said she'd been slipping for some time, but no one ever saw it and she was too proud to ask for help." He shook his head and looked up at the sky.

"Or too scared," I speculated.

Wesley shrugged. "I don't want to talk about her."

I didn't want to talk about marriage either, so I pressed him. "Have you seen her since she's been in there?"

"No." His voice was stern.

"You should. I should—"

"Why would you want to?" He jumped and turned to me, scowling.

"Closure. She wasn't in her right mind," I calmly explained. "Wes, I want to talk to her; forgive her."

"I'll think about it," he huffed, relaxing a little.

A part of me took his response as a reluctant yes. Besides, if it was something I wanted to do, a piece of closure I could find, who was he to act as a barrier? I leaned into him again as he put his arm back around me.

The band had settled and warmed up as the conductor waved her hands and they began playing "God Bless America." The music folded in the soft wind as I sat and admired the meticulous, brick bandstand. As silly as it might have seemed to some, I found the city to be charming. The type of unique I couldn't purchase at an Hermes in Tyson's.

The thought of returning east became increasingly bittersweet each day I stayed with Wesley in the Midwest. As the band started another tune, I thought of how I didn't look forward to leaving the dirt roads, the country restaurants, and the people I'd met. We sat on the green, wooden bench until the band played its last song. When they finished, everyone who came to watch started clapping as the conductor turned and thanked us all.

"One more thing," he said, standing and holding his hand out to me.

I took it. "What?" He grinned and started walking down the trail that led in front of the bandstand. "What?" I asked again.

He pointed to a building across the street from the park. "Ice cream," he finally answered. "They have some of the best."

"Okay," was my response. We both didn't want the afternoon to end. I smirked and let go of his hand, taking off and reaching the door first. I grabbed the handle and held it open. "My turn," I snickered.

He rolled his eyes and entered. We made our way to a square table in the back. Besides the workers, we were the only ones in the restaurant.

A short, freckled boy came up. "Hey, I'm sorry, we just turned the fryers off."

Wesley shrugged. "What about ice cream?"

"Oh, sure! What do y'all want?" Relief came over the boy's face. I checked the time. It was one-thirty and the sign on the door indicated the restaurant closed at two on Sunday. Most restaurants back home would be open until eleven, or later.

"Hmm...a sundae, with chocolate syrup," I responded.

Wesley looked at the boy. "Same, with strawberry, instead." He glanced back at me. The boy nodded and walked behind the counter to make our order.

"Do we have anything in common?" I teased as he slid his feet next to mine and rested his head on his fist.

"Probably not," he smirked. "Let's see...favorite color?"

I smiled. "Blue."

He looked at me. "Green. Would you own a cat or a dog?"

"Are we doing this?" I giggled.

He raised his eyebrows and tapped his foot quietly. "I think we are."

I rolled my eyes. "Fine," I smiled. "Cat," I answered to his dismay.

"Dogs. They're the best."

We both laughed, and our question-answer session was interrupted as the kid brought us the sundaes. We thanked him, and I grazed my spoon against the chocolate as it ran down two scoops of vanilla ice cream and settled in a milky pool at the bottom.

Wesley, however, continued. "Weird hobbies or interests?"

I swallowed my bite before answering. "No, it's totally weird." I didn't want to answer.

"Why? You know my obsession with word puzzles. Your turn," he challenged.

I sighed. He was right. "Fine, it's so nerdy though..."

He raised his eyebrows and sighed. "I'm waiting, Miss Daniels."

I shook my head. The ice cream continued to melt. "Okay, so when I was in middle school, I was really into reading, but not just any reading...I liked V.C. Andrews, Anne

Rice, stuff like that. So...I'd read it at home and then bring things other kids were reading to school so I wouldn't look all weird and..." I laughed, "I *so* don't wanna tell you this," I argued.

"Still waiting..." He sat back and folded his arms.

I blushed. "I also read historical books and became obsessed with *Titanic*. So that's my weird hobby...anything related to the *Titanic*. I'm a pretty big enthusiast."

"What's embarrassing about that?" He shook his head and took another bite.

"I feel like it's nerdy," I answered.

"It's okay to have interests deeper than mall discounts, you know. What fascinates you about it?"

"I don't know..." A couple seconds passed. "The why."

"The 'why'?" He gave me a strange look.

"You know, why did it happen? All the theories, the tragedy. How such a grand ship could hit an iceberg and just... sink!" I finished.

He listened intently, and we continued to discuss the boat. He threw out theories and I did, as well. Obviously, we had different ideas about the sinking of the ocean liner, but in the end, it was kind of nice to have an informed conversation about a topic I was interested in.

Time was easy with Wesley, between the exchange of opinions and the melting ice cream, it drifted passed us like a satin breeze. At one point, Wesley scooped up a strawberry and offered it to me on his spoon. I leaned over and ate it. We both chuckled because it was cheesy.

The relationship surpassed our shared secrets and fears. We'd become fast friends, lovers. Our fear was the depth of which we could hurt one another. Losing my parents taught me several things, the main one being how fleeting life was. Despite our abilities, Wesley and I weren't immortal. One morning we could walk out the door and never see one another again. I couldn't lose him like that.

After some time, Wesley paid our bill and we walked out of the restaurant and into humidity. I stood on the sidewalk facing Main Street and studied the old storefronts.

Wesley stood next to me. "What do you think?"

"I'm in love with it all. I'm not sure I'm going to be able to leave," I half-joked, though, it was mostly truth.

We walked to my door and he placed one hand on the handle and the other against the window, smirking as he did and knowing what he was doing, just like a few weeks prior at the pool. Those deep-sea eyes were fiery against my own. "I'm in love with you," he whispered, moving one hand from the door and pushing my hair back.

"I love you," I responded, the words swirling like the music had as he leaned and kissed me before opening the door. I got in and he shut it behind me like he'd done so many times when we'd been on the run from Sullivan.

Sullivan—God, that name made me shudder. Those slimy eyes. He closed the door behind him and looked at me, "What's wrong?"

"I was thinking about Sullivan. About us, on the run," I admitted.

"I know. It'll take a while to get over it." He looked down. "But we'll make it. He's gone now."

I nodded as he pulled out of the parking space and started down Main Street. Once we arrived at the stoplight at the end of the strip, he prepared to turn right. "This is 54 highway—it runs east and west. If you go west, there's a grocery store."

"Only one?" One grocery store in a town threw me for a loop. Back home we had Wal-Marts on nearly every corner.

"Yep, and you better not need anything after eight on Sunday night," he mused.

I sat up, interested. "Really?"

"Yeah."

"That's so cool!" Everything back home was busy, sirens blaring during the night, stores open twenty-four hours, seven days a week.

"Not to people who run out of things on a Sunday night," he smiled.

I rolled my eyes as he pulled in and parked. We got out and made our way through the automatic doors. I grabbed a basket and followed Wesley, taking a moment to appreciate his backside as he turned up an aisle.

"I don't think we need a basket—I'm only picking up condoms," he whispered as I caught up to him.

"Maybe I should go to a women's health clinic," I suggested. Birth-control would be a good idea.

"Good luck finding that around here," he remarked.

I shrugged, and we walked side-by-side until we came to the 'feminine hygiene' aisle. He grabbed a few boxes and tossed them in the basket.

"Aren't you ambitious." I eyeballed both packs.

"You want to run out again?" he warned, raising his eyebrows.

"I didn't mind so much." I winked at him as we turned, almost running into Tiffani.

Her eyes panned from me to Wesley and back to the basket. Before she could say anything Dalton, Alana, and Connor came from around the corner. "Hey Wes! Lila," he shot me an innocent grin, the freckles across his nose made more prominent under the fluorescent lights. He shyly ran a hand through his shaggy hair. I smiled, hoping Tiffani would just stay quiet until I could talk to him. That was not the case.

She nudged Dalton and cleared her throat. At first, the gesture was met with a look of confusion, until she nodded at the rectangular contents of the basket. Dalton's smile dropped and he pursed his lips. He was hurt.

I could—I pushed my thought out to Wesley.

No! Do not start using them again, he responded.

It'd be so much easier, I argued, but he didn't respond, and I dropped it.

Alana and Connor made grim faces and walked toward the snack aisle. Wesley spoke up, "Tiff, Dalton...hey guys."

Tiffani eyeballed both of us. "Oh, we're just friends," she mocked. "Wow, I guess you're both busted now."

"Wow," Dalton mouthed, perplexed. "You coulda just been honest, Wes...Lila..."

"Dalton I—" I moved toward him and he took a step back.

"Forget it. C'mon, Dalton." Tiffani reached for him, but he pulled away and walked over and stood straight in front of Wesley. "You could have any girl you want, man. Why her? Because I wanted her?"

Tiffani chimed in, "When you're tired of her, you know you'll come back to me. Forget it. I deserve so much better than you," she huffed and pranced away with Dalton.

"I'm so sorry, Wes," I consoled.

We stood for a moment, partially in shock and partially because we didn't want to catch up with them again.

"It's okay, time will heal all...I think." He rubbed my back and we continued to the checkout line, careful to avoid the others. We paid for the condoms and exited the store.

"Hey! Guys!" Alana came running with Connor trying to keep up. Wesley and I turned, bracing ourselves for more backlash. "I'm not saying that lying was right, but for what it's worth, I think you two are really good together. Super chemistry." She looked at Connor who shrugged. Then she turned back to me. "You got my number, right?" I nodded, surprised.

"Kay! Stay in touch, even when you go back East," she added.

"Totally," I answered, relieved that she'd be cool enough to put things behind us. She nodded and jogged back to Connor who waved at us as we loaded up and backed out.

"I feel pretty low," I confessed.

"Well, don't," Wesley stated. "It wasn't a lie. We really didn't know how we felt. We weren't together or anything."

"Wes, we knew how we felt," I argued as my stomach knotted. "You told me already, I just couldn't come to terms with it. I feel like we're too young for any of this." I took in a deep breath. "I mean, do you actually believe this is all Fate's doing? Her grand design?" I paused, trying to make sense of my turning thoughts. "What I'm saying is, is the attraction real? Or designed by fate?"

"Fate doesn't control love," he answered matter-of-factly.

"She sure tries to. What if she didn't care if we were together or not? Would the attraction be this intense?" I'd wondered for some time but was afraid to ruin the euphoria of the past couple days.

"I haven't thought about it." His voice lowered.

"Never? You never questioned it?" I was surprised someone as arrogant as Wesley, would be okay with letting an abstract idea chart the course of his feelings. Was he doing it because, maybe, he didn't want control? Or maybe he was happy and reluctant to ruin a good thing.

"No. To me, it doesn't matter. When I met you, I was happier in general. You challenge me every single day." He sighed, "You don't put up with my shit. I want to work to be a better person, someone you'd be proud to be with... honestly. As long as we're happy, the mechanics of it don't bother me."

They bothered me, a little, and made me question whether the seemingly unrealistic emotions we'd attached to one another were real or just an illusion. The very touch of Wesley's hand on mine seemed like a fantasy, regardless of how many times we held hands. It was a dream a part of me never wanted to wake up from.

"I still could've made them forget," I offered. "I'm not fighting with you, but it would've been so much easier."

"But that's not real life. You want to live like everyone else, you said."

I pushed my thoughts at the radio and flipped it on. Some country music song began playing and Wesley tried to keep from smiling as we pulled up to the house. When we went inside, we found that Billy and Katie weren't home.

"He might have taken her into town or to a friend's," Wesley explained.

"Oh, okay," I answered, walking into the living room and scanning the built-in shelves full of books.

"Dad made these, too." He ran his hand over the trim. "Bet you couldn't have guessed." Wesley moved behind me and wrapped his arms around my stomach. I leaned into him and he kissed the top of my head.

"They're beautiful...and so many books, too," I added, noting there'd be too many to count, much less read.

"Mom enjoys reading...Dad, not so much. But I've read most of them," he bragged.

"Really?" I couldn't say I was surprised.

He sighed, "Nothing else to do. Remember? Pretty much isolated." He cleared his throat. "You hungry?"

I'd been ignoring my stomach and all I'd eaten was ice cream. It was cutting into early evening. "Yeah, what do you have?"

"Let's see." I followed him into the kitchen where he opened the fridge and peeked in the freezer above. "Hmm, nothing," he complained, searching through a few cabinets.

"No food at all?" I was a little surprised.

"Not unless you know what to do with ingredients," he huffed.

"Not really...if you have chicken, I can cook it in a pan with vegetables or something," I offered. "You're smart, shouldn't you know how to cook?" I teased, moving closer toward him.

"Yeah, I somehow skipped that part." He pulled me into his arms, our kiss burning of July heat as he lifted me onto the counter top, and I wrapped my legs around his firm body. He rested his forehead under my chin like he often did when he was thinking.

"Are you okay, Wes?" I asked after a few moments.

"Yeah...I just...I was thinking—"

"I know you were. You should stop doing that so much," I giggled, pulling his head up and distracting him with another kiss.

"Then we should do more of this," he breathed in my ear.

He ran his hands along my waist as I gave in to his warm breath against my neck. Our bodies melted together into a singular motion. We enveloped one another; he was in every part of me and I in him. Our lips moved up and down in syncopated rhythm; his hand clenched my waist and my fingers ruffled his soft hair. After a while, I hopped off the counter, and we embraced, succumbing to the thick layer of passion that pulled us together.

"You don't want this moment to end," he surmised, wiping some loose pieces of hair from my forehead.

"You're in my head." Truth was, I was in his, too. I couldn't stop it. I could feel everything he was feeling.

"I know. I can't stay out of it. It happened the other night, too, but stopped soon after," he confessed.

"Don't worry, I won't dig any deeper than I have to," I remarked.

He smiled, "Wouldn't want you finding out all my secrets, would I?" He chuckled.

"Oh, like what?" My curiosity getting the better of me, I pushed a little harder.

"Hey, stop that," he complained and pushed me out.

"Why?" He piqued my curiosity. "What are you hiding, Wesley?" I teased. "You *are* hiding something."

"It's nothing. Leave it alone," he tensed up.

"Oh, fine. You're no fun," I pouted. I didn't want to make him mad, and Lord knows I had secrets, too.

"I'm not?" he smirked. "I bet that's not what you thought a few minutes ago," he grinned.

"Don't be an ass," I warned.

"Okay, so, want to go get some food?" he offered.

"Anywhere deliver?" I wondered. The answer would be no.

"Does pizza sound good?" I agreed, and he called and ordered a couple pizzas to be delivered.

We decided to watch TV while we waited for the food, but one kiss led to another, that led to another, that led to the touchy-feely stuff, that led to our clothes falling to the floor, and Wesley's eventual scramble to put his back on to answer the door while I sank under a thick blanket on the couch, giggling at his shirt turned inside out. When the door shut, I got dressed and soon after, a flushed Wesley walked into the room with two plates full of pizza and a glass of water.

He looked at me. "You didn't have to go to all the trouble of getting dressed." But it was a good thing I did. Before I could respond, the front door clicked open again and Katie bounced into the living room.

"Pizza!" she squealed and took off into the kitchen.

"Need help, Katie?" Wesley called.

"I'll get it," Billy answered back as he came through the door.

"Hey Dad." Wesley stood as his dad paused in the foyer. "Got a minute?"

He followed him to the kitchen where I couldn't hear what was being said. Soon they came out into the living room and everyone took a seat while I scanned the stations to find a show for everyone and settled on *The Little Mermaid*. Katie's eyes lit up when she saw it.

"Wes," Billy looked over at him. "I need you to go to Kansas City tomorrow to pick up some wood."

"Okay, Dad." And then he went back to watching TV.

'I'd love to see Kansas City," I piped up.

"Actually," Wesley started, "Dad's supplies take a lot of room." He looked down when he saw my face drop.

"Lila there's a ton of stuff to do around here," Billy assured me. "I'm sure you can keep occupied for a couple hours."

It was then that my phone buzzed, and I pulled it from my pocket hoping it'd be Sara. It was a strange number and I opened the message—*Connor's busy tomorrow. Wanna hang?*

"That's weird," I commented out loud.

"What?" Wesley asked, surprised.

"I got a text from Alana wanting to hang out tomorrow. How'd she even get my number?"

"She asked for it at the restaurant. Don't you remember?" I shook my head. "She asked if I had it. Maybe you didn't hear," he offered.

I shrugged. Maybe he was right. The group date was pretty awkward, and I was sufficiently distracted. So, I texted Alana back—*Sure!*

A few minutes passed, and she responded—*Great, pick you up around 1.*

"She'll be here around one," I explained. "What's the lake all about?"

"Stockton Lake—it's about fifteen miles from here. The kids have a lot of fun out there," Billy explained. "There's boating, swimming, cliffs... but don't go jumping off them. It hasn't rained very much this summer, water level's low," he warned.

I turned to Wesley. "I wish you were coming."

He kissed me. "You won't know I'm gone." I caught a strange set of looks being exchanged between him and his dad.

Billy cleared his throat. "It's getting dark and I got an early day tomorrow," he said. "Katie, you want me to tuck you in before I wind down for the night?"

"Daddy," she smiled and batted her eyes, "can Wes and Lila take me to the field to catch fireflies?" How could we say no to her?

"Sure, baby. If they feel like it." He looked at us.

Wesley and I exchanged looks of agreement, and as the sun continued to go down, we slipped our shoes on and walked through the yard to the large, empty field of grass. Katie ran far away from us and shrieked as fireflies lit the dim sky.

"When it gets dark, you'll be able to see the stars better." Wesley explained.

"I've seen stars before, Wesley," I informed him.

"Not like this." He took my hand and spun me around.

"Sit with me for a minute," he asked.

We both sat on freshly mowed grass facing Katie, who was having a blast running through the field. He moved behind me and I lay my back against his chest.

"When I go to college this fall, I want to go to Mary Washington. I've spoken to academic counselors and they have an amazing campus."

"Okay," I started. What was he getting at? "What about Princeton?"

He squeezed me tight. "Mary Wash offers a pre-med program that looks pretty good."

"So, you're staying in Fredericksburg?"

"Will you go back with me? And stay...in my house. It would be *our* house?" He stumbled over his words.

"I'm going to miss it out here. I've fallen in love with it," I confessed. "But I love you more," I finished.

"I want to be honest. I'm going to be in school forever. Two more years at Mary Wash, plus residency hours, studying for the MCAT, and interviews for Medical School. When I get in, it's another four. Then seven years of residency to train in neurosurgery," he groaned.

"I believe in you, Wes. You know that." With Wesley, it was never 'if' I get in a program, it was 'when'. He knew he was smart enough to do anything he wanted.

"Thanks, but I want you to know it won't be easy. I'm talking all-nighters at the library, stress..."

"I'll have goals of my own. If you're worried that I'm going to sit around all day and pine for you, then you can relax," I explained.

"That's how I want it. I don't want you freaking out if I'm gone a lot. But I also don't want you feeling alone because I'm sure as hell going to miss you."

I turned to find him smiling and staring back at me. Even in the darkness, specks of blue danced in his eyes. "What?" I whispered.

He breathed into my ear. "What do you see when you think about the future?"

Moments passed. "God, I don't know," I sighed. "Before any of this happened, I had no idea. I want to travel, a lot. You know? Have new experiences. Reinvent myself. Get my high school diploma. Go to college, for art history. I want to help people, maybe even people who have our abilities. Somehow, I'd like to know I made a difference..." Those things didn't complete my list, but they were a good start. His eyes continued to glisten under a sheet of stars. "What about you? What do you see in your future?"

He gently wiped my hair from my left ear and sighed, "You." His voice was soft wind flowing between blades of grass that swayed into me. "Hopefully you'll keep me around for a while," he finished.

I already retracted my belief that 'being in love' needed to have an age. Before responding to that statement, I thought about the journal and how Delilah had fallen in love with Ashley so easily, becoming giddy when he wanted to court and marry her, I assumed. Maybe there wasn't an age limit on the idea of 'forever' either. "I can see us together for a *long* while, Wesley Turner."

"Honestly?" he gulped.

"Yeah, why?" the lighthearted moment changed with his tense expression.

The serious look on his face didn't ease up. "Forever?"

Why was he pushing the question so far? Was he fishing? With him it was hard to tell unless I pushed into his head. Instead, I did the only other thing I could think of to loosen him up. "Maybe," I teased as I ran my fingers through his hair.

He sat back, half-smiling, leaving the conversation alone and instead insisting that I look up. I leaned back and gazed at the night sky to find he'd been right all along. The single sheet of bright stars I'd grown up with multiplied into a thick blanket, knitted with layer upon layer of shimmering white dots. "I've never seen anything—"

"Quite like it?" he interrupted as my mouth dropped. "Kind of like how I feel about you," he rubbed my back softly and I shivered.

"You say that to all the ladies," I teased.

The moment froze in perfection—myriad stars in the sky, Katie with a jar full of fireflies, Wesley and I in a close embrace as my lips fused with his underneath a glowing canopy woven together by flowing chirps of crickets.

After some time, Katie marched over holding a jar full of the glowing bugs. "I'm sleepy," she proclaimed.

Wesley pulled himself from me. "Well, let's get you to bed, but let the lightning bugs out before we head in."

"Do I have to?" Katie groaned, tilting her jar and peeking through the glass.

"Would you like to live in a jar?" Wesley answered back.

Katie thought about it for a minute and reluctantly unscrewed the lid to release them before we made our way into the house. Wesley followed her to tuck her in and I slipped into my room, curious to know what happened next in the journal. Did the dashing young Ashley come calling on Delilah? It was a total soap opera and I giggled as I flipped to the pages.

October 17th 1666,

Dearest Diary,

The air grows cold as does my heart. For Ashley, my truest love, did come calling on our house. Made he, his appeal to court to my father. For requested I of my maid to overhear the discourse, whereupon she did tell me that Ashley is base born and thereby consider him unfit does my father. Cried did I, all the day. I did not eat. I did not sleep. I wept upon my pillow until my mother thought me quite mad and reminded me, did she, that a lady does not weep over a silly trial. Repaired shall my heart never be, sweet diary, for is he, my truest of loves 'till I shall never have another.

I slammed the book shut as a single tear rolled down my eye. I was sad for this girl from hundreds of years ago that I'd never met, and never would. Her pain was mine, for a moment and heaviness surrounded me as the door creaked open. Wesley came in, looking worried.

"You weren't in my room, and then it was weird... it was like I could feel you were upset."

"I was, but it was just over this stupid diary." I wiped the single tear from my eye, laughing and suddenly felt ridiculous.

He picked it up off the bed and thumbed through pages, stopping on a random entry and read aloud, squinting. "'May 3, 1664, Dearest Diary, Today did father introduce me to my new maid, Mary, who spent all the day complaining of the task of combing through my hair. 'The lady's hair isn't natural, 'twas ne'er a child wit' gold tha' weaves in an' out of dark brown. So thick 'tis t'comb. Green eyes 'o fire. Ne'er have I seen anythin' like 'er.' Confessed she this to our long-time cook who thought it quite the scandal and hastened to send word to me. Take no offense did I. For these observations, she states plainly, are but truth. My eyes are frequently noticed by our overnight guests. For as long shall I breathe, my secret shall remain told to none.'"

Wesley put the book down. "Sounds pretty dramatic to me," he commented sarcastically.

"That wasn't the page. I was two years ahead. She'd met a man with blond hair and blue eyes. He wanted to court her and at first I thought it was silly about her wanting to get married and everything, but..." My voice trailed off—they'd never be together. "He didn't have a dad and apparently it made him not good enough."

"Shouldn't you be happy? You don't believe in being engaged so young and so sudden," he challenged.

"I don't know," I looked down. "It's different. Maybe I'm rethinking my ideas. I guess it depends on how deeply you feel and how much faith you have in the relationship, in the other person, in yourself."

He chuckled. "Don't feel too bad for Delilah."

"And why not?" I scowled that he thought it was funny. Delilah and Ashely not being together was sad, he needed to understand that.

He laughed again. "You realize what her engagement ring would've been?"

I cocked my head. "No," I responded, hesitantly.

"The Puritans, which I suspect she was, didn't wear jewelry. Her engagement ring would've been a thimble." Wesley laughed again. "It was considered practical. She could sew things while she waited around for her man to marry her," he finished.

I rolled my eyes and sighed in disbelief. "No way."

"Want to look it up?" he challenged, holding out his phone.

"No," I smirked, coming closer to him. He was probably right.

"You sure?" he whispered, his lips meeting mine, causing me to forget our squabble.

"Very," I kissed him again.

He combed through my hair and muttered, "Green eyes o' fire and gold that weaves in and out of dark brown. She sounds a lot like—" he stopped. He didn't have to say any more.

"Ashley's eyes were the bluest water... he had hair like the sun," I added, slowly.

Wesley's eyes widened, "Lila, did Delilah conform to Puritan ideals?"

"How so?" What was he getting at?

"Did she rebel against her parents? Anything about her not agreeing to do what they asked of her?" All of a sudden his teasing turned to focus. I could almost feel the spinning of the wheels.

"No, in fact she seemed like she wanted to do right by them," I answered.

"But when she found out Ashley was unsuited for her, she'd be angry with him for not being honest. She'd feel deceived. You said she was heartbroken?"

"Yeah..." I started to answer. Where was he going with the questions?

"Did they end up together?" he asked.

"I haven't made it that far," I revealed, picking the book up and turning it to where I'd left off. "Should you be applying to law school instead?"

But Wesley was too far gone. He was completely focused. "Go a few entries further," he insisted.

I turned the pages, "Here." I read aloud. "'October 29, 1666. Dearest Diary, My heart began to heal. For the young son of the Reverend Baker did come calling, whereupon asked he for my hand in marriage. Father did agree to this. I am overjoyed. Soon, shall I write again. Soon, my name shall be his and shall I be known as Goody Baker...' Then the words fade."

"Skim a few more and read another," Wesley requested.

I sighed and turned through at least a dozen entries. "'December 27, 1666. Dearest Diary, Cold is the weather, but warmth is upon my heart for Clyde Baker is the loveliest of husbands. I dare not venture outside, for fear of taking more ill. For a week past, I have found myself unable to take meals. Weak and tired am I, perhaps from my wifely duties, for Clyde has an insatiable hunger for activities unable to be written among your precious pages. I will share with you an intrigue. For it is shameful. The night past, I took tea before bed to settle my stomach. Slept did I and dreamed of Ashley. Took he, my hand in his, and warmth did I feel. Awake did I, abruptly. I carried shame, all the day. Know I, that if my dearest love found this information, he would have me no more.'"

I finished. Wesley's face was firm, pale even.

"She's pregnant," he concluded, becoming strangely interested.

"No, she's not. How do you know?" I rolled my eyes. There was no way Wesley could deduce that.

"Just keep going," he demanded, growing frustrated.

"Okay, okay...calm down though." I turned through more pages.

"Just flip to the end...please," he added, like 'please' would make his attitude better.

"Fine," I huffed.

"'September 3, 1667. Unable am I to write. Lost have I my husband, my dearest daughter. Weaker I grow each day. Ashley and his wife left for the north with my precious girl. Had they no other choice than to leave me in the woods for death...' Oh my God!" I gasped, slamming the book once more.

Wesley sat, unmoving. "I'll save you some reading. She was pregnant. It was summer, she was in a field, making flowers float...telepathically. Her maid caught her, told the church. She was tried as a witch and cast out. Ashley's wife was a midwife. She delivered the baby...and they raised her."

"You know this how?" I asked, still in shock.

"I've dreamt it." he started. His blue eyes were wider than I'd ever seen them. "You..." he put his hand on top of mine, "you're so familiar, recognizable to me."

It all struck me at once, everything he was getting at. He didn't have to say it, because I said it for both of us. The one dark possibility, too miniscule to take seriously, but hanging in the back of both our minds. "We're fate's do-over..."

Wesley nodded. "Yeah, she fucked it up the first time... and brought versions of us back. And when things didn't go her way, she threw one big ass temper tantrum...and—"

I punched the bed "But *why*? Why does it matter so damn much?" I asked, angered, like Wesley should have the answer. "So everyone else gets free will and we're fate's slaves?"

"We can choose to not be together," he responded.

"We could choose it, but it's like when we weren't together, nothing seemed quite right about my life. I fit in and had friends, but I also kind of didn't fit in. Don't you get it, Wesley? Fate's blackmailing us. Sure, we can break up or go our separate ways, but what if everything falls apart like it did for Delilah and Ashley?" I suddenly regretted eating the pizza as my stomach began to churn.

"Lila, I don't want you to be with me out of fear. I want you to have a choice." He put his arms around me.

I tried to imagine life without Wesley and couldn't. "I don't want a life without you," I whispered in defeat. He smiled, weakly, and leaned in to kiss me.

Our kisses were tender, like we both knew the other felt deceived by some intangible concept. We hoped that the desperate meeting of our lips over and again would repair

273

anger and hurt. Somehow, my body on top of his, as we made love in gentle strokes and the air turned to velvet could compensate. Our souls realized that we weren't teenagers, we weren't people—we represented a bitterness pieced together from an inability to let go.

We finished and held on to one another, tight, in mutual fear that not doing so would not only destroy our own lives but destroy the happiness of those we cared for the most. His soft, warm lips healed my body as they pressed against mine. Making love again, like once we started it was impossible to stop. The confusion that hurt so bad, began to feel good, so good, and a drop of sweat tickled my nose as I lay my head against his chest and kissed his ear to. Intently listening to his heavy breaths, as they became a force that sent warm shivers through my body before we both collapsed.

Even more hopeless was the expectation that from all the tragedy I suffered, there was a payoff. Not just finding Wesley and falling in love, but something deeper—some bigger picture or endgame. It'd been one of the few threads left to hold on to. Sleep was welcomed, his arm around me was a comfort against the hefty slam of truth and I drifted off, content in our make-believe reality.

WESLEY

I kissed her shoulder before rolling out of bed. Was everything my fault? Maybe I should've kept quiet about the dreams. I walked to the bathroom and stepped in the shower, hoping to wash the heaviness down the drain. It wouldn't be possible. I washed up quickly and dressed in the bathroom, not wanting to wake Lila up. My wallet and keys were sitting on the nightstand, so when I grabbed them, I tried to be quiet.

The sun was just coming up, and I waved at dad, who headed toward the shed to pick up some tools. I was reluctant to leave Lila, but a day with Alana at the lake would be good for her.

So far, the setup to my plan had turned out perfect. Dad played his part, and Alana was more than willing to agree to a girls' day out with Lila, even managing to concoct the perfect distraction. I headed west on 54 and merged onto 71 North to Kansas City. The mall would probably be the best place to begin my search.

If someone had approached me two years ago, no, even one year, and told me I'd be heading out to buy a girl I just met an engagement ring, I would've asked them what they were drinking because I wanted some. The only girl I'd been with consistently was Tiff, but even after I'd screw up, and she'd take me back time after time, there wasn't a connection. Sure, I could've let her go, but not doing so was what made me a bad person.

There was something amusing about being able to be with nearly any girl I wanted, but, the first time I laid eyes on her, I couldn't bring myself to think about anyone but Lila. She was a tempting, seductive goddess and being with her would risk the loss of the fantasy, not to mention, concentrating on *her* would distract from everything that had been going on around her.

With Sullivan gone, she was all I needed to focus on, at least until college. The first couple years wouldn't be bad. It'd be medical school, the long hours, the time away from her. The stubbornness and independence, that sometimes annoyed the crap out of me, would come in handy. Like she said, she wouldn't sit around pining for me to come home; she had her own things to do.

The drive time sped by, as two hour drives into Kansas City usually did. I made my way into the Kansas side and eventually pulled into NorthPark Mall. Beads of sweat gathered on my forehead as I made my way through the entrance. I found a nearby bench and sat. Was I having a panic attack?

Another idea crossed my mind and I pulled my phone out and dialed the last person on earth I ever thought I'd call for advice.

"Oh my God! It's like nine o'clock in the morning. Is something wrong? You woke me up!" she cried, nearly blowing the speaker on my cell phone.

I was exasperated. "No, Sara, nothing's wrong. I'm calling because I need your help."

"Can it wait? Peter, Daryll, and I partied a little too hard last night," she explained.

"It can't."

A long pause, then, "Fine...What could Wesley Turner, the end-all-be-all of knowledge, possibly need to consort with little ol' me about?"

"I'm at a mall, alone and—"

"Oh Jesus," she interrupted in a tone so agitated I could feel her rolling her eyes.

"Let me finish. I'm looking for something specific, for Lila."

"What?" I didn't know how to tell her and scanned through all the ways it could go wrong. "Do spill, Wesley... Hello, Wesley?"

"A ring...but not just any kind of ring, an engagement ring," I finished to a quick thud.

"Sara?" I waited. She hung up on me and was speed dialing Lila as I sat there.

A couple seconds passed, and I was preparing to hang up, but then she came back on. "I dropped the phone. Sorry, I thought I heard you say you needed help buying an engagement ring for Lila. Wes, is this a joke?"

"No. I love Lila. More than any person I've ever met."

"You're both so young. And I don't know whether to be excited or drive out there and punch you...hold on a minute." She pulled the phone away and yelled, "Peter! PETER! Wake up and get in here!"

"What? What's wrong?" I heard a cracked voice.

"Wesley, I'm putting you on speaker." I inhaled a deep breath. My simple question was turning into greater fanfare. "Peter, Wesley's at the mall."

"Oh my God. That is an event," he exclaimed in the background. "He didn't hurt himself, did he?"

"No, no, you don't understand. Wesley's at the mall because he wants to buy an engagement ring," she explained. I braced myself once again.

"Excuse me? I didn't hear you right, Sara."

"Wesley wants to propose to Lila," she re-explained.

"You're too young. This totally can't happen," was his response.

I gripped the phone tighter. "You want to fly out here and stop me?" I challenged.

"It's tempting—"

Sara interrupted him. "Peter, stop. It's not up to you, it's Lila's choice. He can ask, but she can say no."

After a long silence, Peter spoke up again. "Why the hell is he looking for a ring at the mall, then? Those rings are so yesterday. You need a specialty store. Turn, leave, and go to your truck. I'll look up a couple places. Where are you?"

"Kansas City," I answered.

"Okay, give me a sec and I'll get back to you."

I sighed and put the phone back in my pocket. I hadn't reached my truck before my phone buzzed. Peter had texted me an address from Sara's phone with a message to call back when I arrived.

I finished walking to my truck, got in, and programmed the address into the GPS. I pulled out and followed the directions until I arrived at a stand-alone brick building. After I parked, I called Sara back.

"Hey there, lover boy!" she sang.

Sara must've kept the speaker phone turned on because I heard Peter's voice in the background. "Wes listen, the place is appointment only, but I was able to get you in. My last piece of advice...go for the Verragios—"

"And good luck," Sara interrupted.

"Thanks, guys." But they'd already hung up.

I stood in the parking lot for a while. Doing what? Wondering if she'd say 'yes'—wondering if I was falling victim to some other-worldly fear mongering. This wasn't supposed to be me. I shouldn't have been there, at nineteen, picking out a diamond ring. Maybe it wasn't me at all, just where life had taken me, where fate had led me. I sighed and headed toward the door. The walls were bright white and aligned with posters of smiling brides and grooms, boasting a particular wedding ring designer. The numerous display cases that lined the room shimmered under the lights.

"Sir, may I help you?" I looked up and saw a guy who appeared to be a little older than myself dressed in a suit. He walked toward me and reached out to shake my hand.

We shook, and I told him I had an appointment. He looked through a book and nodded. "Yes, I see it. Mr. Turner, here for an engagement ring. My name's Josh, and I'm happy to help you find the perfect one," he beamed, exposing his slightly crooked front teeth.

"Thanks, man," I responded, happy to have all the help I could get.

"Do you have any specific style in mind? If not, we can look at a few favorites, or I can show you loose stones we can place into settings."

I shifted my weight and wiped a little sweat from my forehead. My plan hadn't allotted time for me to freak out. "A good friend recommended Verragio," I explained.

"Ah yes, a good company. Beautiful pieces. We keep ours over here." I followed him toward a case in the corner. He walked around the back of the cabinet.

"Would you like to sit down, Mr. Turner?" he asked, seeming concerned.

"Please, just call me Wesley." I was glad he offered a chair because I didn't see myself being able to stand much longer.

"Certainly, Wesley. Are you okay? You seem more nervous than our usual customers."

"I'm okay, really. Being engaged, it's something I couldn't see myself doing...until *her*." My heart flipped thinking of Lila.

"I'm just saying, don't rush into things. You're young, enjoy it." He was loosening up.

"Fate's going to have her way—no matter what," I responded.

"Oh, you're not the 'it's fate that we met' type," he formed quotation marks with his index fingers and cocked his head.

I scowled. Did this guy want commission or not?

"I only say that because I see it day in and day out. Those are the rings that get returned," he scoffed. "We're allowed to make our own choices, ya know? Fate is forever changing based on what you decide. Don't let superstition control you," he advised.

A couple minutes passed as I studied the rings that'd probably cost more than both my trucks combined. The way the diamonds glistened as the fluorescents teased the stones, the beams nearly blinding, like love. *What if he's right? What if fate is just some fear-mongering bitch? Would Lila's parents have died anyway?* Even if everything Josh said was true, none of it changed the feelings I had for Lila; she was worth fighting for.

"Changed your mind?" He raised his eyebrows and leaned back, waiting for my answer.

"Let me see that one." I pointed to the case and he pulled out the two-tone ring I indicated.

He handed it to me and I held it up and studied the center diamond that connected to smaller diamonds going around each side met with intricate gold detailing. How would it look on her finger?

"It's one of the newer styles, but they only make a limited amount of each. It's .70 total weight," he explained. I nodded, pretending to be interested even though I wasn't well versed on the subject of rings.

I gulped. For once, I worried more about my wallet than her answer. "The price?"

"$3,750," he answered and then quickly informed me that the store proudly offered in-house financing.

Yeah with a twenty percent interest rate that goes up to thirty after the first missed payment, I criticized.

"What size is she?" he asked.

I quickly texted Sara who demanded a picture of the ring and said she thought it was six. "I think she's a six," I replied.

"I can check our stock. Give me one second. If we don't have it, I can order it." He stood and walked to the back of the store.

I waited. How long would an order take? "I have a six-and-a-half. If you're wanting it right away, you can purchase it and bring her in with the ring and we could get it sized. That's usually the best option. Especially with the summer heat, fingers tend to swell."

"Three thousand dollars...I could pay more of my truck off with that," I muttered.

Josh raised his eyebrows. "I can show you more affordable options," he offered. "But you better get used to it, women are expensive," he joked.

"No..." I cleared my throat. "This'll be fine. I'll take it and we can bring it back for exact sizing."

I paid Josh, and got in my truck, right as a text came in from Sara—*You better send a pic!!!!!!!!*

So, I texted her a photo.

OMG!!!!! BE-YOU-TI-FUL!!!!!!!!!!!!

I started the truck, happy to discover I was close to 71 south. I pulled out of the parking lot and merged onto the highway. I'd have to keep the ring hidden. I needed to ask at the perfect time. How would I ask? What would I say? Somehow, it'd work out. After all, even Fate, the fear-mongering frigid bitch herself was on our side. What could possibly go wrong?

R J SULLIVAN

She stared at me over a cup of coffee as rain hit the roof, and I thought about grabbing those blonde curls and yanking them until she screamed my name. I gave her a pleasant smile.

"I got your note at work and if you're another reporter, I told them all...I'm done. No more interviews." She rolled her eyes, put her hand on the table, and readied herself to stand up and leave.

I want to grab your arm and twist it until the bone snaps in two, bitch. I placed the palm of my hand gently over hers and patted it reassuringly. "I'm not a reporter. Name's RJ Sullivan." I leaned toward her, "And we both want the same thing."

"Yeah? What do we both want?" she sneered.

We both want to be in that restroom over there. You want me to pound you just like every other piece of ass wearing those short little skirts. I smiled again, "We both want Lila Daniels dead."

"I'm listening," she answered.

"How is it that she was able to convince all your friends they somehow knew her, but not you?" I asked the little whore in front of me.

She shook her head and batted those doe-eyes. "I dunno, really. It's like I could tell she was a freak, ya know? Like there was something really off with her. She'd say things to me over and over—ridiculous stuff like 'you're cool with me being here'. Like I'm just gonna believe that or something," she explained. "After what she did to Linda, I want her to burn in hell. Me and Linda grew up together; we were like sisters." She folded her arms across that silicone chest of hers as it heaved in disgust.

I was on to her, I knew what she was and maybe she didn't even realize it. "I want her dead, but sweetheart, I want you dead, too. You see," I whispered, calmly, "you're like her, but instead of being telekinetic, you're able to block her and those like her out."

Her eyes were wide, and she started to get up. "Where you going, hun?" I said, tauntingly. "I'm with the FDRA; there's surveillance around this whole building. But, I'll tell you what. Let's make a deal, huh? I'll give you an address and you bring me a dead Lila. If you do that, sugar, your life won't be so important to me. You get what you want, and I get what I want. What do you say?" I extended my hand to her.

"What's the FDRA?"

"We're a government agency and that's all you need to know, for now. I mean, you can certainly decline my offer, but it would be terrible if evidence surfaced pinning Linda's death on you," I threatened.

"I-I don't believe you... you can't just make evidence appear," she heaved.

I chuckled and leaned forward. "Dear, one phone call, and I can turn your world upside down." I checked my watch. "Quite frankly, you're wasting my time with questions. Do we have a deal, or not?" I tapped my impatient fingers against the table.

"I think I'm making this deal with the devil," she answered hesitantly, licking a pair of cherry red lips. "But if it's my life or that bitch's, I think the answer's obvious."

We shook hands and I handed her a piece of paper. "The address is where she's staying. The number's mine. Call me when it's taken care of."

"What am I supposed to do? How am I gonna kill her?" The gravity of what I was requesting of her sank into that blonde little head of hers.

"Happy Birthday." I smiled wryly and pulled a box from beside me, wrapped like a gift.

"What the—" she exclaimed.

"Open it at home. Use it to kill her. Remember," I growled and pointed to her, "her or you."

"Fine. At least the bitch will be dead." She left a few dollars on the table and I watched that tight ass wiggled its way out the door.

I sat by myself for a while, thinking about Lila, those long legs, perfect lips, hair thick and long for gripping. Was Wesley banging her? Lucky bastard. It was a shame I couldn't get to her myself, before Amy did. That was the way it had to be.

The lanky waitress came by to collect the money and warm my coffee. She could warm something else. She wanted it too, all women did. The way they'd look at me, those round innocent eyes telling me they wanted it. Bitches.

Thunder rattled the windows as I stood and made my way out the door. I'd see Amy soon enough, and it'd be my turn with her. I smirked as the bells rang, indicating I had made my way out of the corner café in Chicago.

WESLEY

When I pulled into the drive, the side of the house was lit by a warm glow. I put the box in my pocket and walked over to see what was going on. Queen blasted from Dad's old radio, probably a mixed tape. No matter how many times I tried to set my father up on iTunes, he refused to get it, preferring a box of old tapes he'd put together decades ago.

"Hey Dad, what's happening?" I asked as he carried a bag of charcoal.

"I'm grilling, and the girls are changing into swimsuits," he chuckled and looked down to the grill. "Steaks."

"Sounds good. Guess I'll change too, then." I ran up the stairs. Where would I hide the ring? All the way back on the top shelf of my closet. *There's no way she'll find it.* She didn't come off as a snooping type girl.

I changed into swim-trunks just as I heard Katie's door open and her bouncing down the stairs squealing with excitement. I opened my door and was heading to the stairs when Lila came out of her room in a pair of cut-off shorts and her bikini top. I couldn't move as she strolled up to me, her skin tan from the lake.

"I missed you!" She walked over. Pressing her body against mine and smiling an I-know-exactly-what-I'm-doing-to-you type smile.

I answered her with a kiss. "I missed you, too," I responded before kissing her again and taking her hand. I started for my room.

"Where are we going, Wes?" She looked around as though we'd get caught.

"I want to show you how much I missed you," I hummed in her ear.

"But, your dad," she argued.

"He won't notice. We'll be quick," I smiled. "Come on."

She squealed as I picked her up and started for my room, hurrying to shut the door before she changed her mind. We laughed as I made my way over to the bed, still holding her. I straddled her. Memorizing the glow in her eyes.

"Every time I see you...I just...ugh..." I growled in false frustration.

She giggled. Her hair was silk, spread across the pillow. "Someday that won't be the case." She laughed, "Maybe you'll see me and run the other way, fast."

"This will always be the case," I promised her. It was true.

"What if..." she thought for a minute, "all my teeth fall out?"

I smirked. "I wouldn't care," I whispered.

"I could go bald," she tried again.

I stared into her fiery, green eyes that shone like grass beneath layers of quilted stars. "Don't you realize, you're so much more than looks to me?"

"Isn't that what you care about, Wesley Turner?" I pressed my lips together, holding back a smile. She knew me too well. She wasn't in my head.

"Lila Daniels, I'll love you no matter what," I answered.

"If I become a hoarder?" she challenged.

"No matter what." I kept my answer consistent.

"You're confident," she giggled.

"I'm arrogant." We were both laughing.

Like a movie, we stopped. I couldn't stare deep enough into the shining set of green eyes that gazed into my own. My future was somewhere in those compelling blades of grass, but I didn't feel like searching for it then. I ran my hands down her extended arms, her skin liquefying as I made my way to her ribcage and her waist, hips, and up and down the eternity that was her smooth legs.

Our bodies moved in a rhythm so perfect that it never should've been, to some tempo that hadn't yet evolved, but there we were, discovering it in each deep breath, bead of sweat, every time she dug her nails into my back and what should have amounted to pain—I found no more than pleasurable.

The progression of emotion, of love, of passion should never have been. Like Lila's ability, it was too much untainted sensation to be shared between two people. Except, there we were, bodies eternally tangled as our lips met once more, the rush of her fervent breath warm against my skin.

I forced myself to pull away from her. "We should dress and get down there before Dad really does come looking for us." She agreed and soon we were out the door and down the stairs, making our way to the kitchen.

"Hey Billy!" Lila greeted Dad as she worked to smooth down pieces of her rustled hair.

"Looks like someone got some sun today," he commented, looking up from the grill. Lila's cheeks were still flushed. "You might wanna put some aloe on that," he advised.

"Sure thing! I'll definitely look into it," she answered back, probably realizing it wasn't from the sun.

Dad, seemingly oblivious about what took place upstairs, went back to cooking. Katie splashed happily in the pool. I got more time to talk to Lila.

"Bad timing for me to run an errand, huh? How was the lake with Alana?" I wondered if she enjoyed it.

"Amazing! No waves like the ocean, so I actually went in the water. Kind of." I shook my head and smiled. "Okay, I put my feet in the water. Alana's really cool. I'm going to miss her. The day was nice, though. I spent a lot of time thinking," she recalled.

"About us?" secretly hoping the answer was yes.

"No, the Lewis Diagram." A response I was absolutely not expecting but should've been.

"Why? What's interesting about covalent bonds?" Although, her talking science was sexy—*very* sexy.

She laughed, "I'm kidding. I actually tried to get my mind away from us, to clear it. Get a grip on everything before it gets too intense."

I smiled and took her hand. "Isn't it already?"

"Yes, and that's the problem." She ran her thumb across my index finger.

"What? I don't see a problem," I said honestly.

"That I think this is it for me. That *you* are it." She took in a deep breath.

"You say that like it's a bad thing." My thoughts turned to the small box hiding in my bedroom closet.

"Scary; Wes, I'm eighteen," she paused before continuing, "I'd like to go see your mom." She wanted to change the subject.

"Lila...I can't yet." I didn't feel like having the discussion, but something about it was important to her.

"Then don't, but I need to. Wes, please," she contended.

Unable to tell her 'no', and knowing it wouldn't really matter what I said, I replied, "Okay."

She threw her arms around my neck and kissed me once, but that was all it took. Our lips locked tighter than a carbon-nitrogen bond. I couldn't have stopped it if I wanted, but mostly I didn't want to. My hands found their way around her waist and played with the rim of her cut-off shorts. The splash of water against the concrete, the pulse of frogs and crickets, the rustling of the light breeze disappeared—

Until dad cleared his throat. We looked up, embarrassed to have drawn so much attention from him and Katie.

"Oooooh!" she exclaimed while making kissing noises at us from the other end of the pool.

"It's about time to eat." Dad took the steaks off the grill. "Lila, Katie, why don't you go in and sit down? Wes, come help me with the trays." He gave me a warning look.

"Sure, Dad," I hollered back while making my way over to pick up a tray of potatoes wrapped in aluminum foil.

"Things go okay today?" he whispered.

"Yeah," I answered, wanting to change the subject.

"You two...you're good together." He thought for a moment. "Maybe I was wrong."

"Thanks, Dad." He gave my back an encouraging pat and we made our way into the kitchen where Lila and Katie were waiting.

I fought to stay awake during dinner, everything including the afternoon's escapade with Lila, caught up to me and I wasn't even aware of the conversation until Dad pushed his chair out. "I think I'm gonna run up the road for a couple hours. You two okay with putting Katie to bed tonight?"

He didn't say it because of Katie, but I knew he meant Tornado's. I didn't care.

"Sure," Lila answered.

"Will you tell me a bedtime story?" she asked. "Please?" she added.

"Yes. Run upstairs and get ready. I'll be up in a sec," Lila promised her. With the prospect of a story, Katie ran down the hall and up the stairs. Lila stared at me. "You tired?"

"Yeah and I need to get some more work turned in before the semester ends," I added.

I cleaned up the dishes, scraping them off and piling them in the sink. There was one beer left in the fridge, so I grabbed it and unscrewed the top. Giggles sounded from Katie's room and I followed them and listened quietly as I stood outside the door.

"So, tell me the story," Katie whined.

"Okay. Let's see," Lila cleared her throat. "Once upon a time, long ago, there was a lovely young princess who went walking across a bridge one night. Suddenly the clouds covered the moonlight and she was scared."

"Why was she afraid?" Katie scrunched her nose. "I wouldn't be afraid."

"Because princesses didn't leave the castle much and it was dark," Lila explained quickly, caught off guard.

"Oh… why don't princesses leave the castle?"

Welcome to the abyss of telling Katie a bedtime story. I chuckled to myself.

"Because they're princesses," she answered simply, before continuing the story. "She's scared, and she meets an old lady holding an apple. The lady offers it to her and she eats it and falls to the ground."

"Did she die?"

"No…"

"She doesn't die, does she?"

"No, she won't die," Lila cleared her throat.

"Good, so what happened?"

"The lady captured the princess and put her in a tower with an evil dragon. The princess wasn't dead, but instead, she was in a deep sleep. One day a prince entered the castle and came upon the sleeping princess, who, according to legend, could only be awakened by true love's kiss, but the prince couldn't fathom how kissing a sleeping woman who had no voice in the matter could possibly be true love. Instead, he waited until she woke up on her own and rescued herself."

"They became good friends and got to know each other over the course of a few years, while they both pursued degrees and became financially and emotionally independent, after which they decided to begin a relationship based on friendship and trust instead of patriarchal whims that assume a woman should have no agency." I stifled a laugh and took another drink of beer to keep myself quiet.

Katie blinked. "I don't get it, and what does patriotical mean? Did they say the pledge together?"

"It's patriarchal and it means… ugh, never mind." Katie reached her hands up and Lila gave her a warm hug before turning the ballerina lamp off. "It's late and you need to go to sleep."

"So, do they live happily ever after?" Katie yawned.

"Yes, they live happily ever after."

Katie clapped. "I love happily ever after stories. Is that what you and Wes will be like?"

I lingered by the door to hear the answer. "I hope so." Lila pulled the covers over Katie and reached for her stuffed rabbit.

"Me too," she smiled.

I hurried back to my room, clicking on the computer and loading one of the quizzes that would be due in the next few weeks. Of course, answering the questions was mechanical. I already knew them. As I did so, I thought about Lila. Between her comments and her answer to Katie's question, she'd definitely say 'yes', regardless of the feminist fairy tale. Besides, it was ridiculous to think a girl would say 'no' to me. I sat back and waited for my answers to upload onto the college's network and post to the system. She entered the room.

"I think she's asleep and I probably will be, soon," Lila yawned.

"I'm tired, too. It's been a long day," I swiveled my chair around to face her.

She plopped down on my lap, and I rested my hand on her leg. "Whatcha working on?" she batted her eyes.

"Trying to get caught up on my online classes. Haven't been on here in a while," I explained.

"Why's that?" she grinned, crossing those long, sexy-as-hell legs as she did.

"Some girl keeps distracting me." I took her face in my hand and the chair squeaked beneath us as I pulled her closer to me.

"Oh, that sucks," she pouted.

"It's okay. I kind of like it," I grinned.

She leaned against me while I opened another sociology quiz. It was hard to get through the questions with her body leaning against mine. Her sweet vanilla smell broke my concentration.

"What *is* xenocentrism?" she read over my shoulder.

I smiled, "Someone who places more value on another culture than their own." It was a textbook answer, but it'd suffice.

"You don't use many weird words anymore," she frowned. "Why not?"

I thought for a minute. I certainly had more than my share of little known and colorful vocabulary, but being preoccupied with her, I hadn't thought about them as often.

"Because if I use all my energy on lengthy words, I won't have enough left do this," I answered coyly before lifting her up as she squealed in surprise.

"Wes—" she started.

I was lost in her thick hair, its floral scent saturating my lungs. My mind was disoriented, only focused on her sharp breaths. Our lips moved together, failing to separate as we made our way to the bed, falling onto the soft sheets, dissolving into one another. I rolled onto my back pulling her with me and settling us under the sheets.

She giggled and laid her head on the pillow next to my arm. In comparison to what she'd been through, I had it good. I hadn't been lied to my entire life. My parents were both alive, even if Mom had a break down and Dad was struggling to handle it all. How easy my world could've fallen apart without Lila. Because of her, I thought about life differently. It wasn't the mechanical future I'd planned; keeping my nose in the books, girl after girl on weekends, avoiding commitment because, honestly, it terrified me. With her, I had a best friend; someone who understood me in ways no one else would ever be able to. We kept each other from shattering. I drifted to sleep next to her, looking forward to the next day.

"Ashley," she gasped, horrified I'd snuck into the barn.

"Sorry am I not. No, I shall not be sorry." I kissed her as a mare whinnied in the background.

"Ashley, engaged am I to the son of our pastor. If we are discovered, we shall surely be placed in the stocks... I-I could lose my betrothal—"

"Delilah, run with me. To the north where they know not of who we are, for I am to marry Ruth. Daughter to the midwife."

"No, I shall not. My duty is to honor my parents and their wishes for me. Running with you would humiliate my family," she whispered.

"They shall catch you in time," I warned.

"For what shall they catch me, Ashley? For what purpose are you threatening me?"

"Your magic."

She stepped back, horrified. "You know of my powers. I am not of the devil."

"I am the same. I shall speak of you to no one. My love for you is like the sky, endless."

"Don't." She lowered her head and looked away. "I will hear not of your affections."

"I know you love me, too." I stood in front of her, so she'd have to look at me.

"No, Ashley. Go." Tears filled her eyes. "Just go. I must do my duty."

"Our duty is to be together. I saw of it in a dream. At night, dream you, as well."

"Go! Go now!" she screamed in anger. The scornful look on her face being enough to make me turn and go my way, but I didn't want to leave. I had to stay. I couldn't lose her, I couldn't go on…

"No, I can't!" I sat straight up, confused about where I was.

"Wesley!" Lila's hand was on my arm. She sat up, too. "Wes, what's wrong?"

My gut twisted. "Some stupid dream… nothing." I wasn't about to tell her what I'd seen, or the pain I experienced through the nightmare.

"Wesley—"

"Let it go, Lila!" I snapped, only half-realizing I was awake, in the real world. She drew back. Recognizing I yelled, I apologized. "Sorry, it's not anything I want to talk about, but I shouldn't yell at you." *Dammit, keep letting your temper get the better of you. That'll win her over,* I scolded myself. "Shit," I shook my head. *Would I even be able to treat her right*?

"Wes, we can talk about it tomorrow," she yawned. "But, yeah…no more yelling." She went back to sleep quickly, while I stayed awake running the dream through my head.

Something about it was familiar, but so different. I was me, Lila was someone else, as though she didn't recognize me.

Would Lila tell me 'no'? Was that what the dreams were about?

Maybe it was my subconscious warning me that she could say 'no'. My stomach knitted itself together until the strands were unrecognizable.

I glanced at her, already asleep, and sat up. I slipped some boxers on and restarted my computer. Once it was online, I finished the quiz, which was the last thing I wanted to do, but had to do something to keep my mind off the dreams and my plan to propose.

LILA

I woke feeling more rested but anxious because Wesley had agreed to take me to visit his mom; I wasn't sure when we'd go. Pushing the subject didn't seem like a good idea. Anyway, what would I say to the lady who turned me in to Sullivan? I reminded myself she wasn't in her right mind when she did it. Would I do the same thing if I had a child? Would I be willing to do anything to protect them?

I felt something else, an emotion I couldn't place, like something was going to change soon and it would alter my life, forever. I shook the odd feeling off. Wesley wasn't in bed. I sat up and stretched before walking to my room.

I closed the door behind me and pulled my hair up in a messy bun. I picked out a bright sundress with an upbeat, floral pattern and sat it on the end of the bed before running hot water in the antique stand-alone tub. I poured some rosewater bath wash I forgot I'd packed and when it bubbled up, I turned the faucet off and let my towel drop to the floor as I got in and rested my head against the porcelain side.

The soft perfume shyly made its way to my nose, and I inhaled it deeply, focusing on each breath. I pushed things from my mind and relaxed. I took another breath in, and when I pushed it out, I sent more worry with it, until the only thoughts remaining were Sara and I together, giggling and being silly, my mom and dad talking, playing board games on Sunday nights, playing with Katie, and Wes— his looks, his crazy attractive personality, and my pondering stopped on his intelligence. It was undeniable he was insanely smart, and even though I wasn't stupid, I wondered if I'd hold him back. All the years of medical school would be a lot of studying.

I was almost asleep when I heard, *May I come in?*

It was Wesley. I sat up, unsure of why I was so nervous after everything we'd done. *Sure.* I scooted further underneath the bubbles.

The door opened, and he was standing in front of me, a white towel around his waist. His tan skin shone underneath the lights, his tight abs, strong arms, that thick blond hair... were I Wesley, I'd probably be arrogant, too.

"So, can I?" He flashed me a mischievous grin.

I snapped back to the moment, "Huh?"

"If you want to be alone, it's okay," he shrugged.

"No. What? Sorry just spaced out," I answered, not wanting to tell him I was drooling over him, although the look on his face indicated he already knew it was the case.

"I wanted to join you," he shrugged. "May I?"

I smiled at the thought of how erotic everything with Wesley had been—how many firsts I'd had, the shower, sex that wasn't totally awkward. "Sure," I answered, probably blushing as I did.

He unwrapped the towel, and I moved forward so he could slide in behind me. When he was settled, he pulled me to him and I leaned my body against his, resting my head on his chest while he loosened my hair and it fell to my sides. "What do you do to me?" The warmth from his whispered breath filled the air and despite the heat from the water, my body was saturated with goosebumps and my stomach jumped in response to the electricity that pulsed through me.

Running my feet lightly against his, I whispered back, "I seduce you and use you for your body."

He chuckled. "I love your humor." He gently massaged my shoulders. "I love your strength. You've been through so much and I've never had to rescue you. You saved yourself."

"It doesn't feel that way," I argued. "It'll always hurt to think about my parents and the way they were murdered."

"Lila…" He put his arms around me, pulling me to him tighter.

"You filled the hole it left. Wesley," I turned to him, "you complete me."

The soft popping of bubbles was the only sound as our lips met and separated. Wesley looked at me with a serious expression I hadn't seen in some time. "What do you want from me?"

He kissed me again, before I could answer. I didn't want to waste time, so I used a single word—the only one I could think of, the sole statement that seemed to define what everything had been leading up to. "Forever."

I looked away, knowing what my words implied, fully aware of how Wesley could interpret the one thing he might not be able to give. I wanted to avoid any awkward looks or his tense expression. The hurt we'd both endure when he realized he wouldn't want that type of commitment.

He pulled me close to him, again, and caressed my arms gently. "I want that, too."

My heartbeat sped. I shivered and blinked my eyes a few times, trying to make sure I wasn't sleeping, like the bathwater wouldn't turn to blood or he wouldn't be glaring at me. It was real.

"You're cold, we should get out before you get sick," he coaxed.

I laughed because that's all I could do in response.

"What's funny?" He lowered his brows.

"Me getting sick. I've never been sick in my life." I giggled, "Not even a sneeze."

"Weird. Me neither," he laughed. "Look, we have something in common."

"About time." Maybe it was a good end to a moment that had become way too intense.

He stood and grabbed his towel. Once he wrapped it around himself, he handed one to me. "I'm going to get dressed." He turned to me. "I'm taking you out. I'll give you a few minutes to get ready. Then we'll go. I'll be in the living room." My heart skipped a beat at his spontaneity, the unwavering confidence as he grabbed me again, our lips meeting and refusing to part. "Or we could just stay here," he postured.

"Wesley..." I started, looking forward to going out and curious about where he'd take me.

He smiled. "Alright, alright."

I stood for a minute, alone in the tiled bathroom and closed my eyes. I had nothing figured out, no idea about going to college, or getting a job. I hadn't even gotten my diploma. But I could picture everything with Wesley.

I left the room and slipped into the dress and sandals. I brushed my teeth and took the time to apply full makeup, smiling as I blended some mineral eye shadow. I picked a dark lipstick and ran a layer of gloss over it to make it pop. *Why stop here?* I thought as I began pulling up pieces of my hair and pinning them out of the way. When a loose strand fell, I curled it, knowing how much Wes enjoyed twirling my hair in his fingers, and how much I liked when he did, how I turned to liquid at his touch.

As I did this, my phone rang. "Hey!" Sara's voice sang over the phone. "How's farmland USA?" she teased.

"I like it out here," I answered honestly.

"O-kay," and then silence.

"Hello?"

"Sorry, any news?" she inquired, curiously.

"What do you mean?" I wondered what she was hinting at.

"Oh, I dunno...anything big happen? Anything you need to tell your best friend?" she hummed.

"Are you still drunk?" I was a little frustrated that she drunk-dialed me and was holding me up from leaving.

"Ugh, like, no way! Geez! Never mind, call me later though, okay?"

"Umm...okay," I answered before ending one of the most cryptic phone calls I'd ever received. I glanced at myself again in the mirror before leaving the room and walking down the stairs.

Wesley must've heard me coming because he met me at the bottom. His eyebrows raised, and his lips formed 'wow' in slow motion. I was in awe as well. His hair gelled and fixed, he was in a cerulean blue polo with light khakis and tan shoes.

"If you wanted my full attention today... you got it," he remarked, giving me a once over.

"Something tells me I'll be pretty focused on you as well," I replied.

We were only focused on one another as we sat through a movie and went to eat. The humidity mixed with the fantasy of summer as it weaved its way through rainy days where we sat together on the porch swing, doing nothing. Sometimes not speaking and others where we couldn't stop laughing. Listening to a symphonic blend of raindrops settling on blades of grass, floating between chirping birds and a steady tap of the roof while I studied a petal from a begonia as it bent under the weight of clear drops.

I started sketching. The pictures reeked of vivid sadness, loss, frustration, and somewhere hidden in the depiction, an unpolluted contentment I found within the haze of time Wesley and I spent together.

One afternoon, I walked back from the field where I'd been drawing wildflowers. I opened the side door and was met with the smell of basil and garlic. I turned to the stove where Wesley stood, smiling. I narrowed my eyes.

"And what would you be doing?"

He nonchalantly answered, "Learning to cook." I wanted to kiss that gloating smirk off his face. He looked away from the pan for a moment and motioned to the living room. "Go, sit...it's almost finished, and I'll bring it to you."

"Wes—" I giggled.

"Go, woman, you're breakin' my style." He grinned before turning back to the stove.

I sighed, rolled my eyes, and ran the sketchpad and pencils to my room before coming back down and settling on the couch, the smell of marinara and herbs wafting to my nose. *I can totally get used to this,* I told myself.

It wasn't very long before a confident Wesley emerged from the kitchen with two plates, one for me and one for him. "Ce soir, tu manges du poulet étouffé dans la sauce marinara avec des pâtes et des haricots verts. Savourer!"

I pretty much died at his words, and honestly, he could've been serving a plate of dirt and it'd sound delicious. I couldn't speak as he set them on the coffee table in front of us. After a while, I pulled myself together and looked at him. It was obvious he was waiting for me to try it, so I picked up the plate and cut a bite of chicken. "You cooked it through, right?"

He chuckled, "Yes, I've been reading cookbooks. Trust me."

Cooking would take practice, right? No one reads a cookbook and just learns to cook right away. I took a bite of the steaming chicken, so tender it nearly melted when it hit my tongue, the herbs from the sauce dissolving in the meat— no one but Wesley.

"So?" he asked as I chewed, eager to try another bite.

"It's gross." I made my best disgusted face.

He smiled, nervously. "In that case..." he started to grab my plate and take his fork to it.

I sat up. "No, no..."

"You like it, then?" he teased.

My taking my plate back and immediately cutting into the piece of chicken was gesture enough to denote the answer was yes. "I don't get it," I said before taking another bite.

"You don't have to," he joked and picked up the remote control. He scanned the channels while we ate until it came to the news.

"And tonight, on the six 'o clock evening news, water plant workers petition city council for a raise, we'll take a look at the weekly weather... more hot temperatures coming at us, and finally, scientists confirm research proving certain diseases are becoming immune to modern antibiotics. More on that, but first, in breaking news, we have reports of a cattle trailer that jack-knifed on highway 70 North earlier today. Bruce is on the scene..."

The newscaster's perky voice faded out as I motioned to the devastation on the TV. "I could stop things like that," I remarked, remembering how I'd eased the pain of the woman in labor.

"Not really. You can't turn back time, and how could you be everywhere at once?" he challenged.

"I'm just saying. Were I there, I could've stopped it..." I'd been working hard to not use my abilities at all and wanted to talk about something different. "I feel like boring old people—eating dinner and watching the news," I chuckled.

Wesley didn't laugh. He set his plate down and stood up, making his way to the couch I was leaning back against, and gently pulled the plate from my hand and set it down, his eyes never leaving mine. He took one of my wrists in each of his strong hands and pushed them together, lightly pulling me up. The seriousness of his shining blue eyes, his unwavering coolness caused my head to float. Still holding my hands up, he led me as I walked backward until my back ran into the wall. He held my arms against it and whispered. "Don't move them."

His hand maneuvered under my skirt and pushed against my hip. The wall was hot, the room stifling. I started sweating and my breath was steam against the neckline of his t-shirt. He ran his fingers up and down the insides of my thigh and pressed himself against me as I tilted my head to kiss him.

His eyes shattering into mine, he whispered, "Being with me will be a lot of things, but it will never be boring," His lips slid closer to mine, like glass. My body burned in anticipation of what he was about to do, until he pulled away. His voice changed from a deep whisper to conversational tone, "I'm thirsty. Want a drink?"

I released the deep breath I had been holding. "Yeah..." I was parched, but not for water...I wanted *him*.

He grinned and started for the kitchen. I leaned against the wall, wondering what just happened; not understanding how Wesley got to me so easily, how he could just up and take control, how he was so confident about it. I regrouped myself as he walked back into the room.

"Beer or water?" he held up a glass of ice water and two bottles of Bud Light.

"Beer?" I said slowly.

"Was that a question or an answer?" he joked.

I took the beer. He sat on one end of the couch and motioned for me to sit next to him, but I took a seat on the other side.

"What's that for?" He lowered his eyebrows.

It was too easy for him. I liquefied at his touch. "I'm making you work for it," I challenged. "Girl power and stuff," I added.

"You're a bit feminist, huh?" The TV continued to act as background noise until he grabbed the remote and turned it off.

"I think people are individuals, that one person shouldn't define another. I don't think a man should control a woman," I pondered before continuing, "Or vice-versa. That relationships are more like partnerships. You don't like that?"

"It'd be a complete let-down if you thought differently." He moved to where I was sitting and took the back of my head in his hand. "I love you because you're strong. This is the first time I've felt like a gir—woman doesn't need me."

The evening passed. Eventually Wesley won and I gave in to him and his blue eyes, and his perfect face, and his even more perfect muscles. It faded into the next day, and the next. We kept an eye on the news, from major outlets. The story from Evansville and the Facility was dying out among speculation about future ineffectiveness of vaccines, unrest in the Middle East, and of course… local weather. Wesley continued to study coursework and in the meantime, I sketched, and no matter how terrible I thought they were, he did nothing but compliment them.

I'd draw in the mornings and evenings, spending my afternoons indoors to avoid the wrenching humidity. No doubt we had humidity in Virginia, but God, one step outside and I might as well have been drowning. After heating up some of Wesley's leftovers—miso-glazed black cod, I sat at the table, surrounded by quiet, and was missing his company as I often did in the afternoon, but in all fairness, I knew college would be like that for him. Fortunately, July was winding down, and I hoped to get a couple uninterrupted days with him before we went back to Virginia.

I pulled my phone from my pocket and dialed Sara. "Hello?" came the familiar voice on the other end.

"Hey girl!" I greeted, happy to hear from my friend.

"What's up? How's prairie life?" she teased.

"I love it out here. Don't judge."

"No, you just love who you're out there with. Oh, by the way," her voice was sing-song. "Any news for me?"

I shook my head. "No…" I answered, not understanding why she kept asking.

"Oh." She was disappointed. "I thought that's why you were calling…hmm."

"No, just calling because I miss you. I can't wait to hang out again in a couple weeks."

"Seriously!" Her voice excited once again. "Me neither! We totally need to hit up the mall!" she squealed as Wesley came around the corner in nothing but jean shorts hugging his perfectly designed waist. His hair was frazzled, his face tense.

"Hey, I'll call you later," I remarked and ended the call.

"You didn't have to get off the phone," he sighed, rubbing his head with his fingers.

"You okay?" I set my phone on the table and walked toward him.

"Yeah," he answered, his hand still pressing against his head. "Finished my last final. Just stressed out." His face was unmoving. I stood in front of him, placing my fingers firmly into his thick shoulders and massaged. He tilted his head back and groaned.

"Tell me if it hurts."

"No, it feels good," he sighed, taking my hands in his and kissing my fingers until he reached my index finger, which started the tingling throughout my body. "How do you know what I need?" he whispered after he kissed both hands.

I took his hands and placed them on my hips and kissed him, an answer he found fitting as he responded by lifting me and somehow managing to carry me up the stairs and into his room where hours drifted over our heads while we made love.

"How do you feel now?" I asked him as I rolled over and rested my arm on his chest.

He pushed my hair behind my ears. "Come to the lake with me."

I wanted to lie there next to him all day. "Why?" I whispered, tracing his chest.

"Because if you don't," he remarked as he suddenly rolled over, so his body hovered over mine, "I'm going to do this... again." His hand ran over my ribs and I shivered.

"And that would be terrible," I added.

"Very." His warm lips met mine and I answered by returning his kiss with a deeper one. Before I could do more, he pushed off the bed. "So, we should go," he added disappearing into the bathroom.

The shower turned on. It was silly to clean up before going to the lake. Regardless, I put one of Wesley's spicy smelling t-shirts on and went to my room to grab a bikini. I picked a neon pink one that I found uncomfortable, as far as where it landed on my waist, but loved how much the top boosted my breasts. When I returned to his room, he was out of the shower, nothing but a towel separating me from his perfect body. He noticed me blushing as I walked to the bathroom. I showered, dressed in the bikini, and pulled a white sundress over it. I clipped my hair in a messy bun and opened the door to Wesley's room.

"Ready?" he asked as he finished gathering some towels and sunscreen.

We drove to the lake, which wasn't far from his house, and pulled into a spot at the same area Alana had called 'the beach'. It was lined with sand that I found coarser than the sand at the ocean, but the view was still gorgeous. The beach faced a dam and was sectioned off by a yellow line that formed a semi-circle, and out farther than those, were buoys. Occasionally, a sailboat or small motor boat would pass by and cause waves in the lake.

Wesley and I strolled to the sand and picked a spot. We laid our towels down and I bent to sit. "Hey, c'mon," he held out his hand.

"You know I don't actually go in the water," I reminded him, unsure how he'd forget.

Wesley pulled his shirt off and to the side of us, a couple girls were already checking him out, but he was only looking at me. He held his hand out. "You're with me. You're safe," he answered genuinely. I hesitated for a moment before pulling my cover-up off. "Damn," Wesley muttered.

I self-consciously checked the bikini, making sure nothing was exposed. "What is it?"

"You're just fucking hot," he responded, to my relief.

I took his hand and we treaded lightly on the hot sand until we arrived at the water. Lakes didn't have a lot of waves, but I was certain there'd still be an undertow. My stomach jumped to my throat, "Wes, I—" I didn't have time to pull back. He scooped me up and I squealed, surprised.

"Trust me," he insisted and pressed me up against his strong body. God, I wanted to believe him. He walked farther out until the water was just at his ribs. "Ready?" he asked.

"No," I answered.

"Hold onto me." He lowered me into the water, wrapping my legs around his body as he did. The way my chin rested on his neck, his arms around my waist, his unending eyes staring back at mine, everything about being that close to Wesley screamed safe. The water lapped against our bodies and everyone vanished as our lips met. "I won't let you fall," he promised.

They met again and when they parted I told him, "I know."

"Want to go back?" he whispered. I nodded as he picked me back up and walked until the water stopped at his knees. He put me down. "I think you're safe here."

I bat my eyes and fanned myself. "If anything happens, will you rescue me?" I mocked.

He answered by splashing me. I splashed him back; the water hitting us both and spattering hard against the surface of the lake. I ran to the shore as I continued splashing him and he chased me until we reached the towels. My stomach was sore from laughing and eyes watered from being splashed. I grabbed a towel and wiped them, offering it to Wesley when I was finished. He took it and wiped sand off my face.

"Hey! Guys!" a voice shouted as it neared us. It was Alana.

I waved at her as Connor came running behind her. I giggled because it seemed like she was always a few steps ahead, everywhere they went. "Hi!" I greeted.

Wesley quickly began scanning the beach for Tiffani and Dalton. Alana noticed this. "Yes, they're here."

Connor made his way to us. "Hey guys, didn't know you'd be here today," he remarked.

"Umm, since you're here," Alana looked at Wesley. "There's someone you need to talk to," she finished cautiously.

I looked up. Dalton approached us. Wes walked toward him, and I couldn't hear what they were saying. I considered listening in, remotely, but fought the urge. Relief washed over me when they high-fived.

Connor glanced my way. "They've been friends too long to lose it over you. We were all watching you and Wes..." he took a deep breath before finishing. "We've never seen him like that." He paused as Wesley made his way back to us. Connor glanced at him. "Everything okay, man?"

Wesley shrugged. "Yeah, sort of." We all watched as Dalton started for his truck. I should've talked to him, but what could I possibly say? I messed up, big time.

Alana and Connor hung out with us the rest of the day and that evening, we stopped at a local Chinese buffet where I learned of a unique variation of Cashew Chicken. It was basically fried chicken over rice with gravy, cashews, and onions, but it was amazing. Just another thing I'd miss going back East.

He hadn't driven far when he slowed down and pulled over. "What are we doing?" I asked looking out the window where a roadside stand sat, surrounded by shelves. They were filled with crafts and what looked like baked goods.

"It's a Mennonite stand. Everything's homemade; it's amazing. Come on, you'll see," he said as he popped his door open and got out. I followed, and we made our way to the stand.

I smiled at a couple of the ladies. "Hey!" I greeted.

They both returned my expression and nodded as I browsed loaves of fresh baked bread. Wesley had picked up some jars of jam. I went behind the stand and over to the shelves of crafts. A younger girl was leaning against a tree, holding a pen and paper. Every so often, she'd look up and then down. Her dark hair was in braids and pushed behind her back, but when the breeze came through, she'd fight with a few loose pieces that threatened to get in her eyes.

Just sit and draw, Emma, that'll keep you from trouble. Focus on the rich white clouds; anything to keep Mama and Pa from finding out about you.

Her unsure voice flowed to me. *Emma?* I asked.

She looked up sharply from her paper. *You hear me?* She glanced over at the older women who were busy answering some questions for Wesley. *How can you hear me?*

I smiled at her. *Because I'm like you,* I explained. *But if you don't want attention, you better keep drawing and I'll continue to browse.*

I'm evil. This is magic, and magic is a thing of the devil; it's a sin. I'm going to Hell.

It's not like that at all. I glanced at her, reassuringly. *You were born with this. It's nothing you had a choice in, and I'd venture to guess at least one of your parents can also do this.*

I wouldn't know, she answered. *They passed away when I was a baby.*

That sounded familiar. *You're not alone. Just know that, and you're not going to hell either. Don't believe is for one second.* She looked up briefly and smiled. A single tear appeared and ran down her cheek and she wiped it away. I pushed my energy into her, I wanted a better sense of how she felt. *Never be ashamed of who you are.*

What's your name?

Lila. And it's very nice to meet you, Emma.

Her face lightened. Relief spread through her small body and I felt strong arms around mine. "You ready?" he whispered in my ear.

"Yes, let's go," I replied. And then I looked at Emma. "Bye," I said in a low voice.

"Bye." returned her timid one.

Wesley and I headed back to his truck and when we were both in he asked, "What was that about?"

I pressed my lips together. "Emma, that little girl, is telepathic. She thought it was dark magic and that she was going to Hell." I shook my head. "I reassured her that this is occurring naturally. It's not a choice." My voice grew heated. "It's not like we wake up one day and decide to ourselves, 'Hmm, I think I'll be a telekinetic today.' Why should we have to feel so alienated and confused about who we are?"

"Whoa," he held a hand up. "Off the soap box. That sucks she has no one to talk to, but at least she ran into you. I don't think the world's ready to be told about this."

"So we have to hide and have people believing we're evil. It's not fair." I was beginning to calm down.

"It starts small. Like what you did with Emma... baby steps. Maybe we'll see change within our lifetime," he remarked, taking one of my hands in his and causing a thick current of electricity to weave its way to the bottoms of my feet.

I yawned and leaned my head against his arm. "I'm tired."

"Rest up," he laughed. "Tomorrow's going to be a busy day."

"How so?"

"You wanted to see Mom. She's in Springfield and just a little bit south of there is Branson. I want to take you down there. We can go eat and then maybe go to a few of the 'tourist traps'," he chuckled.

"Okay." We rode the rest of the way home in silence. I thought about Emma and how this part of evolution didn't discriminate based on gender, ethnicity, religion... my mind turned to Peter, even sexuality. So why should we face discrimination if we were honest with people about what we could do?

I'd eaten too much cashew chicken; it turned in my stomach. I had to think about something different. Branson sounded fun, but meeting Wesley's mom, while something I wanted to do, was unnerving at best. His mind was spinning, also; I could feel it, the product of the connection we shared was all thanks to some warped idea propagated by Fate. He felt my nerves, as well.

"You don't have to see her," he started.

"I don't have to. it's what I *need* to do. I want to talk to her," I explained, much to his disapproval.

He brought it up one more time, that night, when he met me in his room, with a bottle of beer and a frown. "I still don't like it."

I shrugged. "You don't have to like it."

His jaw tightened as he moved toward me. "I don't."

It was fascinating how we could fall asleep in the midst of tension and awaken in the middle of the night, me in his arms, or his head on my chest. I opened my eyes, my nerves still grinding inside. I combed through his hair, it was soft on my fingertips. He groaned quietly and yawned before looking up at me.

He smiled sleepily and whispered, "Hey."

"Hey, yourself."

He stretched and kissed me before taking me in his arms. Immediately, I fell back asleep and when I woke again, it was morning.

I was up before Wesley, who was probably in no hurry to get going, so I took a shower. When finished, I thumbed through my clothing, which, needless-to-say, had migrated slowly, but surely, to Wesley's room.

I jumped when his voice came from behind me. He held up a strapless dress with a floral top and black skirt, trimmed in lace. "I think you should wear this."

I took it, giving him a sarcastic smile. "Alright," I said.

He tossed it on his bed and added, "It looks better right there, though."

I narrowed my eyes. "Then what should I wear?"

He neared me, a towel separating his bare chest from my body. He sighed and pulled the top of the it apart and as it dropped to the floor, he took the back of my head in his hands, combing his fingers into my hair and pushing my mouth to his. "This," he answered in a tone so low it was barely audible.

Not breaking the stare, I reached behind me and grabbed the dress. "I think you're trying to charm me into not going."

"Is it working?" he whispered in my ear.

"No," I stated, still smiling, but turning sharply and hurrying to the bathroom because, truthfully it was working, and I had to get away. I dressed and opened the door back up, walking over to my hairdryer and line of hairsprays and brushes that overtook the top of his once empty dresser.

"You always wear it up."

"So?" I plugged the hairdryer into the wall and started combing through wet tangles.

Wesley came up behind me, gently taking the brush out of my hand and leaning into my ear, combing through my hair softly. "The first day of school, I wanted to skip— to grab a drink and stay home, to start college, like retaking high school courses wasn't enough, I had online classes to keep up with as well. The last thing I wanted to do was keep an eye on you. Spanish was the first class of the day... you walked in, your hair long and curly, still wet. Your eyes shimmered, and a plain tank top with shorts never looked so good. Keeping an eye on *you*, wasn't such a chore. It was more difficult to keep them off you. I should've approached you sooner."

"Why didn't you?" I let him keep brushing through my hair.

"I finally did, and look what happened," he responded. "Wear it down." He set the brush down and gathered clothes to take before disappearing into the bathroom.

Not one to take direction from most people, especially a guy, I thought strongly about pinning it up, but Wesley was right, I always shoved it straight into a messy bun. When it was finally untangled, I scrunched it, sprayed it with sea salt, and spread a little mousse through my roots to give it volume.

With my face already bronzed from the sun, I only bothered to add a little bit of makeup to even the tone, and, of course, mascara. Unsure of how much walking we'd do, I went for light brown, flat sandals, and finished my look with a silver necklace and the charm bracelet.

I waited, pacing in anticipation, not bothering to eat breakfast because my nerves eliminated any inkling of hunger. When Wesley came out of the bathroom, he was dressed in black dress pants and a gray shirt, his hair gelled.

I eyed his look for a while. "I feel underdressed," I finally concluded.

He shook his head. "You're not. I'll meet you downstairs. I just have to get a couple things."

Not thinking anything of it, I headed downstairs and waited for him in the foyer. It wasn't long at all before he came down and we headed for the car. He backed out and started down the rough driveway.

"I still don't get it." He was talking about his mom.

I put my hand on top of his free one. "It'll be okay. We won't be long. It'll be good for you to see her."

"I don't want to see her. This was your idea." He tensed up.

Determined not to start a fight on a potentially nice day, I sat back. The trees waved us down the gravel road and onto the highway.

After a while, Wesley spoke up. "This is highway 54, going east. It'll take us to Bolivar and on to Branson."

"I've heard of Branson; I think my grandparents visited it."

"It's changed a lot. I wanted to take you to eat there and then I have something special planned. I hope you enjoy it."

I smiled, because truthfully, I enjoyed anything I did with Wesley. "I'll love it."

He seemed to be more at ease. What had he been so uptight about? Visiting his mom? Maybe pushing him to see his her was wrong. He was acting like his old self, and with Sullivan dead and no other threats, there was no reason to stress. I didn't feel too guilty, though. I hoped seeing her again would give me some closure. I needed to erase some of the pain and hurt.

We came to an intersection, eventually, and Wesley turned right onto Highway 13.

"Only twenty minutes or so and we'll be there. Are you sure you want to do this?"

"Wes, I understand how uncomfortable it's making you. I can tell from how you're acting, but this is something I have to do. I want her to know I'm not angry, I'm not a threat... that I love you."

He sighed and shook his head. "Just be careful. Promise me that?"

"Promise."

After a while longer we pulled off the highway and down a few side roads until we came to a parking lot that sat in front of a brick building, 'Bolivar Regional Mental Health Center'. We saw a sign for In-Patient Services and he pulled closer to that end of the establishment.

He parked, and we got out. I slipped my hand into his as we approached the building. "I can feel you're nervous." He stopped walking and faced me.

"Of course I am," I confirmed. "But I have to do it, Wes."

"I know." His lips were light as they grazed my cheek. I ran my hand down his arm before we started walking again. He pushed a green button and the door buzzed open.

"Who are ya here to see?" asked a middle-aged woman at the desk.

"Turner, Anne Turner," Wesley answered.

"Come on through," she responded as another set of doors buzzed open to reveal a lounge area with couches, a television, and fireplace. "A nurse'll be right with you."

We walked through the doors and stood in the hall. The entire place smelled like soup. After a few uncomfortable minutes, an attendant met us at the front. He was young and lanky. "She's in her room. Follow me." He started down the main aisle and turned left at a corridor. Once we reached the end, he told us, "She's stable, again, and has been for a couple days. If you need anything, there's a red button by the door you can press for immediate assistance."

"Thanks," Wesley muttered, and the man nodded and walked away.

"Wes?" I started.

"I'm not going in there." He was short and refused to even look through the window.

I sighed and pushed the door open. When I entered, I'd never have known she was a patient. Her hair was in a neat pony-tail and she wore capris and a t-shirt. I even detected a hint of blush and mascara as she turned from the window and faced me.

"Look at you...guess you got out after all." Her monotonous tone was the ticking of the plain clock resting on the wall.

Annoyed with the indifference in her voice, I replied, "Of course, did you think I couldn't?"

She shrugged. "I suppose Wes brought ya here." She shook her head and leaned against the wall, crossing her arms.

"Yes. I asked him to. I needed to let you know I forgive you and that I love Wesley, and that we—" Everything poured from my mouth before I could stop it.

"Forgive me?" she interrupted. "You should thank me. I got ya away from him."

"I want to be with him. I know I've only known him a short time, but I love him," I admitted.

The unforgiving pause before her response lent itself to her continued scrutiny of what I was telling her. "Maybe so, but why'd ya want to put him through all that?" She beaded her eyes and pursed her lips. "What do you think you'll do? Date him forever?" She fanned her hand. "Eventually you'll get married...then what?" she scoffed. "Children?"

"Well...I d-don't know..." I stuttered, feeling totally cornered between the cold walls and her challenging expression.

"Of course you don't know!" she shouted unexpectedly. I jumped. My reaction amused her. She cackled like one of those witch characters in a scary movie, but it wasn't a film. It was real, and I was terrified. "Why would you do that to my son? Force him to live a life on the run. Then you have a child. Do you want to put a baby through what you and Wesley went through?" she sneered.

"Sullivan's dead!" I shouted, getting annoyed. I wasn't hearing what she had to say. Sullivan was gone and the FDRA along with him. There was no one left to come after us.

"Honey." She moved closer to me, her eyes bullets that shot themselves into my own. Her gravy breath crept up my nose as she whispered, "There'll always be a Sullivan. It's only been a couple months since your escape. Does it feel like your first trip out here?" she hummed, "Everything a little too quiet? Lila, honey, you have the ability to destroy the world. That's not something that's gonna slip through the cracks."

"I don't b-believe you," I stammered. I was on the verge of having what I wanted— Wesley and I wouldn't allow myself to admit how much danger I could put him in if she was correct. If there really was someone else that knew about the abilities, or me, then they'd never stop.

What if we stayed together? My mind dreamed up a little girl with Wesley's shining ocean eyes and my tangled mess of hair, just a smidge lighter than my own. What kind of abilities would she have? What would she be capable of and who would find out? Would we have to give her up to kind strangers to ensure her safety? My heart sped.

"You're doubting yourself, because even you know how your life's gonna be. Do you love Wesley?" I nodded. "Then don't put him through that. He's smart, handsome, he could have a good life, have a family, live in a house in suburbia with a minivan and a dog. He can have everything you can't. Don't take that away from my son," she warned as she walked over to the wall and crossed her arms again.

A tear formed in my eyes as they grew warm and I fought it away as I turned and buzzed myself out of the room. She was wrong, totally wrong. Sullivan was gone. *Gone.* No one would have to run again. Wesley and I could be together, happy, living in some cookie-cutter home, like normal people. Quiet, normal people, working nine to five, raising a couple kids, or having a dog.

I walked down the hall and wasn't watching where I was going when I bumped into a hard body. "Wesley," I sighed.

He put his hands on my arms. "What? What's wrong, Lila?"

She was right, everything she said. My eyes hit Wesley's. It was all true. We couldn't have any type of life together. It was all the other Sullivans who wouldn't give up, and we'd be on the run, always. If I let him go, he could be happy, and that was what I wanted for him.

I couldn't tell him there. "Nothing," I lied. "She just wasn't very nice," I continued the story.

"Figures," he shrugged, giving me one of those hugs where my face rested perfectly on his shoulders and I could take in the spicy-citrus fibers imbued in his shirt.

Instead of pulling away, he kept his arms around me and pulled me closer. I died a little when his lips met mine and tried to imagine not feeling that every day. Like life would punish me for something I couldn't help, an ability I was born with. How could we be bound by Fate? Where was she? It was all lies, pitiless lies that tore what was left of my heart into pieces.

We exited the building in silence and he kissed me again as he opened the door and I got in the truck. He backed out of the lot and eventually we were on the highway.

I'd have to tell him, eventually, the reasons we couldn't be together. The white flash of his teeth behind his boyish grin, the way words twirled between his lips, his super-model fresh scent would talk me out of it again and again. He wasn't going to agree as easily as I did because he wouldn't see what he'd miss if we were together. If I couldn't have a life, then what I wanted more than anything was for him to have one.

"Lila, talk to me. What did she say?" He glanced at me

"I told you, nothing. Well, at least nothing I want to talk about right now." It just wasn't the time.

"Did she threaten you?" His face was stern.

"No, not exactly. She warned me," I finally admitted.

"About?" he fished for more information.

"Nothing, Wes," I sighed and studied the rocky cliffs racing by the window.

"Remember, she's in there for a reason. Don't put too much weight into what she says."

Wes was right. Maybe the future wasn't as grim as she predicted, but how could I be sure? It did seem odd that they'd put so much effort into finding me just to give up after I destroyed the Facility; but, then again, maybe I sent a clear message that capturing me was impossible.

It didn't seem like very long until we came to Branson city limits. My thoughts were lost amid the attractions and shows. People played mini-golf and I read the names of storefronts boasting beef jerky and discount tourist tickets.

"Damn!" I jumped at Wesley's exclamation.

"What's wrong?" My stomach unlaced as I looked around, afraid that perhaps he saw someone odd following us.

"Hold on, I think I got a little lost."

"Really?" I sighed.

"What? I don't know everything." He shook his head and switched lanes.

"You don't say." I raised my eyebrows.

"What's that supposed to mean?" A confused expression came over his face.

"Never mind," I laughed, temporarily forgetting the conversation with his mom.

He backed out of an empty parking lot and turned around and before I knew it, we were pulling into a resort. "I made dinner reservations for later, but in the meantime, I thought you'd enjoy this..."

I looked up at the large replica. "Oh my God! Wesley, that's the *Titanic*." From the car window, I was facing the bow of the gigantic ship, a near perfect imitation— at least from the black and white pictures and the movie with Kate and Leo.

He grinned, "It's a museum. But they restored the grand staircase and made it accessible. I hoped you'd enjoy it."

"Oh! More than the movie, even! Wes, this is amazing." I couldn't believe he'd think to bring me here, but then again, I kind of could believe it, since I did admit to being an enthusiast. As we made our way onto the ship, a staff member handed us a boarding pass. "This is incredible, Wes!"

"The tour is mostly interactive, but I may have pulled strings and arranged for our own private guide," he revealed as he ran a hand through his hair.

A man dressed like a crew member approached. He was tall and thin with long silver hair pulled back into a pony tail. "Hello, Sir, Madam. My name is Paul and I'll be your guide aboard the *RMS Titanic* this afternoon. Feel free to ask me anything you'd like."

I gave Wesley a hug. Having been interested in the *Titanic* since I was young, getting to board a replica was one of the most fantastic things I'd ever done. We held hands as he walked us through a main room and I turned to give Wesley another big hug as he beamed in response.

As quickly as 'forever' seemed to go away, it began to come back. It wasn't as though he'd proposed. We could take it one day at a time, until he got tired of being on the run or tired of me.

Wesley turned as a hand tapped his shoulder. "Sir, there's been a billing issue."

"Oh? Strange." He looked at me. "I'll get this straightened out."

"We can wait here, right, Paul?" My stomach kind of sank.

"No, it's okay. Start the tour and I'll catch up," Wesley nodded in reassurance and walked off with the staff member.

It seemed odd, but stuff happens. He probably typed in a wrong card expiration date or something. I shrugged as Paul distracted me by pointing to a closed door in front of us.

"This way to the staircase, ma'am." He opened it and I stood at the bottom of an ornate wooden staircase and suddenly, I was in the movie. I wanted to squeal in excitement but held myself back thinking the reaction would be completely inappropriate.

"Paul, this is gorgeous!" I exclaimed, grinning at him.

"You can walk up the steps." He motioned toward the beautiful staircase with its shiny banister and iron detailing swirled between the rails. I looked at him to double check, in disbelief that I was about to ascend the iconic staircase. "Go on, go ahead," he urged.

I felt strange; there were some onlookers standing around. None of them were walking up the stairs. *Oh well, their loss*, I thought, as I took the first step. I stared at the clock at the top of the stairs, feeling a little empty doing so without Wesley escorting me.

Regardless, I continued, and as I made my way to the top, Wesley stepped down a couple stairs on the side. I'd never seen him like that, his expression somewhere between frightened out of his mind, and happy.

"I'm—" he interrupted me before I could tell him I was glad he made it back. He took both my hands. What was happening? A lady at the bottom, gasped.

"Lila Jeanette Daniels, when I see the rest of my life, I see you." His eyes shone in the elegant lighting. "And all I want is to make you happy. I know we're young, but I promised you 'forever'..." His hands shook as he struggled to pull a small black box from his pocket. He dropped to one knee. "M-marry me?"

The chilling blue in his eyes hurtled at mine and I wanted to say 'yes' more than anything as I stared at the two-toned, glittering ring. "Wesley...I..." Time stopped, and my heart sank into an ocean of uncertainty. His mom's warning rang through my head and as it did, all the late-night conversations in bed, strawberried moments in the field, the day at the lake, the possibilities of a little girl with dirty-blonde hair and chilling eyes drifted until I could no longer reach them.

"Say 'yes', Lila. I love you," he smiled, his eyes glistening, hands still shaking.

"I'm—" I glanced at the faces of everyone watching as the floor swayed until I couldn't. I ran down the stairs, nearly tripping on the bottom one, and quickly got off the ship. I kept going until I saw his truck. I leaned against it, hiding my head and my tears.

A hand touched my shoulder and I jumped. "Wesley... I...I just can't—"

"Why? Why now? Every time we talked..." he interrupted.

"Things changed, Wes. Your mom—"

"Oh, so *now* you're going to listen to my mother?" His face tightened.

"You should, too. She's right. She's right about everything, Wes. What kind of life would you have? Always on the run with me."

"We'll figure it out! Jesus, Lila...please." His cheeks were red.

"I—" I wanted to explain more, but he interrupted.

"I don't want to hear it. Get in." He sulked, walking over to his side of the truck and opening the door. I got in, as well.

"Wes, listen, please—"

"You listen...look at Delilah and Ashley. She said 'no' and ended up dead. He ended up raising her child. I had all year to talk to you. Don't you get it? I wasn't just keeping an eye on you...I fell in love with you. I did nothing about it, and the day I did, your parents were murdered. What will Fate do now that you said 'no'?" Anger shot from his face as his jaw tightened.

"So now you're fear mongering me?" He was unbelievable.

"No. Nothing like that. I'm telling you how things went down."

"It's not true, Wesley. I'm allowed to make my own choices. I'm not ready to be engaged, I'm eighteen," I contended. Though, it was a lie. That even though I realized eighteen was young, I didn't care. He was everything I wanted.

I thought through the past few weeks, a time when I would've said yes. Before I talked to his mom and considered the grim outcomes. He didn't say anything; the tension grew on his face.

"Don't do this, Wes. Don't close up." I reached my hand to touch his, but he pulled it back.

He shook his head, the same rigid expression on his face. "This was a mistake."

"No..."

"It was all a mistake. I was done with all this back in Fredericksburg. It was you all who showed up at my house. I'm not doing this again, Lila." He laid his head against the steering wheel.

"Wes—"

He didn't look up. "Just don't," he requested.

Silence.

I was angry, too. Irate, that he was thinking bad things would happen if we weren't together; pissed that he would use that to corner me into a decision. He was as much at fault as me, but I'm talking about Wesley Turner; he'd be stubborn before he'd admit to being wrong, especially when he was hurt. I could feel his pain. He put himself out there and I refused the gesture.

Since we'd known one another, I lied to him and rejected him time after time. Honestly, I was scared. We were both young, my world had basically been torn apart, we were different from everyone else, and I knew how fast everything could change. The doubt and uncertainty clouded the desire to be with Wesley. It had from the beginning. It was like each time we got close, I put up a wall, gave him some reason to step away from me. It wasn't as though I didn't love him, it stemmed from the hate for myself—who I was and what happened because of it. As much as he didn't think he deserved me, I didn't believe I deserved him. At least, not if I couldn't forgive myself, because it was only through that forgiveness that I could genuinely be in love with him. It was the only way I could stop hurting him.

I never felt so lost. Out of all the times we argued, even after I killed Linda, he'd forgiven me, somehow. I wondered if I could sneak in his head, though it would probably be a bad idea. His eyes were focused straight ahead, so I gently pushed. He didn't move, and I was able to graze the surface of his thoughts—anger. I slipped in a little further, past the sheer rage. My body was filled with more hurt and fear than I could've imagined.

"You haven't done enough," he said steadily as energy was thrust back at me hard enough to push me against the seat.

"Wes, I just—"

"It's not enough you invest so much in what my mom, of all people says, you use it as an excuse to tell me 'no'," his voice was unusually calm. "I get the whole 'being young' thing. It's not like I planned to get married in a year. Proposing is something I wanted to do, after all I told you about loving you, and only you, Lila...it was the only way I could think to *show* you."

"We should—" Again, he interrupted before I could finish.

"There's not a 'we'. Since I saw you, the first day I started at that high school, *you* were who I thought about when I went home at night. Not the cheerleading skirts, not the crop tops, not the girls flirting and talking to me...Sure, they were hot, but it wasn't about any of them. It was you and something about you so inexplicable, no matter how many crazy words I knew, you didn't fit any of them. I'd think about talking to you, asking you on a date, but I didn't want you to end up as another one night stand. I couldn't do that to you, and I convinced myself I didn't deserve you because I was just another 'player' and you were too good for that.

Now that I've gotten to know you, I realize I was wrong. I opened up to you, and you lied to my face. I was honest about my feelings and you lied about yours. Every single time I try to get close to you and show you how much you mean to me, you lie. You were either lying when you told me you wanted me forever, or you're lying right now. And I realize one thing— I don't care either way. There's obviously something going on with you that you don't trust me enough to talk about or have enough faith that I'll help you get through it. No more, Lila."

He said it all. I had no comeback, no excuse. He never raised his voice and what he said was true. I didn't know if he was hoping I'd talk or if he was glad I didn't. The pieces of me that'd began to heal started to shred once more. My eyes were hot, and I fought to not sniffle when my nose started to run. I refused to let him see how bad the truth had hurt. How devastating the thought that I'd actually lost him that time was; the reality of it—a nail pounding into my gut while I struggled not to throw up and kept my focus on the road ahead.

WESLEY

I had nothing to say. I was a dumbass for not ditching her in Fredericksburg, but the attraction was too strong, or I was too weak. I couldn't tell her 'no', but she, apparently, had no problem saying it to me. No other option existed— I had to make myself leave and not look back.

I needed to take off, get out of Missouri, get to college. My foot remained heavy on the gas pedal as I made the quickest trip from Branson to El Dorado ever known.

I pulled up to the house and put the truck in park. I didn't move. I looked away from her as though, in less than a glimpse, she could ensnare my emotions, pull me back in with a simple glance from those striking green eyes. I couldn't talk to her or let her speak. I had to avoid anything that would draw me back to her.

She opened the door and stepped out, slamming it behind her. As soon as she moved a couple steps back, I peeled out. *Get out of here. Get as far away from her as you can. But where?*

I pulled into the lit parking lot of Tornado's and opened the door. Garth Brooks soared through the speakers singing some sappy, slow song. I couldn't get to the alcohol soon enough. I made my way to the bar.

"What can I get for ya tonight, Wes?"

"Hey Ben," I nodded. "Make me a Seven-Seven and I need more *Seven* than Seven," I requested.

"Rough day?" He eyed me over. "You look good. Why you all cleaned up?" He smiled. "Is it that lady-friend you were tellin' me all about?"

"Long story," I answered as he poured the whiskey in a glass and 7-Up over it.

"I'm here all night." He tossed a rag in the sink below the bar. "I know you, get a few a' these in ya and you'll pour out your heart." He chuckled, "What about what's-her-name? Did y'all get back together and break up again?"

"What's-her-name is called Tiffani," came a soft voice from behind. I sighed. My place of refuge was infiltrated by a pair of tan cowboy boots and a sundress.

"Oh...my bad." I chuckled as Ben held his hands up sarcastically and Tiff rolled her eyes in annoyance.

"No, this isn't about her. It's someone else...it *was* someone else," I admitted.

"Oh, did you finally tire of her?" She tried to sound sorry but failed.

"Knock it off, Tiff," I groaned. "Ben, get her a drink...on me, whatever she wants." I looked at her and pat the seat next to me. Surprisingly, she sat, and I wasn't sure why, but it made me feel a little better.

She ordered some type of cocktail and looked at me while Ben mixed it for her. "Wanna tell me about it?" Her painted nails touched my shoulder and I shrugged her off.

"Maybe in a few drinks?" It'd only take a couple and she wouldn't be able to talk clear enough to ask anything.

She shrugged. "Hey Benny-boy. We all know Wes is gonna get hammered and spill, so can we hurry the process along? Get us a couple a' shots...how about Three Wisemen?"

Ben's eyes widened as Johnnie, Jack, and Jim swirled inside double-shot glasses. "Stuff's going to hit ya hard," he warned.

I didn't care, anything to forget about Lila, her body against mine, her clothes on my floor. Ben put the shots on the counter and I took one after another. "Two more, bud," I requested.

"'Kay, but lay off after this," Tiff demanded.

"We'll see," I took another gulp of my drink and waited for the shots. When he put them up, I took both, not offering one to her. Halfway through the Seven-Seven, the room started spinning.

"So...Wes, ready to talk?" Tiff grabbed my shoulder while Ben leaned over the counter, waiting, and she gave him an annoyed glance.

"What?" he questioned. "The way Wes is puttin' 'em down, this'll be good," he laughed. "It always is."

Tiff nodded in agreement while the counter swayed. "So, spill..."

Needless to say, I didn't care anymore. "I thought I loved her..." I started, shaking my ringing head.

"You think you love a lot of people," Tiffani scoffed. "You love them for a night. Whatever, you'll get over it," she paused. "It's not like you proposed," she added, laughing.

I worked hard to raise my head up and meet her eyes as they widened, and her jaw clanked against the top of the bar. "You *proposed?*" She nearly fell backward as she leaned away from me. "Are you insane?" she screamed.

"No..." I mumbled, "in love. Another shot?" I managed.

"Oh, my God," Ben said. "I'm making you two and one for myself," he muttered as he walked off and returned with the shots. I took one after the other.

"Wes, you've had enough," Tiff whined, resting her hand on my numb shoulder.

"You're right. I've had more than enough," I slurred, "of everything."

"Come dance with me." She tried to pull me up and I stumbled back down.

"I don't think..." I wanted to be with Lila but didn't care as the alcohol poured down my throat, she remained in the empty glass. I pushed it away. I didn't want to dance with Tiff. My connection with her amounted to sex, but, she'd never lied to me, never let me down. She was safe.

"It'll be like old times. None of this drama." She put her hands on my cheeks and pulled my head up, whispering, "You remember the old times." I caught the gleam of her candied lip gloss.

I remembered, quite vividly, but even those afternoons between the legs of Tiffani Newham weren't enough to make me forget Lila. I sighed, "Fine, if I can walk, I'll dance with ya."

She squealed and threw her arms around my neck. "Yay! Let's go."

"Have fun!" Ben called out and as I turned to nod, I caught him shaking his head and taking another shot.

I stumbled over to the small dance floor, glad the music had sped up. As it played on, it wasn't long before my only focus was on the floral sundress grinding against me as the alcohol convinced me I was a good dancer. Lights spun against the floorboards and I didn't realize another girl was behind me until it was too late, but Tiffani didn't seem to care, and I certainly didn't mind.

Maybe I'd been right all along, playing the field was better than locking it down with one person and that evening served as the perfect example. The back of her red head rested against my chest, giving me the perfect angle down the front of her shirt until after God knows how long I whispered, "Let's get outta here."

She turned. "No second chances, Wes," her voice curled with the music.

I grinned the grin that'd persuaded her into bed too many times to count. "How about a hundredth chance?" I ran my hand down the curve of her waist. Would one night with her would make me forget all about Lila?

"No, Wes," She pressed her lips together.

I poured warm breath in her ear. "T'as de beaux yeux, tu sais?"

She loosened up. "It's not working, Wes," she smiled.

I tried again. "J'ai envie de t'embrasser."

She giggled. "You know I don't un—"

She understood well enough when I turned to face her and pressed my intoxicated lips against her own, and like always, she nearly liquefied when I did.

When we finished, she whispered, "I'll get my brother to take us to my house. Parents are outta town." She turned and left the dance floor to talk to Adam.

As soon as she did, another girl took her place. I hadn't seen her before, but she turned and smiled, her curly blonde hair sweaty from dancing. "Hey there!"

I smiled and pulled her closer. "Hi," I managed while studying the tilted floor. The eyes would get her before anything else.

"Name's Carla," she whispered and grabbed my hand, pressing her tight jeans against me.

I didn't care for blondes, but in my drunken stupor, I slurred the stupidest line ever spoken in the history of Tornado's. "I've never been to heaven, but your body's angelic enough to take me there." It worked. I grinned again, the room spinning faster as she led me through the humidity and to the back of the building.

She pulled my head toward hers and soon we were kissing. I explored her curvy body and appreciated the roundness of her ass as I rested a hand on it. She wasn't afraid, rather, she seemed experienced; she knew how and where to touch. She un-tucked my shirt and started running her hands up my chest as I wasted no time kissing her neck and moving down.

"Get off him, whore!" an angry voice commanded as Tiff stomped around the corner and pulled her away from me. "Wesley Turner! I swear to God...I'm taking you back to your house. You're not coming with me!"

To my dismay, Carla took off into the bar and I moved closer to Tiffani. "C'mon Tiff, Lila's there," I pleaded. "Take me back to your place and I'll be good." I leaned into her, running my hand up her arm. "*Real* good."

She dissolved and sighed, "How do you always get me to forgive you?" She took my hand and walked me to Adam's truck.

We got in and he backed out. The cab spun so fast. I was going to puke. As fast as we left, we were at her place and exiting the truck. She led me up the sidewalk and into the house. Her lips met mine in fast, desperate kisses, and everything went black.

LILA

His tires spit gravel like curse words as he peeled out. I turned and went into the house. He wouldn't be back anytime soon. Where was he going? A part of me didn't care. I stood in the foyer until the red glow from his taillights vanished behind trees.

I sighed and walked into the kitchen. Pulling a chair from the table, I stared out the picture window into the night. I scolded myself. How would the evening have differed if I just said 'yes' to him? I would've been happy. My mom and dad would've been happy for me.

I rested my cheek against my hand and counted the feathers on a picture of a rooster hanging on the wall. I didn't think about things like how the delicate two-tone diamond ring would've looked on my finger, or if denying him was an overreaction. How good would his lips have tasted after going to dinner and eating cake for dessert? I avoided those thoughts like I avoided the notion that the truth was in front of me, that afternoon, challenging me with glittered eyes and two letters slapped it away.

"Lila." The voice made me jump, I turned and stared at a brunette, older version of myself. She stood, her forehead crinkled along with her eyebrows. Her nose flared, and her mouth was at the beginning of a smile. I knew immediately who it was. I lied to Wesley when I told him 'no' and I lied to myself when I thought the night couldn't get worse.

"Jennie," I nodded because I wasn't going to contribute to the tension by ignoring her. I got up from my chair and looked again at what seemed to be myself. Even though I hated her, I just couldn't stop staring.

"It's really you." Her soft voice was piercing.

I held my hands out to my sides. "Yep, sure is."

Her smile faded. "No denying, you have Tom's sarcasm." She paused. "Lila, I know you hate me and Tom for leaving you, but you have to give me one chance."

"Why?" I crossed my arms. A defensive posture, but what more could I do? Humor her? I couldn't. Okay. I could've. I didn't want to. What if she was right? What if Wesley was? I experienced, firsthand, the danger her and Tom were in, but somewhere, I didn't want to know they were justified in the decision to abandoned me. I wasn't ready.

"Please, *one* chance. I have something to show you." Her face tightened.

Outside had darkened, but it was still warm. I could've walked away. Just, taken off down the road and continued until exhaustion set in. I had nothing left, there. Of course—I looked out the window and into the darkness, lit only by a few stray fireflies—I had little left elsewhere. Both options suffocated me. *'You wouldn't want to spend your life in a glass jar, would you?'* Wes had asked Katie that evening in the field. The same night he asked me to move in with him. *Why not?* I told myself. *I already screwed everything up with him. What harm will this do?* "Fine," I agreed.

"Come in the living room." She turned to walk down the hall and I followed. We sat on the soft couch and all I could remember was making love to Wesley there. I gulped.

"What happened with Wesley?" Jennie gave me a concerned look that seemed genuine.

"Nothing." I turned away and fought back tears. I needed him there so badly. I thought about sending him a text but decided against it.

"Let me show you this." She held her hand out for me and I took it. When I did, a deep hole penetrated my soul. Darkness, loneliness, and almost two decades of seething pain shot through my body as scenes fast forwarded in my mind, kaleidoscopic agony, I couldn't bear.

She let go and I opened my eyes. I could breathe again, the hurt taken away with her hand. "That's how it feels to let your baby go." A tear filled her eye and I finally understood.

My mom was there, sitting in front of me. She loved me and wanted me, but she wanted me to be safe. It was everything Wesley had said, and I was too afraid to believe. Overwhelmed with it all, I burst into tears.

"Wesley..." I sobbed.

She hesitated before putting her arm around me, but I moved closer to let her know it was okay. "What about him?"

Before I could answer, Billy walked around the corner accompanied by Tom. I stared into my own bright green eyes. "Did he hurt you?" Billy asked.

I looked up at him. "No, I hurt him."

Billy didn't say anything and neither did Tom, but Jennie stroked my hair. I wanted to talk to her, just like I used to talk to Mom. I put my head back against her arm. She smelled like lavender. "He asked me if I'd marry him, and I told him 'no', but I don't think I meant it." I wiped some tears away. "I don't know what I want."

Tom looked at Billy, confused. "Wes did this?" he huffed. "The same Wesley I knew a couple years ago who went through women like socks?" Billy shrugged.

A strange silence made its way into the room, but Jennie spoke up. "Stop, guys." She looked at Tom and stroked my hair. "There's no doubt she and Wesley should be together. They'll destroy themselves without one another, but they're both young."

My stomach turned. "I have no choice," I stated softly, although it was more of a question.

"You do have a choice, but if you love him like I believe you do, do you need a choice?"

Tom and Billy stood together, awkward as men are when discussing emotions. "He's not coming back from this; he won't forgive me."

Jennie pat my shoulder. "I've known Wes his entire life." She laughed a little. "He doesn't like the word no. Let him pout in whatever way he fools himself into thinking will work. He'll be back," she reassured.

I didn't say anything just laid my head down on her lap and let her stroke my hair. For a moment, I wasn't worried about Wesley. It seemed as if everything would work out. Like he'd come back. Tom turned at a knock on the door.

Billy rolled his eyes. "Probably him right now. Bet he went down to that bar again and had to get a ride home." He looked to me. "He won't be in any shape to talk." I nodded, understanding.

Billy walked over to the door and opened it to a girl who nearly knocked him over as she ran inside and slammed it behind her. Her eyes were wild, almost crazed. She held up a gun, shaking. I recognized her immediately as I flew off the couch and Jennie jumped up.

Her hand trembled, uncontrollably. "You guys can't get into my head." The gun panned from Tom to me.

Jenny took a step forward. "Don't do this."

"Amy, leave them alone. You're after me," I coaxed.

"Nothing is happenin' to no one," Tom finally spoke up. He looked at Amy. "Put the gun down. You don't want to do this."

"You can't persuade me," she threatened.

"You're right. I can't, and I don't want to," he took another step toward her. "Who put you up to this? A man named Sullivan?"

Sullivan, the name blasted my mind. It was a grenade, my thoughts—the fallout. He wasn't dead. How? I didn't know. Didn't care. I failed, again. The opportunity I had to end everything, botched. He was a coward, sending Amy to finish a job he couldn't do.

"It's you guys or me...and since she killed my best friend, I guess the answer's obvious." She pointed the gun at me.

"You have every right to be angry. I didn't know...I didn't know any of it," I tried to explain. "I'm sorry. I know it doesn't make it right, but I am and killing me isn't going to bring Linda back."

In one tense moment, my thoughts attacked me; life can change in the matter of one breath. Hours ago, I was safe with Wesley. No doubt we'd be in the same situation with Amy, but at least we'd have been together.

Her finger pressed the trigger, harder than before. I squinted. *Bye, Wesley. I really do love you.* Nothing happened. I opened my eyes, slowly. Amy's eyes swirled with intensity and confusion, full of questions anyone would have if they were holding another person at gun point.

Her hand weakened, and she lowered the gun. Tom ran to take it from her, in case she changed her mind, again. "I know!" she screamed. "Don't you get that I know? I don't understand any of this, but if I don't kill you, Sullivan will kill me."

Billy looked from me to Jennie and finally to Amy. "They have to go. They have to get far away from here. If Sullivan thinks they're here, they shouldn't be. If they want to live, they have to get out of here." Jennie shook her head.

"No," I started. "I have to find Wesley."

Tom looked at me. "You can't right now. We can explain to him what happened, but you two can't be around."

It was everything Wesley's mom had said. Even if Sullivan wasn't after me, it'd always be someone. I looked at Amy. "You coming?"

"Do I have a choice?" she responded in defeat.

"Not if you want to live." I'd taken Wesley's role, ready to explain everything to her on the run.

She shrugged. "What are we waiting for?"

"One second," I said, taking off for the stairs.

"It'd better only be one second," Billy warned as I reached the top.

I grabbed a duffle bag and filled it with pictures I'd brought, grabbed the old book, and as many clothes as I could. When I left the room, I started for Wesley's door, needing one final look around, but changed my mind. There was no time.

When I came downstairs, Billy met me with a set of keys. "There's a car out back. It's old." I nodded before taking them from him. "I'm sure you can get a hold of a better one later," he finished.

"Head west. Don't go east," Jennie advised. "Whoever's after you would expect you to go somewhere familiar to you."

Amy headed toward the door. I started to follow, but hesitated, looking back at Jennie and Tom. I walked toward her and threw my arms around her. She hugged me back and Tom joined her. I should've cried but didn't. Couldn't. When would life make sense?

"Will I see you guys again?" I asked.

Tom rubbed my cheek with his thumb and stared deep into my eyes. "Yes," he promised.

I just met them and didn't want to leave. "Mom, Dad...I love you." I pulled away and looked at Billy whose eyes were filled with relief. "Thank you," I whispered.

He gave me a reassuring smile and nodded for me to get going. "What about Sullivan? What if he comes here?"

"We know his tricks. We'll be just fine," Tom asserted.

I nodded and turned, hesitating at the door before following Amy. We ran across the yard and behind Billy's shed. I'd seen the Ford Aspire sitting back there before and wondered why no one drove it. Amy stood by the passenger door and waited for me to unlock it. I looked for the lock button.

"Are you stupid? They're not automatic. You have to reach over and pop the lock," she rolled her eyes. I pulled the lock open on her door and she got in. "Let's go," she directed.

"Do you know where we're going?" I asked.

She shrugged. The motor strained. How long the old car would last? I pulled through the grass and onto the bumpy driveway.

"You know the tires need air," Amy remarked. "We'll have to stop soon."

"I'm not riding in this thing the entire time. These locks aren't my thing," I huffed as I pulled onto the driveway.

"What do you mean?"

I glanced at her. "I mean what I said. We're getting a new car."

"How? Steal it?" she glared at me.

"Basically," I answered.

"How do you sleep at night?" she seethed.

"My parents were killed, I didn't graduate high school because I was caught by Sullivan and forced to be his guinea pig. He's killed thousands of people like us. Now, he's coming after me again, after I thought I killed him." I kept my eyes focused. "I don't sleep at night. When I do, I have nightmares. I'll do what I have to do to keep us safe. Are you coming or not?"

She didn't say anything. She was quiet, like I was at first. "I don't get it, but I suppose I should. The guy I met, Sullivan, was a real creeper..."

"I'll explain it all later," I assured her as we passed by an old bar—Tornadoes. A shiny blue pickup was parked in the lot. I slowed down.

"What is it now?" she complained.

I didn't answer, the thought of stopping heavy on my mind. The turn signal screeched as I forced it down. I'd tell him what was going on and then he'd know. He'd realize I wasn't just running off. I was ready to turn the wheel when a tall, blond guy in a gray shirt came stumbling from around the corner, hands all over Tiffani.

Rage flooded my body. *Don't stop or things will get bad*, I told myself. I was in disbelief that I believed him when he said he loved me, incredulous that I regretted telling him 'no'. The car rumbled and the engine roared as I peeled down the highway, trying to get away from the bar as fast as possible. I was chasing regret as it snaked down the curvy lanes of the Southwestern Missouri backroads. *We'll head west.*

"What was that about?" Amy griped again. "Let me guess, you'll tell me later." She crossed her legs and folded her arms over her chest.

I pulled my phone out and dialed the only other person I could talk to. "Hello?" came the familiar voice.

"Sara," I panicked. "Are you okay?"

"Uh...not really?" her soft voice came through the speaker.

"Why? What's wrong?" I was terrified for her.

"Peter drank the last of the vodka last night... there's nothing left."

I breathed a sigh of relief. "Sullivan's not dead."

"Are you with Wesley?" she asked, suddenly concerned.

"No, it's a long story. I'm with Amy—don't ask. Just know I love you. I'll get a hold of you as soon as I can. If you hear from Wes, tell him I'm safe," I requested, hanging up the phone and tossing it out of the car window and into the trees.

"What the hell did you do?" Amy screamed.

"The same thing you need to do. Give me the phone," I urged.

"No...that's my lifeline," she argued.

"Exactly."

"Well, you're not getting it," she reiterated.

Before she could do anything, I pulled the phone from her purse. "What the—"

"Told you I'd get it anyway." The phone floated into my left hand and I tossed it out the window.

"You bitch!" she squealed again.

"You don't have to come with me. It's your life." I glanced at her and she gulped. "Literally," I added. She didn't say anything else.

I'd have to tell her everything, later—my thoughts returned to Wesley, how bad I'd felt and how enraged I'd become— much, much later.

RJ SULLIVAN

Never trust anyone to do your own work. Especially not some loud-mouthed bitch.

I sat up the road a ways, waiting for her phone call, listening for a gun shot. Nothing. *Stupid bitch.* I'd dealt with those who had abilities long enough to learn the only way to trick them out was to step out of my own mind—wait to make choices, think about nothing, picture darkness. That's what experience had taught me.

I'll kill every single fucking one of them. I allowed the motivating thought to escape before turning my mind off. Besides my gun, which I always carried, I had no plan. No speculating who I'd shoot first or what I'd do after.

I wasn't going toward a house. I wasn't walking down a road. I wasn't anywhere. I just happened to turn right and stroll up a driveway located nowhere in particular, until I came upon a door and knocked.

A brunette answered. "Li—"

I didn't give the bitch a chance to get the words out before I took my shot, nearly point-blank, to her forehead. The two men were next, one after the other. Tom, Jennie, and Billy— dead. Decades of chasing Tom and Jennie came to an end in a quick, less than satisfying second, but I couldn't give them a chance to try their tricks.

I searched the house, carefully, keeping my mind shut off as I did. I was in his room, Wesley, the blond kid who nearly took me down in Lowndes. I picked up a pink and white bra from his bed—C cup—*lucky bastard.* I contemplated, almost forgetting to keep my thoughts boarded up, but envying the guy as I took in the rubbery-sweat smell of sex that overpowered the room.

No one was in the house. They were gone. I'd have to pull them out of the woodwork. Wherever he was, I'd find Lila. I went back downstairs and outside where I discovered a shed with a jug of gasoline. I trudged it back to the house and poured it throughout, flicking a match and igniting the liquid as I closed the door behind me. I left quickly, before anyone called the fire department.

I reached my car, out of breath, opened the door, and made my way a little farther south. I'd find him, then her, his little sister, and probably that Amy bitch, too. But as a token of retaliation, I had one more stop to make—one last thing to take from Wesley Turner.

WESLEY

The sharp ring from my phone caused my head to throb harder. I reached around without opening my eyes until I found it and sent the call to voicemail. I rolled over, not caring where the hell I was. My head pounded. A warm body scooted next to me. Lila—it wasn't Lila.

I moved closer and pulled her to me. She moaned and whispered, "This is unexpected." Her voice weighed on my ear. She wasn't Lila, but I was too tired to move. I didn't say anything, just tried to go back to sleep.

My phone buzzed again, jarring me awake. "Shit," I complained, dismissing the caller. I sat up and opened my eyes slowly, the severity of my hangover telling me it'd been too long since I'd been that drunk.

"Where ya goin', Wes?" her voice cracked.

"Water," was all I could manage. If I forced myself to drink enough, the pounding in my head would dissipate. I squinted and fished around for boxers until I found them and slipped them on. The walls slanted as I made my way to the kitchen.

I grabbed a glass from the counter and ran cold water in the sink, filling it while a pair of slender hands ran themselves around my weak stomach. "You know," she whispered, "we have bottled water in the fridge. The stuff from the sink's crap."

I stepped to the side and continued drinking. "This is fine," I replied, her smile faded when I moved away from her. I wanted to tell her it wasn't anything against her. She was perfect, standing in front of me in a black tank top and underwear—gorgeous, the type of girl who could walk into a gas station with her hair pulled up, wearing sweats and a hoodie and every guy in the place would want her.

I ran my free hand through my hair, fighting to ignore the gurgle in my stomach as the cool water shocked it. I held back waves of nausea. Only a fool would believe he could make amends to a girl like Lila after what I'd done the night before. What would I say?

'I got shitfaced because I was pissed you said 'no' to me so I made out with a strange girl and had drunk sex with my ex. Sorry...' Yeah, that'd work. What else? Flowers? Candy? How does one apologize to the person he loved for revenge fucking someone else? I pressed my temples to keep my head from throbbing.

"You're thinking about her, aren't you?" Tiff asked. Her voice still resonated with the same sexy cracking sound.

I didn't want to lie. "Yeah."

She shook her head, turned, and walked down the hall and into her bedroom. I poured another glass of water, determined to make myself keep drinking it.

"Wes!" she hollered. I set my glass down and went to see what she wanted. When I reached the doorway, she was holding my phone and scrolling. "Your phone's blowing up."

Hoping it was Lila, I walked to Tiff and took it from her hand. The screen displayed several missed calls and a couple voicemails from a number I didn't recognize. Just as I was getting ready to play a message, the phone vibrated and lit up. I accepted the call.

"Wesley Turner?" A man's voice boomed from the other end.

"Yeah..." I answered, hesitating.

"This is Sheriff Mitchell with the Cedar County Sheriff's Department. Drive careful, but get home as soon as you can," the serious voice commanded through the speaker.

"Okay," was all I said and ended the call. My heart dropped. Suddenly, the walls stopped tilting and I looked at Tiff as I started pulling on my clothes. My first thoughts were Katie and Lila. Had something happened to them? Why I was getting a call from the Sheriff and not my dad? I shook off all the possibilities, so I could focus on getting home.

"What's going on?" She looked concerned.

"I need a ride to my truck." I pulled my socks and shoes on.

"Umm, sure…is everything okay?" She started to get dressed as well and was twisting her hair up. "It's Lila, isn't it? She called you?"

"No," I answered, irritated. "I don't know," I muttered, grabbing my wallet and picking my phone back up.

"I'll come with," she offered, but I shook my head, indicating I didn't want her too.

She slipped on sandals and grabbed her purse and keys. We headed to her car and I got in. The ride to the bar was a silence that indicated it'd be our last time together. We both recognized it and knew it. The realization wasn't bittersweet, there was no loss or regret, just finality that acted as relief.

She pulled up next to my truck and I looked at the glossy-eyed redhead sitting next to me. Somewhere between the on and offs, my encounters with other girls, her threats to never take me back again, and the nights she did, she'd become a woman. I'd failed to notice that as I studied her green-blue eyes. "Tiff…"

"Wesley, it's okay. I'm okay," her smile was hazy at best. "We're okay."

I breathed deep and reached across the car and hugged her, pulling back slowly and looking in her eyes one last time. "Thanks," I said as I opened the door and got out.

She didn't pull away immediately, but when I got in my truck, she waved before backing out and turning toward her house. I went the opposite direction and sped up when I got off the gravel. I fought to not speculate about what I'd find when I arrived home. Perhaps, I was having another nightmare. Soon I'd wake up.

I took the curves faster than I should've, swerving out of my lane a couple times. Once, an oncoming car honked and I pulled back across the yellow lines. The closer to home I came, the harder and quicker my heart thumped. I pushed the nausea and dizziness away.

I turned up the drive and stopped the truck. Passed emergency vehicles, flashing lights, and the few neighbors standing around, a burnt frame took the place of where my house once stood. For a second, I froze. The gravel pulled my shoes into it and held them in place. When I did move, I ran. I took off as fast as I could. "Katie! Lila!" I yelled.

A short, middle-aged man stepped in front of me. "Wesley Turner?" He pressed his lips together.

"Yeah." I blinked. "What's going on?" I blinked again. The answer was obvious; my house had burned down. "Katie?" my voice grew louder, another hard blink.

"We have no reason to believe she was in the home at the time of the incident. We're trying to locate her," he informed me.

A small weight lifted. "Was *anyone* in the house?" Maybe Dad went out or Lila had left to find me, any excuse for them to not have been in the home when it caught on fire.

"Our team found one female, two males," he explained.

"Dad, Lila..."

"I'm sorry, son. One was your Dad. We're working to identify the other two; no luck yet."

Words went as far as my throat and fell apart before they made it out of my mouth.

"We're working on it, though. So far, the coroner is putting the other two in their late forties," he explained.

Was it possible that Tom and Jennie had returned? Could it have been them and not Lila?

"Did you have any guests staying with you?" Sheriff Mitchell fumbled with a notebook and pen.

"Just Lila Daniels. She's a friend from school," I answered.

"And where was she?" He eyeballed me.

Knowing she didn't do any of that, I lied. "She left yesterday afternoon. Back to college, I dropped her off at the airport myself."

"Okay," he muttered. Then his eyes turned to me. "Where did you go after that?" He raised an eyebrow, waiting for my answer.

"I left. Went to Tornados. I went home with Tiffani. I was with her all night."

"Uh huh. The Newham girl?" I nodded as he shut his notebook, a white truck pulled up.

The door opened, and a blonde ball of curls ran to me, arms straight out. I scooped her up, memorizing the powdered scent of her hair. "Wesley, what happened? Where's Daddy?"

"I don't know...umm, Katie, I'm going to talk to you, but not yet," I answered her, but how would I really tell her? How could I tell my six-year-old sister her father was dead?

"I want Mommy," she cried as I hugged her tighter.

Sheriff Mitchell spoke up. "That's another thing, Mr. Turner. There's no easy way to tell you this, but when we contacted the center where your mom was staying, they advised of their attempts to contact your father. Your mother passed away early this morning—looks like suicide."

I looked at him, incredulous. "What?"

"Yeah, the staff reported no indication of behavioral changes. No reason to believe she harbored suicidal tendencies." He gulped. "No signs of foul play, either. Police down south said it's one of the most horrific cases they've ever seen, what, with it being compacted with the death of your father."

Thoughts spun into pain and anger. Lila's words filled my head, *'There'll always be a Sullivan. Someone wanting something from us.'*

Unless, I thought. *Sullivan's still alive.*

"Son, Paula Anderson from social services is on her way. Since Katie's a minor, we'll place her temporarily—"

I cut him off. "No...No. I'm her next of kin. I'm nineteen. Can't I take her? Legally?"

He shrugged and looked down at his notepad. He wasn't going to take me seriously. "We've been through enough!" I yelled at him.

"Wes, don't leave me," Katie sobbed.

The sheriff's face softened. "When she gets here, we'll talk. I don't see why she couldn't go with you."

"I have a home in Virginia. It's a rental, but it's big enough for her," I stated, hoping it'd help my case.

A black Ford Escort pulled up the driveway and a well-dressed lady, probably mid-thirties wearing glasses got out. "My God!" she exclaimed as she made her way to our small group. "What on earth?"

"That's what we're trying to find out," the sheriff answered as he filled her in on everything they knew. Katie held me tight.

The lady looked from me to Katie. "I'm Paula Anderson from Cedar County Social Services." She held a hand out and I shook it, hoping it would get on her good side.

"Wesley Turner." If I lost it on her, I'd have no chance of staying with my sister. "This is Katie."

"Well," she started.

"I know you're here to take her, but I'm her next closest relative. I'm nineteen and capable of watching her," I interrupted.

She stared at me for a while and studied Katie's red, swollen face. She cleared her throat. "Normally, we don't do this, but I looked her up through her social security number before I arrived and you're right; there's no immediate family." She thought for a minute. "It's Saturday, we can't see a judge until Monday. Even then, it's a long shot, but if I can get a clean background check on you, there's a chance I can put this in front of a judge Monday morning. Now, it'll only be temporary custody. When you get back home, I expect you to comply with DSS protocol if you want full custody of your sister."

I smiled for the first time that day. "Thank you."

"Mr. Turner, out here, you have quite a reputation with the ladies." She studied me. "For obvious reasons," she muttered more to herself than us. She cleared her throat and recovered, "However, having custody of a small child, you take on a higher level of responsibility. You must see to it that you're providing her with good examples, not young girls running in and out of your house all day and night like it's one of those party clubs. That's not a safe environment."

I nodded. "Okay..."

"She must be properly fed and cared for. You must enroll her in school and it wouldn't hurt for you to be involved with the school as well," she finished.

"I have to be in Virginia soon, college starts in a couple weeks," I explained.

"Oh, details. That'll be fine. Give me your mailing address and I'll have the paperwork sent to you. They'll assign you a caseworker out there. Mr. Turner, I do, however, expect you to show up at court on Monday morning. You are *not* to leave this county."

"Yes ma'am." It was the best news I'd had. I turned to Katie. "You're staying with me," I told her.

"Yes!" She wiped her eyes and put her arms around me.

After a long time, I let her go. "Stay here for a minute," I told her.

I made my way up to the scene. The lady from the white truck who'd brought Katie home was talking to a few neighbors. The voices turned to whispers and stares as I passed them.

"Sir, this is a crime scene," the officer's voice blurred into piles of ashes. I ignored him and continued. I walked past the yellow tape. "Sir!" he called out again.

I stood on what used to be the front porch. There was nothing to look at, everything was decimated save for a few fixtures in the home that'd been charred. The shed was still standing, and I went over to it. No one was over there as I pulled the heavy door open. Dad's equipment was still intact. I ran my hands over one of the metal machines until something scratched my index finger. I pulled back quickly.

Could it be possible that Sullivan didn't die after all? If he was back, he'd have the ability to work with law enforcement. Katie was sitting in the grass playing with her friend; the mom hadn't left yet. I walked over and rested a hand on her shoulder.

"Let's drive to the gas station and get a drink," I coaxed her.

"I'm not thirsty," Katie piped up. I picked Katie up and walked past him. I put her in the back of my truck and got in, glad I'd gotten gas already as I backed out of the driveway.

"We're never going back, are we, Wes?" her little voice asked meekly from the back.

"No," I whispered. "We can't."

She didn't say anything else, but my phone buzzed. "OMG! Wesley, are you okay?" Sara's shrill voice shrieked.

"Yes, you?" I answered.

"Lila called last night," she began.

"Sara, where is she?"

"I don't know, but she's with a girl named Amy. She said she'd be in touch. What's going on?" Her voice was tired, but worried.

"Sullivan's back, that's what I think," I replied. "Look, we'll be in Fredericksburg, soon. Meet us at my house when I get in touch with you."

"We?" her voice changed from worry to curiosity.

"Me and Katie, my sister." I ended the call and focused on the road.

Amy was from the casino, if it was the same Amy. Nothing made sense. Lila was gone, Mom was gone, Dad, Tom, Jennie, everyone I knew, everything I knew. I could only look ahead into the foggy, Saturday morning distance.

What would the judge say? Yes? What if the answer was no? Katie was all I had; I wasn't going to lose her to the system.

My thoughts were a disconnect. We had to leave, but could we return to Fredericksburg? They'd have cops waiting. How much did Katie understand? How much had she dug around in the sheriff's mind? How could I break news to my baby sister that I couldn't negotiate myself?

I pulled over on the curb and unbuckled her from the car seat. We couldn't leave. I had to take her back, find somewhere to stay. There was too much to do—funeral arrangements, court... Lila. No, not Lila. It was all about Katie. I had to make it about her.

I hugged her tight. I didn't cry. I wouldn't. Katie smelled like baby powder and wind. "Wes," she sniffled into my shirt. "I'm really scared."

"So am I," came my honest response as we gripped each other tightly in the umbrella of August humidity.